M000214978

Enigma Books

Also published by Enigma Books

Nicholas Anderson

NOC

Non-Official Cover: British Secret Operations

A Documentary Thriller

Enigma Books

Copyright © 2009 by Nicholas Anderson

First Edition

ISBN 978-1-929631-85-8

Library of Congress Cataloguing in Publication Available

Introduction by the Author

"Military Intelligence" is an oxymoron,
just like "Government Organisation" is.
A bloody game with no rules.

The Secret Intelligence Service (SIS) of the United Kingdom of Great Britain and Northern Ireland doesn't have a logo though verification of staff on its dark green triangular badges clearly states *"Semper Occultus"* ("Always Secret"); doesn't have its name on the door though it works from a crystal palace on London's River Thames; doesn't have to report its cheques and balances to any government ministry nor to the denizens of the Houses of Parliament it stares at across the water; and is largely unknown even to its own country's citizens, much less the rest of the world. The only external notion that it even exists is that its personnel's salaries are paid by the Foreign & Commonwealth Office through Hambro's Bank. And much like its famous American cousin, the Central Intelligence Agency, its employees are sworn to never talk or write about their work and are bound so by signing the UK Official Secrets Act.

When I first joined SIS (also known as MI6 for Military Intelligence Department Six, its original name) from the Royal Navy in 1973, following extensive training, I was originally assigned to the Special Political Action section. But within a few months it was closed down.

Most of SPA's younger officers were then integrated into a newly formed secret sub-division with no official name (to this day it still cannot be published) but was later externally known as "Operational Support Branch", an updated version of the old Section D (for destruction) in World War II, which specialised in sabotage. For American readers the US equivalent of the UK's now defunct SPA and SD is the Special Activities Division of the CIA's Clandestine Service, which is under the dominion of its Directorate of Operations. I was one of the few who were actually SIS officers and not special forces-trained, so I used my head more than brawn. We were institutional killers* that undertook disruptive actions on the black, that is to say we made illegal entries across borders to perform dirty work then returned home mostly without the knowledge nor connection to the local British embassy's staff assigned to other covert affairs.

Then I was promoted. The main job description was called deep cover within SIS though the US-led NATO preferred NOC or non-official cover—either description was undeclared. SIS' dozen NOCs were then and still are subservient to the whims of NATO and the US government's policies but operate separately from the CIA's Office of External Development, which runs the US' 150 or so own NOCs. Amazingly though, the CIA's London-based Chief-of-Station gets to sit in on the UK's Joint Intelligence Committee's weekly analysis report, the Red Book, for the eyes only of the British Prime Minister and select cabinet ministers to be assessed over each weekend. The American version is the early morning President's Daily Brief. My countrymen have no reciprocal access to this and thank goodness they drew the line at full divulgence between the CIA's OED's secret operations and ours when it comes to NOCs.

As far as I am aware I am the only NOC in both the UK and the US to be recruited from the armed forces who graduated through the spy system to the most secret of the secret intelligence officers…and the sole person to chronicle it. *But I did so for a more than noble cause: ideological, not for riches or fame.*

Nevertheless, the distribution list for disclosure of chain of command information within SIS was limited to two—the teller and the receiver— usually the line officer at Requirements & Production and myself. Who was above him I'll never know but it was purposely designed to stay that way. Note: Eventually I did get to learn the name of the man at the top issuing

---

* A licence to kill is known at SIS as "supreme breach of law" was written in the employment contract as: "In extreme situations of *summum jus, summa injuria,* laws may be disobeyed if said disobedience is deemed legitimate and in furtherance to the cause."

the orders but let me just call him "Martin Mackenzie", a take on his real name. Insiders can figure it out and know that I know, OK?

From there I served in various SIS divisions in charge of different continents, often living like a mole. I suppose I was known to be good under pressure and not soil myself when the going got muddy. I got to know a lot of what went on, most of it was unpleasant and would shock ordinary people if they knew. These days when sceptics ask me to provide evidence, I can only smile. SIS files don't link its officers or its agents' code names to their real identities, so it's well nigh impossible to provide the elusive proof. Instead every dossier is colour coded, for example, green means it is still active while those with a yellow card indicate it's still an accountable document rather than a draft proposal, and so on. Pink files are the most sensitive of the top secret category.

(Do you really think an experienced hacker can access Chronos, NATO's coded computer system? I think not. It's virtually the same thing for me. But what is in my head is permanently imprinted.)

Besides my favourite response to cynics is, "If you have not been informed about it then how could you comment and deny it?"

Plus there are those in the know who will say, preceded by clearing of their ruling class throats, "Ah, yes, this is somewhat of a selective telling of a story—yours—and it is supported by multiple hearsay. Moreover we can't admit your disclosures, old chap, as our jobs, mortgages and reputations are at stake...therefore we hope you understand why you are deemed completely and utterly misinformed."

So it's my word against theirs. That's what it boils down to in the end. It slowly dawned on me that I was being employed by a criminal organisation—they believe they had the right to be above the law.

They can't actually prove I did not, while I can't prove I actually did either. But I do invite investigative journalists to closely follow my story: They will see truth emerge and that my 'imagined characters' do exist in real life. By the end of my narrative, even though I presented it in what I term "informed fiction" for easier dissemination, individuals checking the facts will be convinced beyond reasonable doubt that I am sincerely imparting inner knowledge while, at the same time, hopefully they will understand why I had to write it in this manner. It is accurate to the spirit and the letter of what transpired.

Yet "Mr Mackenzie", a Cabinet Office mandarin, and his SIS lackeys in tow (me included down the bottom of the totem pole) were more often than not following directives themselves—always issued by Americans either at NATO, mainly from its Mons HQ, Belgium, though other orders originated from the naval intelligence unit at Verona (far from an Italian port), with additional input from Stuttgart in Germany where the US European Command is based (which is linked to US Central Command in Tampa, Florida). All have a say about how European lives are to be lived. This does not include all the military bases and spy satellite gathering posts dotted throughout all the continents like the pox. War mongering is its chief business globally.

In the end, there's not a lot of difference between history and fiction anyway because the former has been written by people with the latter in mind. Secret intelligence, especially in non-traditional platform programmes, in a supposed liberal democracy does not equal evidence that it can be presented. It especially should be known that any unprocessed SIS, CIA or NATO file has no number assigned to it therefore officially it does not exist. Ultra top secret SIS records that are actually processed are withheld from the UK Public Record Office for 50 years after their date of creation and then may be designated another 30 years or more, if assessed to be extraordinarily sensitive. I know the Duke of Edinburgh, the Queen of England's husband, and a Royal Navy officer himself, is allocated 300 years holdback. The US government believes that the Constitution allows it to defer secret covert action notification to Congress indefinitely if it felt circumstances so warranted.

Enough! Please feel free to pigeonhole my book whatever you wish. I have told my "memoirs" as I know it to be. Is it an admission of guilt or a case of just following formatted orders (a euphemism meaning it was verbalised and not written), the latter in itself a response to an effective command that can't be legally translated to include accountability? You be the judge. But I do know that by writing this account I feel as if I have finally lifted a great weight off my shoulders. And there is so much more too to tell than I've narrated herein so retaining that information will be my saving grace.

—Nicholas Anderson (pseudonym)

THE BRITISH GOVERNMENT'S
DOUBLE "DAMAGE LIMITATION" LEGAL SYSTEM

In the United Kingdom of Great Britain and Northern Ireland it is mandatory that manuscripts of any kind by former professionals from the security, intelligence services and special forces be submitted for clearance to the Ministry of Defence, per Official Secrets Act requirements and other Secret Intelligence Service confidentiality covenants. Every state in the world has its version of same.

Likewise, a DA-Notice—assumed to stand for "Defence Advisory"—is a voluntary edict of self-censorship by British nationals who are authors of any subjects pertaining to the nation's military- and intelligence-related matters, and are similarly reviewed by the 13-member Defence, Press and Broadcasting Advisory Committee. The UK is the only country to have such a decree.

British government policy is never to confirm nor deny its espionage operations, past or present— until it has been declassified.

I, herein, confirm that the contents of this book is a fictional memoir and based on OSINT (Open Source Intelligence), and duly swear that because I believe in a truly democratic constitution—as it is my human right to do so—I therefore willingly refused to defer my script for analyses to both the aforementioned MOD and the DPBAC. However, if existing ops, systems, codes and individuals lives were possibly to be endangered by my actions I censored myself by replacing the word with asterisks or changing the details. For obvious reasons this was applied too for likely legal suits and other blocking devises.

Furthermore, I would like to believe Article 10 of the European Convention on Human Rights that guarantees freedom of expression protects me.

I also hereby authenticate that the author's name is a nom de plume, which I so chose to do to safeguard my family.

Symbolically, in writing my "autobiographical tale" you are walking in my invisible footsteps. - NA

"Intelligence ends with the first shot fired. Real Intelligence much more resembles a fascinating chess game, much complicated by the fact that the figures and their positions are not known to the players…"

– Victor Sheymov, *former KGB officer*
who defected to the United States

* * * * * * * * *

To the five women in my life:
my Mum—who always knew;
my deceased fiancée—who will never know;
my ex-wife—who didn't know;
my lady—who knows; and
my daughter—who will know.

* * * * * * * * *

NOC

Non-Official Cover: British Secret Operations

Prologue

Courage is a quiet sound made with grace,
heard by those who behold it.

I'd free-fallen blindly through dense rain clouds from a HALO (High Altitude, Low Opening jump from 30,000 feet for approximately 2½ minutes with 60 lbs. baggage at a speed exceeding 160 miles an hour with temperature below 50F before opening the parachute at under 4,000 feet). The Chinese-made Chuji Jiaolianji trainer turboprop AC (aircraft) with extra fuel tanks added, and false Chinese insignias had returned south to Peshawar, Pakistan, following the windy peaks that separated the USSR and China.

My marker was a plastic-looking blurred ink spill, a distant lake called Zhaysang koli, on a white carpet. I'd tugged the cord and spun uncontrollably before settling into a slower descent by black parachute at night into Soviet Kazakhstan.

The plan was to get to Semipalatinsk, 200 miles away and I'd done so by commercial bus routes over the next two days. My photo identification in Cyrillic stated that I was a cadet in *Voyenno-Vozdushbye Sily* (VVS, the Soviet Air Force) and attached to *Dalnaya Aviatsiya* (Strategic Aviation, the wing for long-range bombers). Documents showed I had graduated from a *Sovetskaya Akademiya Vozdushbye Sily* (Soviet Air Force officer training academy) near Moscow, that I was from Rostovskaya Oblast and the signed

Yuridichskaya (from the Judiciary) stated I was "temporarily transferred to an unspecified VVS air station." Best still, I carried a week old copy of *Shcit y Mech gazeta*, the KGB's Shield & Sword weekly newspaper.

In a country of Slavic peasants that couldn't read, I had the accent and demeanour of a high-class apparatchik, even in my plain clothes. Those few authorities in these barren lands who could read wouldn't dare question my papers and attitude. If they did I was fully authorised to practice my SAMBO (*Samozaschchita Bez Oruzhiya* or Self-Defence Without Weapons, a Russian form of 25 different hand-to-hand combat systems) with no questions asked. It never came close to application and at no time did I feel overly apprehensive but I did have to take several necessary common sense precautions at critical junctions and situations.

Using a long-range portable telescope I had duly verified that there were 40 long-range high-altitude Tupolev TU-95 (Bear-H designated by NATO) strategic reconnaissance bombers equipped with nuclear warheads on standby, discreetly parked inside hangars at a secret VVS base near Semey. The satellites couldn't spot them through the steel roofs so somebody had to go to see it at ground level. The tail numbers of the front half dozen that I could observe were duly memorised (one, I concede, couldn't exactly be recollected later).

Phase One completed, it took another five lonely days to get my arse from there to the desolate location for Phase Two.

That was six time zones east of Moscow and several hundred miles north of the mountainous borders where China and Mongolia meet. Eight hours of wretched trekking and just east of Chita railway station. The *khanovey—the wind of winds* in Siberia—was wailing white soot every which way.

Through the fog, at minus eight degrees Fahrenheit, the town of Amazar in the Russian Far East was empty, bar the thousands upon thousands of forlorn dark steam engines standing obediently in unmoving queues as far as the eye could see, an eerie graveyard for the state's retired iron locomotive servants dating to the previous century. It was so cold that flocks of greyish frozen birds looked like they were still in flight as they laid dead on the canvas of the snow.

Blending into my background with only my breath to signal my presence, I shifted from my perch in the hills overlooking the strange foreboding sight two miles away, and hung the binoculars momentarily around my neck to adjust my hardened *shapka* (a fur hat with ear muffs tied around the jaw). The satellite picture expert in London had explained that, according to information received from the imaging craft and due to months of unclear weather in this region, it was believed the Soviets had used the opportunity of a 'free roof' over their heads to reconstruct a previously obsolete silo. It was now perceived to be a hidden home to hundreds of warheads from the Soviet Union's long-overdue to be dismantled and recycled SS-18 ICBMs (Inter-Continental Ballistic Missiles). It was supposed that they were hidden around here somewhere.

As a party of one ferret, my assignment was only to identify its exact location and get on the next *Transsibirska Magistral,* the Trans-Siberian Railway, still in civilian dress, to the necropolis of Vladivostock, which was frost-bound for an average of 110 days a year. Afterwards, my mission was to make my way to the commercial port next to the naval shipyard at nearby Daizavod, rendezvous with a corrupt Japanese merchant navy second-mate who would clandestinely arrange my boarding an ice-cutting freighter to Hitachi and home—bringing the data in my head. Another miserable uncomfortable week or so before reaching safety. What a bloody way to float in the New Year, I thought. It was Christmas Day, December 1977.

To my left, less than half a mile below me, a covered Ulanjov jeep skidded into a clearing, then stopped. It wasn't any of the armed-forces vehicles that I recognised. Four men, whom I initially thought were *kolkhozniks* (collective farm workers)—tumbled out. However, as I spied upon them through the field glasses, I observed that two of them were joined by heavy leg-irons and all had one-half of their heads shaved. From their dirty striped garb, I could only surmise this skinny group was comprised of either *katorzhniki* or *poselentsi*—hard labour convicts or penal colonists exiled to these sparse outposts—now on the run.

Then, the bunch of monkeyshines pulled out some poor sod in a uniform—perhaps a prison guard. Based on the clouds of smoke vented from his mouth, he was squealing at the top of his lungs. They stripped him bare like hyenas ripping meat, and then, two of the bastards forcibly stood the shivering fellow on top of what was left of a chopped tree.

The fettered duo laughed drunkenly as they poured bottles of mineral water from a crate in the boot over the naked man, and within minutes he was a bowing ice statue on an imaginary cross—minus the crown of thorns.

Then the goons enjoyed a frenzied party of sorts—sucking down what remained of the *mineralye vodi* (mineral water) pretending it was vodka, dancing around their sculpture of liquid marble. It was probably a long time since they'd had even reasonable water and even longer since they'd been treated like human beings; they no longer acted like humans.

After the sickest hour or so I've ever witnessed, it was their time to be off after they'd all had a piss.

Before they got back in the stolen jeep, one of the fuckers snapped off one of the dead man's arms and waved it around like a trophy to the cheering triad. Then, he threw the slowly dripping hard meat in the back of the getaway vehicle as if it was a memento of their brief visit to hell, and off they disappeared in a swirl of milky dust. I was left staring at the white scarecrow with an overcoat of ice and the single outstretched limb—alone in a cemetery of one.

As hard as I searched for the next 48 hours I never did find the whereabouts of that damn silo. I stayed as an uninvited guest in a deserted *izba* (log cabin with a corrugated roof)—perhaps some factory manager's summer hut—with that pathetic glacial effigy still there waving at me when I left for the railway station and the *Transsib* again to make my own escape from this frigid netherworld.

Before reaching the safety of Japan I had already concluded that this entire deep cover exercise was only to discover whether or not I could survive extreme conditions, as well as return home in one piece for some extended operation in the future.

Chapter One

At last the sun was straining through the dull morning mist. Last night's storm was over. I folded the *Los Angeles Times* and strolled down the steps to the beach barefoot, in yesterday's worn tee-shirt and cut-off jeans, gripping the usual plastic travel mug of coffee. Too early in the day for the few tourists and too late for the many surfers—they were probably headed up to the year-round snow peaks at Bear Mountain with their other boards. The ruffled breakers were nearly non-existent compared to the thunderous 15-footers the day before.

An unusually quiet February morning in 1992 for Balboa's peninsula where the millionaire's cottages are neatly clogged, Manhattan-style, along the Pacific shore. But I was thankful on this Monday, for the weekend had been the normal helter-skelter in this avant-garde Californian artist community. Still, I always relished walking on the edge of the waves most mornings, even when it rained, surf pounding or licking ripples as today's was. The water's coldness gave the feet a regular kick-start. I imagined it stimulated my brain too.

I looked back behind me a hundred yards across the football field at the small grey beach house I'd lived in for five years. A far cry from my native northeast of England; the fog was much heavier there and the locals were far more robust than the carefree inhabitants here. It seemed another lifetime; it doesn't relate to me now.

Sipping from the container, I gazed out over the wintry pastel grey sea, feet tickling through the cool soft sand. I loved squatting down meditation-style taking in this semi-fictional world, it unfailingly gave me the creative juices for my next entrepreneurial business venture.

An English voice said calmly, "Excuse me for troubling you, sir, 'Box 500' designated me to fly out and see you immediately." Yes, I thought to myself, *I remember them, those bloody bastards at British domestic intelligence headquarters. MI5 were always blaming we international lads for something or other...* "Sir!" The English accent was definitely posh London. I looked up with my hand shielding my eyes...shadow of a broad body...the kind usually found in the rugby scrums...dark suit 'n' tie on the sand didn't fit...chubby manual sportsman's hands. The gleaming sun obscured the face. Probably Eton College boy, typical upper class; Daddy's influence got him a nice comfy civil servant post stateside, attached to the head of some station. Maybe they wanted to see if he could run errands properly before assigning him a little bit of real sweat on a jungle job.

"Lieutenant-Commander Anderson." I nodded at No Face. "DC Embassy sent me out this morning to see you, sir, I just got here a quarter of an hour ago. Al and Colleen at the coffee place said I'd find you out here, if you weren't home." He was ramrod straight the whole time.

I kept nodding, I'd been through a moment like this before. Yeah, I remember now, Bulgaria in 1976. I downed the last of the cold coffee and patted the sand next to me. "Alright, what's sucking the devil's cock now?" I sighed. Into the shade beside me, as he came into focus, was a clear, blue-eyed, rugged face, with short, sandy, curly hair and the word "anxiety" in bold letters all over his young freckled forehead.

His name was Higgins, I think, or Hinton, or something beginning with "H". Basically a nice chap, inexperienced, not worldly at all. Who knows where the diplomatic business finds them these days, probably through the United Kingdom's upper classes' daily newspaper advertisements. Been in Washington only a few months pretending to push papers in the Commerce Department in the US office, "After graduating from the Government Code and Cipher School in Bletchley Park, near Milton Keynes, Buckinghamshire, in the UK." His vague job combinations didn't add up to me. Probably was told to say that. I knew which damn county and country it was in, for crissakes! Nervous bloke, talked a lot, never failed to call me "sir" despite my polite requests to stop. After all, it had been a long time since I wore the blue-black officer's uniform of the British Royal Navy Fleet Air Arm designed by Gieves & Hawkes of 1 Savile Row. Obviously a blueblood, as I'd guessed right, and the rugby part was spot on judging from the two slight scars over his nose. If you looked closely at the right angle, they looked like a faint permanent band-aid of off-colour skin pigment. Then I spotted a tiny metal badge on his lapel—the London-based Harlequins rugby team logo. The old gut still worked right after nearly 10 years out of the spy business.

The lad droned on. Nowadays I only wanted the fat without the trimmings and switched off the rest of the sermon people generally gave. I was always that way and will never change. Living life at the point end of a spear had honed me into a person who cut straight to the problem at hand. Had to be that way, basically just to survive another day.

"H" had patiently stood waiting for me on the veranda, back to me the entire time, while I showered and packed. He never told me his first name and I never asked. Couldn't tell me how long I'd be gone for, "Maybe two weeks or so, sir, but you'll need warmer things in England." I rubbed Buddha's belly for luck and headed down the wooden steps briskly towards the rent-a-car.

The drive up the traffic-choked 405 freeway was uneventful and the young Englishman had finally shut-up.

L.A.—the city of the car—loomed out of the worsening smog with its asphalt tendons stretching through its body. Yesterday's storm had failed to blow the captive carbon monoxide up out of the basin and over the surrounding hills. Jets on their twin flight paths could be seen dotted out like glowing fireflies in two regimented lines on the right. As we approached the first Los Angeles International Airport—LAX—exit, circling around over Sepulveda Boulevard, a descending Boeing 747 roared low over our heads to screech its smoking tyres on the runway to the west of the road.

First class seats and all on British Airways. Pads my frequent flyer programme account nicely, I smiled to myself. My my, it must be important this one—Category A—plus the young chauffeur "H" personally sent to collect me. *I'm impressed*, I thought sarcastically. The airline employee at the check-in desk profusely apologised that she could not seat the apparently relieved English fellow next to me for the flight. With the messenger "H" safely ensconced the other side of the aisle three rows back, I could be allowed to think for the next half a day on the way to London's Heathrow. What was so damn urgent?

I couldn't sleep as everybody else in the floating metal capsule's cabin dozed around me. Outside was blank space with not even the stars to stare back at me. I was in a state of tabula rasa myself and as close as Man gets to heaven, to the inaudible music of the spheres. Flying miles above uninhabited landscapes and sleeping populations, I thought of my life, a remarkably different life that had got off to a start like no other and had shaped me well for future adventures.

Products of the British Empire's colonial tentacles, my English father had met my Scottish mother in Aden, the southernmost point of the Arab Middle East, in the Yemen. I'm not certain where they married, but they did so fairly soon after happening across each other in that wretched stinking hellhole of a city. I do know I was conceived during their month-long honeymoon not far from Kathmandu, Nepal, on that border between heaven and earth known as the Himalayas. And so by happenstance of their spur-of-the-moment lifestyle, I was born in Bombay, India—and not in Colombo, Ceylon, now Sri Lanka, where they had originally anticipated my birthplace. Baptised as "India" by its conquerors, the traditionalists preferred to call their country *Bharat* where a sixth of humanity calls home, we lived for a few years in the affluent Malabar Hill suburb near the beautiful big bay—*Mumbai*—for which the city of Bombay was named. There, apparently when I was a baby, a maharaja in Cochin in the deep Indian south, gave me a tiger tooth for luck. I still carry that symbol with me.

When I was old enough to remember, we next lived like royalty almost on the Equator, in humid Singapore, then another colony of the British imperialists. My father's office was at the Phoenix Park complex there. I even had my own personal driver and a turquoise two-door Studebaker with fancy fins at my disposal, while my parents had a black one between them. On a recent visit there as an adult, I went to the unchanged Raffles Hotel where I could still visualise young Master Anderson running down the outdoor corridors. Much like my petite mother did, as I was growing up, little old ladies dressed mainly in frilly cotton whites continue to hold court at four o'clock for tea and scones, with imported Cornwall jam and Devon cream from England.

Sometime in between, the family relocated to Hong Kong's lofty Victoria district—locally it was called Xianggang—overlooking the 'fragrant harbour', which is what that city was named after, while Dad's work place was in Little Sai Wan. As I was the only child, I was dispatched to a private boarding school in the northeast of England half way around the world, to Hurworth House to be exact, in County Durham not far from the old market town of Darlington. At the start of every summer and every winter holiday I began a life of boarding BOAC Comet 4's, TWA Constellations (Connies) and Air India's "Lemonade Specials"—so called because they ferried brats like me—to spend months wherever my parents happened to be at the time. In those days I disembarked at airports in Beirut, Baghdad, Tehran and Tashkent during stopovers and never thought anything unusual about it. Nowadays people would faint to think of a 7 to 12-year old British boy wandering around unattended in these wayward last frontiers among the fierce local tribesmen and their lazy camels with chewing gum grins.

While "home", wherever it was during my visits to the Far East, I recall I would occasionally accompany my father, supposedly an emissary, on his business trips to some very exotic places. I remember with vivid detail being in Kuala Lumpur, Jakarta and Rangoon. Two week-long, gruelling hikes to Canton and Peking were particularly memorable. Adventures in living dangerously were normal to me, though I was not a teenager yet.

I was constantly left in the company of our dozen or so ethnic Chinese "servants"—a word I have great reluctance to utter but they were indeed servile—while my mother and father were on the society circuit. One of the employees I distinctly liked was Kao Liang. An older man, he taught me the fine art of self-defence in choy li fut, tai-chi exercises, and reasonably good Mandarin Chinese at a fairly young age, fairly useful to have under one's belt later as an adult. At times my clearly dismayed father would have to angrily remind me that I was mixing knife, fork and chopsticks.

By the age of 10, during the first few weeks of returning to school in England, I'd be strolling along the banks of the gentle River Tees flowing through Hurworth, with Yorkshire on the other bank, and would reflect on the abject hunger and underlying feeling of anger of the peasants in remote, poverty-stricken villages in southeast Asia. Now, here I was without a care in the world and far from danger in the peaceful pastures of a rural European civilisation.

Fortunately I did not suffer from the Dickensian emotional rot of the English boarding school system. But the brutal gap I experienced with left-and-right and black-and-white and top-and-bottom mesmerised me early. I do remember philosophising about this and my English literature teacher then forced me to write down what I was thinking, no matter how absurd it was, and so I did, not knowing the power of words.

My first ode ever was: *Life is like an ocean, and the waves go up and down and no wave stays up forever.*

But as an adult I can reflect that it continues to still be a strange sensation, after a spate of travelling in strange exotic places, to suddenly find oneself in a typically English country location with peace and a peculiar type of silence.

Still, Sundays at boarding school were particularly bad days. In the morning, two school buses appeared. The largest was for the Catholic live-in boarders who gingerly went to their Mass many miles away; the handful of Jewish boys clambered in the mini-bus to be delivered to the synagogue an even further distance away; and we Protestants, encompassing the largest denomination of all the boys at the school, walked down less than an eighth of a mile to the local church with its tolling bells. I always looked back to glance up at the top floor windows of the school to spot the single Buddhist attendee of our school, a Burmese boy who remained alone, often crying with fright in the echoing cavern of the empty school dormitories. Guilty by innocence. The image of his face is seared in my mind's eye. I was in the church choir, which could be fun at times, I did find the religious ceremonies unappealing and downright boring. Not watching the unmoving clock became a trying art and gum chewing without moving your mouth was perfection personified.

Sundays also meant long walks in chattering groups along the steep riverbanks or through the country lanes with high hedges. We would dress in our "Sunday best" as typical British private school boys do, in regimented uniforms and caps, followed by writing the required letters to our faraway loved ones. Having re-read some of these correspondences years later, I see they were filled with detailed descriptions of the frequent fights at school, on Sundays only, it seemed. *Jihad*, I called it once in a letter to Mum and Dad, "erupted between the various warring religious factions and I found myself always in the middle separating the fighters". For some strange reason I can't recall ever seeing our school teachers present on these nights, as if they had wisely left us alone to settle our differences without their arbitration, while they rested in peace.

I was so filled with distaste at the abject nonsense of the priests, rabbis and reverends, that at 12 I declared in writing to my parents that I was a devout atheist. I had added then a short prose, for which I was caned by a teacher, derived in part from a school library history book on Vladimir Lenin: "Religions were formed to control the masses thinking and to keep those in power in control."

Far from teaching young minds to fully understand each other, the school seemed to promote animosities. Perhaps that was the purpose. Meanwhile, competition between the school's two "houses" was intense enough, as it was, I was one of the "Dark Blue" of Oxford University while the "Light Blue" represented Cambridge.

So I have remained an atheist all my life, never seeing any reason to change this opinion, and as the years pass I find I am getting deeper entrenched in this belief. I am me and I have nobody else to rely upon, never having to seek spiritual help, yet strong in the belief that I will always find the right answer and be alright. I believe wholeheartedly in the underlying idea that where there is a problem, there must be a solution waiting to be discovered.

I remember my father turned up at my school on one of his many trips to England and showed me a letter postmarked Dharmsala, India. It was from the Panchen Lama informing me that I was "by virtue of my place of conception and birth, the reincarnation of a Nepalese Highlander warrior-prince's soul who became a reclusive philosopher". The Panchen Lama, I was told, was number two on the totem pole to a living god, the Dalai Lama, and the Panchen Lama was Tibet's second most important religious official. They were in-exile in the Indian Himalayan hills waiting to go home to Tibet, and that's where my Dad had met them. I remained nonchalant at this information, already having declared this "as a rather silly matter", while Dad appeared quite chuffed by my attitude. Nothing more was ever said about it again.

Still, when I was presented with an opportunity to buy a lucky all-bone Buddha as an ornament while I was in the free economic zone of China's Shenzen as a tourist in my mid-forties, I did so based on the strength of the memoirs of my private school days in England. Since then I discovered something about myself, about *Kundan*—the name for "The Presence" or the Dalai Lama—and that is I have inherited his same three gifts: knowledge, intimacy and friendship.

The British Airways captain's baritone voice suddenly awoke me from my deep sleep, announcing our descent. I tore off my sweat soaked eye-patches and rubbed my sore eyes. The Chinese servants had taught me to dip my fingers in my own saliva just under the tongue, rub it gently all around my tired top and bottom eyelids and they would magically come alive.

From the air, I had always loved watching the meandering, murky River Thames peaking through the clouds. This particular flight approach to LHR was my favourite: The history tour route, miniature Tower of London, toy-like Houses of Parliament, tiny grass patch of a Fulham football ground, glimpse of early morning row boat training, outstretched oars like a slowly climbing white centipede on a dark glass window. The sight of the low-lying fields and multiple greens of glorious England rising up closer made my back tingle. Whenever I had been away for any length of time, this green vastness had never failed to strike a peculiar sense of awe in me—my heart belonged there.

But my head and soul didn't want to be here anymore. I snapped back to reality.

My minder "H" was tapping me gently on the back handing me a regulation raincoat, which had mysteriously appeared.

Hello, London, it's nice to be back.

* * * * * * * * * *

Of course we had to arrive during the Tuesday morning rush hour traffic into central London. As we crawled bumper-to-bumper eastbound along the M4 motorway, "H" more than once muttered to himself that we should have got on the underground train at the new tube station right inside Heathrow Airport, instead of sitting motionless together in the back of the black cab.

I was strangely relaxed for I had always adopted the philosophy that "only with the perspective of time can cause and consequence be clearly seen," so why worry unnecessarily. It was drizzling but then it always did at this time of the year. I had always had admiration for the cool way the British drove their cars—hard, fast, courteous, and all the while, not a horn to be heard. London had plenty of both kinds of mini's still: cars and skirts. With time the black bowler hats and dark suits had all but disappeared, to be replaced by plentiful white turbans trailed by colourful saris in an atmosphere of steel drums and Rastafarians.

Finally we were approaching The White House. From Euston Road I could see the building across the small park in front of it. When I'd stayed here before, I used to jog daily in Regent's Park, just a few minutes north. It had been many years since I'd last been here and I was surprised to see the golden garlic-shaped dome of a mosque directly behind it on the skyline. On my right I caught glimpses, between the skyscrapers, of the Post Office Tower, a silver needle puncturing a stab in the London clouds of the same colour.

As we were climbing out of the cab, I had begun to wonder how long young man "H" was going to be hanging around. I mean we didn't really have much in common, as it were, and he had delivered me to the master's den, so to speak. A generation gap was the reason for the mental space between us. As if I had sixth sense, right on cue he offered me his hand. "Well, that's as far as I go, sir, you're booked in under your own name and in the name of the Firm's export business, of course," he stuttered. "I'll keep the cab, if you don't mind, on to my digs in South Ken."

I didn't say much, couldn't think of anything really, and instead muttered some sweet polite nonsense. Finally, I mocked an English upper class accent, "I'm happy I wasn't stuck at the posh Basil Street Hotel in bloody Knightsbridge, hey what." He looked as if he was surprised I knew the existence of the Edwardian-style, first class establishment where the SIS booked guests they wanted to impress. I guessed it was important enough for me to be brought here in first class, but a customer I was not. We shook hands briefly and his hefty back was turned and I thought that would be the last I would see of the lad with the still quizzical face.

Up in the Firm's luxury hotel room-cum-small flat—they had several at The White House—there was the expected envelope on the kitchenette's table. Usual stuff—be ready at 11 o'clock downstairs in the lobby. I wondered which person would be assigned to brief me about whatever it was that had cropped up. After all it had been nine years since I'd "gone private" as they say, or retired from the service.

The screaming kettle rudely invaded my consciousness. While the Fortnum & Mason brand Darjeeling tea bag brewed in the real china cup, I unpacked what little I had brought with me from Balboa. I spread-eagled myself on the bed intending to take an hour nap before taking a shower.

Curiosity killed the cat, but not me I thought. I'm officially out of this game. In addition to signing the UK Official Secrets Act when I joined the Royal Navy in 1971, later seconded to the Secret Intelligence Service; and when I left the SIS in 1983 I had supposedly been granted immunity from prosecution so long as I kept my mouth shut, and I had thus far. This jaunt was just going to be another exercise in picking my brain about something

I'm purported to be knowledgeable about, only it was to be conducted in person. Over the years while I had lived in America I had screened my incoming calls on my telephone answering machine carefully and ignored those that preceded with the distinct click of encryption devices, followed by long-distance static and echoing British accents. Twice though I had mistakenly spoken to SIS staff that did not follow the standard procedure and had been sucked into giving them the free advice they were seeking. But this time they sent somebody so there was no avoiding it.

I'm "an expert on Chinese, Arabic and Russian affairs specialising in new technology mainly relating to defence programmes", with an occasional spattering of involvement in the medical field. That was the official term to describe my apparent understanding of matters and human beings, but what it really meant was: I observed developments of international concern behind enemy lines. I was a "NOC-cer", which alternatively rhymes between soccer and no sir. NOC was a US-influenced NATO term for spies who operated in the interest of their country with non-official cover status in foreign lands; unlike those privileged others who had diplomatic immunity in case something went wrong.

Sometimes when going down into the ground like a mole for weeks and months at a time, the British SIS—the "Foreign Service"—internally, liked to alluringly label blokes like me as deep cover. Sounded like a name of a safe position on the cricket field. But I would duly transform myself into its eyes, its ears and its nose when I had to and catch people out. Despite all that jargon, contrary to popular notion, the world of espionage is a relentlessly bleak world where truth is equally hard to discern, as well as to conceal.

Well past the horizons of personal achievements I thought I would reach one day, I had a unique combination of charisma, skill and luck, and a rare knack to perceive the emotion of the moment. *Chance favours the prepared mind.*

I also had several gifts well suited for intelligence: Near photographic memory; athletic guile; mental agility; adaptability; and confidence, plus that rare capacity to establish rapport with almost anybody from every walk of life. What I really was: a person who's real objective is to change and influence the opinions of people in other countries, by whatever dastardly deeds the mandarins of the British hierarchy had devised. In doing these tasks I had visited well over 50 foreign nations in 10 years within the employ of MI6, SIS' old World War II's name (when it was Military Intelligence Department Six), in accordance with the various projects which had clearly defined political and economic goals on behalf of—and to further enrich—Her Majesty's government.

When I was back downstairs standing near the entrance-exit, a woman's voice dryly intoned, "Your hair is much longer, my God you look like a hippie with that outdated Edwardian moustache." I turned around to face Mrs Blyton, a portly very smiling Ellen Blyton, the personal assistant for nearly two decades to three "C"'s, the male heads of SIS who never used their real names. Publicly each had only used the equally wonderfully unassuming cover title of 'Counsellor, Foreign and Commonwealth Office', instead of their real title, that of 'Chief'.

We hugged each with feeling. "Nicholas, I know you could get away with being any one of 100 different nationalities—as it states in your personal file—but I'd never have thought you were an Englishman today, and that tan, my goodness! You must have a nice white line down there too," she giggled, taking delight in ribbing me, as she put her arm in mine leading us to the revolving doors and outside. "How was your flight across?" she asked not expecting an answer, while gently touching my elbow with a childlike delight.

"How's things at Box 850?" I replied, meaning MI6 as a whole. To which I knew she wouldn't answer. Small talk stuff. By now I knew she was working for her third successive boss in her career. Retirement couldn't be far away.

Instead of riding in the Firm's expected maroon Ford Sierra, we went on a foxtrot past the parked vehicle slowly and strolled slowly north towards Regent's Park and the Zoo. Passers-by would have mistaken us for a middle-class holidaymaking son and his loving mother, or with an aunt at the very least, if it wasn't for the supposedly nondescript single security detail with bloodhound's eyes 100 paces or so behind us. *So the drivers double these days*, I thought, as I glanced back at an infrequent car horn-blowing infraction.

I'd always thought she must have been some humdinger in her youth, much younger looking than her age betrayed. Her hair peeked specks of grey through the fading burgundy, her hazel eyes still sparkled brightly. Mrs Ellen Blyton must be in her early-sixties by now—five years over the mandatory retirement for active intelligence officers—and whenever I pictured the first "C" I ever knew, in my mind, I pictured this affable frame of sophisticated bubbliness just to his right, notebook in hand. Together at work, rest and play, I thought. It was rumoured for years they were an item even though satisfactorily married to non-involved others, who were conveniently not well versed in the secrecy business.

"Nicholas, I know you too well by now, and while you couldn't give a damn about anything most of the time, at the same time some *things* do piqué your interest."

I thought about that paradox for a bit and took the easy way out, "Well that's why I'm here, love." I white-lied not really knowing why I was there at all, but I kept looking at her for an explanation.

She continued not looking at me but at some mythical object in the distant as if trying to choose the right words. "I know you've point blank turned down a couple of requests to help in past crises, in fact not returning my phone call once I recall," she chided me with a quick glance sideways. "You're perfectly entitled to do whatever you want, of course, but this time we sent somebody to get you as you know."

I must have looked a bit impatient so she increased her verbal pace. "First of all, this is 'official and not official' at the same time which I know you understand." She cleared her throat. "Remember Dr Molody? He's requested you to be involved in something he's doing now and, well, again it's not something you have to do for him and us. Only if you want to..."

I cut her off, "Where is he now, Ellen?"

"Back home again in Moscow, would you believe it?" her tone was low, almost whispered.

She continued to talk, filling in the gaps while I went through the process of bringing text and data back from my memory banks. He wasn't Russian as Ellen implied. Wasn't even a true Soviet either but he was adamantly a Czechoslovak citizen back then, always defending that fact whenever anybody addressed him as a Russian, even though he spoke spotless Russian as well as good English, passable French and flawless German. He was today perhaps reminding the misinformed that he was and had indeed been "a Slovak" all along, and had checked off the first part.

Eldar Michal Molody, Jr. was born in Bratislava, then in Czechoslovakia, during the early days of World War II. Both his parents were die-hard nationalist patriots. As the Red Army advanced west towards Berlin, his father, an anti-Nazi, had been forcibly repatriated, under the threat of immediate death, as a low-ranking officer into the then retreating German Wehrmacht. To the day he died, the old man never forgave himself his "sins".

His effervescent mother, whom I had the pleasure of once meeting, was an intellectual. Well ingrained in the local Bohemian literary society of that era.

Michal—who liked to be known as Mike—was extremely pro-English in everything from its history to its football teams. His knowledge about its royal family and their personal lives was a hobby. He knew more about Great Britain than most Brits. Despite his father's hatred for all things German, Michal grew to love the thundering Germanic music of Wagner, another slight contradiction at the time, for all his quiet but towering academic accomplishments.

A genius in every meaning of the word but he was also one of the boys and could drink, swear and pretend to be a lout with the best of them. Molody, as everybody in his family knew all along that he would, graduated with the state's supreme top honours as a doctor not only of medicine but also of philosophy from the University of Bratislava, itself recognised as one of the world's finest schools of medicine. I recalled that only an unusual man could come up with a classic line like, "Eventually, the ability to download consciousness into a computer will finally free people from their bodies, signifying the next great leap forward in human evolution".

Two aspects of the man always remained with me to this day: He was modestly unassuming and he was very much a humanitarian.

"You say he's gone back to Russia, after all this time?" She took an embossed specially printed folder out of her handbag and sat down promptly on the nearest park bench, while I chose to stand directly in front of her, my hands remaining inside the coat pockets. Our following friend too had found a seat not too far away. It appeared that he had become overly interested in pigeons and their flying methods. "Insanity at its finest," I quietly mumbled.

According to the report, after Dr Eldar Michal Molody and his wife, Caterina, defected from the Soviet Union in 1978, they had elected to live the life of nomads. It began with a fiscal quarter in Switzerland, then two years in Britain, a year each in New York City and Chicago, six years in Los Angeles, and the last three back in Switzerland again. All of his time spent in the United States was in introducing plastic surgery to the rich and famous. He was one of the first to make it fashionable and he became very wealthy from his burgeoning practice in Encino in the San Fernando Valley, just over the lip of the hill from Hollywood and Beverly Hills. They had become parents of a girl named Kristina, born in Illinois, USA. The year previous in 1991, when the Soviet economy collapsed with communism effectively ended there, he almost immediately went back to the reborn Russia and struck a capitalist deal for himself and his Swiss-based Institute of Bio-Cellular Research under the joint auspices of Moscow's Academy of Science and the Academy of Medical Science.

For the past 12 months he had commuted every other week from his established residence in Geneva, departing on a Monday morning for Moscow, spending four nights in a Russian government-supplied flat, with a couple of drivers and Ladas at his disposal, and returning Friday night. The weeks interspersing these trips he spent either at his modest home on Lake Geneva or some other destination in the world. When he's not in his adopted Mother Russia, he's escorted by between two and four security personnel at all times. All of this travel, accommodation and bodyguard service there and overseas was sponsored by the Russian Federation.

"Obviously they've forgiven him his 'sins' and value his contribution even more now." Ellen paused for a moment, looked up at me and handed me a set of blown-up black and white photographs, "A long lens close-up of Dr Molody and his wife taken last month in St Maarten." She continued reading snippets from the file in her lap, as I abruptly relented and quickly sat down purposefully besides her, resisting a thought to put an arm behind her.

"SIS delved deeply into his background, most of it you already know. Dr EM Molody became one of the Soviet Union's top scientists, rising to the top of his field of medicine in just under a decade. They depended greatly on his innovative scientific research. He almost single-handedly invented the replication of human genes as the West knows it." Her voice droned on and I started to drift away.

I looked at one of the photographs. He had not aged well. For a man with access to plastic surgery you'd think he'd take advantage of it. Caterina—he lovingly called her Catty—looked stunningly beautiful as usual. As teenagers, she was his first and last girlfriend back in their home-town and that was that. They'd been together over 40-something years. Mike's face showed traces of the strain he'd endured in his eventful and fascinating life. His always thinning blonde hair had thinned dramatically, his blue eyes now wore metal rimmed glasses. I couldn't see the rest of his body in the photo but I imagined he'd filled out to match his heavier face. He looked more like a medical doctor than ever before.

He'd once told me his favourite book was Sigmund Freud's *Die Traumdeutung* (The Interpretation of Dreams) and that it wasn't about dreams at all. More about what our lives mean in general. "If one has a dream and wishes to turn it into reality, then over a period of time it becomes a fact." The point for me was that over my own life I'd found his insightful statements to be true. During dangerous moments I had him to thank for my positive thinking and ultimate survival.

A long straight-haired brunette with big brown doe eyes, the curvaceous pixie-like Cat was a total extrovert to compliment her husband's introverted personality. While he was a workaholic, she was an art and theatre groupie, always heading off to some gallery or opening for the apparatchiks of Moscow, the privileged class. Caterina had every opportunity to meet other men, but she remained totally devoted to "her genius physician husband", as she lovingly dubbed him. I had spent time in her enjoyable company and noticed many men look at her admiringly but she never really heeded the attention.

My focus returned to Ellen. "A month ago at a British Embassy cocktail reception in Moscow thrown by Ambassador Roderick Postlethwaite, Dr Molody specifically sought a private audience with the cultural attaché and requested you by name. The enquiry in turn was passed on to H/MOS (the Head of SIS operations in Moscow who was declared to the Russian government), Jonathan Redman, and then eventually H/RUS/OPS (the Head of SIS' operations in Russia and based in London) here at home," Ellen Blyton smiled, looking directly into my eyes. "Not that you care about such protocol, young man," she admonished, "but you should be so honoured that such a world renowned scientist should want to see you and go through the highest diplomatic channels to make certain he finds you."

I didn't say anything but just gazed right back into her twinkling eyes, waiting for the words which were to come.

"We have no idea what he wants to talk to you about or why, but it would be only fitting of him to ask for the man who helped him defect in the first place."

* * * * * * * * * *

How I first met Mrs Blyton was interesting. Following the formality of an interview in 1973, undertaken more for the sake of protocol (as I was a junior officer in the armed forces), with the Coordinating Staff at the Foreign & Commonwealth Office at Queen Anne's Gate in London SW1, I was sent straightaway to SIS spy training school at Fort Monckton on Gosport's southernmost peninsula in Hampshire for six months. Because I had a military background and experienced warfare, stints were also served both at the British Army's Intelligence Corps training centre in Ashford, Kent, and Bletchley Park's Station X, a Royal Navy code and cipher special unit—among others. As a result I well versed in SIS paramilitary practices, at least on paper, which the average new intelligence officer did not undergo. A week in St Albans in Hertfordshire at Operational Research Department among the "Major Boothroyd's techie Q's" revealed that MI6 really had a unit that developed unusual weaponry and gadgets. But in a nutshell the main lessons were: ninety per cent of information comes from vision—the remaining ten per cent comes from hearing and touching—and that the SIS operate at zero estimate (stands for "starting from a blank piece of paper"). *Most people communicate about what they already want to hear, having an opinion before the facts.*

Soon after completion—I am a graduate of the "class of 54" (not a year but the designated number of the intelligence officers new entry course I attended)—they then transferred me overseas quickly once they learned I had a flair for languages and could play sports. Two years stationed as the number three (coded COP/2)—the most junior rank of the SIS station trio even though I was a P Officer (P stands for Production, in charge of planning ops and carrying them out) and not an R Officer (R stands for Requirements, in charge of dissemination of the production gathered)—in Copenhagen, the Danish capital, had been okay. The problem with Denmark and its close neighbour, Sweden, was that the nationals spoke excellent English and preferred it to their mother tongue. Children learned Americanisms by watching TV in the original language with Danish subtitles. A good way to learn early and a clever matrix of modern imperialism.

Most of my early time was spent office-bound, head burrowed in assessments, analyses, and monitoring Scandinavian developments in the

SCIF* zone in the basement. Then from time to time I'd be part of the human link in cut-out methods whereupon one person delivered something small, obvious confidential, to take it to another—like in a chain of delivery boys. Classified as dangerous but actually standard drill stuff, I can look back now and see how they broke me in slowly, bit-by-bit. *The presence of the person changes everything.*

By far the most exciting moments there for me was in my first year—1974—when I collaborated three times with a to-be defector called Oleg Antonovich Gordievsky, a KGB operational staff Line PR colonel, a political intelligence espionage specialist from its foreign unit, the First Chief Directorate, reporting to its Department R. I was rated as an above average badminton player and was scheduled in games to play him, once in a foursome and twice with just him against me. The whole point on every occasion was to collect small Kodak film canisters from him and give it to my SIS number two (COP/1) right after the matches were over. I can't remember if I won or lost against the older Russian but he continued to play the game for 11 more years before making the break to our side of the court, stepping under the net from Moscow, even though—oddly—at the time he was already based in London. I was starting to see that espionage is a strange game even from the first serve.

Then one day I received a telex asking me—kind of read as a directive really—if I would be interested in finishing my education. As a result, I commuted daily by hovercraft across the few miles of water to Lund University in Sweden. Naturally the idea of having me study for a PhD in Social Intelligence was to ultimately benefit the British Royal Navy and the Secret Intelligence Service jointly. Even my thesis was communist eastern bloc-related and my professor, it was rumoured was an ex-patriot former spy for JNA, the old Yugoslav Army. Old fart Dedijer, the senior lecturer, originally from *Jugoslavija*, opened my eyes to the fact that "where there is no division; possibilities multiply". He had greatly helped me in my understanding of how the various structures of political life worked on both sides

---

* SCIF is a restricted top secret/sensitive category camera-monitored Secure Compartmented Information Facility where all manner of critical infrastructure equipment is housed, ie: a paper, plastics and metal shredder; all filing cabinets had alphabet combination dials that were changed weekly; iron safes outer door activated by key and inner door by voice; a photocopier that duplicated approved documents on a certain type of paper and noted the time. A red-lighted body heat sensor flashed when more than three personnel occupied it.

of the imaginary east-west line, during which I juggled my own two existences on a divided part-time basis while on full pay.

The best part of all was that I fell in love for the first time. Consistent with the rest of my life it had to be a strange happenstance. Only a few weeks into my transfer there, on a Friday evening I visited Tivoli Gardens alone in the centre of town, eaten there, then on the spur of the moment gone to a discotheque. I'd quickly found that the Nordic beauties don't wait for their heavy drinking Viking men to ask them for a dance. The custom was polite and in a non-sleazy way, reversed. If you were other than the norm—fair hair and blue eyes—you were in big demand. A bit like happening to be good-looking blonde woman in the middle of Rome, among all those Latin bottom-pinching lotharios.

In the days before AIDS awareness, I had found myself spending the night with a Christina. A Scandinavian Airlines System air hostess who had forewarned me that she wouldn't be there when I woke up as she would be off flying. So trustworthy was the Danish way in those times that I was told to please help myself to breakfast and then make certain the door was locked when I left.

Sure enough, at mid-morning the redhead had disappeared and I gingerly prepared coffee and whatnot in the buff. Standing in the kitchen buttering toast I became aware of being watched. A tired SAS flight attendant in her blue uniform was standing in the doorway but smiling wickedly at my full glory. She had just returned from a transatlantic trip that morning and shared the flat with Christina. I didn't try to cover up myself as my hands were holding a knife and food. As she raised her eyebrows, her only comment was simply, "Nice bottom half."

I was to live with that very stunning platinum blonde, sapphire-eyed Dane on-and-off for eight years. After donning a black kimono she had thrown me, and after she had showered and changed into a dressing gown, we had spent the rest of morning chatting gaily at the kitchen table. And it went on like a rocket from there. Her name was Vibeke Brink, the Danish Christian name for Rebecca. Christina? I never ever saw her again as within one week Vibeke had moved into my place permanently.

It was three years later when she discovered my real occupation, and even then she wasn't to learn everything. Ordinarily in Britain my cover was provided by a claim to work in assessments for the Ministry of Defence. While in Denmark it was such officially described as "under a Royal Navy joint security programme with the Danish Navy". The MOD and RN even gave me ID pertaining to this. But initially I only told her about my "other alias" work.

All the while she had thought I was an English music publishing executive—my original story to her—given leave to "study international commerce while undertaking occasional royalty and creative tasks abroad". It was enough for her to have to comprehend why her live-in lover disappeared for silent weeks and months at a time, but couldn't tell her why.

What had gnawed at her for a lengthy time was that some of the obscure places I reportedly went to were not exactly known for music. It was true. At the time there were no pop music charts in the third world and probably still are not. But what she was to never learn was that she had long ago been vetted by internal security and cleared to have a relationship with me.

In those days I would also return to London for a few days generally once every couple of months. More often than not I would drive the Firm's Audi west to the port of Esbjerg and take the overnight ferry into Harwich, where I'd be in my Stanmore flat in the northern London suburb of Middlesex early the next afternoon. From there it would be a Bakerloo Line tube ride into the city down to Baker Street and a short walk to the square where "worldwide music operations" were conducted. I had to learn the trade after all, to know what I was talking about in times when my cover came into play on the turntable. I was only "one of our men in Denmark", an inconsequential posting on the SIS totem pole, and still learning my new trade.

Then, by late-afternoon I would be at the old SIS headquarters— boarding another brown line train, this time down to Lambeth North tube station and in a few minutes I'd be at Century House on Westminster Bridge Road—not that far from the Houses of Parliament, which was just down the road across the river.

It was at this location where I first met Mrs Blyton not long after I'd been seconded to the SIS.

* * * * * * * * *

In the mid-seventies I had been sent on a mission to Tunisia on Africa's northern shores. Strangely it was only a hundred and fifty miles south of the

Italian island of Sicily, which was in Europe. My only real preparation was a week's crash course in basic Arabic at The School of Oriental & African Studies in London's Russell Square.

I loved Tunisia. It had plenty of French influence but not without its own beauty. The Tunis Air 737 came into Tunis over pearly white beaches and creamy white buildings on a breezy sunny Sunday morning. Soon it was to be rightfully promoted as a delightful holiday destination.

On the way into the city, there was a football match not that far away from the hotel, so I quickly unpacked and joined the crowd African-style. It was a professional game between Club Africain and Etoile Sportive du *Sahel*, the last word was the local name for the Sahara Desert.

After the match I spent time people watching. It was a harmonious mixture of liberal attitude and Islam, the way it should be—being what you want to be without pressure from anybody. Its fundamentalist religious neighbours all saw it quite differently however.

The next morning I was driven south to *Susah*, a fabulous holiday spot on the Mediterranean known now to tourists as Sousse. I promised I would one day return for a well-deserved break with Vibeke. There, my driver Khamais introduced me to my Berber guide Faozi, who never spoke English; and I never tried conversing with him in either French or his brand of Arabic. Then Khamais left me with him. That night it was just he and I in a cool decrepit hut in the middle of darkness.

At cockcrow the escort and I set off walking for the border. I thought of the Japanese word for mirage when I first saw it. *Maborosi* was an illusory light on the ken, which lured its fishermen out to sea; and I took it as an omen of things to come. The memory-forming photograph of the lone Tunisian fisherman standing in his boat against dawn's light stuck like a fishhook in the gullet of the mind. The mystic island of Djerba could be seen on the horizon. Like a mental videotape put on stop, my recollection is freeze-framed at strategic moments, and I can remember it all.

Tunisia's arid southern Matamata region has harsh searing desert winds, but it projected a ravishing quality against the background of the hills. Somewhere there, carved twenty feet down into the rock, are natural wind-ventilated tunnels that lead into Libya.

In Arabic head-dress and clothes, I crossed the *Libya* border under-ground. It was fifteen minutes of speedy footsteps in the dark. At the sight of sunlight beaming brightly down the tunnel, my unfriendly pal Faozi gave me a hand-traced copy of the route, bade *"au revoir"* and turned on his heels and disappeared back into the airy blackness. I tried to focus at the piece of paper, bit my lips in apprehension at doing the return journey alone, then put it in my pocket.

At the top I made a psychic picture of the all-important exit point and built a stone marker with a series of pebbles made to resemble the Eiffel Tower, at least to me it did. I hoped the sand wouldn't cover it and make it unrecognisable when I got back in a few days time. I made sure the molly (a German-made electronically controlled automatic exposure mode 35-mm Minox C micro-camera the size of a matchbox with 36 shots per roll) was functioning, the special preparations suicide pills called L-Tablets—thought to be named so because it was lethal but was actually for luteolin—and local money was secured properly to both my legs, just below the knee, and I set off afoot shuffling. The culture boys in London had made certain my natural swaggering style didn't attract attention. They had even given me something that coloured my teeth, which gave it an unclean look. The sun took care of my tan quickly, as expected.

The first place where there were any houses in the sandy flatness was Tiji, a nondescript deserted town at the height of the sun burning down. Light green poorly printed torn posters dotted the centre of town with the portrait of Muammar el-Qaddafi, the Libyan leader, posturing with his customary female bodyguards. He wore an Arab cape over a blazer and slacks while they grandly posed around him with rifles, wearing Bedouin-style scarves. You'd think the publicity boys in Libya would come up with a wider range of shots; not use the same one. I found myself trying to come across another posed angle, but failed. They were all identical.

According to the MI6 directive, Tiji was exactly two hundred miles from my objective. An hour later I was sitting at the back of a full bumpy bus, accompanied by chickens and goats. The dusty non-air conditioned vehicle slowly followed directions to *Tarabulus*, otherwise known as Tripoli, the capital of Libya. It was a fine way to see the country, doing it as the Romans do, though I pretended to be asleep.

At dusk I hopped off just south of the city where lights could be seen ten or so miles in the distance. I was thirty miles away from my ultimate destination. It was such a lovely evening that I slept on a wall and washed myself from one of the many wells. There were at least five other men with me out there on that mortar. I didn't have to talk to anybody if I didn't want to. Arab custom respects that choice. Again at sunrise I was on my way once more.

The SIS report had provided plenty of satellite photographs. According to the intelligence office-bound experts, and verified by both US and UK militaries, it was stated that the world's largest underground chemical weapons plant was emerging here in Tarhunah. They had wanted somebody to go right up to it and take a look-see, and that's precisely what I was doing. *A single fact changes the perception of anything.*

From a few miles away, it was a simple natural rocky pyramid. It was what was going on under the coned lid was the problem. I wasn't expected to go into the interior of the mountain; nor did I think I could. Nor would I know the difference between chemical production and a water irrigation storage system the Libyan diplomatic channels had claimed it was. American and British hydro wizards had specifically written, "a 100 tons had been removed to date and that water containment doesn't need that much space". The war boys had added, "biological manufactured weapons can produce tons of poison gas per day". All of it speculation thus far.

Up close, right at the electric fence, I'd estimated it was around six square miles of construction activity underway. By chance some three-dozen Arab workers were going into the compound and I simply joined the end of the queue unnoticed. While not actually inside the belly of the beast, I was on its dinner plate—better than I'd ever hoped to do. I took several photos and merged with other workers, even carrying some metal rods to nowhere in particular, as it served my circulation process.

The two Asian gents and the blonde Caucasian couple in safety helmets didn't fit at all out there in the Libyan desert mound range. I made my way towards them. I got a beautiful colour slide of all four of them posing together. As much as I tried I couldn't get the oriental guy nearest to me into a separate frame and besides how long could I keep bending over in-conspicuously. It was his blue helmet that bore an unusual logo, which I wanted to record on film; instead I made a note of it in my head's filing cabinet. As he walked away, the older man called after him in Japanese something about *"yama san"* and followed it with, *"moshiwake gozaimasen."* I knew a little of the language, as many of the words derived from China, and he clearly referred to the "mountain" and that "there was no excuse." As he turned again the man accidentally walked right into me standing there and I apologetically responded without looking at him, "Peace be upon you"—

"Salam alekhum." He ignored my stupid bowing. In his hands on the clipboard were clearly the Roman letters "WET" in bold capitals, which I thought uncommon for a Japanese company.

I kept taking dozens of discreet photographs, then decided to get out, as I'd stayed too long. Eventually I ended up filing out with another group of Arab workers waiting for a security guard to open the gate. However, standing next to us, some seven feet away, was a foreign threesome smoking foul-smelling *Byelomore Canals* (a Soviet brand of cigarettes named after canals built by Stalin) who were having a discussion in Russian. Though I couldn't get every word, the snippets I got were: "Kolya, the Fourth Directorate should be happy with our work," one said seriously. The other later stated in an overstated jocular way, "Chicken's neurological pathways are similar to those in humans." The third man didn't speak but his briefcase carried a tag which in Cyrillic read, 'Ural Mining & One Dressing Combine.' His first name was Pyotr but his thumb was over the last. They walked out of the site with us and boarded the same worker's bus back to camp.

I thought I'd done a reasonably good job for the day and treated myself to a tasty meal of lamb kebab and rice that night by the side of the road. I hadn't expected to go that close but snaps always came out better the closer you got to the object.

Unfortunately the morning commuter bus to Tiji never came, or maybe I'd missed it. I didn't bother asking anybody what was up. Standing at the bus stop I saw a fairly new bicycle parked outside a store. Just when I'd decided to take it, an Arab lad about fifteen years old got on it, coming towards me ten feet away. I pretended to walk in front of him "by mistake" which made him brake as he toppled to the side. Quickly checking nobody was looking, I had both my arms on his shoulders. He passed out from the hard squeeze I administered him, as I gently "prevented his fall". I placed him on the shaded side of a high wall and arranged him as if he was taking a nap. The bag of flour he was carrying became a convenient pillow under his head. I hoped his Mum wouldn't scold him later for being a slacker.

It took me a while, but I eventually found the road heading southwest to Tiji and the Tunisian border. An hour and a half later I wheeled past a military training camp in progress by the side of the sparse road. I stopped for a breather to watch the exercise. As I had some film left, it turned out to be another photo opportunity. Who knows what the blow-ups may contain. After a quarter of an hour I was on my way again.

Having abandoned the bike in Tiji, I walked the rest of the way to the border. There the "Eiffel Tower" was still standing and I re-traced the same route through the tunnel. Minus the guide and the driver I had before, I quickly made it all the way back to Tunis. I was back in rainy London two days later, giving myself a deserved half-day off at the Firm's expense before turning up at the office.

While the microfilm was being processed, I wrote my report on my routine assignment and turned it in. When I returned the next morning from a second night at the White House, the duty officer in reception told me to go straight to Mrs Blyton's office. Everybody knew she was "C"'s personal assistant. That became the first time I'd met her.

On the way up, the call of nature came, so I stopped into the men's toilet to take a leak. I was a bit nervous, as this was the big boss' secretary I was going to see. As I tapped on the door and entered, I happened to catch her doing up her blouse's top button. So I stupidly said while raising my eyebrows, "Oops, sorry about dropping in, love. I knocker-ed." It was a cocky northern English reference to her nice breasts.

She sat there open-mouthed while staring over her glasses. Finally, she looked down at a file in front of her and mumbled, "Are you Anderson, just back from Libya yesterday?" I stood there mutely at attention and nodded. I was kicking myself for the off-hand remark; it was a damn stupid thing to say. But she was smiling wickedly now—which puzzled me—and deliberately in a sexy manner leaned forward over her desk to take in my full view. "My, so what do we have here?" as she stared at my pants. It was then that I realised embarrassingly, that in my haste, I hadn't zipped up.

I did so immediately, but wise-cracked back, without looking at her, "Seems that we *are* letting it all hang out today, aren't *we*?" For some reason that made her grin and ever since that time, whenever I had the infrequent occasion to see her, we have had a fecund sexual rivalry which has never got past the spoken or assumed. *Even unintelligent remarks make a point too!*

The outcome of that first all-morning episode was most productive in the business sense though. She handed me two telexes, plus the same drawing I'd made to diagram the design I'd seen on the Asian's helmet close up. "These intercourse's are from *Kempetai* and *KISS*," as she pursed her lips ever so slightly at me, while gazing innocently into my eyes. "They are respectfully the Japanese secret service and the Korean Intelligence & Security Service. Your logo was evaluated and confirmed as that of a South Korean company based in Japan called Chosen Soren. They have helped communist North Korea acquire technology, especially materials for ballistic missiles as well as biological and chemical weaponry."

Next up was a copy of the exact replica of the WET initials I'd witnessed. "WET is based in Hamburg, West Germany. Exports machines for manufacturing mustard gas, bombs and rockets—in violation of West German export regulations." That explained the two blonde Aryan men. The Asian must have been holding a clipboard they'd given him.

The filched photograph of the four men came out perfectly. I wished they'd smiled though. I would have captioned it, 'Asia and Europe enjoying time together in Africa.' "They will all be fully identified shortly and questioned upon their return to South Korea or Japan and Germany," was all she offered. *They'll be wondering how they got singled out too*, I thought to myself.

"The Fourth Directorate is indeed a unit of the KGB. They are in charge of maintenance of nuclear war bunkers for high level Soviet government officials. Their presence indicates they built the same for the Libyans in there. As for the 'chicken' joke, the language department thinks it refers to implementation of a real gaseous nature inside that mountain. I would respectfully agree with them based on the evidence you've picked up.

"There *is* an enterprise unbelievably entitled Ural Mining & One Dressing Combine. They are based in Beloretsk in the Yamantau Mountains, not far from the Soviet satellite region of Kazakhstan.

"As for 'Kolya', which is the diminutive for Nicholas, and 'Petya', as Pyotr was probably called…are *usually* false as they never use their real names on foreign assignments. However, as you know, when Russians don't know somebody well enough to use their nicknames, they use the patronymic—meaning they say the full first, middle and last name. It sounded like they knew each other quite well, as if they'd worked together before."

She shuffled some more blown-up photographs and handed me one. "Lastly, those photographs at the training camp you happened upon yielded the most promising fact of all." I was looking at a close-up shot of two men sitting in a jeep, both Bedouin camouflages over their heads. Next she gave me another closer shot of the lighter skinned man on the left. He very clearly had blue eyes and a straight white man's nose. It was accompanied by a full shot of his face from another period, paper clipped underneath it. Whoever took the latter full facial must have been right in his mug. It was that clear a photograph.

"This man has been identified as Patrick 'Paddy' O'Neill. Head of the Provisional Irish Republican Army. The other man is from the Libyan *Moukhabarat*, their intelligence service, or the 'listening post' as they like to call it. We quickly did some homework after seeing this. It answers the ages old question of where the IRA is getting their limited nerve gas supplies from. Some of those other young men out there have also been tentatively identified as Irishmen based on their fair complexions. There were an estimated dozen of them altogether. Obviously it means the Libyans are either funding the IRA and/or also training them. I would think it safe to conclude they are really doing both and it confirms there is a link between them."

She leaned back finally. "You've done an excellent job, young man. It's plain to me you have a knack for spotting clues. It's quite uncanny. We're lucky to have you with us."

Chapter Two

Most people find it difficult to understand
why anyone would fight against a superior enemy
but we do so refuse to accept defeat
through the psychology of submission.
We do not respect those who force us to do anything ever.
Perhaps nobody may understand this passion,
this calm, this controlled madness,
but Lord Byron, Garibaldi, Spartacus and Tolstoy
would have understood us easily.

Back to the present in 1992, I closed the door behind me in the flat at The White House. Ellen Blyton and I had strolled briskly back from Regent's Park, followed obediently by The Dog, as the rain had started to bucket down. We arranged to meet again in 24 hours, same place, same time. Obviously without her having to say it out loud, "C" was going to want to know whether I wanted to be in or out. I chuckled to myself over the part about "it's official and not official at the same time". In all my years I'd never heard or read anything in SIS quite put like that. *Even oxymorons exist in extremely focused spy organisations where a word out of place could make a difference.*

It was only mid-afternoon still in London, even though I felt I'd been here much longer. I've actually been here since only the morning, I reflected. Long distance flying had a habit of playing these topsy-turvy tricks on the mind and body. Made a mental note to follow up on taking over-the-counter dietary supplement melatonin pills which Molody himself had recommended years ago. Still hadn't tried it after all this time. Something to do with the melatonin hormone being a master hormone which is secreted by the pea-sized pineal gland in the brain. He said it helped reset the body's clock as well as fight common diseases of ageing.

The jet lag was starting to kick in and I felt drowsy. I slipped off my western cowboy boots and blue jeans. Mrs Blyton thought I "looked like a hippie" when I thought I was trying to create the free image of the American wild west.

I switched on the telly. Good old "Auntie Beeb"—the BBC—hadn't changed its format much over the years. Still had a bit of an upper crust image despite the non-discernible English accents of its news readers. The same old damn problems remained with the Irish Republican Army in Belfast. Catholic minority versus Protestants majority. The politicians still trying to achieve their own agenda. If you asked me, there were three things they all should at least try but hadn't so far: Educate the kids from kindergarten age and up to play with each other, so they felt less inclined when they grew up to knock the other guy's block off just because they were a different denomination; in the name of economic progress make a truly concentrated effort to create more jobs for both sides and not for one side only; and stop the flow of funding coming from well-meaning affluent Irish-Americans and their organisations who truly believed their donations were going for reasons other than purchasing of weaponry. I shook my head.

Those dumb theories could be applied to the Israeli-Palestinian problem too with their respective money-raising brothers in the US, as well as to other bitter religious frictions elsewhere. They won't listen to someone like me anyway, though I'd been to both Northern Ireland and the Gaza Strip, and had felt the pulse of the streets first-hand. A damn pity really. I shook my head. I hit the off button on the remote control and sub-consciously did the same to myself, falling into an instantaneous deep sleep.

In my dreams I found myself floating down the turbulent river of life to my childhood and the delta widening to the ocean of young adulthood. It was here in London that my father and I drove four hundred miles from Stockton-on-Tees in the northeast of England, to a hotel near Harrods, for a one-day university fair. Actually it was related to American universities only, and I was invited to attend given my college grades were not bad but my sporting achievements were excellent. At 18 I had aspired to being a professional football player and at the time had played a couple of seasons as an expenses-paid amateur for the reserve team of Newcastle United Football Club. Three years prior I was a member of the British Schools swimming team, having won the national championship in the butterfly stroke. So I guess that put me up there as a natural sportsman. I'd heard they'd awarded high-level educational scholarships in America for those with superior sporting ability and I'd fitted the bill.

The day of interviews went so-so. On the long drive back up the A1 motorway in the rumbling Humber, Dad and I had been silent for most of the trip north when he quietly posed the question. "So which American university may you pick, young man?"

Given my mature background so far in life, I was truly shocked at the deeply offensive manner in which several of the many American educational institutions representatives had spoken to me earlier that afternoon. I wasn't at all prepared for the frequent god-worshipping quotes of the US bible belt interviewers, who struck me as rabid reactionaries and worse. It was quite unlike the average British way of life. Duke and Auburn made their verbal pitches to me, with a possible third tendered at a later date from Brigham Young. If North Carolina, Alabama and Utah represented the best I could attract and this was their normal speech...I simply couldn't find the precise words to express my controlled feelings of disgust and anger.

My thinking was that my father would not understand my mixed emotions but, to my utter and complete surprise, he simply said, "I know *exactly* how you feel, because I got the same bad reaction, son." Later he added, "We're going to have a chat with your Uncle Len." And that was that.

Len was my Dad's older brother by 13 years, at that time he was a labour union leader representing the large majority of northeast England's left-leaning iron, steel, coal mining and dock workers. Uncle Len was a dominant powerhouse in the world of the locally repressed working-class.

Up to that point I hadn't given it much thought really, I mean I knew the man was the complete opposite of my Dad. In physical terms he was bigger, rounder than his younger brother's slim frame. In attitude he seemed both extremely jovial and extrovert, a comedian at heart, compared to the reserved corporate director demeanour of my father. Lastly, he appeared to be the very epitome of the almost bald, sleeves rolled up, blue-collar working man in a boiler suit while Dad was a prim 'n' proper suit 'n' tie man with slicked back perfectly combed hair. I'd pictured them as Laurel and Hardy, and it so happened that Stan Laurel was originally from Hartlepool in the northeast of England too, so perhaps it was a local trait.

Apparently, during the reign of Harold Wilson, Britain's then Prime Minister, there was a oft renewed and frequently broken bond between the British trade unions and the Soviet Union. It was often speculated that Wilson was really a communist and it was later printed by the right-wing pro-Conservative press in Fleet Street (the British media's conclave) later reported that this pipe-smoking Labour leader had "visited Moscow eighteen times since World War II". Such was the contradictory political and economic climate in Great Britain in those tumultuous days.

Well, it came at no great surprise that my Uncle Len was a die-hard Trotskyite Red too. While I did laugh at the thinly-veiled revelation, I shut up when Dad disclosed he himself was a liberal-minded Conservative party voter. What was the bloody difference in the end? But the crux of the matter was that my uncle managed to finagle a one-year induction course in Economic Geography at Patrice Lumumba University in Moscow, without me having to complete an entry application or examination—much to my obvious delight.

Less than a month later, I remember that my father said something to the effect that "if I didn't like it there—I had a non-restricted return BOAC (British Overseas Airways Corporation, the predecessor to British Airways' long-distance routes) airline ticket in my hands". It meant I could just go to the airport in Moscow and leave when I wanted to.

Well, I stayed for the entire year much to his and my surprise.

And that was when I first met the good Doctor Molody...

My mental alarm clock woke me up exactly at the time I'd wanted it to. I tried to jump-start my brain by recalling events in the past twenty-four hours. I finally rose from the bed, still a little groggy. Southern California was now a distant dream. Having just completed the necessary urinary relief, and contemplating seeking my favourite first-day-back-wish for a combination of fish 'n' chips, washed down by Newcastle Brown Ale with a top of lemonade—when lo and behold, the telephone rang.

"Nick, you're back, you rotten scoundrel."

I admit I had to think for a second or two, before slowly responding with uncertainty, "Is that you Dave, Dave Brennan?"

We both laughed like excited schoolboys. It had been about six years since we last saw each other but I thought of him constantly. We had gone through naval academy in Devon together, and our lives took on almost the exact same paths at SIS and we had successfully survived a couple of dangerous covert missions together. He was the same age and I thought of him as a twin brother. We both shared an interest in spending the wee hours of the mornings coming up with funny epigrams. Once even, we arrived at a part-statement or half-motto, which evolved into our official slogan:

"We have been through so many things together
that we don't really care about anything
and hereby decide to call it
our 'kamikaze psychology.'"

But we really *did* deeply care about the world around us. Without asking him, I'd put two and two together and naturally assumed Mrs Blyton had told him of my whereabouts and he had called immediately.

Less than three-quarters of an hour later, freshly showered and shaved, I went to meet my long lost buddy from MI6 in the Masons Arms pub, just off Great Portland Street, only a 10-minute quick walk south from The White House.

When I walked into the smoke-filled lounge, I couldn't see him. I scanned the cosy bar looking for his six-foot gangling frame. The last time I saw him he had nondescript sandy coloured hair that was always in need of styling. The girls had always liked to ruffle his thatch fondly to try and give it some shape, a fruitless task. A modest, gung-ho, dry-humoured, lagoon-blue eyed bright mick from near Larne, Northern Ireland, he never failed to blast off one of his donkey he-haw howls. When he did occasionally so bray loudly, everybody present would stand still in mock horror at this awful sound.

I shrugged and made my way to the bar and ordered a pint of beer. A quarter of a way down the drink, while still pressed to my lips, I gazed alternatively at the two doors through the clear beer glass clouded with spotted foam. In entered the plain-clothed Lieutenant-Commander David Desmond

Brennan, Royal Navy, retired, and much to my open-mouthed amazement, in a hand-mobilised wheelchair.

Following the howls of laughter and hugs, much to the amusement of the regulars in the pub, we found a quiet corner, away from the din of the early evening after work crowd. I sat there speechless, a delayed reaction to seeing him an invalid. It even crossed my mind that it could have been one of his strange jokes. I mean what do you say to one of the most athletic persons you've ever known and he's confined to pushing himself around like this? "So I'm a cripple, so what, I know what you're thinking Anderson, you can't fool me." He read my mind as usual and held my look with dogged impunity on his face. The typical Brennan-style stare told me to button-up and I did so obligingly.

In rapt uninterrupted muteness I literally sat there gawking as his story unfolded.

As it turned out, he'd been stationed in Belize in 1988, the only truly democratic country in Central America, formerly known as British Honduras. He was the resident SIS intelligence officer in the newly formed Counter Narcotics Section at the makeshift British Consulate in the new capital of Belmopan. As he put it, there was only him and a couple of other blokes sharing a crammed office. The British High Commissioner never knew he existed. It was a routine posting of small consequence in world affairs, or so he thought. Recently amicably divorced with no children, he had welcomed a year or two in the sub-tropics and expected to spend a lot of his free time snorkelling in the azure Caribbean Sea. After all the world's longest *living coral* barrier reef was there—which was only a few miles offshore. It was his favourite pastime, second only to his love of drinking. "Booze. It's what the right hand's for," he would quip before sucking down a pint in one go.

His main role was to regularly check close-up on the several violent peasant uprisings in Central America and off he went into the wilderness of mirrors. His tales of intrigue in Nicaragua were particularly spellbinding. He'd conducted a study of the Stalinist Sandinistas rebels involvement with the sale of narcotics, supposedly supported by Gorbachev's Soviet Union, including a similar report on the US under Reagan's leadership and their official US$50 million-plus financing of the little government army of 12,000 Contras who were also in the drug distribution trade. "Puppets strung up on the world's stage manipulated by self-serving others and falsely described as a holy war," he grimaced. He had also spent a couple of days each week travelling clandestinely to nearby Guatemala, and from there on south in longer jaunts to Honduras, El Salvador and Nicaragua, usually sitting for days in a dusty bus, monitoring the activities under the guise as a neutral United Nations observer using a false Norwegian passport.

He discovered the CIA had ties to corrupt Guatemalan military officers. "The amount of Israeli armoury imported into Guatemala was quite astonishing and it was a wonder that it was never stopped. But being the 'US in the Middle East', the Americans weren't going to block the sales to the Guat army.

"The point of telling you all this is that over 200 tons of cocaine a year flows to the United States through the Central American nations from South America, accounting for about 40% of the total coke entering the US. A further 100 tons is estimated to find its way from there to Europe.

He had worried about his own welfare which was increasingly getting more on-the-line by his mere continuous presence, not to mention his fair complexion which stood out a mile in the unfriendly environment.

"Finally," he said resignedly, "I'd used up most of my nine lives. I was ultimately in the wrong place at the wrong time. Actually, as silly as it sounds, I was momentarily side-tracked with fascination at watching these sea-faring bull sharks so far up river in a freshwater lake trying to attack a group of peasants wading across…I wasn't paying full attention to my surroundings and I stupidly walked blindly into an illegal checkpoint where they must've paid off the army guards. They blindfolded me…"

"Who is *they*?" I enquired. My paraplegic pal stared at the floor and then smiled grimly at me, glassy-eyed. "Nothing to do with what I've been talking to you about so far—unrelated—but not quite totally unrelated though. The fucking *rearmados,* the 'rearmed fighters' in an area in Nicaragua called La Cruz de Rio Grande. The warlord there is one José de Jesus Ochoa who was hand-in-hand with the Colombian drug cartel's self-appointed 'security' guys, the FARC, you know the *Fuerzas Armadas Revolucionarias Colombias* or 'Armed Revolutionary Forces of Colombia'. It's a fascinating story really, if you care. And I did. At the end of the Cold War, FARC's ideological focus sapped. I mean they had their representative offices in Mexico, Costa Rica and some European countries. They'd continued to rob banks, extort cash from wealthy landowners from the results of kidnapping their kin, much like the IRA." Then almost to himself, he added, "A pretty spooky way of making a living..."

He took a big gulp of ale before continuing. "They're only some 110 men and 10 women, each allotted about one US dollar a day for food. The guerrillas always claimed not to be involved in doing drug trafficking and don't get paid cash for their mostly 'security services'. That's how ideological FARC were. But *why* they provided services was because a AK-47 rifle, for example, costs US$2,000 on the black market and both the Medellin and Cali cartels paid them in guns and ammunition which, to them, was better for them overall as they didn't have to haggle over prices.

"Their traditional heroes are Ché Guevara and Simon Bolivar, at least that's what the T-shirts proclaim. I didn't know until that point that *ché* was Argentine slang for 'buddy' which frequently replaced 'comrade.' Many join FARC as young as 13 and 14, mainly due to the influences of the much older leaders like Manuel "Sureshot" Marulanda. His number two was Alfonso Cano and the number three on the totem pole, Jorge "Mono JoJoy" Briceño. You see, I still have a memory for names, unlike you Anderson," he mocked.

I found myself touching his sweating palms lightly to bring himself back thousands of miles to the jolly pub atmosphere in London.

"You know, you and I have had a lifetime fighting against the marijuana and cocaine industry..." He broke off, almost fighting back tears, finally blurting, "The arseholes that captured me played with my life like I was some kind of cockroach caught inside an upside down glass jar. I'll never forget it. Too horrible to relate to you. I hope nobody else ever has to survive being slowly crushed by being bound by duct tape and rope to a boulder of rock and rolled down a steep ravine. I was left to rot in excruciating pain and I have nightmares about them giggling like it was a fun thing to do. They were all screaming in Spanish, 'Dogs die like dogs!' *Perros mueren como perros!* God almighty, Nick, I hate those bastards and the world's biggest market they supply there in the US. If there wasn't an ever increasing market for the stuff there, I'd still have my legs," he trailed off. He never got into who found him and I guessed he'd blanked that from his instant recall memory.

"The danger of communism in Central America during the five decades of the Cold War was greatly exaggerated by the United States government. After all these years, now that I had the actual time to sit down and think for once. I finally figured it out that all that Central American war nonsense was just a smokescreen to keep everybody focused away from the real reason. And that was where the heavy-duty money was. There was definitely a link between the so-called terrorism-slash-so-called holy war and drugs from Colombia on its way to North America. I have to also assume that they thought it would be a matter of time before I stumbled across the truth and exposed it. There's nothing else I can fathom, for them taking it out on me in the way they did. I'm sure they thought they'd eliminated me from the scene. But I'm still here, as is my fate," he trailed off again. "I've coined it as my narc-farc concerto." Brennan had regained his Irish comic composure.

"You're starting to sound like a MI6 musician waiting for an encore, Brennan," I said jokingly, referring to CIA jargon for a radio operator.

He laughed his loud laugh. "Yes, the Russians and the Americans could not agree to build a bridge, so they dug a hole for all of us." This was the lively David Brennan I knew. "To Poland and Czechoslovakia," he mimicked a mock cry, raising his pint glass "to that mad, mad escape from the Commie bastards down the river torrents to freedom. Jeez, that was a crazy time. I can still hear the whitewater whizzing past." His eyes were filled with fire momentarily.

We spent the rest of the evening wandering the surrounding streets of London W1 with me pushing him. Cod 'n' chips we had north of Baker Street tube, followed by lots more brown ale and a chaser of vodka at the nearby Euston Road pub's last call at closing time. He told me how much he missed the rhythm of walking. He reminisced that I would always write all sorts of unintelligible nonsense down, when we had travelled to points unknown, and how he had contributed his Irish wit to help. Later on that night he asked me to compose a prose to fit his 'current dilemma,' as he positively called it, so I surprised myself by saying unrehearsed:

> "To those who want to destroy their lives on drugs
>   and its profitable related cousins;
>   reality metes out the punishment they deserve
>   and I gladly have no sympathy."

"You were always good at coming up with that kind of stuff, you know," he stopped and suddenly stared at me. Then he wheeled away while trying to memorise it periodically in his semi-stupor. I, in turn, divulged my inner thoughts about going to Moscow—he was definitely all for it—and he came up with his own witty line in the form of another toast, "I wouldn't start from here, if I were you! "

But he said this only after I had asked him if he had been planted to influence my decision. He swore "on his children" that he wasn't sent by anybody. I later recalled in my alcoholic haze that he didn't have any children. An evening I will remember to my dying day.

That night I went back to bed with not a care in the world, having been happily reacquainted with Dave Brennan. He did not want to go to bed that night I learned, instead, deciding he was happy to end his life on a high note when he got home and not having to care ever again. Lt. Cmdr. D. D. Brennan, RN, (ret.) you didn't have to retire yourself by suicide. *If you had reached out your hand; I would have given you mine to pull you away from despair.*

I miss you so very very much, lad, and I'm so sorry I missed the clue you gave me with your very last toast..., "Life is alright if you can stand it."

* * * * * * * * *

She came swinging through the revolving doors in a hurry, her dulling red-brown hair tied straight back as if she was in a wild rush. Looking unusually ashen-faced, the normally upbeat Mrs Blyton appeared distraught. I instinctively knew something was seriously wrong.

"It's David Brennan," she said matter-of-factly, her voice without life, avoiding my eyes. "During therapy he had been classified as having 'suicidal tendencies' during periods of temporary depression. Had been that way for years now and he finally did it, last night." She was fighting back tears, trying not to be emotional in the unemotional business she was in; but every now and then, one hits the bull's eye right in the heart. Ellen looked up at me ponderously as if it was an after thought, "I gave him your telephone number here, if you don't mind, I can't imagine that he never called you."

If it was a question, I answered her by nodding dumbly, but I felt as if the hotel foyer was spinning and I was falling into a labyrinth. I leaned against the wall.

"He looked really buoyant when we said good-bye," was all I could repeat to myself. I don't know if I said it out loud or I was saying it to myself but it was a faraway echo. I was trying to get a hold of myself because the dam had cracked wide in front of me with Ellen and her tears were starting to well up. An expensive white lace handkerchief appeared quickly as we led each other to a settee. It had never occurred to me for a second that he would think of it, never mind kill himself. Brennan was a fighter; not a quitter. Not my buddy Dave. I can't believe it. "Quitters never win and winners never quit," could have been his motto. Hell, he repeated it often enough to me when I'd had enough. But he never remotely touched on thinking of the Big Moment, at least never voicing his thoughts. But that was when he had usable legs.

"His next door neighbour smelled gas when he was getting ready for work this morning. After banging on Dave's door for an eternity, he called the police and his worst fears were confirmed," she sniffed. "His body was found lying on the kitchen floor with his head resting on the open oven door. The constable I spoke on the phone to said he looked strangely peaceful when other gassing victims he'd seen were grotesque twists."

I don't know what triggered me but I suddenly blurted out, "Ellen, I *will* go to Moscow but not on the Firm's terms or anybody else's for that matter. I don't want anything to do with MI6. I woke up this morning in two minds, not having given it much thought really as I was...was..." I stopped for a deep breath. "As we *were* having such a good time last night. It was an absolutely brilliant evening. I think he would have wanted me to make this decision, so I will. Now that I've thought about it, Molody's a great bloke too. Might be into strange stuff but if he's asking for me then it must be well worth it or he wouldn't go through such lengths to make contact."

Ellen Blyton stared at me as if I'd slapped her suddenly. My mind was racing: "Yes," I clenched my teeth, "it'll be on my terms or not at all. The doctor will understand, and Dave most certainly would have. I know you too must know what drives people like me, don't you, sweet? Tell 'C' he can pick up my tab on this one, return flight business class to Moscow this coming Monday morning. BA please, not Aeroflot, and a room at the Hotel President for as long as I choose to stay. No pay, no owing him for what-not, no food allowance, no special privileges, no 'in's' of any kind, nothing else. Understand, Ellen? It's Wednesday, isn't it? But he can arrange a car for me for a few days until after Dave's funeral. Yes, I'll take advantage of that comp though, why not? Then I'll head on to Russia."

"Is that it? Are you finished? Just like that you decide, in the middle of this horrible news?" We sat there just looking dumbly at each other for a few seconds. "OK," she said finally, "I'm sure he'll say yes to all that but I'll tell you something too, "C" said you would do it anyway, and he wasn't too far off on guessing about on whose terms they'd be on. I'll call you in a few hours with all the details and itinerary."

We got up and kissed each other softly on both cheeks European-style, trying hard not to hug each other. After all this was meant to be business. "Just be careful, will you. I'll be thinking of you young man. Take care." While standing waiting for somebody to come through the doors, she glanced back and gave me a short graceful wave and then was gone. I knew then I wouldn't see her ever again in person.

I sat back on the couch and took a big intake of breath and tried to recollect my thoughts on Dave Brennan. Somebody had left the day's *Daily Mail* newspaper on the table so I tried reading it. Between flipping the pages, images of his happy face kept haunting me in bursts of light. Funnily enough, Michal Molody's face interspersed Dave's every once in a while, too. I gave up trying to read the damn paper and decided to go outside for a walk and get some fresh air, even if it was a windy day and I didn't have an overcoat on.

I found myself retracing the same steps we had enjoyed in the grey shades of sunset last night in each other's spectacular company. *If you were going to do it one day my friend, I'm glad it was after a night like yesterday's.*

I could only attempt to understand the frustration he must have felt and knew I couldn't have remained so positive as he in the face of such adversarial crippling odds. I realised then I was crying in the fierce wind and my body had gone cold. I abruptly turned around on Devonshire Street and headed back in the direction of The White House.

Less than a quarter of an hour later as I entered the hotel, the alert concierge waved for my attention. He gave me a message from Ellen Blyton. It simply read: 'Approved—car ready when you want. Usual pick-up garage in The City. Blackfriars Bridge tube station. Funeral in the province on Friday at 11:00 AM. Love. EB.'

I went upstairs and packed what little I had brought with me. I was going to the land of the notorious *Óglaigh na hÉireann*, Army of Ireland, as the Irish Republican Army stood for in Gaelic. Still battling for their day to come to this day.

Chapter Three

Terrorism is warfare by the powerless,
warfare is terrorism by the powerful.

The Caledonian Line car ferry steamed up Loch Ryan on its short voyage across the North Channel which linked the Atlantic to the Irish Sea. I'd left the Ford at the car park in Stranraer, as I would be back in Scotland, hopefully awake, on the last ferry tonight when the "party" after the funeral in Northern Ireland was over.

I looked back following the twin lines of churning water from the stern winding its way in the direction of the small Scottish port we'd departed and it was already a distant haze. The tiny village of Cairn Ryan was barely visible on the right of the disappearing shoreline. I shivered in the bone-chilling February morn.

A steaming cup of hot coffee cupped in both hands I decided to continue braving the freezing elements alone out on the starboard side after-deck. It was a nice chance to meditate until my body told my brain to go inside where it was warmer. I had after all, effectively withdrawn mentally from active life to devote intense effort and concentration to ponder the basic riddles of human experience, all for my own sake. I put my collar up and turned around to lean on the railing with my back to the disappearing shores of bonny Scotland, home of my ancestors.

A closer look at the glistening glass where the sliding doors were positioned revealed a clear full-length still-life painting of myself dressed in a knee-length Shetlands-made all-wool Harris Tweed overcoat. Ironically I had bought it during the last and only time I was in Northern Ireland in the seventies.

I spent an awful long time looking at this faded intriguing Raphaelite-like portrait. My long dark brown shoulder-length curly hair was the only movement in the wind. A 20th-century British d'Artignan-Voltaire cross-breed gazed back at me. Time stood still for agonising minutes as I waited for motion to commence. What I saw was a healthy medium built fellow with a light olive complexion and expressive dark brown eyes. I had a small uneven nose that had been broken twice and still had not been fixed. The unsmiling mouth and black Edwardian moustache complimented fox-style sideburns stolen from Zorro. Women had often commented how lucky I was to be born with such smooth flawless skin and females I had just met sometimes extended their palms to feel the smoothness of my face. For a bloke in his early-forties, the opposite sex told me I was handsome and for that I was grateful.

Meanwhile I had hoped my personality was the main attraction, as I'd felt I could mix freely with both ends of the spectrum of society. When I tried, I suppose I really could look quite dapper, but I was a real Bohemian at heart and preferred tee-shirts and jeans with no socks or underpants most of the time and would go in the all-together in the confines of home.

No matter which dress code I adopted, I pretty much knew there was something about me that created resentment and annoyed some sorry individuals. Perhaps it was because whenever I talked about anything, I'd present it in a semi-factual way, which is slightly unnerving to the sadly insecure. The secure personalities were fine in my presence and I with them. I had always noticed too, the jealousy almost always came from men. *What should I do to change this vexing pattern?* I would ask myself. *Absolutely nothing*, I'd resolve, *it is their problem, not mine.*

Since I had quit SIS, I had never bothered to own a tie, never missing the stupid worthless piece of cloth which in the past I'd frequently got caught in slammed car doors.

When I turned around again, Island Magee was looming out of the lifting fog.

In the taxi looking over the stone walls and low hedges, I recalled an eloquent Provisional Irish Republican Army gunman I'd spoken to the last time I was in the province over 15 years ago. It was at the height of the Troubles as it was still known.

He was from the tiny Catholic enclave in East Belfast called the Short Strand and had been sent to jail for life for killing three British soldiers during a riot on a West Belfast street. Though he responded to my questions with patience and thoughtfulness, a sliver of edgy wariness never left the corners of his wide cool blue eyes, and leaden eclipses of frightening silence sometimes descended. Yet he remained defiant in the hopeless hope of a united Ireland as he fixed a hard stare into my equally quiescent gaze from across the cell's table. He whispered lyrically:

"The ice on the trees will glitter like Waterford crystal
and when the sun shines on the ice on the frozen ponds we pass,
it will sparkle again like Dublin diamonds,
the Irish spring still to come to sadly melt thee Ulster,
and you know in your heart our day will come."

He had ached for the chance to achieve his dream and did whatever lay within his ability and that was his offering. The terrorist's world does not much revolve as bump and bounce from pothole to abyss.

I cringed from the colourless flashback of being a foreigner in your own country, and I raised my collar as we passed the black and white rectangle sign signalling that we were entering the clachan of Glenoe.

Standing for a few moments taking in my surroundings, I thought this is where one of my best friends grew up, and it wasn't that much different to Hurworth in England's County Durham where I'd attended boarding school for years. It was more a hamlet than a village and completely deserted. I headed in the direction of the sound of the bells and the lone church spire.

It was cold and overcast and as I walked around the corner, suddenly the clouds parted and there was a big rainbow arching over the small church. It was so beautiful that I stopped dead in my tracks. As there was no one else around, I almost cried. It seemed it was only there for me, with manly love from Brennan. *He's getting his own back on me*, I cynically said to myself.

I looked over the stone wall at the cemetery at the far end and over the dozens of crosses and headstones I could see a couple of lads busy working. It looked like they were preparing a grave, ready for a ceremony, so I assumed that bleak spot under the frozen leafless tree was to be the mark for the ex-helicopter pilot's last descent to the ground.

A hatless, black-robed priest came vector at me, head down from the opposite direction, and we met precisely where the right-angled path led to the church doors. He nodded curtly and had a rather abrupt tone, "Morning, sire, here for the funeral? Well you're early. Doesn't start until another 45 minutes. And you are?"

"Nick, er, Nicholas Anderson." I had stupidly not considered an alias. Damn stupid fool, it's a known fact that mothers don't call out their children's names here because certain names are identified as favoured by one group or the other. I deserved a brick falling on my head. "Nicholas Anderson" was as Protestant a Christian and a surname as it gets.

"You're not from these parts, I can tell. You worked with him, I suppose," sniffed the white-haired spectacled man with the white collar. He was looking at me for a response, which wasn't forthcoming. "You'll have to hang around out here, I'm afraid, until the others come. I've just returned from his Mum's place. They're nailing down the coffin at the moment. They'll be along in a while. They say he was a popular lad, Davy boy, always in some place or other at the far ends of God's country." I put down my untouched hand slowly. He never introduced himself nor did he bade "cheerio". My eyes bore into his back as he shuffled away.

To think the "Orangemen" Protestants and the "Emerald Isle" Catholics, led by church leaders like this guy, annually organises marches in each other's communities, one of the chief causes of fresh disruptions. Each think their own colour is more than a colour and is a way of life, and that's the way it is.

When I'd visited Ireland before, it was at the suggestion of Britain's domestic intelligence service, MI5, on the pretence that "being on the outside looking in, you may come up with something we haven't thought of". At the time I had been between jobs, and several highly observant MI6 international men like me were assigned a week or two in Northern Ireland. We each were required to give an oral and written report upon our return to London, including a personal overview on each of Northern Ireland's political parties: Ulster Democratic; Progressive Unionist; Ulster Unionists; Social Democrats; and Sinn Féin—the latter legally being the IRA's official political wing. The report would take place at my favourite sub-office of SIS, the one in Cromwell Road in Kensington where the bugging section lads were based, so you knew, for sure, it would be recorded for posterity. In many ways it was akin to a school test but the big head honcho "C" was trying to be creative. "You never know what might happen and who may come up with what" was the outline of the general game plan. Plus the exercise gave guys in their mid-20's, like me, on-the-job anti-terrorist training. There was also plenty to do too in the evenings afterwards around that neighbourhood in the London Borough of SW7.

In downtown Belfast I'd been given a room for ten nights at the Europa Hotel, ignominiously claiming to be, with bitter pride, the "most bombed hotel in Europe". Walking between layers of sandbags into the hotel grounds was a feat in itself, even though the pass issued by SIS saved many minutes and elicited a couple of brief unwarranted and unwanted salutes. Funnily enough my first meal in the restaurant defiantly offered a BLAST sandwich which came layered between soda bread. Unbelievable Irish dry humour during dark times. I ordered it and later regretted I had done so.

But the most ominous part of the whole first-time visit was the fact that in battle one could usually tell who the enemy was, yet here the Catholics and the Protestants looked the same, ate the same food, drank the same beer and had the same identical accents—just different Christian names and surnames.

Another massively overlooked fact was that the Irish Republican Army had Marxist-Leninist ideals, as clearly stated in their manifesto, which I'm certain most of their Catholic supporters never read. The head guy at their own political wing, which was based in the Belfast district of Lower Ormeau, a Catholic enclave, was always telling associates to address him as comrade. As a lover of rock music, even most record buyers I'd talked to never knew that U2's explosive hit song "Sunday, Bloody Sunday" was all about when British troops fired on Irish civil rights marchers in 1972, killing 13 and injuring hundreds. Such is the continuing blissful ignorance of the world we live in.

I'd been given broad authority to go where I pleased and did exactly that by spending several days in the Catholic strongholds of Armagh, and in Shankill Row, a staunchly loyalist area of Belfast. Other mainly Catholic bastions were in Drumcee, and in the second largest city in Northern Ireland, Londonderry. The most noticeable landmark was the thirty-yard long graffiti on a wall in Derry's Bogside ghetto which read "God made the

Catholics, but the Armalite made them equal" in reference to the American-made AR-16 5.56-mm rifles which were in abundance among IRA snipers. Interestingly, if you were a Protestant, you'd say Londonderry and if you were a Catholic, it was simply Derry.

I'd also spent quite a bit of time in the cages of prisons in and around Belfast, primarily at the Castlereagh holding centre; Maghaberry; Long Kesh's the "Maze" H-blocks; and the Crum (Crumlin Road). I'd also undergone a rushed two-night Aer Lingus trip down early and back up late the next day to southern Ireland's Mountjoy Prison, including visits to Dublin's Special Criminal Court and the offices of their counter-insurgency agency, C3. It was a most eventful day and then some.

While in the Irish Republic, also known as Eire—Dublin was *Baile Atha Cliath* in Gaelic—I also took a couple of unauthorised strolls past *An Cumann Cabhrach*—The Helpful Organisation—offices at 44 Parnell Street, near the centre of Dublin, the address to where New York City and Boston Irish-American policemen were known to deliver hard cash twice a month from Noraid in NYC on the pretence of being on holiday. The reason the local authorities hadn't busted the IRA fundraising and publicity arms on both sides of the Atlantic was that it was better to know about these things rather than drive them underground, where it became harder to track.

During a break of eating a home-made meat pie in a working man's pub within view of the dark prison and gulping down the black stuff called Guinness—brewed in this same fair city—I was told by an outgoing *Gaelach*-speaking laddie leaning on the bar near me, that the Pale stood for *that* part of Ireland colonised by the English. When I asked him in my fake Scottish brogue how that came about, all his response—as if I should have known—was, "'Beyond the pale' is the wild world beyond the enclosed stalked out area around your home." Very clearly I'm in Ireland, home of illogical logic, I thought then to myself, 'Welcome to *the* island.' *Failte chuig an Oilean*. There is no translation for the word "a" either in their national tongue—go figure.

The visits to the prisons came about because one of the first items on my agenda was to investigate the British Army's controversial practice known as non-selective internment. They had arbitrarily rounded up and detained some seven hundred Catholics known as IRA sympathisers and thrown them into jail, without a real trial, with unusually long sentences, sometimes with solitary confinement given to the louder protestors. Personally I thought it was a gross violation of human rights, and stated this in my final report that "probably less international sympathy with the resulting hunger strikes would have been attracted with *selective* detainment of known IRA *guerrillas* and not arresting all plain sympathisers, who were only really *nationalists* anyway." But it didn't seem to elicit any response from anybody at the SIS at the time. That's also when I heard the young Catholic recite his interesting, eloquent prose at the Maze, which I'd recalled earlier in this day.

Had the SIS taken the time to really *want to* get inside my head I could have told them much more then I'd let on. You see, at that early stage in my career I'd already developed the rare ability to see things in an off-the-wall but relatively unbiased fashion, usually where everybody could get a piece of a pie instead of one getting to eat all of it. My way was to basically look at both sides of the coin before passing judgement. But in lay-man terms I got the utmost impression then that they already knew most of the variables which were in *their* favour; were not ever going to consider anything remotely counter productive to upset the already pre-approved set game plan; and were going through the motions of the verbal and typed report for the pleasure of having me repeat my unheeded findings in the interests of wasting British tax payers money. And, of course, they have to justify it by perpetuating the clichés.

Besides little do they know, they made up my mind for me based on a lone incident I'd accidentally witnessed on the last day of the two I'd been in Dublin...Wednesday, 21st of July 1976. At the time I was 25.

The parish bells in Glenoe rang loudly to bring me back to present day Ireland. I could see a procession of about 50 people approaching in my direction. In the middle of the crowd amid audible cries, carried aloft in a brown box laid my friend David Brennan on his last tour through the village of his youth. He was probably having a ball as the centre of attention for once.

Mairead Brennan was the first person I recognised at the front of the pack. She was Dave's ex-wife of only a couple of years, after over a decade of marriage. They remained as friends, after all they were childhood sweethearts and grew up together here in Glenoe. I suspected they continued to remain lovers on the few occasions when they did meet, as neither had a companion still. "Love, the most terrible demon of all," I murmured under my breath. It was a quote from a book I'd read recently.

She was a Protestant—a Prod—and he a Taig—a derogatory nickname
for a Roman Catholic. After they married, they were considered pariahs and
suffered threatening phone calls, found graffiti sprayed on their house and
were spat at in the streets. Finally they moved lock-stock-and-barrel to the
northwest London Irish suburb of Kilburn to escape the persecution from
their own people. Over the years he spent much time overseas with his job,
while she, being a homebody, pestered him to consider returning to the
home country...but not to Glenoe. Dave had confided to me once that if
they had indeed been able to conceive, leaving his wife with a child to raise
while he was away would have made a difference to her loneliness. With
that, along with the distractions of modern civilisation, they found themselves drifting apart. Finally they severed the cord that bound them by
selling the house, then filed for divorce, with him obtaining a low-key
posting to Belize and she returning at long last to live in the place down the
road from her origins, that capital with the lower case "c"—Belfast.

Despite the haggard face and rather heavy figure, she remained a distinctive fair Irish lass with her bright blue eyes, reddish-blonde shoulder-
length straight hair, with a ruddy complexion. When she saw me standing
there she waved enthusiastically, even gently tugging at the sleeve of the
younger woman that was walking alongside her.

Not too far behind them I was extremely perturbed to see Danny
O'Malley, the former director of the Sinn Féin publicity machine, the
political wing of the Provisional IRA, the Provos. I was so surprised to see
him here at David Brennan's funeral procession, I almost choked myself.
After all this man was my friend's sworn enemy. There was a dark balding
man wearing sunglasses in deep whisper-like discussion with O'Malley as
they walked and it struck me instinctively that perhaps he was Middle
Eastern. Certainly, he like me, very clearly wasn't from these parts either.
O'Malley, who had served five years time in Long Kesh for kidnapping, had
reportedly retired to write novels and review books.

Mairead Brennan ran to me and hugged me emotionally for what
seemed like several long minutes. The smell of a woman engulfed me.
Finally she whispered in my left ear, "It's more than enough dealing with
my grief without having to deal with my anger too, right dear?"

Then she kissed my cheek and released her embrace. I glanced at her
quizzically for further explanation but none was forthcoming, so I put it
down to her experience of the pain of death.

Standing directly behind stood a younger version of Mairead. She held my eyes provocatively. *She has to be her sister or relative of some kind*, I surmised, but sexy body politics didn't fit the equation right at this inopportune minute.

When Dave's ex-wife's eyes finally did meet mine, her face was a strange brew of joy, fear and sadness. Her white, pretty face was cruelly highlighted by smeared grey, watered-down mascara. Her eyes were the expected tinged pink with her fading orange lips bitten purple from anguish. "Nicholas, I knew you'd come somehow," she croaked, while her smile remained sheepish.

She looked across at her companion standing next to us and started, "Oh, I'd like you to meet my sister Caitlin, er, you might remember you met once in London, not long after we'd moved there?"

Her hair was much redder and fuller than her older sister, her eyes a much deeper cobalt blue. While an attractive woman, her eyes had a metallic coldness to them, but I couldn't recall ever having met her.

Caitlin said, "Remember the little girl that slept on your sofa while my sister and husband were out for the night?"

That night a decade ago, came back to me suddenly and I went through all the motions of forged embarrassment—just as O'Malley and the Arabic gent entered the church gates not noticing us. The girls and I then mingled with the silent crowd scuffling to get through the tiny wooden parish double doors.

During the long drawn out Roman Catholic funeral service I deliberately stationed myself in the last row. I'd always done that so I wouldn't have to partake in any religious recitations and kneeling. It was my peaceful form of compromise, as I could just stand there in deference to the feelings of whoever, while not offending anybody at the same time.

With difficulty, my thoughts went to my dear friend lying serenely in that polished coffin suspended near the altar. I half expected him to open the lid and sit up and laugh at everybody, draw perverted pleasure from witnessing who fainted and who didn't. It was within his nature to pull a cruel stunt like that in the name of fun. A Catholic boy married to a Protestant girl, attended by an IRA member and possibly an Arab, plus one of his long lost best English friends living in America, all under one roof at his good-bye rites right here in his home town. It was the perfect stage for a stunt. As much as David and I were the same in so many aspects, he'd love this kind of scenario while I hated it. Sadly he never popped up.

Danny O'Malley's presence bothered the living hell out of me. This was the man who wrote Sinn Féin's manifesto. While idealistic in its many points, it was very close in actual fact to the Soviet Union's communist ideals. O'Malley was the same person who had reportedly concocted the idea of a prison hunger strike for Bernadette Devlin and from the resulting worldwide publicity she'd gone on to become a British Member of Parliament. The idea bore temporary fruition until the British government quickly passed a law banning prisoners from becoming MP's. Danny "Bangers" O'Malley had a fertile mind, that devious little plot nearly blew up the British political system.

Switching off the sermon, I reminisced that this must be the same priest Brennan had over for tea at his mother's house when he was a kid. The story went, as told by him, that while his liberal-minded Mum had said she wanted to send her son to non-denominational school, the hometown priest had been against the idea, and Dave recalled the statement ad nauseam, "Catholic schools are for Catholic children." As a result of this defining moment he remained physically segregated and mentally suspicious of the other half of his nation's countrymen, until the day, as a teenager, he met his future wife-to-be. Being a basically open-minded chap, because of the ethnically biased advice, he conceded it "was implanting a virulent virus in my young cancerous head which took a half a life time to expel."

Last to leave the parish aisles, I had followed the procession slowly outside. You could see the breath rising as they passed the doors. As I walked on the path I could feel a soft thin layer of soil sliding over the frost-bound dirt beneath it, tightly like the flesh of the forehead on my uncovered face. I touched darkly on a sobering thought of seeing the sight of 50 Irish Catholics and Protestants standing in relative peace and unity. If I hadn't seen it with my own eyes, I'd never have believed it.

Slowly scanning the surrounding black-clad audience, I locked on to Caitlin. She was looking at me, too. I moved my head ever so slightly in acknowledgement and kept my human radar scanning in motion going to her left. Mairead Brennan was a sorry sight, crying and wailing, being supported by an elderly man who could have been her father. I chose not to look, it was too painful to watch.

The weeping older couple over there must be Mr & Mrs Brennan, Senior. He took after his mother not only in spirit but I absurdly imagined for a nano-second I was looking at Dave dressed in drag.

There was no sign of O'Malley and his olive-skinned buddy, at least not on my screen in the ringside section. I hoped he hadn't departed yet and was in the back of the crowd somewhere. At an inopportune time like this, I was intrigued at what brought him to a dead invalid MI6 officer's burial. I saw them on the slight ridge inside the cemetery's perimeter wall to my right, in deep conversation. I tried lip reading but couldn't. I was too far away and in their animation they had shifted to their profiles. I ground my teeth at the irony of the English meaning of the Gaelic words, *Sinn Féin*, which meant "Ourselves Alone". This whole situation summed it up for me.

I was human Gamma Guppy-ing, a code word for a seventies' American spy programme where they were eavesdropping on Soviet leaders—and adopted by we British as a fun in-house word too. While the priest prattled on, I smiled again to myself about the irony and wished I had the technical means of the CIA to hear those two up there behind me. *The enemy of one's enemy is one's friend.*

They were starting to lower the coffin into the black hole slowly. I wanted to picture Dave Brennan as he was in the prime of his life; not in this negative way. The pall bearers had pulled up the ropes used to drop the casket and had mutely erased themselves from the scene.

When I turned to look back at how the ceremony was proceeding, I caught Mairead throwing a red rose on top of David down there. My own held-back emotions up to that moment had been held in check...but her symbolic gesture forced mistiness over me and for a few seconds my vision blurred as I clenched my fists.

What was said, done and angered by the demon inside these two lovers yesterday has no effect on them today. Despite the loss, love is the winner.

* * * * * * * * * *

The pub in Glenoe was a few minutes down the narrow cobblestone road from the parish. As I entered it was jammed full of Irish men and women in celebration, clinking pints of beer while their children sucked down lemonade and stuffed their faces with potato crisps. I always admired the fact that they could have so much song and dance at so miserable a time. I was told once that the whole idea of having a ribald party, such as the one I was in the middle of, was to think the deceased were still amongst them. This practice of The Wake evolved centuries ago when they actually propped up the dead bodies in the middle of the festivities while they drank themselves into a stupor. I figured it was better to celebrate death this way than the many mournful days of dramatic overacting at various prolonged ceremonies that the Italians, for example, suffered themselves through. The latter, in a perverse way, seem to enjoy undergoing such sadness as opposed to the Irish banter now. I know because I'd been through a couple of Italian-style funerals in Naples and the Bronx.

This *craic* was well underway. It was Irish slang for belly laugh or good time. Before long the singing group started up loudly from the tiny stage that had been assembled especially in honour of the deceased David Brennan. Raucous out-of-tune songs were in full flow sung in unison by all and sundry, like a football crowd behind the goal. Several were about joining the IRA, "where the helmets glisten in the sun, where the bayonets flash, and the rifles crash to the echo of a Thompson gun". They surprisingly sang the mournful "Only Our Rivers Run Free" with feeling, and then launched into "The Fields of Atheny", about a man imprisoned by the British for stealing corn during the famine. "Four Green Fields", a ballad that decried the separation of Ulster in the north from Eire's other bordering provinces, followed that. Even the IRA's unofficial anthem *"Faine Gael An Lae"* ("Bright Ring of Day") made a guest appearance. When "The Celtic Symphony" was half way through, I decided I'd heard them all before and I'd had enough. I threaded my way through the throngs towards the quieter half of the pub.

With a pint of draft Killian's Red in my hand I fortunately found an empty seat in the corner next to the window. I'd sat on a newspaper and when I lifted my bottom to pull it out, found myself holding up a crumpled issue of yesterday's *Andersonstown News* and tucked inside that was a beer-stained old red and white copy of *An Phoblacht*, the weekly *"The Republican News"* voice of Sinn Féin. It had been many years since I'd flipped through a copy and the articles pretty much remained the same in its hatred of the British. The contents covered all things referring to the dream of a united Ireland. Sitting there ardently reading almost every line, it invoked a wide range of responses in me, even as I sat inconspicuously among them. *How vulnerable we are to those who think of the gun as a legitimate political device.*

Had those old farts from SIS *wanted to* hear more about my ten days in Belfast and Dublin, I could have told them that the IRA leaders spent their social time drinking in the Pound Lovey bar and is only one of 22 such bars with snooker halls they have since opened in West Belfast. Instead of depending entirely on Irish-American monetary support—which we Brits thought was the sole source of revenue—the reality was only a maximum of 50% of the IRA's budget comes from America, and dwindling just as fast as the local coffers swell. In a few years time, perchance they'll be closing down the fundraising office of Irish Northern Aid, or Noraid, which in my days, used to be at East 194th Street, the Bronx, New York City, USA— before they moved to Seventh Avenue, Manhattan—with its paid membership of 5,000 Hibernians in chapters across the United States. The Helpful Organisation ably represented them in Dublin, in the Irish Republic.

If only the British government had opened their closed eyes, they would have seen that the bigger balance clearly comes from bank robberies, extortion, tax exempt frauds and faulty gaming machines throughout Ulster. The monies derived from these seemingly normal business operations gave the Gerry Kelly administered Army Council, the seven-seat IRA ruling body, a working budget of UK£5 million *each year* and marginally increasing annually. They paid their murderous gunmen and bomb-makers to indirectly create revenues and sympathy and therefore generate more revenues. Ask Joe Cahill, he's the gun-running numbers cruncher. Go knock on the door of the Navan branch at the Bank of Ireland and ask to see the IRA's bank balance—SIS' auditors found it there once. While their accounting methods *were* excellent, they had since been halted. Why wasn't Pat Doherty watched closer? Everybody knew he was heavily involved. A vicious little cycle it is. Meanwhile this little racket costs the short-sighted British government UK£5 million *per day* in attempts to control the Troubles. *Even way back then I used to think: Is there not something very wrong with this out-of-focus financial image? Is war worth continuing to make money?*

A diamond-ringed female hand appeared slowly over the top of the paper, blocking the article I was reading. Looking directly down at my face was Caitlin, her face flushed rosy with drink. "So here's where you've been hiding, you bad lad, I've been looking all around for you. Just when I thought you'd gone, your face popped out from behind the paper." She plonked herself down groggily. The Irish lass, glancing at the paper which lay in my lap and seeing it was *An Phoblacht* casually remarked, "The fact that Catholics aren't angry every day, 24 hours a day, says a lot about their reasonable nature. If it wasn't for Dave's funeral I wouldn't be seen dead listening to that fucking nonsense next door. If I wasn't sitting in this stupid pub, I'd have both the UDA and UFF come in and take it off the face of the earth." Without missing a break from her softly spoken, violent statement, she slipped nonchalantly into chatting about how long drawn out the Catholic services were and what to do with the fucking priest.

As I watched her boozy face, I pondered what the Ulster Defence Association, the 50,000-strong paramilitary Protestant response to the IRA would have done, had she called them to complain. These blokes wanted Ulster to remain part of Great Britain. And what about the exceptionally violent splinter group of killers who broke away from the UDA family years ago, the Ulster Freedom Fighters? They were worse than the IRA.

Clearly this 26-year old was also making a no-holds barred unpretentious play for me. It registered in my loins immediately. No doubt about it, she was a sexy lassie in an obvious come-and-get-it-now way. Her overcoat removed, the surprise underneath revealed a tight black top with her well-rounded breasts and hard nipples pointing out like buttons attractively through the garment. She wore a black leather mini skirt and black nylon fishnet stockings that were obviously not tights— I confirmed that as I peeked a glimpse of ample white skin up her slim legs the moment she sat down.

Not used to such wanton attention, I nervously glanced around the noisy lounge packed with all sizes and shapes to see if anybody was watching. Men put in these far and few desired moments often utter stupid things, and so I did right on cue by babbling, "Have you come with your boyfriend, have you." It didn't come out as a question at all and she thankfully ignored the idiocy of my grade A dumb statement. Another underlying sexually charged man-woman discussion ensued for half an hour between us, thankfully oblivious to the loud din of the pub.

It soon became apparent that her main fascination was the fact she knew via her sister and her sister's ex-hubby that I was a former clandestine operative and it excited her. The gist of her dialogue centred on James Bond, The Saint and other action movie characters, and she even expressed a desire to eventually live in the South of France "among all the spies". She was not an idiot by any means but clearly her life sought wider boundaries, well away from the confines of Belfast, and she wanted it immediately and was going to get it.

On my earlier trip to the bar, I'd glimpsed Danny Boy standing at the bar with his Arabic shadow still in tow, so I took an opportunity by its horns.

"Caitlin, love, let's see how good you are at this spy thing," I cajoled her, squeezing her knee closest to me. "You see that dark gentleman over there by the bar near the door to the toilets, the one in a medium grey suit and red tie, see him?" It took her a few seconds of leaning forward, half off her seat, her breasts pressed on my shoulder, to see who I was talking about and then she finally nodded and sat down hard again, giggling.

My demeanour took on a sudden hardness to show I was serious. "I want to know who he is, his name, anything at all, what's he doing here in Glenoe. I mean, I'm sure he didn't even know your brother-in-law Dave, so why'd he come here today of all days."

Caitlin snickered wickedly again slightly and then when she saw I meant it, her blue eyes widened with anticipation. "Righto, I'll do it, anything short of sleeping with him, I'll be back so don't go away 'cos I want you," she winked all too obviously. She kissed me full on the mouth hard and got up.

I watched her make her way through the maddening crowd, stopping to joke with a couple of men and then she disappeared down the hallway into the ladies room. A full two minutes later, out she bounded, refreshed and hair combed. She pulled her dress down and actually tweaked her nipples brazenly. Less than a minute later the lass had parked herself between O'Malley and her designated target. Straight off they stopped their deep conversation and switched their attention to the sensuous girl with the biggest come on I'd seen in ages. I suppressed a laugh at the sight of these two grown men panting at the girl. After about a minute of viewing their interaction, I looked out of the window towards the cemetery still visible down the street.

A fresh crowd of visitors coming into the pub had blocked my view of them and she was gone for what seemed ages. I began to look at my watch. Soon time to get going. Suddenly Caitlin dropped herself next to me with a round of drinks from the bar. "Couldn't find out any thing about him but after he'd touched my arm more than a couple of times, which told me he fancied me, I asked him his name right out of the blue, and then he told me," she seemed proud of herself.

I waited an eternity and said finally, almost laughing, "So what was it?"

"Oh, right, I never told you did I, what a git I am," she feigned embarrassment and thought for a brief moment, frowning slightly, "let's see, it was something like 'Moo Mohammed Abu Fart.' I did ask him to repeat it twice before telling him my name was Linda." I in turn repeated the name to her and she softly said it again back to me, licking her lips slowly and touching my mouth with the tip of her varnished forefinger. A few silent minutes followed and then she said bluntly, "We leaving now?" I told her I had to get the ferry from Larne in an hour, and she was much the worse for the alcohol... She interrupted me by blurting that she'd volunteered already to take me in her sister's car and without hesitation jumped up and went looking for Mairead.

After her dark red mane and leather skirted backside disappeared around the pub wall, I glanced out of the window once more. A green Vauxhall Cavalier had pulled up since I had last looked out. Leaning on the car was a burly middle-aged man wearing a tweed cap and an anorak, smoking a cigarette, with his back turned to me. He could have been a gentleman farmer. Checking back inside the pub, I saw "Danny Boy" O'Malley and Mohammed Moose Whatsit winding their way out to the exit.

As they came out into the open street, the driver of the car turned his craggy profile to face them and walked around the parked car to greet them. It was then that I realised that the driver was none other than Patrick "Paddy" O'Neill. The very person that so considerately telephones the day's code and verbally signs off with his name as "P. O'Neill" each and every time the IRA warns the British police of a bomb about to explode in less than ten minutes time, nearly always maiming and killing innocent citizens.

As I stared out of the pub window at him, and as he opened his driver's side door, he turned his face and we momentarily locked eyes on each other. There was no sign of anything on his face and he got in unhurriedly.

A rush of adrenaline hit me. I didn't quite know what to do. Then before I knew it they all jumped in the car and whizzed off in a hurry. I sat there dumbfounded staring at the dregs of my beer glass, my mind racing.

The entire British Secret Intelligence Service roams the world actively looking for this man and I've actually seen him for the third time in person right before my very eyes: Tripoli, Libya. Larnaca, Cyprus. And now here on his home turf right here in Glenoe, Northern Ireland. Blimey, each time he looks remarkably different, but I'd been to many surveillance courses about how to spot through disguises—it was definitely him each time. To run to a phone will accomplish nothing by the time I get the damn message through and besides, I reminded myself once again, I don't want to be drawn into the melee right now.

The mind puts things away until it can deal with it but there's fate alive and in progress here somewhere, I told myself. *It has to be my destiny and only time will prove why this man crosses my path so often.*

Caitlin and Mairead rolled up together. For sisters they seemed an underlying strain between them from the first minute we'd all met.

"You look like you've just been hit in the stomach," said Mairead. "You OK?"

I stopped short of spilling the beans. She'd already had a rough day and was trying to keep a stiff upper lip. We said our good-byes at length. Mairead hugged me somewhat stiffly too, more than a couple of times. We never exchanged addresses or telephone numbers. Instead we accepted that this tense poignant moment signalled the end of a chapter in our lives.

Her last words were to yell over to tell her sister to "come over to Dave's Aunt's house later and not to drive too fast."

I was still reeling from witnessing O'Neill once again.

My slightly tipsy sex kitten of a driver volunteered straight at the windscreen, "Can I come with you to Stranraer or wherever you're spending the night?" she turned to look at me longingly, almost pleadingly.

My temptation was to howl yes at the top of my lungs and leap into the sack with this slim curvaceous vixen. Though I thought about the threat of AIDS certainly I was attracted to her. What heterosexual man wouldn't want to spend a night with a young woman this attractive and willing? A decision to consider.

"Well?" she breathed, glancing over for an answer as a car headlight shone on her face as we stopped at a traffic light. I thought about it and said, "Caitlin, I don't think it's a smart idea. You're the sister of my best buddy's ex-wife. It doesn't seem right, you know, not after a day like today." I stopped, searching for a better explanation, "If it's adventure you want, it's not something you must travel to find, it's something you take with you. If you like maybe I'll give you my address and phone number in California and I might write back. Who knows?"

Then I waited a few seconds, "Who was the nice Irish fellow Moose Mohammed Whatsit was with at the bar? I got the distinct feeling you both knew each other but you both played strangely dumb and you never mentioned his participation in your conversations."

The girl had visibly stiffened up and dangerously ran a red traffic light. The side of her jaw flexed. I looked ahead and I could see the ship's funnel about a mile away.

She started babbling. "I'm not a slut or whatever you're thinking, Nick... That was a fucking great chicken-shit observation you gave me and it pisses me off, it really does, you know..." Caitlin was suddenly screaming epithets at me and then started to sob, breaking down, wiping tears, her body shaking with anger. A dramatic performance indeed. In the dockyard the car came to a full stop close to the ship's blackened hull.

I calmly continued. "I mean, *I* know he's Danny O'Malley from the Provisional IRA but how do *you* know him, Caitlin?" I said it softly while beginning to gently but slowly bend her spare hand in a Chinese grip, "Come on, I haven't got all day, tell me, love?"

The pain was in her eyes but she foolishly resisted. I applied more pressure delicately. She shook quietly in agony this time, then like a tigress she hissed at me, "He's Dave Brennan's Mum's older brother by ten years, Dave Brennan's uncle. They hated each other with a passion since David was kid, but Danny came to see him off anyway as a favour to his younger sister."

I closed my eyes slowly with the pain of hearing that unexpected news. I waited about ten seconds then opened them again. Finally I said quietly, "There's more, keep coming with it, Caitlin, if that's your real name."

She sneered and spat in my face and with venom snarled, "I'm not Mairead's sister either, arsehole." She started to laugh cynically and hysterically.

"I know," I said calmly, not wiping the spittle, not giving her the satisfaction, "Mairead Brennan never had a sister. The little girl who slept on my couch 15 years ago had brown eyes and was her cousin. You guys figured I wouldn't remember the particulars. I didn't think much of it either admittedly, at the beginning. But it dawned on me when I saw the, oh so brief, interaction between O'Malley and you. *Then I knew.* Something was wrong. Plus you mistakenly gave me another slight clue. The UFF are not part of the UDA any more. Haven't been for years. The UDA find their random senseless killings politically unacceptable and therefore shun them officially. Any self-respecting Protestant would know that, and you didn't. Which either makes you a Roman Catholic, a Jew or a Muslim. Me thinks it's a Catholic. Am I right, love?"

I sat looking across at this petulant little sulking girl and eventually let go of her crooked hand, "So who and what are you?"

She stubbornly ruffled her hair nervously, rubbing her hand with the other, not responding to me, looking blankly away out of the other side window. So I reached over and touched my hand lightly again on hers again. A torrent of words came gushing out of her mouth like an aqueduct. "We were blackmailing Mairead Brennan to tell us everything about her life with her ex-husband. Since they were no longer married, the sacred vow is broken, and she's a fucking Protestant anyway. He still had access to finding out how we get our funding and we want to know how much is known about our international network. So last week we went with her to London to get David Brennan to assist us but he refused to cooperate. So we waited a few days to let him think about it, then you showed up out of the blue, and the next thing he's done himself away. Seeing you most likely would turn up for the funeral, I was told to pillow talk with you. But, I suppose, you were smarter than we all thought. Anyway, it looks like it's a dead end now he's gone. We'll probably try some other means and we'll let Mairead off."

She seemed relieved, giving herself the sign of the cross, then remembered one more thing. "That Arab guy. I really haven't a fucking clue who he is and that really was what he said his name was. I don't think they thought I'd tell you his name and I was getting cocky, thinking I was winning with you. So I stupidly told it to you. And, by the way, my name really is Linda too."

"Yes, I know that too Linda Coughlin." Out of my pocket I took her Republic of Ireland driver's licence marked Eire in green and waved it at her. "I removed it from your hand bag when you went to find Mairead. A lousy photograph of you, my dear. I must say you look much better in the flesh."

She sighed, heaving her fragile shoulders back on the seat, a defeated smile on her gaunt pretty face. I bucked the desire to slap her but instead gave her a full deep-thrust long kiss into the mouth and then bounced out of the car. I ran up the ship's gangplank for the second time in a day—this time a light evening fog shrouded my ascent. The last ferry's deck was eerily void of passengers.

Shaking with anger from what I'd just heard, when I looked back down from the top, she and the car had vanished in the mist. I wanted to voice out loud, for everybody to hear, *By the way, Mairead doesn't have an Aunt anywhere on this planet for you to go to, sweetheart. She was throwing me a clue and I caught the message with both hands.*

As I entered the ship's warm cabin, I also smiled too about my bullshit line of the connection between the UDA and UFF. I hadn't a clue if that was true or not. I completely made it up and the silly moo caught it with her fingerless hoofs.

The person I was had just returned through the left-open door.

Chapter Four

I have learned more from failure than from success;
failure is a component of success.

After my first overseas stint at the Copenhagen station I was assigned to the capital city of Switzerland, Berne. My codename was BEN/1 from which BENNY—the cryptonym for Dr and Mrs Molody was derived. (At SIS a "cryptonym"—a codename for internal use—is selected for every agent and defector, who never knows what theirs are. Today they are randomly computer generated and not chosen by the officers responsible as it was previously. It is uncommon for two persons to get a singular cryptonym.)

Vibeke had taken my transfer well. Due to her seniority she had exclusively scheduled herself on all flights departing Copenhagen for Geneva and Zürich with overnight stays. For two months it took its toll on her, for as soon as she reached Berne late at night, it was almost time to return to work early the next morning. Plus I wasn't always home for weeks and months at a time. Later she had switched to Scandinavian Airlines' long haul routes to Africa and South America. It gave her, on average, four days off for five days work, sometimes more depending on rank, which she pulled often. She had always said she preferred Berne over Copenhagen any day, without actually saying that it was where I was too. She was as devoted to me as I was to her.

We never went to Sousse in Tunisia as I had hoped. Instead, when we had holidays we went by car from central Switzerland through the Alps, via Austria or Italy, to either Pula or Rovinj in Istria, northern Yugoslavia. She'd had enough of flying. On one trip we'd gone down to visit my old Swedish university professor, himself on holiday in his hometown of Dubrovnik. A visit to see its medieval history was a must.

When it came to breaking that annual pattern, despite my preference again for Tunisia, she had especially wanted to go to Cyprus. I was always game to travel to anywhere I'd never been to. So following a brief stay at her parents farm in northern Denmark, we had flown SAS gratis in first class, under employee privileges—as I was now regarded as her common-law husband—from Copenhagen to Larnaca for two weeks of sun.

Two days from the end of that holiday she had to return early to the farm, as her closest childhood friend in Denmark had a serious accident. She insisted I stay and finish my well-deserved rest. I did.

Being me, I thought I would break the monotony of nothing for a whole day and drive out to the war zone hidden from the thriving tourist sector. Unbeknown to many visitors, the Cypriots had been picking at old scabs for years. Like the Catholics and the Protestants in Northern Ireland, for decades the Greeks and the Turks of Cyprus had the same prolonged hatred for one another ably fuelled by history and religion.

It was so bad that the good old British Army once again were in the middle preventing them from roasting each other. To help the policing efforts, the Brits had established a no man's land by drawing a line right down the middle between the warring parties, sometimes officially splitting houses into two different enforced areas. The world media never reported much on the violence but it was never-ending. It would boil over then peter out. A storm in a caffeinated tea cup which kept everybody at the international kitchen tables awake.

The Greek-Cypriots and the Turkish-Cypriots had lost sight of what the hell they were doing completely and were stuck in a time warp. Their respective bloods on the mainland sometimes forgot them as an insignificant pinprick, as they continued to focus their loathing directly at each other from Athens and Ankara. *Kipros*, the small beautiful island peppered all over with Cypress trees, was the real loser as they continued to rub salt into its unhealed wounds regularly.

I'd phoned the company commander and identified my rank and reason for requesting a tour of the area. It was completely out of the realms of SIS but the army man had seen no problem with my visit. Following the directions I'd been given by him scribbled on a piece of hotel stationery paper I'd rented a mini car at the hotel in my real name and headed out to the army base.

The tour of the battlefields had gone fairly normally. I looked like a typical tourist, which I was, with a uniformed official guide. I had no specific agenda and was taking in the sights. It was over inside an hour.

Driving out of the compound and saluting the guards, I headed back to my hotel. There were plenty of cars on the road but minutes later I passed a parked vehicle in a lay-by offering a good view over the British army base. For some reason I had turned to look at the two men sitting in it and I thought I saw Paddy O'Neill and the Libyan from years ago sitting in a jeep plus binoculars.

A sixth sense made me do a U-turn and look again. As I went by again in the opposite direction, the hair on the back of my neck sprang up. I was convinced it was him. Their car had just started off slowly, so I had to turn around once again and I followed them several cars back.

Fifty minutes later, their Ford Capri pulled up outside the terminal at Larnaca Airport. As he got out of the passenger side into the sunlight, lo and behold, I was looking into the face of the Provos IRA leader in the flesh. I hit the steering wheel with my fists, both frustrated and excited.

He leaned back inside the front seat and shook the hand of the driver and then took an oversized duffel bag out of the back seat. With a wave he disappeared into the building.

I wrote down the number of the Cypriot-registered car's plates. That simple little act, of hastily penning a note on the back of the directions from the hotel to the army camp was to come to my rescue months later.

I drove to the car park across from the terminal and quickly went in. I found him just leaving the Cyprus Airways check-in. Checking his watch against the arrival and departure board, he ambled towards passport control. I watched him pull out the green cover for citizens of the Republic of Ireland and clear the inspection area, to the bored glance of the sole Cypriot immigration officer.

I wanted to make a phone call but didn't know to whom. I thought about that British CO who had arranged the brief sightseeing trip, but his number was on that same bit of paper I'd written the registration plate number on, and I had left it back on the car seat.

Still I had to see which gate he went to. There was only one orange and white Boeing 727 on the dusty tarmac, on the side he wandered towards. A Cyprus Airways baggage worker in overalls came past me on his lunch break, and I took the opportunity to say, as if I was an excited British tourist, "Is that the plane I'll fly on back to London? I'd like to take a photo of it."

With his mouth full of food, he waved his hand in denial, pointing to the blind side of the annex, "No, it'll be the other side. It doesn't leave for another hour." I thanked him as he tried to catch up with the sexy uniformed girl walking ahead.

Rapidly I went back to look at the arrival and departure board. The only other Cyprus Airways plane listed before the London Heathrow flight was to Rome and it was going in fifteen minutes time. It had to be his plane.

I had to make a decision. I had my wallet on me: it contained my credit card and all other identification in my real name. Fortunately, I had taken my passport with me to prove to the army I was who I was. So I went back to the same desk where O'Neill had checked in and enquired if there was room on the Rome-bound flight. After idly looking at a screen hidden from me, she nodded, telling me it was only half-full but it was leaving soon. I quickly produced my credit card. She seemed puzzled I didn't have any bag to check, nor was I holding any carry-on. Then I took off walking post-haste towards the departure gate. Just me and the clothes I walked in.

At the immigration desk, I identified myself to the passport control officer. "This is an official request from the UK's Secret Intelligence Service. On Her Majesty's duty I command you to inform the British Consulate here in Cyprus of my imminent unexpected departure to Rome. Please make a note of my name and provide these details to them immediately."

That seemed to wake him out of his slumber and he could see I wasn't kidding, and proceeded to jot down my name and passport number. When he finished and handed me back my British passport, as I turned to leave him with documents in hand, I suddenly remembered the car keys and gave them to him. "Please apologise for me and tell the consulate to inform the rental company that I've left their car across the road. It is extremely important for you to also note that there is a car registration plate written on a piece of paper on the front seat that I'd like them to check. Thanks so much for everything. You'll get a notation for this, I can assure you." I left him jotting that down too as I ran down the corridor to the plane.

With the back of Patrick O'Neill's head in full view across the aisle and in front, less than two and half hours later the Cyprus Airways jet landed in *Italia* at *Aeroporti di Roma—Leonardo di Vinci*.

We disembarked from the back of the plane so I found myself in front of him. I fully expected him to collect his bag at the carousel and decided to wait for him up there. But by shooting further ahead I could take in a quick visit to the loo on the way. As I came out of the men's he had just come level with me and I tucked in a step behind him with a bunch of passengers from the same flight. To my utmost surprise he turned off at the transit signs towards a connecting flight. My ticket terminated here. If I had a bag I know I would have checked it in as far as here, not thinking maybe he was only transferring through Rome. How fucking stupid of me! Anybody heading to another terminal would have to show their new destination's tickets to the security control at the gate there before being allowed access on from this point. I cursed myself. *I have no idea how I got so lucky as to exist; and I will never know.*

I stayed on this side of the barrier as a handful of travellers went through the proof of on-bound tickets at the transfer control desk. I needed time to think. On the other side I saw my prey turn left under the men's sign there. Seconds later a double announcement was heard, "Message for Mr Malachy Kinsella arriving from Cyprus. Message for Mr Malachy Kinsella, please."

There couldn't be that many Irish names floating around inside Rome's international airport coming from Cyprus. Without thinking I headed to the nearby intercom telephone and picked it up, "Yes, I am Mr Kinsella. You have a message for me?"

The Italian woman's voice put me on hold for a second then came back on in accented English, "Yes, Mr Kinsella. Mr Nikolay Valkanov will be unable to travel with you to Bulgaria this afternoon as he is remaining in Italy for further business tonight. He suggests you please check-in at the Hotel Vitosha-New Otani in Sofia and he will join you there tomorrow. He sends his utmost apologies. If you wish to get in touch with him, Mr Valkanov suggests you call his office number in Sofia and speak to his secretary, who will then contact him for you."

I repeated most of it back to her in faked annoyance in a bogus Irish brogue, thanked her and hung up. All the while I was looking down the hallway at the men's toilet exit. O'Neill came out and went straight across to the internal phone and snatch it up. So he *was* travelling under the name of "Malachy Kinsella"! I saw him talk into the unit and wait. His back was turned to me a hundred yards down the airport walkway. After several minutes he eventually hung up, pushed his hand through his hair in an act of irritation and kept on down the hallway.

The same Italian lady must have informed him she had *just* given him the message, I was sure of that given his exasperated hand movement. Hopefully, he would put in down to a misunderstanding by the Italian switchboard staff. It was a blind risk I was prepared to take. I had no choice.

I wasn't really sure what I was doing following him around. In surveillance training it had been repeatedly stressed to go with your gut, and that's all I was basing it on messing around here in Rome Airport. If I was travelling on to Bulgaria I was going to need a visa. I followed the last of the straggling passengers that had deplaned from Cyprus and were filing towards the main arrival hall signs.

I cleared Italian immigration and customs fast. With beads of sweat on my brow, after fiddling around with the local telephone directories, I finally went to the British Airways reception and asked them for the British Embassy's telephone number. The Italian girl had written it down for me instantly and invited me to call from their phone. After gallivanting around foreign climes one truly appreciates the efficiency of such professionalism. The embassy picked up on the first ring. I asked for the military attaché and hoped he was in. He was, and after a brief exchange while the STU-111 (secure phone on GSM mobile) kicked in I gave him my parole (code name to identify yourself followed by a password), urgently requesting a visa for Bulgaria and the immediate issuance of a false passport. As I thought, that man was actually the SIS head of station and he didn't fuck around. If it wasn't the right person then the individual would have passed me to the correct one. The bloke even said that he expected a call from me anytime soon following receiving a message via London from Cyprus. He then told me to stay put and that he'd have somebody contact me back at the British Airways desk within forty-five minutes. I told the same *Italiano* brunette in the BA uniform where I would sitting when the call came in.

No call came. Right on the 45th minute, a young man in a fashionable Italian suit and silk tie but so obviously snobby private school British was standing at the reception desk. I saw the brunette point him to me.

As he came towards me I stood up and he gave me a weak handshake. He was all prim and proper and smelling of something nice as he went through the security procedures as I produced my real passport. I signed for the envelope he proffered and he kept my passport in exchange. I opened it right then and there in his presence. Unbelievably, my own photograph was imposed on the ID page in the name of Kenneth Cavanaugh, a travel agent born in County Durham, England, on my real date of birth. A short-term visa for Bulgaria was stamped in there too. Still in his company I had to sign 'Kenny Cavanaugh' on the signature section in the passport and the same on another document he produced. Inside was a return Alitalia airline ticket for today, from Rome to Sofia, with an open departure date back to Rome and on to London. The used outbound London-Rome segment had been torn out. Also enclosed were some *lev* and *stotinki* Bulgarian money, five hundred Pounds Sterling in cash, a valid Midland Bank credit card, an assortment of receipts, an unwritten postcard of the Coliseum and so on and so forth. The usual Department of Trade booklet on the country of destination was tucked in to educate the reader on various cultural aspects and ways of doing business. A handy thing to have which I always referred to.

We shook hands and off he went. The only words he said, other than "sign here" was to snootily say, "The Balkan Air flight just left, so you'll have to wait two hours for the next plane. In the meantime the embassy requests you to complete this form and seal it in this same envelope, and leave it for collection at the BA desk over there." It was a standard form to update head office for my reasons in alerting them to an emergency request. It also covered the Rome station's backsides in case I screwed up.

After filling in my report, I then used the newly received cash and went and bought some fancy Italian clothes to call my own, plus purchasing my favourite *Fragonard eau de toilette* in the duty-free. I did it so that I wouldn't be embarrassed anymore by an underling in superior dress code compared to bum-like me in a sweaty tennis top and jeans. My objection to the British class system contributed to this feeling once again.

It was another two hours of flying before I got off that night in Sofia looking quite dapper in my new Italian-version of a Savile Row outfit. But it was to be the beginning of an emotional death row for me.

* * * * * * * * * *

Writing about this part of my life was hard.
Because I had to go back to see it, to live it.
I didn't want to go back there again to tell the story.
Be that I am now challenged to complete it.
…I have never been so scared in all my life.

Bulgaria, the basket case of communism. Sofia is full of drab and soulless Soviet-style high-rises, the colour of factories. Plenty of unattractive grey Stalinist ornate architecture, a city completely void of character. Dismal surroundings produced equally dismal faces, the nearest thing I'd seen to fit with George Orwell's bleak "1984", in the mechanical first person.

Balgarija, despite being a bastion of extreme communism, was associated with major crime movements in Europe and the Middle East. A capitalist tool which was of considerable importance to *Darjavna Sugarnost,* the Bulgarian state security service—sometimes known as *Drzaven Sigurnost*—and ultimately that of its masters, the KGB.

On the flight over to *Sofija* I had been trying to remember the exact wording of a report I'd once read years prior. To the best of my recall, it was about Turkish intelligence believing that as many as six drug-smuggling rings operated brazenly from the very hotel I was going to stay at.

During checking in at the Hotel Vitosha's modern reception under the name Cavanaugh, I asked innocently if my associate from Ireland, a Mr Kinsella, had already arrived. The fairly sexy black-haired Bulgarian girl in a bulky uniform, flipped down a list, and confirmed he was here, before casually picking up the ringing receiver.

Peripherally I'd seen the man's face close on my right as I felt a pinprick in my neck. My vision blurred and another bloke on my left was supporting me before I blanked out.

I came to stark naked. Two dark strong men lifted me off the bunk and sat me at a bare table in the middle of the room. When I raised my spinning head, even with vertigo, in the crepuscular gloom of the windowless room, I faced a giant whose slicked head gleamed with a kind of shining grease.

He slapped me so hard I nearly fell off the chair. It was then I noticed the single bare light bulb swaying above me. I think I faded out then.

Sometime during that hazy time, he or somebody else had loudly read in broken perfunctory English, the fact that I was charged with "spying against the state at Kozlodui"? The shrill speech had mentioned there were four nuclear reactors at the plant. I was trying to drum up a map in my head on where the hell the place was but the page was blanketed white...

It was a beautiful trip, which suddenly became surreal, as faces familiar to me didn't make any sign of recognition as they glided past. An overweight female singer I knew, who was dressed as a court jester, was whispering, "The official view is that we must wait and see what the position is at the time the decision has to be made." It was repeated over and over again to me. "I understand, you don't have to keep telling me," my voice was heard. "Decisions are only as good as the information received. Without dialogue there will never be a solution. A lie often repeated is often believed. Yes, the worst opinion is silence. No, you cannot set a dangerous precedent by deciding to abandon the right to confront evidence against me." My voice said that? "Wasn't it Sigmund Freud who said it, I think?" echoed the woman's tuneful voice. "Freidrich Nietzche? Franz Kafka? It had an 'f...'"

Her image was starting to slide up the roof away from me, not down... The ceiling was twitching slightly when I opened my eyes. "Jeez, what a fucking dream," I croaked. My throat felt parched. I was cold so my fingers searched for a blanket but only found my open crotch.

I sat up groggily and realised I had been lying there hyperventilating with nothing on. I wobbled on to my feet and staggered at what represented an entrance-exit. I wouldn't have called it a door as it was too small.

The soles of my feet were swollen. I must have been administered *bastinado* or *falaqa*, depending on whether one was South American or Arab. I squirmed at the thought, it was the caning of the bottom of your foot, of which there was no one word for it in English. No football injury I'd ever had felt like this. I found myself leaning on the damp wall.

I was dying for a drink and searched the room but there was nothing. But I could hear running water on the other side of the thick partition—it was like an inviting waterfall.

Most of the ground was covered with a quarter of an inch of watery slime and floating filth. The mildew flowed grimy lava down the side and curved around on to the bottom as one. For a second I tried to spot where the walls began and the floor ended. It was a game I was to play many times to pass the time; sometimes vice versa to make it interesting. A cement bunk of sorts with no mattress was what I had laid on. It matched the colour of the greenish walls. I was beginning to understand my lot: I am in a cramped, damp cell with no natural light, inserted here by my captors to rot. I will survive.

This was to be my Hilton-Suite-by-the-Sea through rose-tinted glasses. It had to be that as a way to exist in spite of adversity. Alone you go through a process: a sense of discovery about yourself. Every time I awoke—whether it was daytime or nightmare I went through the checking-in procedures daily with a ghostly vigour. A triptych within a square existence, as I watched myself go through the motions like a puppeteer peering down. *Anderson, old chap, you are still imprisoned in your own mind*, a spoken sound in my head would reverberate. *You are incarcerated in the jailhouse of your imagination. But you will survive, lad.*

Every time my eyes opened from sleep, I never failed to check for a blanket, but I remained nude. I kept thinking I would snap out of this sick fantasy. I shall never know why but I reasoned with myself that as from the first minute I was born, and every day after, it was a brand new day. I will wear nice clothes again though.

Then the sound of water would end. The silence was such that I could hear sounds within my head. At times I would become breathless with the pain of missing the clinks of glasses and the clanks of the service of making the drinks. It felt like I had already been kicked in the mouth. Yet I knew that I would get out of this hell *soon*, or whenever that soon would come, so I willed myself in continuing to persist in this self-imposed noire psyche. Newcastle Brown Ale will touch my lips once more—I guarantee it.

The mind games endured. They used sleep deprivation and an interminable stream of conversation to keep me awake, hitting the body often, while shackled in excruciating positions I didn't know the body was capable of. They knew sleep would freshen my resolve. The violent shaking rattled my teeth till I fainted into sleep. An MI6 course had warned us this was a method to be expected, if captured. It doesn't really help you to know it ahead of time when you're the recipient. Of course it wasn't really me; it was somebody else in my body taking a beating.

Every week, there was a day I was given no water, later on that day I would be blindfolded in a rag soaked in urine that stung my eyes, and tied standing up facing a wall: There I was compelled to catch drops of water from a tap high up on the wall above me, while laughter rang around me. Later they would place me on a stool and my mouth was forced around that metal tap while they held my head hard. Then they would turn it on full. The only way to avoid drowning was to drink. When my belly was full, the interrogators would punch my abdomen while uttering obscenities, making me collapse to the floor. Squirming, I would almost be submerged in my own vomit, which I could feel trickling in thick sticky streams down and around my nakedness beneath.

Harsh words rained down non-stop, but it was like pouring crushed ice cubes with razor sharp edges over me as I lay frozen still. I knew they would eventually melt. Once, I wished I were water-soluble so I could turn into light jelly and escape by washing freely down the drain.

The muffled fright sledgehammers you and you come to terms with the muddied factors of the past. A rhythmical thumping engulfs the senses like tottering on the edge of a bottomless darkness with an anvil attached to your ankles. There are no sentences to utter about this watery shallow grave, which has sunk to the bed of the mind. The dulled sound is dampened by a cordoned steel cloth over the eyes and ears like a clamp across the crossbones of the skull. I won't mention the stench of fear in its mixed forms.

Unbeknown to those cruel men, I actually welcomed their company, plus the regularity of their visits, coupled with my own sleep pattern, for it informed me that indeed another week just passed and I was still alive.

There are dumb things to think about in solitary. The paradox while I was in jail was that my captors were earning around £30 a month; while I earned 166 times theirs—even as I sat on the bare floor fantasising the rotating numbers on an imaginary TV screen.

Occasionally I tried to keep my sanity by psyching myself to watch that same fake blank monitor as I replayed certain favourite movie scenes in my mind. I had saw them once again as if they were transmitting to me in the comfort of my home— no popcorn with it.

Prison is a very degrading environment for human values but also a place where you really get to know the human fibre—your own and that of others. It was a learning experience at its worst.

A guardian of philosophy guided my moral compass. You can picture yourself as an insignificant dot from the deadness of the heavens; scouring below from 22,300 miles above the Earth from a tin can at 6,879 digits over the speed limit...depending on the phase of the moon and the state you were in.

Over the weeks I'd got to talk statically in Russian to a stubby bearded Bulgarian. From the confines of the floor, I only ever could see the bottom half of his face. He was the guard who fed me slop once a day and rewarded me a half-bucket of water to do whatever I wished with: wash or drink. But I had to shuffle my faeces from the corner with bare hands into that bucket afterwards, so they got filthy again. I'd kept a mouth full in me to spit on my befouled hands. But I understood what they were trying to do by treating me like shit.

His name was Slavcho. His wife's name was Ilina. Their daughter was Maya. It took me all of three weeks to get those three names from him. Little does he know how much he helped me. I survived on those three names putting imagined faces to them like a child sitting at their kitchen table talking to them in my world of unresponsive dolls.

Once, just once, enough to raise my spirit—oh, how it did—my jailer played a flute. Clearly he was practising, but it was all I needed to compose an instrumental sound in the recording studio of my mind. I would hum it for hours, which became days, then weeks.

I survived simply because I refused to give up hope. I kept finding things to think about. Trivial games with tiny pebbles, stupid designs drawn in the dried dust areas pretending it was a desert island and that I was responsible for its imminent architecture. I'd fall asleep looking *forward* to the next day, if indeed it was day, because the dim light bulb stayed on forever. It could have been night when I awoke for all I knew.

The occasional insects would come to introduce themselves—a welcome diversion or two—but entering my mouth while I slept was not one of them. It happened a couple of times. They taste quite acrid.

I developed an understanding companionship with the ceaseless curiosity of my solitude. It certainly allowed me to analyse its psychic uses; a mental transformation of my own intellect. It was to ignite into a motor that drove my desire to want to expound these thoughts into motion in the future.

It is the wisdom of the survivor, you do not even know how much a prisoner you are to your struggle for survival. Provoked by an intermittent definite dread, the starkness of my surroundings at times did sink me, and the possibilities existing in my mind would come momentarily to an all time low for that particular day only. Weeks would pass where the hours were the same and you no longer care what the next few minutes will bring, allowing your captors to in part achieve their goals. *The biggest enemies of all are the mistresses of emotions and mastering its fears.*

In my estimation it had been eleven weeks. A sentence of gross simplification as it was much more gruesome and tedious than mentioned.

For all the things that go on in this world, I would say the gods have a wicked sense of humour. The blindfold day in the week came again for the eleventh time. The same faceless figures' movements could be heard. Pain was to come soon. But today was slightly different, they'd given me a colourless blanket. Oh fuck what now?

The black hole came quickly this day, no gagging smell, but in the form of an unseeing careless hurtful jab of a needle. I was faintly aware of being thrown into the back of a vehicle, it had to be a van. Oh great, the sound of its motor rumbled. I loved the rocking and rolling. It's a different motion for once; makes a nice change. I was smiling insanely.

Then an animated alarm clock with a happy face suddenly screamed, "Hey, Anderson you should be proud of yourself, you didn't break. Wake up! Now they are taking you and me and are going to smash both of us..." Me? That's me lying here. Fuck, I *am* going to die! That's what going on here. I am going to die with my head in shreds, here in this unimaginative country. Why couldn't I just pass away of natural old age in England with the family around a village heath watching cricket with tea and strawberries? I was still smiling at the irony and stinging tears welled up under the tight cloth over my shut eyes. It was so nice of them not to piss on it for once.

The effect of the drug wore off. I lay there waiting with no anticipation. I couldn't think of anything in particular. I couldn't recall what my Mum and Dad looked like as much as I tried for one last picture, then Vibeke's name vibrated by in graffiti. A thin layer of sweat betrayed my fear and a trickle was forming, soon to make its slippery way down my bare-back.

The movement ceased and it was some time before the doors of the van squeaked slowly open. It's a chilling feeling. Hands were helping me out to my feet, tying the rough blanket around my bare waist.

I was crying. I didn't want to die, not yet. Please give me a few more years at least. Just a wee bit more please? Jeez, what a fucking way to go. Um, well, the warmth was invigorating nevertheless.

Being blindfolded, hearing accented voices speaking English words suddenly for the first time in months is very confusing. I have forgotten that language, how it sounds so weirdly clipped. I used to speak it once.

The knot was being untied. The rush of sunlight hurt my pupils as I shield away from it. But somebody shoved me away. It was like awakening to an experience both fresh and familiar; the animalistic and animistic wonder pole-ended my being. But still I cringed away from the aching rays.

My knees felt like crumbling upon delivery of a male voice heavily accentuated but in perfect English it said, "I wish you to confirm you are Nicholas Anderson, a British citizen?"

He's just checking before the bullet is reserved with my name on it. I was amused, somehow proudly to myself to not allow his humour to con me. Yet it was nice to hear my name once more...but no face was attached to its image. Yes, I think I will respond anyway.

I turned slowly towards that façade standing there, with the sun behind him beaming around that imposing human statue. I couldn't speak, I'd briefly forgotten how to form words in English. My mouth was moving but still it emitted silence. Cautiously I started to nod, then I responded with dignity, "Yes, I am he."

He had stepped aside and his hand's wrist proffered the same way *maître d's* do it. That sun smashed me in its full glory. It felt so good, like I was ice cream melting itself. My feet's toes were savouring the earth. I don't know, I felt relieved to know them again before death came.

I still wasn't fully focusing yet but another man shuffled past me going in the opposite direction. My puzzled eyes peered at him and the well-dressed man accompanying him, but he didn't look up. I never looked back. He must be dying with me today. I laughed internally at that.

The sign in front of me read in Roman letters 'Kapitan Andreevo border post.' Another sign stated that this was the 'Bulgaria-Turkey crossing.' A couple of armed uniformed men stood watching pitiful me. I began to walk straighter then, out of my pride to be here.

There was a physical check then right out there in the open by a doctor dressed in army fatigues, stethoscope around his neck. Why would they check my health, I'm going to die, don't you know? Fussing over me, I couldn't understand him that well. He didn't sound Bulgarian or Turkish. Was he Greek, maybe Yugoslav? I asked him where he was from. He stopped a fraction and smiled at me quizzically, taking my fragile hand in his, "My name is Chaim and I am from Israel. You are in the care of *ha-Mossad le-Modiin ale-Tafkidim Meyuhadim*, the Israeli Institute for Intelligence and Special Tasks. You are going home to England, sir." I passed out at those words.

Those four Israelis who came to get me spirited me by a private jet from an airport in Edirne, northwest Turkey, into Tel Nof air base just south of Tel Aviv. I stayed awake for I didn't want to miss anything, as I had missed so much. I didn't expect anybody to understand that I was screaming with joy inside.

The main topic among the Mossad men was the current status of a Lufthansa Boeing, which had been highjacked by four Palestinians, one being a woman. They mentioned a string of cities across the world that the plane had flown to while the terrorists sought asylum. The only places that stuck in my head was Rome and Larnaca...

My memory of the ordeal was already elusive and blurry. A shaky home video recording that doesn't come into focus. Obviously I screwed up at that Sofia hotel. The Bulgarians were alerted to look for anybody following "Kinsella". O'Neill was sufficiently aroused by his message being possibly intercepted at Rome Airport. I hate that man when I think of him.

I was like a child. One of the Mossad lads did something on the aircraft's table which fascinated me. Folk wisdom says that on the vernal equinox an egg will balance on end, but that day I saw him balance an Israeli bank note on the vibrating plastic table in front of me. It reminded me of my own life very much.

Eating the *pitzuhim* they'd offered me had been difficult. I couldn't crack the seed shell open in my clumsiness. They did it for me and fed me like a baby.

They made me laugh though, to prove a point that I wasn't the only one going through hardship. The true story about a woman in Jerusalem who threw a cockroach into the toilet was best. When the creepy-crawly wouldn't drown, she sprayed the toilet bowl with insecticide. Later on, the husband while sitting and shitting there, dropped a lit cigarette into the toilet and had to be rushed to hospital when sparks ignited the pesticide, seriously scorching his sensitive parts. Worse was to follow: the injured husband later suffered a broken pelvis and ribs when the paramedics, reportedly in fits of laughter, dropped the stretcher while carrying him down the stairs.

It felt good to giggle for the first time in many months. It hurt.

For reasons I don't know I had ogled and toyed with, over and over, a small paperweight that had somehow found its way into my hands. Israel's state telephone company, Bezeq's design was on it, and it had held me in awe. I had cradled it lovingly and it felt good rubbing against the side of my face.

Strange shit happened. When I sat on the aircraft's small toilet seat I nearly fell off it as I hadn't used a real loo for so long. I initially forgot to use the roll of tissue too. The soap was like holding gold. In there, obviously alone, I had stared in embarrassment at myself in the mirror for long minutes. I didn't know me for a split second, as ridiculous as it sounds. I looked haggard and undernourished, understandably. My beard was most unkempt and straggly, and the matted hair on top was worse. The army overalls they gave me hung loose, I appeared like Ché Guevara. I felt dirty as hell and hallucinated briefly about a good steaming hot bath.

I got my wish later, splashing in water in a hospital in Israel, including a long-awaited shave. Then I had slept uncomfortably for an unknown number of hours. I couldn't get used to the softness of the mattress and every time I turned over, I thought I was falling off as I gripped the side of the bed.

The only event to speak of about my stay in that institution was being questioned briefly the next morning by a polite bald chap from *Sherut ha Bitachon ha Klali*, the Israeli domestic intelligence unit, which translated to General Security Service—but liked to call itself by its simple acronym *Shabak*. He shuffled into my room quietly and without introducing himself softly asked me not about my horrid stay in Bulgaria nor about my well-being, but whether or not I knew the present whereabouts on one Abu Nidal. With a straight face I responded that I did not know the answer to where the Father of Struggle was but that the Palestinian bomb-maker's real name was actually Sabril Khalil al-Banna and I didn't know where he was either. The Israeli mildly stared at me for a few seconds, then shrugged and left silently.

Later that same day I was being whisked through security gates at Bournemouth Airport on the south coast of England. The evening drizzle never seemed so invigorating on me. I was still getting used to clothes draped over my being. I felt odd in them, as if I was invisible. Yet I felt everybody was overly staring at me, even a stray cat.

From the back seat of the pick-up car I did look back at the executive aircraft that had flown me home for five hours non-stop, as it was already taxiing to take-off again without refuelling. It was the same one that had collected me in Turkey. It was a four-engine Israeli government-registered unmarked all-white Lockheed Jetstar with twin drop tanks on both wings that looked like missiles (but were actually for petrol storage). It also had an extremely comprehensive communications system along with special electronic jamming devices, for sure, otherwise the armed escorts in the cabin wouldn't have said half the politically sensitive things that I heard them transmit over the airwaves in English. The other fifty per cent were obscenities about the recent shenanigans of the terrorist Carlos the Jackal. Half the world was hunting for his scalp including these Israeli gunmen.

In Hampshire we had pulled into a secluded gravel-lined driveway outside Beaulieu leading up to a house in the woods. An elderly, kind-looking man came out of the brass-handled double front doors before the black Rover came to a stop.

Strangely I cannot recall his name. But I was to spend five days and nights alone with him before I was allowed anywhere. It was a record at the time for the release of a former-prisoner of the communist bloc. That is only for those that got out...

After dinner, out of the blue, he had asked me if I knew how long I had been incarcerated. I said straight away, "Eleven weeks exactly."

He had looked at me at length, as if seeing into me, and replied, "Not bad, you are off by just three days. I find that pretty remarkable, I have to say."

He asked me to explain how I'd managed to estimate the time so well. I'd been stumped for a reply, then I remembered why, "The cockroaches came out at night to party, without fail. I would pass the time watching them network with each other for hours. Then at the end of the evening I killed one with my hands, neatly lining the bodies up. Each one represented an imagined night. I had seventy-seven of them. A graveyard for insects."

Then he began the following words, preceded by clearing his throat, "Now let's discuss the applied physical pressure you went through…"

Over the days I got to learn that he was an expert in debriefing, finding out what was lodged in there and weaning it out of you, whether nicely or not, depending on how deep down the crap was hooked in. He had cut his teeth with MI19, a British World War II intelligence unit—the German Department—that oversaw the return of prisoners of war back into normal life. He called Germans "Bonzos".

Despite the mental blockages, that master of psychology fascinated me. He pieced together my jigsaw puzzle, which came through hazy flashbacks; old letters by and to me; news clippings leading up to my capture; utilising real and mystical characters that challenged my perception of a right and wrong move. He declared me as good as could be considering what I had endured.

It was the United States Air Force's Global Positioning System of 24 satellites which had located my exact holding pen, or within 300 yards of where I was. In one of my teeth was a device emitting a signal to find me.

The British government's top secret spy centre, GCHQ—Government Communications Headquarters—in nearby Cheltenham had 95% access to the GPS' information. Regrettably, using a selective availability policy, which was the remaining unclear 5% of the political picture, it had to be approved first by the Pentagon. This bureaucracy explained why it took so long to come and get me. The GPS had also managed to overcome strong scrambled radio jamming by the Bulgarians. I was to discover then that the Russian equivalent is called Glonass, which had the same number of orbiting birds whizzing 11,000 miles out in space—half way between the American tin cans and Earth. A second group of three satellites called KH-9 HEXAGON Crystals were utilised which provided powerful high-resolution large format pictures of my approximate site, in a location which was just south of an industrial city in Bulgaria called Plovdiv.

As for Nikolay Valkanov, the Bulgarian meeting Malachy Kinsella a.k.a. Patrick O'Neill, he turned out to be attached to the Bulgarian army and based in Sofia. A prototype Igla MANPAD was shipped later by air from Burgas via Amsterdam on its way to Shannon but Dutch customs officers confiscated it before the IRA collected the small container. (The Igla is a

Bulgarian-made Man-Portable Air Defence System, a shoulder-fired surface-to-air anti-aircraft missile launcher that can fit into an average-size suitcase.)

Apparently another Bulgarian, a diplomat called Raiko Nikolov, was heavily involved in the negotiations for my release, but it had all been supervised through the aegis of the Israeli government. I thank you with my heart, sir.

The reason the Israelis were involved was because the slip of hotel paper I left on my rental car's front seat in Cyprus was traced to a wanted Palestinian who had been convicted in absentia of murdering a top officer of *Agaf ha-Modiin*, better known as Aman, which was Israel's military-intelligence agency. They were more than grateful for the tip given to them by MI6, courtesy of me, and kindly repaid the deed.

I was grateful that I had never thought about biting my wrists with my teeth to commit suicide…because I had a capsule of poison tucked within a second hidden false tooth in my mouth all that miserable time. Such was my utmost belief that I would survive the horror of Bulgaria.

Plus, as dumb as it may have sounded, (and I never would have admitted it to that older man who debriefed me) but I didn't want to die with the last stench of sweaty armpits in my nostrils, which the compound cyanidenon stinks of. I'd always particularly detested that awful smell. The world is a much sweeter place than that and it gave me the impetus to savour more of her in my life. I am appreciative for that opportunity once more.

When you are exposed to cruelty,
you begin to feel the law of the jungle beating inside you
and it makes you angry, vengeful, full of despair,
the sense of no hope; and to forget quickly.

Chapter Five

There's no need for tabernacles,
no need for complicated philosophy.
My own brain, my own heart is my temple.
From me I emanate the answer to the moment,
and along it comes on cue.

The loud scream of a jet engine coming down to land above me brought me back down to earth too with a jolt. I found myself back in the present day driving on the outskirts of Heathrow Airport's new Terminal Four having gone bumper-to-bumper in the Monday morning traffic. I parked the Ford Cortina in the spanking-new, covered car park and made a mental note of its numbered location, while admiring the terminal's modern exterior architecture.

Off I went to get *The Guardian* at WH Smith's newsagents. I had a habit of stocking up on plenty of Cadbury's whenever I went to any foreign clime. Besides Russia's Red October chocolate wasn't too appealing taste-wise. I checked my watch and headed to a pay phone.

"Ellen? It's me, Nicholas." I related everything about the funeral in Northern Ireland, including actually seeing O'Malley with O'Neill.

At one point I had to ask if she was still there on the line as I was getting no response at her end. I noticed too there had been a long silence again when I'd finished. To fill in the awkward void in the conversation, I went on to tell her where the car could be picked up when she interrupted me by saying tinnily, "Anything else?"

I stopped and thought for a second. "Oh, yes, I nearly forgot. Have you ever heard of an Arab, possibly Lebanese, maybe Jordanian, with a name which phonetically sounds like 'Moo Mohammed Abu Fart'-something? Description: Prematurely balding, early-forties, well-trimmed black beard, not the usual crooked Arab nose, tubby, about five-eight, speaks English well but with a slight American accent."

She injected, "And why may I ask do you think it's those particular nationalities, dear, and not others?"

So I simply said the first thing that came to my head, "Because I lip-read him say *'taybeth'* after sipping a beer. Only western Arabs say that it's 'delicious' and the others don't even put it to their lips anyway, never mind saying how nice it tasted. At one point they even clinked glasses and, I believe, they may have made a mention of an unintelligible word in English beginning with 'Coal'. The other clue was that I distinctly heard him say 'gotten' when he passed me going into the parish as opposed to 'got', which is not the way we Brits say it. Well, is it, luv?"

Again another silence, as if she was making notes. Finally the sound of Mrs Blyton's slow chortling her familiar sexy girlish laugh came down the line. "Only you could say things like that, Nick, honestly truly. Facts only the facts." I could picture her rolling her brown eyes. Then she sternly told me to call her back in half an hour before hanging up suddenly. I didn't like the sound of that at all and cursed under my breath as I hung up.

So I took the opportunity to buy a cup of espresso at the new continental coffee bar in the far corner and read the paper. Right on the 30-minute dot I was speaking to her again from the phone bank. She was chuckling now, her usual self again. "You are something else, Nicholas! The 'coal-word', that's Coalisland. It just happened a few days ago and had been withheld from the media until further information is forthcoming. Apparently our Special Air Service's undercover Intelligence & Security Group fellows shot and killed four IRA there. Yet you pick up a mention of it from the other side of a pub just like that. The 'moo' and 'fart' though, darling, was Moueen Mohammed Abu Farkh. Palestinian. Not PLO but Hamas, a new hybrid of the older model. Its full name is *Harakat al-Muqawama al-Islamiyyah*, Movement of Islamic Resistance, that's also an acronym for zeal. We've got a lot on him though. But we have to admit we didn't know he was on our beloved soil and talking to the Irish laddies, plus privy to their insider news like Coalisland." She hesitated before adding, "According to Big Ben your plane physically leaves the ground in about forty minutes even though they'll be boarding in about five from now. Do you remember young Hinton from the Washington station, well, he left on the tube well over a quarter of an hour ago with the file update for you. He'll pick up your car to drive it back into town."

Before I could protest about being sent confidential information I didn't want to see, Ellen Blyton, the woman behind "C"'s throne, I'm sure had anticipated this so she conveniently had ready the made-up excuse that she had an important call coming in and abruptly had to end our conversation by signing off with that sweet English innocent voice of hers, "Nicholas, have a safe flight to Moscow and call in with news on Molody, that is if you want to tell us what happened. God-speed." Then the line went dead.

I uttered an obscenity for the second time in an early day.

I was standing anxiously at the gate when the last handful of passengers were boarding the 767 when I saw young "H" running down the airport hallways sliding a little bit on the slippery floor, just like a wagging dog does in the rush to the back door to the garden heading for a walkie. He was waving a large manila envelope.

It always seems like I'm the last to board the aircraft every time. I grabbed it from him rather nastily.

I made my way to my portside first class seat. My boarding pass number had an "A" which meant I had a window seat. As I gave my jacket and carry-on bag to the attentive male attendant, a petite attractive lady in her red-brown fox fur hat stood up gracefully next to me holding both the same day's copies of the liberal *L'Humanité* and *Le Figaro*, a right-wing rag— a confusing political message to knowledgeable on-lookers as the papers had extreme viewpoints. I discreetly watched her take off her hat and her straight medium-length honey hair tumbled out and I noticed her eyes were warm brown, obviously she was French to my mind. Besides, most Russian blondes usually have blue eyes. I had always liked to determine the person who is next to me on a long flight.

The cool fixed smile of a pale young English stewardess appeared with the unfashionably uncool Queen Mother's hat on her head, offering us our drink of choice. I ordered a Stolichnaya and orange juice with no ice in

French. The Fox next to me said in English "the same please", which naturally told me that she had heard my choice of drink and we smiled at each other with our eyes. Older than me, no doubt, but a sexy good-looker nevertheless, then I turned away to look out of the hole in the wall.

The light brown sealed envelope was resting on my lap and my fingers played lazily on it piano-style as the 767 cruised along the ground. As the jet took off and my head was pressed against the headrest, my hands were ignoring my left brain's signals to talk to her and had started to split the seal with zeal, obedient to my right brain telling me to concentrate on business. Oh thank goodness, I noted it was the white card file, which meant either non-adversarial or containing not so top secret stuff. Blue was confidential while pink was top secret. The latter colour's files marked with the codes 'UK Eyes Alpha' or 'UMBRA' were respectively the most sensitive and highest classified security or signals intelligence material. I leaned away from possible female prying eyes next to me, perhaps reading through the newspaper and resigned myself to a long read. Not recalling what food was served thereafter, time was suspended, every second in flight was an hour, which elongated to something like three. Finally I peered left out of the window.

I gazed away from the snow-peaked Tatra Mountains down below and closed the folder. There are adventures to tell about everywhere, even Poland below. Everybody was sleeping including the absolute corker on my right. I watched her pretty face and whistled to myself in secret silent admiration momentarily before turning away again.

The political chaos in the country below me had a lot to do with my reading matter for the past several hours. I levered the seat back and I reflected on its contents. No doubt it wasn't top secret because I hadn't signed clearance to accept it, but clearly a helluva lot had changed in the Middle East since I was last there a decade ago. What was intriguing to me was that the report I was holding in my hands was produced by the British Secret Intelligence Service with added assistance from two wide-ranging cooperating national intelligence agencies: RASD, Jordan's Jihaz Al-Rasad; and Sluzba Bezpieczenstwa from Poland. Things had changed. Years back it was unthinkable all three would have been cohorts in putting a report together.

The first few pages told me the usual known facts and moved quickly on. I flipped through a series of single small black and white camera shots of obviously dead men. I recognised two even with their foolishly ghoulish masks, both in the trademark black and white chequered scarves around their necks, or what was left of the torn cloth: Zuheir Muhsin (ex-head of the Saiqa faction of the PLO—assassinated by us on the French Riviera in 1979); and Abu Jihad (late second-in-command to Abu Amar, otherwise also known as Yasser Arafat, at PLO headquarters in Tunis in 1988). The guy Jihad named himself with the word for the holy war, I mused. He found out, finally, whether the Koran's *sharia*—laws of Islam—teaches the truth about Islamic soldiers who die in *jihad* against the western infidels. Did he find paradise in the afterlife? Surely it was a most decisive moment of basic fundamental enlightenment, *al manar*.

I skipped forward a few pages and found myself gazing at nine distinctively familiar colour enlarged photographs. A silent circus. "All the big bad baddies from the PLO presented in a innocuous series of celebrity publicity snaps, an Arabic chimera," I smirked to myself. Mamdouh Nofel (inscription: attempted 19 attacks against Israel, including a school massacre that killed 27 children in 1974); Dr. George Habash (head of the radical Popular Front for the Liberation of Palestine); Farouk Kaddoumi (former head of the PLO's political department); Mahmoud Darwish (a Palestinian leftist poet); Mohammed Dief (number one in the Hamas military operation, a sheikh); Ahmed Yassin (another Hamas chief with the fancy title of Sheikh of the Uprising); Fath Shikaki (head of Islamic Holy War); and Yahya Ayyash (simply labelled The Engineer). Both Shikaki's and Ayyash's faces were curiously circled in green crayon for some unexplained reason. It's possible "C" was considering their assassination, he always wrote in green. The last photograph on the right intrigued me immensely as I leaned forward again to look closer at it.

Moueen Mohammed Abu Farkh: Educated in the USA, Doctorate in Engineering, University of Louisiana, lived in Virginia many years. I could very well have taken the enclosed photo at the Glenoe pub. He hadn't changed much, even though the credit in Arabic stated it was taken five years ago outside the Al Aqsa mosque in Jerusalem's old city, *Al Quds*—the Palestinian name for the Israeli *Yerushalaim*. Only difference is he looked more defiant then. He was estimated to be number two in the Hamas family tree, assuming the reins temporarily from the aforementioned number one, the sheikh, who currently lingered in an Israeli prison cell.

It seemed ol' Mohammed here was a big fish. A native of Gaza, Palestine. He was the main guy for nurturing foreign funding based in the good ol' US of Arabic-America for years. Apparently operated smartly in drips and drabs amounting to a total of millions of dollars. As there weren't many Arab-American cops around willing to carry cases of cash to their brothers in need, this clever arse funnelled under US$10,000 per transaction from a bank in Richardson, Texas, via the lax offshore IBC (international business corporation) tax haven of Belize. He then alternated the continued flow between the many one-man-operated independent banks in the Netherlands Antilles' ABC—either Aruba, Bonaire or Curaçao; it then found itself at Interpal in liberal London, a bonafide registered charity for Hamas, who channelled the paper gold, after deducting a donated commission; from there they electronically transferred legally to non-restrictive Polish and/or Russian banks, who welcomed the interim benefits of hard currency. It finally found its way to Damascus, Syria, and Amman, Jordan, where Hamas openly had administrative offices. From there the spoor was spotty. The report never addressed how the lucrative pipeline's green oil eventually spouted out onto the streets of Area C (the Gaza Strip), but I suspected they lead-footed the loot by various transportation over the hills into Area B (the West Bank) at night using the moon and the stars with headlights turned off, maybe even utilising donkeys. Once in Palestine, a large portion of the laundered money was distributed to Hamas' military wing, Al-Qassem, who faced off against Shin Beth, the domestic Israeli security service—who are no angels themselves. Israel was known as Area A.

Not all the dough ends up in the gun-powdered hands of Al-Qassem, who were named after another sheikh, a Muslim preacher who led a revolt against we Brits in the thirties. The sweet children, whom Hamas serves under the auspices of charity, are being taught hatred along with their prayers. These same youngsters grow into human bombers and die in the name of Allah's will. In fact the goal of Hamas, as stated by their charter, "Is to kill all Jews and replace Israel with a pure Arab fundamental state." It goes on to declare, "All Jews are devils, not people." The appendix following asserted, "Israel is the only dominion in the world with no officially declared borders, which is because it plans to bloat at its leisure with its everlasting US$5 billion a year support by the American taxpayer."

The next page had a list of euphemisms that made me grimace: "non-Jews" was the Israeli descriptive term for Arabs, "under debate" their words for the continued control by Israel of occupied Palestine, and "the Zionist entity" was the Arabs descriptive term for Israel.

One aspect that was not covered, I noted, was the numbers game. Hadn't anybody noticed that the Palestinians were breeding like rabbits? When I was last there, it seemed each Arab mother had a handful of kids around their ankles. With four million Jews living actually in Israel itself and 2.5 million Palestinians in the Occupied Territories, how many years will it take to overrun them? There's a minority populace of 750,000 Muslims, Druze and Christians already in Israel, who are only too willing to help their underdog cousins, if Israel keeps up their bad treatment of them and continues its illegal expansion.

The suffering the Israelis have experienced over their short history is being passed on to Palestinians today. The Arabs are entitled to the same rights that were once demanded by Jews, resulting in a holocaust of both races and a tangled mess of contradictions.

The story of how the Israelis themselves were responsible for Hamas' growth up to this point of no return was interesting, too. In the 1970's and early in the Palestinian uprising, the Israelis allowed this surging Islamic movement to flourish and even covertly supported it. By doing so they calculated that this and other new Muslim groups would both undermine and draw local support away from the Palestine Liberation Organisation, which was perceived then as the more immediate threat. Talk about punching yourself in the face. The tactic failed miserably because Hamas, with its tighter-knit cells and even more zealous devotion to Islam, proved much harder to infiltrate and influence than the more secular and corrupt PLO. In fact, according to the neutral SIS report at the time of filing, the Israelis had recently assumed the physical costs of deporting over four hundred of Hamas' activists for some kind of cool off period away from the hotbed to a snowy hillside in Lebanon. There they all quickly enrolled in guerrilla training camps and soon afterwards hotfooted their way back to haunt Israel once more, but this time as better-trained revolutionary fighters.

A fascinating piece of data on Hamas had inadvertently come from the day Israeli troops were shifting through the debris of the newly abandoned Rashadiye refugee camp outside Tyre, near Israeli-occupied Lebanon. There they found the half-burnt service card of a young IRA member, with details on his date of birth in Northern Ireland and full physical description. While there had been no actual evidence in the form of Irish or Arab confessions up to the day of this discovery, it did establish that there was a link between the two terrorist groups. It also confirmed the paperwork evidence on file that numerous IRA Provos had been on six-week training courses, organised by the PLO's Fatah (*fatah* is conquer) wing at between US$5,000 and US$10,000 per man. Payments from US based Irish organisations had made payments to untraceable accounts through a Pakistani bank named BCCI.

There was a brief mention that an SIS operative called Anderson fifteen years ago had been inside Libya on undercover duty and had purportedly sighted the IRA's Paddy O'Neill outside a reported terrorist training camp 25 miles from the Tunisian border. The photographs he had supplied of two men sitting smoking in a dilapidated German Afrika Corps vehicle didn't confirm O'Neill's identification properly as he was wearing a pulled-down Arab head-dress during a sand storm, but the eyes were thought by many in-house identification experts to match the same cold blue and shape as the IRA boss. The other man in the picture was a leading decision maker with Muammar el-Qaaddafi's Moukhabarat, the Libyan secret service. An odd couple if there ever was sitting innocently having a Sunday afternoon tea break in the middle of a desert while plotting mayhem.

* * * * * * * * *

A rare sunny sky was giving way to a flat dismal grey as we approached Russia, where the suppressing enormity of power and emptiness of space seems to reach out to the far horizon.

Sheremetyevo Airport hadn't changed in the slightest. The frozen stationary Ilyushins and Tupolevs of the Aeroflot fleet sat cross-legged on the edge of a hard icy lake of tarmac, like unused tired decoys, suspicious of the sleek Boeing. The British jet—a blue, red and white-clad long distance runner—smilingly maintained a sprinter's pace past them to the distant gate.

The fast walk by the early exiting passengers to beat each other to the baggage hall developed into a stupid dash as usual and I was no exception. The experienced traveller, knows that Moscow's international airport means long spluttering queues for those last stragglers off the plane.

I saw the first bodyguard before his gaze locked on mine for those recognisable timeless few moments when two strangers magnetically know that that's *the* right person. Frankly, he looked like an off-duty armed services man to me in every descriptive manner possible, but I'd learned over the years that what I see isn't what my fellow man sees. I'd obviously had the knack for details and spotting the out-of-place and this was no exception.

Then I saw the second one, a little younger but in the same school of relaxed stiffness. As I stared at him I realised that the couple standing to his right were Dr and Mrs Molody waving enthusiastically at me and I motioned back like a long lost cousin returning home.

Caterina hugged me like an excited schoolgirl, by bouncing from one foot to the other all the while holding both my hands tightly. She retained a mature collegiate-look despite being in her mid-fifties, while her eyes shone.

Mike Molody appeared a little sheepish yet upbeat as usual. It's almost as if he had two personalities at once—I don't mean either schizophrenic— but he could be two people simultaneously; the mild workaholic medical professor and the mad after hours gent entertaining himself at the ballet, the opera or an extravagant dinner lasting five hours and peppered by saucy but intelligent conversation.

Outside, out of thin air came a vehicle with more doors than wheels, a sleek black stretch ZIL limousine. I had a split second mental image of the assembly lines I'd covertly inspected at the Likhachev Motor Works in a Moscow suburb many moons ago. I momentarily tried to remember what ZIL stood for…*Zavod Imeni* Likhachev, that was it! We all piled in, where unsurprisingly, two more men, including the driver, sat in the front seats maintaining respectful silence, neither acknowledging my greetings.

"Four support service guys, wow, Mike and Catty," I remarked sarcastically. "You must be a bigwig now. Either that or you've temporarily been let out of jail for a mortuary visit."

They both smiled politely at the understatement and quickly glanced at each other. The love was still there burning brightly, I noted.

The doctor volunteered, "You must be tired, Nick, so we'll drop you at the hotel now and we'll come back and pick you up for dinner. Is that OK with you?" I nodded sincere approval.

During the ride into the city centre, from time to time everybody took turns at pointing and commenting on some landmark or other. Moscow is littered with monuments and statues of fallen Russian heroes; never a today's hero. The perceived villains in stone had already met crushing demises as rubble under the current people's hammers and swept away with sickles. This mood, of course, historically depended on the respective modern generations political leanings of the moment.

Almost on cue Catty touched my knee and said, punctuating at a distant spot, "That's where Feliks Dzerzhinsky's statue was." There was nothing to see and nothing to say. I could only nod. The founder of the KGB was himself toppled to the ground by the very people who feared him, even in rock form.

The KGB had been reconstructed over a half a dozen times and it still remained a state within a state. SVR and SVRR had been the KGB's successors; now it was Federal Security Service and Foreign Intelligence Service—one domestic; the other international. Before it was called the KGB, it was the OGPU (State Political Administration). Before that it was CHEKA (Extraordinary Commission for Combating Counter-Revolution and Sabotage).

Russian people were long accustomed to Soviet censorship and are probably still adept at interpreting what wasn't said. As a result, everybody had a habit of speaking between the lines rather than on them, leaving the listener guessing at what was meant, implied and intoned. A sombre existence to have to live with.

Moscow looked sick but its heart was still beating. It had been more than a decade since I'd last been here and the city had changed tremendously for the worse since the latest modern revolution when the Soviet Union collapsed. The restructuring—*perestroika*—had little apparent effect. If anything, things looked pretty grim on this overcast afternoon and the potholes were gigantic after yet another cruel winter. Only Manhattan's was comparable to this humourless joy ride as I held onto the door handles after another jolt to the ceiling. We were nearing the main artery to downtown where the crowds swelled.

The little peasant-like, grandmotherly *babushkas* were still on every street corner flogging *matrushkas* dolls to tourists. I reminded myself to get one for my American daughter. As long as I'd been visiting Moscow, I'd always noticed more women than men, a strange observation even though I was aware of the millions of male fallen heroes in the last world war. Some things just don't change over half a century despite progress.

Many observers try to untangle the disparate strands of the dark Russian character. I simply accept them the way they are. They have good reasons to look at strangers the way they do based on their unfortunate and frequently vicious cycles of history. If stares were pistols, I'd be dead long ago. The West calls it xenophobia; Russians call it nationalist anxiety.

Sitting in the heavy exhaust-smoking ZIL, I thought they ought to think about introducing ZEV's, like in California where I lived—Zero Emission Vehicles. Every time a damn GAZ heavy goods lorry rumbled past we were gagging from the fumes. The VAZ', AZLK's and Izhmash, domestically made cars, dominated. I spied an old *Topolino*, the original Italian-made Fiat 500, dubbed Mickey Mouse for its toy-store looks and roller-skate wheels. Russian-made Lada's, Polski-Fiat's and Seat's (Spanish-produced Fiat's) were also in abundance. The building sites' bulldozers sported Fiat-Hitachi logos too. Seems like the Italians in their initial burst of entrepreneurial enthusiasm towards capitalism were everywhere in Russia, their emblems sprouting all over the place, even spaghetti brand logos on billboards.

I could only smile to myself at seeing so much of the Fiat name. In my time in this country, I would get numerous coded messages stating AT&T (also now a famous world brand) and FIAT. But neither meant what others would readily assume today: The former signalled me to go to British Airways and collect a ticket and passport and come home for a meeting for it stood for Aircraft Transport and Travel, actually the first name for the airline before it was called BOAC and/or BEA. The latter acronym translated to Field Information Agency (Technical), which meant we have some news for you, go and get it at the designated pick-up location.

Yaroslavl Station, the main railway station, cruised by. Next door to it was still Kazan Station, the gateway to Siberia and the Russian Far East. The famous *Gosudarstvenny Universalny Magazin, GUM* (State Universal Store) hadn't moved either. Then we passed the main building where the KGB had its school on Leningradsky Prospekt, which got me wondering about what they were up to under the guise of their new names.

It also occurred to me that we were not undergoing any surveillance detection route (to see if we were being followed) and were black (free of surveillance) from the usually beige Zhiguli that followed a few cars back with the standard duo of cut-outs that blended into the front seats.

Suddenly we were in front of the concrete sarcophagus called the President Hotel at 24 Dimitrova Street. The sad attempt at palace-like hospice was especially built for the apparatchiks of Moscow, the bureau-crats of the Russian political system, no matter which guise it hid under. The only way one got to stay here was to be invited, so the local British embassy had obviously finagled its way once again to get me in at my hotel of choice. No doubt Mrs Blyton had pulled out all the stops to get me met properly as well as accommodated here. How nice.

The hotel security guards wouldn't allow the car to enter the hotel's immaculate grounds for security reasons despite the presence of our four drivers with their noticeable *propusks* (security ID badges) in place. So I gingerly jumped out without further ado at the huge metal gate and hauled my bags out of the boot myself. I cheerily waved to Mike and Caterina as they called out of the window "to be ready for dinner at 7:00 PM." I stood at the foot of the marble-like steps for a long minute looking up at the hotel's ugly structure, contemplating. Whenever the barrel of a gun belches in this big country; it was first burped at the council meetings at the dining tables right here.

Chapter Six

"Marijuana, heroin and cocaine kill brain cells with every intake. This loss is permanent and in certain societies—the United States especially—we are beginning to witness the results of this short-term memory asphyxiation with thousands of trance-like individuals doing their daily chores. The damage is already done and the clock cannot be turned back. Of course America always had more cash to spend on these kind of items and, well, it was only a matter of time, in this case about 20 years of steady recreational abuse and now that time is already here."

Molody shrugged and kept chewing on his food while deep in thought. "I am exploring its effect on the DNA that controls which genes are switched on and off. Changes in genes from drug abuse can show up as changes in emotions and actions. Anyway its effect on brain cells has been known for decades but little is done to educate the public. It's the reason I've never taken recreational drugs and seriously advise against it."

My mind always was on a natural high so I never needed a boost to make me feel any higher. But I couldn't remember for the life of me what got us on this subject. Meanwhile, the drug of leisure alcohol was starting to affect me so I ate some more *vobla*—a dried, salted, smoked carp—to counter the effects.

I looked around the rather large restaurant in the Hotel Baltschug Kempinski where we sat having dinner. It was a throwback in time of at least half-a-century. Waiters in black bow-ties and high white collars, some even with neatly trimmed black moustaches, the customary white napkin on their left arms and bowing ever so slightly at every command of the new decadent bourgeoisie munching beneath them.

Michal's face came back into focus slowly across the table in front of me. He had the ability to totally dazzle listeners with his rhetoric and astounding facts. There was absolutely nothing the listening party could do when he'd finished talking but to stare back in wonder. I'd seen it before and could see myself falling for the same trick by this ace conjurer of wondrous scientific discovery.

"Mike," I finally croaked. It had been some time since it had been my turn to speak. "I've flown half-way around the world to be sitting here," I hesitated. "Surely that wasn't what you wanted to tell me?"

He looked at me intently, then knocked back another neat full glass of vodka. He, she and I all winced. "My dear Nicholas, of course not. There is so much to tell you. So much to show you. I want you to know I've been planning your visit for many many months but still I wonder where to begin."

I quickly injected, "Well for starters, what have you two done for the past 13 years which is when we all last saw each other." They looked at each other and both voiced simultaneously, "Has it really been *that* long?" All three of us laughed in unison at the memory and drank a toast.

We bade farewell to each other in 1979 on a beautifully sunny day at a Royal Navy helicopter training air station in Portland, Dorset, in south England. The looks on their faces were a mix of trepidation and joy. The British government had officially cleared them as *personas gratis* and gave them temporary UK false passports at their request. When it was thought that he had shared his vast knowledge to the fullest extent of his scientific abilities to the British, it would then be the Americans turn to learn first-hand from the horse's mouth.

It was their lifelong dream to start a new life together in the United States, and it was also agreed by the parties to not alter their physical appearances whatsoever…only their names. He elected for Martin and she wanted Georgia while their surnames were a simple Anglicisation of their original Czechoslovakian last name.

We formally shook hands with each other just before they boarded the old semi-retired Westland Wessex helicopter, which took them east towards The Fort in Fort Monckton, near Gosport in Hampshire where induction courses awaited the pair before being allowed to enter into normal British society. I, a small rapidly fading figure in my full-dress Fleet Air Arm flight officer's uniform with white cap on, stood at ease, allowing myself to give them one slowly conducted blown kiss, fingers to mouth to air. Another mission successfully completed. I wished them the best of luck. I would miss their ebullient company.

It was clear they didn't have a good time in America, contrary to their expectations. Their daughter was born shortly after arrival in Chicago, but they spent most of their time in and around Southern California, mainly San Diego and Los Angeles. Because he was able to organise his time and condition himself to work like a walking computer, he found he always had time to do everything on his personal agenda and achieved many goals simultaneously. I noticed that he enjoyed peppering his still-heavily accented English dialogue with a play on a popular communist slogan—"I am a miner, who is more?"—by saying frequently, "I am a doctor, who is less." Though he said it as a statement rather than a question. I could only smile back at the oft-used pun.

It took Martin many years to fully understand that in the US' health care system care for the sick is last in order of importance. "You have to follow the orders or you are thrown out as a misfit." He observed that US medicine was indeed best when it came to the treatment of acute diseases and esoteric surgical procedures but it was failing when it came to the treatment of chronic diseases. "The rules of the diagnosis and therapy were, from year to year, more and more rigidly prescribed by medical organisations. No new ideas were allowed to be used and the whole system became sclerotic without a chance of success."

He confessed at that time that he wondered what happened to professional relationships between doctors in the US as opposed to the camaraderie that was so normal in Czechoslovakia, the Soviet Union and Great Britain. "I missed that interaction. To this day I don't really know why it was largely absent. I can only think that excessive individual income coupled with highly specialised fields may have caused the separation between physicians."

Being a new capitalist and finally free from the restrictive shackles of the CIA's National Resettlement Operations Center regulations, Martin drifted into the burgeoning field of plastic surgery becoming an expert in changing the male face into a female face. "Which was in great demand by male transsexuals in Hollywood!" he exclaimed theatrically, before swigging down another vodka followed by another wince.

"No doubt a whole separate story right there," I sniggered. He nodded.

Catty who had remained silent thus far, injected flatly, "They are a nation of cathode ray junkies; people watching television too much."

"The stupidity of American TV is criminal. Everybody there lives in the world of instant coffee and expects immediate results," her husband agreed, before continuing his dialogue uninterrupted.

"The demand for illicit drugs in the United States remains extensive. The federal authorities have failed to eradicate the supply, which would not exist without voracious demand. Sadly millions of Americans are demanding to alter their consciousness, to numb their brains, to 'feel' something beyond what they must believe is the vacuity of their empty existence."

Certainly I got the impression his income hovered in the many hundreds of thousands of dollars, maybe the guy even made a few million. The man wanted the American Dream and it sounded like he achieved it despite the complaints.

"Nicholas, the whole medical industry in the US is hopelessly infiltrated by the cancer of politics. I simply could not see myself playing games by their rules. I was wasting myself ethically and professionally while, ironically, raking in a lot of money. I mean the Americans would pay me several thousands for a 10-minute nose job. It was insane! I could not and did not play the game of benign neglect of my patients.

"Then my father died prematurely of diabetes in Bratislava. My mother never told me until two weeks after they cremated him. She mailed a letter only afterwards to make sure I would not come for the funeral and face arrest." Martin and Georgia were holding hands tightly as tears welled in their eyes.

I poured vodka in everybody's glass waiting for him to regain his composure. He stared into his empty glass for several long minutes, a faraway glaze on his face. *When you see that stare into the middle distance, do not interrupt the train of thought as an idea can disappear in a puff. That fleeting thought is worth pursuing and is a cradle of a beginning...*

"Around then I became deeply interested in a medical revitalisation. I had plenty of human foetal tissue research knowledge from the leftovers of the Soviet Olympic team's sexploits. Anyway I recognised that if the body, hands, demeanour, behaviour and overall appearance give an impression of old age, then it is ridiculous to make the face look young. It means that if you treat only the exterior and do nothing for the interior, you are like a house painter trying to rejuvenate an old building. One layer of paint will not cover the fact that the building is simply antiquated and in need of a general in-depth reconstruction.

"I then realised that the cornerstone of everything is a regeneration of the damaged or underdeveloped structures and that can be helped by the implantation of the foetal tissues." He licked his lips in excitement. "I continued to read avidly about the subject which only confirmed my earlier scientific intuition that the key element of the therapeutic scheme was indeed the implantation of foetal tissues in some way and form, whether it be animal or human."

So far, I thought, it had been a logical evolution of his life's medical experience research and discoveries to date. The main reason we elected to get him out and on to our side in the first place. *Genius is only great patience.*

"It took me years to slowly discover that all the therapies I proposed were being prohibited by the US' Federal Drug Administration. While I continued to provide details of my findings to them *carte blanche*, as I was still under the auspices of the Central Intelligence Agency programme which brought me originally to America; the FDA were starting to make my life hell, yet all the while, never told me to stop. So I kept going along this imaginary path towards a goal with no net.

"Finally I got wise about what was going on around me. I mean, *nothing* would happen; my information would go into the FDA's mouth and be digested while I got thrown the faeces. Eventually I contacted the World Health Organisation in Switzerland. WHO ultimately referred me to the Russian chief of the respective department of non-communicable diseases, a professor. He fell in love with my project, which he in turn presented it to the last ever Soviet Minister of Health who approved it, too—not knowing one iota about my past as it was submitted under my alter-ego's name.

"Then the Iron Curtain fell over a year ago. Within a few weeks of the news, I took the opportunity and moved back to the new Russia to work on my programme without any persecution nor prosecution for defecting."

"But what exactly *was* the precise goal of this programme, Mike?" I asked him point blank, sitting up in my chair.

"Of course, it was to try to eventually clone human beings and to learn from its many side effect modalities."

When he said that so naïvely, I just sat there trying to utter something but nothing was emitted. One expected such world-beating statements from

Molody and there was nothing to say immediately. The rest of dinner was a complete blank.

I lay in semi-drunken haze on the hotel bed back at the President. I knew verisimilitude when I experienced it. Molody never knowingly lied. Trying to sleep was impossible. Though there was silence in the room, inside my head there was a loud party in full throng. Nameless faces came and went; words were being said but not heard above the din; I was trying to get a perspective on what I'd heard at dinner and I was failing miserably.

* * * * * * * * *

When Dr Molody's chauffeur-driven ZIL pulled up at the outside gate in the morning frigidity, I was down the President's steps and inside the car in a few seconds. A typical cold Russian morning with fog swirling off the nearby Moscow River. Caterina had stayed home with a headache and would join us for lunch. Three men sat up front not talking. The glass gate separated us.

"Sleep well last night?" asked Mike.

I looked at him and said, "Actually for once, I remembered everything in my dream quite vividly. I can't really explain why it's so." There was a little space of time so I added as I looked over again at Mike sitting next to me, "Do you know where we're going?"

He hadn't fully acknowledged my presence and was facing away from me taking in the magnificent domes and outside walls of the *Kremlin*— which in English translated to the Citadel. "We're going to my institute just outside town…

"So what was the dream?" he faced me finally.

I hesitated and stared back at him, "You don't *really* want to know, do you?" The sights of Moscow by day were more interesting but his body language and eyes showed genuine keenness.

"I could always attach an electroencephalogram to find out," his smile creased marginally.

I ignored that because I didn't know the instrument he was referring to. He had a habit of drawing these statements out of unsuspecting people. I thought for a moment and duly submitted, "Well, when I'm awake I remember myself encased in a glowing halo walking in slow motion among the darkness of cacti and other vaguely outlined desert plants. I find I'm in the middle of a big night sky with stars glittering like I'm on a stage addressing an audience, all the while a single silent white cockatoo sits obediently on my shoulder. The sound is muted but the picture on the television set is not fully freeze-framed. Yet I did find myself in that scene in real life once in Joshua Tree National Park in California."

He nodded at my comments. "Interesting. It is said that dreams are messages from the gods. The fact that you are awake and recall a dreamlike sequence, of course, is different from the norm. There must be some quantum-mechanical loophole in your neurology system. One explanation could be an unconscious clairvoyance you may have genetically inherited. Another is simply that you found the actual experience enlightening and you continue to refer to it as if it was a movie set constructed especially for you to freely walk around in it—an euphoric feeling—yet your brain tries to make sense of that time, but cannot to date."

I looked to him for further comprehension. Molody shrugged and added, "Scientists have found that memories are processed by a part of the brain called the limbic system. Dreams are symbolic messages sent to us from the blackness of mankind's unconscious brain which has developed over the history of evolution. Its important lessons are recorded in the archives of long-term memory."

We'd passed over the loops in the Moscow River twice and had just left the western outskirts of the city limits. Passing through open freshly painted gates, the newly paved tarmac road went straight and disappeared into a pristine white birch forest. We passed an inconspicuous small green sign in Russian, which announced we were at Serebtyanny Bor, a research department of the Russian Academy of Medical Science. A stone monastery-like fortress, clearly it used to be a dacha belonging to a former high-ranking Soviet official. They don't just give country estates of this calibre to just anybody.

The doors opened and morning's revitalising chill surged into my lungs. It was a hauntingly beautiful preserve atop a hill, surrounded by various kinds of trees standing in their naked winter austerity with moat-like iced lakes. A peasant woodcutter was in progress swinging an axe at a collapsed birch, its branches, like arms, preventing further assault. *When chopped trees fall, they make the sounds of pain and agony.*

Two white-clad nurses, one nondescript sturdy swarthy male and a stunning platinum blonde woman immediately surrounded Molody. They were deep in conversation over the reports he was handed. The three who accompanied us in the car were smoking cigarettes idly leaning on the ZIL watching the death of a tree.

I wandered slowly towards the nearby water with a light mist floating on it. I shivered as I stood on a crunchy panhandle. The bewitching aroma of damp leaves permeated the air. Oddly the suburbs of Moscow never feel quite so immense, or so familiar, as when the dew closes in.

It was seconds before I realised that Mike was gyrating his arms frantically at me, beckoning my presence, before heading in. My meditation time was over.

By the time I reached the door, the lone male nurse indicated for me to stand and face the camera. He explained that it was scanning my iris, which was as exclusive as my fingerprints, before the buzzer opened the door. Once inside the building, it resembled a convalescent home. He was telling me that Dr Molody had to go to an important meeting with the staff and to make myself feel at home. Escorting me into a room which obviously was an employee's canteen of sorts there were refreshments including, much to my surprise, the regulatory bottle of opened lime vodka with an assortment of biscuits. I felt like eating an American-style everything-on-it bagel with cream cheese and lox but it wasn't on the menu.

"Might be a couple of hours," called out Mike as he came past the open door donned in a starched coat, ever the busy physician. "Have a coffee, it compensates for lack of sunshine in cold climates and it contains serotonin, a neuro-chemical which raises our spirits." I only nodded, understanding nothing. I was getting frustrated and wanted to be doing something with myself, like he was.

* * * * * * * * *

I first met Molody in 1970 when I was a student, who had just turned 19, at Patrice Lumumba University in a south Moscow suburb, the ramshackle Marxist version of NYC's South Bronx or Brixton in South London. PLU had some 7,000 students enrolled of which the large majority were foreigners like me, though I believe I was the only one from England.

At the time he must have been over 30. We used to work out at the vast training complex at *Associaciya Sportivnyh Sostazanij Dinamo* (Dinamo Sports Association) in Petrovski Park, which in is the northwest of the city, but we never really knew each other. His was another face in the crowd I'd recognise occasionally. The reason why I practised football and swam there was that, simply, it was close to my living quarters and many of my fellow students had joined the complex too. I'd always liked the colours of black, white and blue, which was that of the club. So you had to join first before you got the attractive all-black outdoor tracksuit with white and blue trimmings. I never got to know how Molody chose Dinamo as there was so many others to choose from in Moscow, especially Spartak, Lokomotiv and Torpedo—CSKA would have been out of the question as it was the club for Red Army personnel only.

Still, we never formally met until a couple of months before I returned home. There was somebody's going-away-party-cum-birthday bash— thrown by a popular chemistry student called *El Gordo* (Fatso was from Venezuela I learnt later) who was on his way to make a name for himself in Palestine—at a loud bar close to the sports complex, and somehow or other we all got talking for a ribald half an hour above the din of music. Subject matter was strictly football. After that it was always a little wave of acknowledgement whenever Michal and I saw each other but no further conversation took place, to the best of my recollection.

I don't know if he knew I was English or not because my Russian was by then quite fluent and everybody at the gym and the campus was from somewhere else. To ask where you were from on first meeting was almost taboo as according to the Soviet doctrine we were the children of the world, and so the subject was never broached. *There is no data on the future.*

It wasn't until I had trained to be a British Royal Navy helicopter pilot, been recruited from the armed forces by SIS and experienced adventure in various hell holes around the world, that I was transferred to Moscow as a non-official deep cover agent of influence. My fluency in Russian was perhaps a major factor for this assignment.

I should add that the British secret service's head hunters in London were actively searching its army, navy and air force officers for talented individuals with university degrees in economics or related subjects, fluency in foreign languages, depth in political science or international relations, a hunger for information, a certain creative twist of mind, the damned ability to write a 500-word synopsis on a current event deemed of importance to national security (always at the department head's discretion) and the *sangfroid* to pass a lie-detector test on a monthly basis.

It was easier, supposedly, for ex-armed forces personnel to recognise its operative intelligence needs rather than selecting from those in the sphere of administration policies. I had come through the ranks of the analytical directorate's watchful and stringent tests over nine months with flying colours and was, without hesitation, rewarded with a promotion to the overseas clandestine duties side of SIS. The international covert operations unit I was assigned to had the simple job of persuading foreigners to betray their countries and work for us. The first interesting lesson learned was that some foreigners act from noble motives while some are scum, and with that in mind, you are sent out in search of them.

Still spy training wasn't complete without a month under the tutelage of the science and technology directorate who normally trained engineers and scientists to build state-of-the-art gadgets for stealing, processing and transmitting secret information.

It wasn't until my second stint in Moscow—silly as it sounds—that I belatedly discovered that the Dinamo Sports Association was an offshoot of an organisation called *Komitet Gosudarstvennoy Bezopasnosti*, or in English it was the Soviet Committee for State Security, otherwise known as the KGB, who had its own main social club in ulica Dzerzhinsky in the city centre. I laughed as loud as I have ever done in my life when I found that fact out.

As fortune would have it, I met Molody eight years after we'd originally met—and it was in the very same bar. We recognised each other instantly. We resumed our much delayed dialogue, starting from where we left off with a discussion about football and evolved from there to deeper thoughts pertaining to world affairs. But this time the fact that I was British was a non-issue as he thought I was from the Russian South as beget my accent and pretence.

Before long I'd been invited to his flat in a nice section of Moscow, where I met his Czechoslovak mother who was visiting on a holiday, and from whom I was discreetly informed not to ever talk of anything related to having babies. The reason being her daughter-in-law Caterina Molody had suffered a couple of miscarriages. Mike later once also told me that his wife was approaching her late-30's and they were resigned to never having a natural child of their own, in fact they were considering adoption.

The fact that they were listed a few thousand names down the list when only a dozen or so babies were available annually had something to do with their decision to consider leaving. The seed to leave was inadvertently planted then by their close neighbours, a KGB officer and his pregnant wife who apparently in a mindless drunken stupor insulted Cat and Mike as being "unwelcome Czechoslovak foreigners who can't have real Soviet babies", or ugly abusive words to that effect.

My specific job was to find and exploit these kinds of situations for the express gain of my country, without excessive loss of life. The trick for an intelligence officer undercover overseas in a trading company is to be high enough to see everything and low enough not to be seen. This mainly entailed avoiding arrest for spying and staying alive. Because the Molody's situation had, in a sense, fallen in my lap, I was initially extremely suspicious of their motives.

So I started the ball rolling by having London do background checks on this unassuming doctor, while I did what I could at my end without attracting attention. After all my cover was that I was a fledgling, Moscow-based businessman-merchant from the southern Soviet city of Rostov-na-Donu, 600 miles away, representing a national wholesale import-export company which dealt in bartered internationally-recognised brands of small music equipment such as horns, violins and orchestra-related accessories, which in turn were distributed throughout the vast music-loving country.

On the wall of my small office was a faded official photograph of a football team; a home-made sticker in my car; and proud possession of an old jersey tacked on the wall of my flat further indicated my steadfast passion for SKA Rostov, the top flight army football club from my home town. Every weekend I would faithfully check their results, just so I would be knowledgeable.

I had to be ultra careful when I listened in to the Americans broadcasting from West Germany on Radio Liberty, a Russian-language station, often having the volume low and listening to it with a towel over my head in case prying neighbours heard it. The same went for when I picked up a copy of *La Pensée Russe* (The Russian Thought), an anti-Communist weekly printed in France in Russian and circulated in certain Moscow underground circles. Both of them were really open secrets and frowned upon by the authorities but they did communicate coded messages for the likes of me on a regular basis.

What I had to especially be careful of was my West German-made Taschenmikroskop Wetzlar 47451 microdot reader with a magnification of 225 times the object, which was about the size and length of my hand.

Found on my being or in my residence or car the Tami advertised what I did for a living.

By an interesting quirk of fate, my business did better than expected by virtue of a Kremlin study at the time, which showed that classroom lessons undertaken with a background of baroque music increased learning capacity by one third, especially achieving excellence in mathematics. I later learned, through Molody, that it was scientifically proven that the rhythm and the beat enjoins the left and right areas of the brain and apparently there is an increased passage of information to long-term memory storage. A fact, I believe, which is still not widespread in the West but is commonly known now as the Mozart Effect in the East.

On paper, this import trading activity in return was paid for by three unrelated exported Russian products: The first was bulk damaged and second-grade sturgeon roe available for repackaged re-export of canned caviar paste, a concentrated salty Russian staple locally called *payusnaya*—this appealed to Iran especially—who couldn't produce enough of their own and paid my company in Persian rugs and carpets; the second was an excellent little known vodka brand called Tarkhuna produced in the Soviet satellite state of Georgia for export worldwide, mainly to the United States; and the third was the re-export of now cheap Russian Near East-made rugs and carpets to Western Europe. I had to know my stuff inside and out on these subjects, and I did. Today I'm an expert on beluga, osetra, golden osetra and sevruga—even salmon roe—the fake red caviar. Ironically, foods considered synonymous with capitalist luxury and decadence…

Guided by unseen forces manipulated by my London-based masters on behalf of the grandmasters in Washington and Brussels, there were many other one-off ventures too, like once representing the export of Armenian petroleum waste product as industrial-grade lubricating oil to Angola. I never asked what that was about, and accepted that I would be never told anyway. All this was the result of having a soft-currency rouble worth nothing outside the Soviet Union, giving SIS an opportunity to send a covert representative of theirs there to help Britain make more money. Meanwhile my income, plus the insurance coverage plans I had, was well above the average. It was paid in British Pounds, of course, into my Swiss Bank Corporation account in Berne, and I got to keep the Soviet roubles I earned, which was as good as toilet paper elsewhere in the world, due to its worthless soft currency value as deemed by the World Bank and the International Monetary Group, US-run institutions.

Perhaps my best coup while there was the order book (SIS jargon for agent-running) handling of important nuclear-related data from a retired training professor at Voroshilov Naval Academy in Leningrad—the old and new St. Petersburg—when I purchased the information from him in return for UK£50,000 value in mixed western currencies. He needed the cash; we needed the fat. What I learned was precisely where the Soviet Navy's 62 Northern and Pacific Fleets nuclear-warhead Typhoon and Delta submarines were based. Until that time nobody had any idea where their Nerpichya, Yagelnaya, Olenya, Ostrovnov, Rybacki and Pavlovsk installations were—but the British Royal Navy had been pleased with my work.

From this same agent I also later uncovered the fact that the Soviet Navy had successfully developed a fast wave skimmer submarine seeker, which used laser beams to spot enemy submarines up to 500 feet below the surface. Turned out to be useful discovery for the Royal Navy to know and good for bogus runs.

The British Royal Air Force had been more than happy on my follow-up lead that SS-25 nuclear intercontinental ballistic missiles were manufactured at a factory in Votkinsk, another obscure out-of-the-way place; while SS-24's were made in Pavlolgrad and SS-18's came from Dnepro-petrovsk—both in the Soviet Ukraine.

Still this and my other objectives behind the Iron Curtain kept me busy, as well as giving me a legitimate reason to travel within the country. Not to mention the twice-a-year official government approved foreign trips to selected friendly nations, always communist, using my perfectly legal red passport belonging to the Soviet Union. So I visited East Germany and Poland once under this very gracious bending of the rigid rules. *One needs to comprehend the face of the object before one proceeds to conquer it.*

In fact I had a well-deserved holiday as a Russian tourist in Sopot—the Polish beach resort near Gdansk, or should I say Danzig. There one got the sense that the locals didn't see themselves as really a part of Poland. Lots of German was being spoken in defiance to my Russian, and plenty of quizzical looks to my attempts at Polish. I reminded myself that the French do this to the British in France too.

My funniest discovery was a summer's day trip 50 miles southeast of Moscow to the hamlet of Malakhovka to listen to hundreds of Russians speaking in nothing but English. Anybody that was going to be transferred abroad was assigned to learn the language there. More ominously, 50 miles east of Moscow in Pokrov was where they produced 200 tons of Anthrax bacteria and small pox virus a year in a building without fences and no security.

However despite my travails, for the domestic Soviet élite, travel was not a right but merely a reward for good behaviour and an annual thank you for their continued servility to the state.

This all had absolutely nothing to do with the times when I was called back to London usually on AT&T by a FIAT dead drop message, urgently requiring my presence for personal briefings, whereupon I collected a real British passport from British Airways in Moscow and had to change my hairstyle and clothes to suit the enclosed photograph. (My main dead drop was a rusty but hollow iron bolt at a badly lit corner bus stop I frequented at night. Larger materials were put into a watertight plastic bag inserted in an old paint can that was submerged in a derelict pond at an industrial site that was walking distance from same bus stop.) When I didn't fly directly out I'd take any one of the dozen illegal exit-entry routes in Poland, Czechoslovakia and Hungary that were carefully arranged by expert MI6 operatives and conveniently rotated on a coded monthly basis to avoid detection, and who gave me other temporary UK identities to use to get on to Finland, West Germany and Austria.

Then, of course, once there, I'd switch again to use a real dark blue British passport which was always conveniently ready inside an official-looking sealed envelope at the local aforementioned airline manager's office in Helsinki, West Berlin and Vienna. British Airways in those days was an active unit of the British government and wholly owned by it.

Once signed for, I'd then travel onwards, usually under the normal guise of an English music industry international development executive whose entrance stamp into that country had always mysteriously been already entered in my passport. Little does the world know that music is Britain's third largest export—including musical equipment, manufactured recordings, publishing rights and royalties—which amounts to hundreds of millions of British Pounds Sterling annually, and still does to this day.

Molody, as it turned out, was the kind of character who had no desire to succeed as a trapped poster boy. He was a real find and wanted to get on with his life. London actually got quite excited on the secretly coded telex about the possibilities of having he and his wife over to stay and have a getting-to-know-you chat in the West. His credentials were evidently classified A-Cat (category A) in the field of not only neurology-related matters but as a respected medical physician attached at various times in his career to the Soviet space, nuclear and sports programmes. My specific instructions were to proceed as I saw fit and report back updates of the situation, whether it be positive, negative or remaining unchanged. Their SIS cryptonym BENNY was assigned.

It is my understanding that because of Molody's top rated categorisation, I was the first UK NOC to receive a then-experimental Discus,* which became of such great advantage for me in the field that others were soon issued them.

It was a bitterly cold night when I returned from another clandestine operation, this time in Gorky, a city on the Volga River several hundred miles from Moscow named after the famous writer (which has since been romantically re-named Nizhny Novgorod). It was then that I was convinced the man was for real myself and warranted a probable upgrade to internal SIS defection alert status.

It all started when Dr Molody spoke to me at a moment when I was beginning to think that I was spending my time skating too close to the edge. I realised then we were on the same wavelength of trust.

He said, "What does your soul look like?"

---

* Discus is a high-tech low-power device for a high-speed VHF one-second air transmission of a maximum of 2,300 text characters to another Discus that was placed less than a mile away. I believe it was at a British diplomat's residence. I would pass the location in a taxi and communicate my message once a week on a given day when he had his on to receive. Later on I could receive from his too on a another date and time. Today they are called SRAC's (Short Range Agent Communication) and are about the size of a cigarette packet. My early model Discus' was the size of a videocassette, heavier and wider, and far more difficult to conceal.

Chapter Seven

I was taught the infinite nuances of subtle strength and quiet courage,
about that power of conviction and the value of sincerity,
and to understand with my gut and my heart.

Here I was in the present day entering his typical professor's quarters, our past still quite vivid. There were books and papers neatly stacked on every available non-walking space. Dr Molody had always been a voracious reader but this was mind-boggling. A grey-haired, academic spinster closed the door behind us, his understanding secretary. She tipped her head so briefly at me accompanied with a colourless smile, ice blue eyes over the rim of steel pince-nez.

Molody dumped himself down in the old leather chair behind the overcrowded desk and ran his hands through his hair, clearing his throat.

"I, we, have a cure and potential cures for Parkinson's disease, Down's Syndrome, Diabetes—type one. We also have effective treatments so far for acquired immunodeficiency syndrome—AIDS—and malaria, among others." He paused to add, "There are also promising findings on being able to actually see diseases for the first time with powerful microscopes. Plus the results from electromagnetic rays in therapy has been just incredible, to say the least." He was standing up slowly looking down at me fixedly.

I sat there returning his stare blankly. I felt I was starring in a real-life version of an Aldous Huxley science-fiction novel. What could I say in response? "Are you nuts? Have you lost it? It was trying to clone humans before, wasn't it, or was I drunk?" I shifted in my seat uncomfortably.

Instead a calm, controlled voice spoke and I was amazed to learn it was my own. "Are they the results of your findings from artificial twinning using human embryos or some other procedures?" I knew that it was possible that identical twins could be produced when a fertilised egg divides for the first time and instead of remaining one organism splits into two independent cells. A similar procedure has been performed in animals for decades.

"Almost the same effect—close—we removed the protective layer around the developing *zona pellucida*—embryo if you like—by splitting the cells apart and replacing the outer coating with an artificial shell. Exact multiple copies of the same anything would enable us to make precise comparisons of the effect of drugs and disease. Unfortunately most cloned embryos die." Mike was in that middle distance again. "It's pursued in order to assist couples seeking in vitro fertilisation. Many eggs are produced so we experiment with one implant and freeze the rest. If the original fails then you can always thaw one of the frozen identical twins and keep trying until successful. It's not quite cloning in a strict sense but my findings have certainly been derived from it. Though I'm making progress towards that area too. I will be the first to do it. Regarding embryonic stem cells, we're trying to reverse engineer the human being by analysing the genetic programme that guides its development from egg form. We've now isolated human embryonic stem cells which grows molecules, genes and pathways and we've started repairing ordinary tissues in the human body... But in terms of the diseases I mentioned, I have found that cancers arise when the cells' genetic code is damaged. It is from these findings that has allowed me to evolve to effective treatments, initially—which one of them has unofficially been declared a flat-out cure today."

I took a slow deep breath and then calmly released the air out. "Mike, why are you telling me this? What can I do about it, honestly...?"

He cut me off with an agitated swathe movement with both his hands, as if directing an advancing aircraft on the tarmac to switch its engines dead. Then a loud silence descended before he spoke. "Nicholas, not only do we need you, we need your personality and your vision. You are the *only* individual on this planet I personally know who could orchestrate a non-medical strategy to see these findings through to worldwide acceptability, from A to Z. Right now we are standing on a runway before take-off, laden with exciting discoveries for the global public. The wide open sky is ahead in front of us and which way to decide to pilot this thing is up to us from this moment on. Humanity needs to know this."

It was my turn to interrupt. "You *have to* prove *all* this to me before I do anything. You have to show me and I have to touch it to believe. You have to be there with me and I have to be with you too. And, I mean—show me. No stones must be left upturned. No 'Mickey Mouse' unsubstantiated stuff, please. If I ask you a question, I want the answer immediately. No winging things by the seat of our pants. I need to fully understand all this. You have to also consider we could get eliminated for this by the Establishment. They'll protect their assets and kill any news of this knowledge before it even bubbles to the surface."

The doctor thumped the desk hard. "Why do you think I have all those plainclothes ex-Soviet army commandos around me, young man? It's driving my wife crazy already! We can't even take a pleasant evening stroll on Prospekt Mira in Moscow or on Lake Geneva's boardwalk without them accompanying us. Very intrusive, believe me. But for us right now, it's a case of either put up or shut up. We chose to suffer the minor inconveniences in order to see my life's work through. The Russian Federation government fully supports this because they stand to make a lot of money from this, naturally, its people are already benefiting. One of the problems, however, is that it's propriety and not patent-able. But it's such a huge long-term project that the only person I trusted to know more about everything I'm doing, *was you.*"

I sat there stumped. Truly disconnected between my head and my heart. But my mind was racing at breakneck speed, considering the angles. I squeezed my eyes at Mike, weighing up his incredible announcement. It was something a major television network should have videotaped for immediate live transmission.

I nodded; listening to my own scared inner self. "OK. It's okay provisionally, until you prove it to me first so I can venture forth with the power of my convictions," my steady voice resonated, like a solid rock.

Molody was on his feet, smiling broadly as if a weight was off his shoulders. He rubbed his hands together in an act of glee, almost child-like. "Good, good, I will. I will, of course. Do you want to start now?"

We shot out of his study, making the little old lady sitting at her desk outside the door jump with fright. He was chatting away gaily but I wasn't taking it in. His was just a mouth moving with no sound. I was saying to *myself, I have no reason to doubt you, sir, but my main thrust right now is that my buddy Brennan died a few days ago, and he'd fought ferociously all his life so that things like this came through. I'm dedicated to doing this for other people I knew like him; not for you; not for me; not for the unpitying world, goddammit.*

At the end of the day, Michal elected to stay behind at the institute while I was escorted back into Moscow's city centre. He had said he was going to give me a lot to read but I hadn't anticipated that he meant 150 thick and thin files in four open cardboard boxes full of files. Just to get a bellboy to come and carry the stuff up to my hotel room from the garden was a job in itself.

As I approached the reception desk in the spacious lobby to get my room key, I passed a very striking woman sitting on the divan who smiled widely at me. On receipt of the key and as I was heading towards the elevator, it dawned on me that it was the foxy French lady who'd sat next to me for four and a half hours on the plane en route from London the day before, and we never actually spoke to each other the whole time. She was still obviously smiling at me with her eyes as if to transmit the message, "well, come on over."

So I sauntered over, much to the disgust of the waiting bellboy who gave the appearance that he'd much rather be doing something else, whatever it was. A small tip, or nothing, from me was in the cards for him for being an ace at impudence.

She remained seated but had leaned forward to half extend her jewelled hand graciously in anticipation, several feet before I stopped in front of her. Our eyes had held each other's all the way across the spacious reception area and I was fortunate not to trip over something. As I took her slight hand, I could feel that tingling warmth again and a light sensuous perfume aroused me.

Big brown eyes, straight honey-blonde cut, chopped-style *á la* Anouk Aimee in the movie "A Man and A Woman". Her modest tan required minimal make-up. The tiny wee gap between her two front teeth gave her a teenage look but her outgoing personality is clearly what dominated this woman. I'd say she was about 5-10 years older than me, around her late 40's, maybe. Her hands told me so.

"*Allo*, I am Ursula, I hope you remember me from yesterday, even though you barely looked up from that file the young man gave you at the airport."

"You saw that? You're quite observant," I replied. We still held hands, inducing tiny electrodes in me. "But you're wrong, I *did* watch your face while you slept next to me—for several moments in fact." That *was* true. I crossed my heart rather elaborately with my spare hand when I said it. Jolts of electricity were now sparking up from my right hand.

"Ooh, la la," she giggled, taking her hand away from mine to discreetly cover the space in her teeth.

"You haven't told me your name yet," Ursula was still smiling shyly.

I took her hand again and clicked my heels and bowed in an overly done Russian-style of greeting. "Nicholas, as in Romanov."

That seemed to make her laugh, a sweet appealing jingle. The tingling feeling resumed throughout my body. The bellboy glared once again.

"I like men who make me laugh. There's not many out there, believe it or not. So many take themselves too seriously. You are British, of course, even though there's a American twang in there. I'd guess you *are* indeed a Limey but you live in America, am I right?"

"Ooh, la la. I'd guess you're right on. How'd you know?" I was genuinely surprised at both her forthrightness and astute perception. I was beginning to think perhaps she knew something about me beforehand. Did some homework on me maybe, read a file herself? I penetrated deeper into her eyes for an explanation. This woman smiled with both her twinkling eyes and slightly goofy teeth. I more than liked her, or was it lust, I thought to myself.

"Oh, I used to live in Manhattan for ten years," she said disarmingly. "Before that I was an Icelandair air stewardess who flew the Reykjavik-New York City corridor all the time. In fact I met my husband, an envoy, on a flight I was working on from Reykjavik to Luxembourg." Her innocence was captivating.

"Are you still married?" I asked, meaning it.

She nodded. "Oh, but he's so old in his body and getting old in his head now. He's 23 years older than me. My son is like him too and he's 23 years younger." She flapped her arms extravagantly like an endangered southern European species, while I tried to figure her age. "They never want to go anywhere and do anything. Just stay home and moan about I don't know what. From now on I will just remember them as they used to be."

"How depressing that it's so difficult to discuss the subject of depression," my dry voice offered.

She paused to look at me, somewhat taken aback, and then grinned. "But *I'm* still young! I want to go and see places, do things. Travel is the spice of life. I've seen one third of this planet and I want to see at least another one third before I get too old to savour it. I notice rare people like you, who exude a cosmopolitan air about them, that they've clearly done a lot in their life. You've also a tendency to philosophise as a result I see."

I stood looking down at her and arced a little bashfully like a musketeer at her compliment. The courtier before the princess. All I could offer lamely was, "The world is a place you look at while you are looking for yourself…and you are way to youthful for senility."

Very unlike myself…I couldn't properly gauge my thoughts all the while standing there. I was slightly mesmerised by this beautiful beast of femininity.

The bellboy was signalling for my key to go up with the boxes on his trolley. Ursula couldn't help but notice the exchange.

"Would you like to have dinner with me tonight before you end up reading all that?" she volunteered openly.

I remember thinking again that I was slightly shocked at this attractive lady's approaches, but it wasn't sleazy in any form or fashion. Indeed I felt privileged to be asked so politely by so nice an individual. *Hell, I've already done enough reading for the day*, I reasoned with myself. I needed to have female company. *Here is my reward.*

"Yes, I'd like that." I replied. "Do you have anywhere in mind?"

Another Latin-style gesticulation of the hands. "Of course not, we should just see where we end up. *Au contraire.* Planning is boring!"

Well, that's all there was to it and we agreed to meet in the same place in an hour which would give me enough time to recharge my batteries, shower, shave and change. I must have surprised the bellboy like hell because his face told me I gave him many roubles more than he expected.

Sixty minutes later, I was sitting in exactly the same spot where Ursula had sat. Good, I said to myself, I need to collect my thoughts about this situation. The woman was remarkably forward. Travelling the world by herself? Hard to think that. I could be setting myself up for a fall here, so long as I land on my own two feet. I decided I would play it by ear, like her dinner plans for us.

All of a sudden I had a sense that she was standing slightly off to the side of me and I turned slowly to look at her for the first time in full-length. A petite girl's body, too, and no hips. Very slim figure, shapely breasts and an expensive body-hugging white dress, probably bought at one of the top fashion houses in the boulevards of Paris. About 5' 2" even though she's wearing light brown leather riding-style boots, in preparation for the sludge outside. The dress accented her style and I'd noticed the jewels had gone. Her neck and hands were void of glitter, which made her look even better, to me. Pretty women don't need accessories to accent themselves.

She twirled around expansively, like a model on the catwalk, and laughed gaily. I stood up and we kissed on both cheeks Continental-style. She glided her palms across my newly shaved skin and commented on its baby bottom feel. Boy that really turned me on, I have to say. I'd only known her an hour and already we communicated like lovers. I helped her on with the same red fox coat and hat she wore on the British Airways jet.

Instead of hailing a taxi, we elected to walk towards the Kremlin, about a quarter of an hour away. The gate man gawked at her, not noticing me, his silent breath steaming into the cold air. When we got to the bridge over the frozen Moscow River, we stood there in admiration, staring at the magnificent view all lit up. A glossy picture postcard to send home.

"Do you mind if I put my arm in yours, Nicholas." It didn't sound like a question. I took a deep breath and proffered an arm. Again that alluring waft of perfume. I later ascertained it was Nina Ricci L'Air du Temps and that her married surname was Durance. "The same name as the beautiful French river that meanders in my neck of the woods in Provence," she smiled sexily. It was also the same as Jones elsewhere in France and meant imprisonment in English, I thought rather capriciously.

We never actually ate in a fancy restaurant. Much to my chagrin, we chowed down standing up at a cheap outdoor mobile café frequented by workers in overalls, before continuing to walk aimlessly around Moscow at night. The chatter and humour never faltered. She never asked me much about myself strangely, not even why I was there. Not that I could answer that question had it come. But it did turn out that she was just eight and a half years my elder. The compliant life of a diplomat's wife, I surmised.

Nor was I surprised to learn that when she lived in New York City, her husband was France's Ambassador to the United Nations—for a whole decade, too—and that they considered Cannes, on the French Riviera, their permanent home returning every quarter from places like Haiti, the Cameroon, India and Romania. Surprisingly she wasn't French. She was German from Baden-Wuttemberg but had spent most of her life in France. Naturally she spoke fluent German, French and English as well as Spanish. A couple of times I was trying to link covert possibilities as to why she had taken such an instant liking to me, but as time wore on the feeling dissipated, while the excitement stayed. Ursula was apparently on a five-day package holiday on her own and had always wanted to visit Russia. Her next overseas trip, whenever it was, was going to see the pyramids of Egypt.

About the only tourist attraction we took in was to Dead Fred, the stiff in the mausoleum. Vladimir Ilyich Ulyanov looked more deceased than animated to us, despite his heirs proclaiming "Lenin more alive than all the living".

I don't know if she knew it or not, so I never brought it up it directly to her...but three minutes after we strolled past the main underground station at Kuznetsky Most, we walked right past the ex-KGB's two L-shaped nine-story buildings where they no longer maintained a staff with the neo-classical dirty yellow stone façade known as *Dom Odin* and *Dom Dva* (House 1 and House 2), the latter otherwise known as Lubyanka, on one side of Dzerzhinsky Square. (The KGB's Moscow Centre or "the Centre" had moved in 1972 to the southwest suburb of Yasenevo. Offices were still kept at this location until around 1976.) The original occupant's name, Russia Insurance Company was still there on the door in Cyrillic, *Strahovaya Kompaniya Rossia*. To test her, I said we were "getting physically close." All she did was to snuggle up to me closer by squeezing my arm. What I intimated by those three words was really KGB jargon for assassination. Just to double check Ursula, I innocuously asked her if she'd ever heard of a Russian emigrant living in France called Roger Orlov. She simply said, "No, should I have?" But she never asked me what he did either. Had she done so, I don't think I would have mentioned that Orlov was a reference to any Soviet Illegal operating abroad, while "Roger" was KGB slang for a local agent.

"Why do you read French newspapers at both ends of the political spectrum?" I asked eventually. Her response was alarming in its innocence, "Oh, my husband taught me to want to know how the other side thinks." But she didn't add which side she was on to start with so I was no clearer on that one.

The next day Ursula was taking a one-night train trip to stay at the Pechory Monastery, near the small town of Pskov, a fiefdom of Russian Orthodoxy on the border with Lutheran Estonia. She'd be back the day after. "It was founded in 1473 by Ivan and Maria, two Muscovites, who changed their names to Ioann and Vasa, shaved their heads and traded in their marriage for a new life as brother and sister," intoned Ursula quaintly. "I love fairy tales like that."

All I could say back was, "Like all good myths, the story of fantasy is false but true." Another glamorous grin from the lady was forthcoming as she playfully punched my ribs in response to my sarcasm.

We'd graduated to holding hands by the time we arrived back at the President. I have to admit I would have welcomed lovemaking with Ursula but I wasn't going to push it. Even though we had rooms on the same floor, we kissed lightly and bade each other good night. I stood looking at her closed door—number 96—for many minutes knowing that her back was against it on the other side. I could make out her immobile faint shadow under the poorly designed door. I kept hoping she would open it again, but it didn't sesame, and finally I silently tiptoed away in a semi-swoon from the silhouette still standing there, alone in her own isolated romance.

I laid on the bed naked trying to read the first file Molody had urged me to read. He'd actually had them all numbered, 1-150, in the order he'd wanted me to read them with the cover note's words scribbled, "You'll have to compartmentalise them yourself in your head because this material will piece together in your mind, like a jigsaw. " I gave up, I had her on the brain, which may have been the whole point of Ursula's exercise, for all I knew.

In my sleep I decided I would have to return to Balboa, California. It would be for a few days only, so I could lease my beach house to a friend that needed a place to live following a sudden separation from his unfaithful wife. The man was sleeping on the floor with no mattress in a temporary hovel. Also I had to take care of many things, like put my car and certain belongings in storage.

I could see that Molody's little proposed project was not going to take the fortnight or so that SIS anticipated. This was going to be many months, at least. I needed to withdraw cash. I could also die for the cause and nobody would ever know. But it was a risk I was prepared to take. *Everything in my life had pointed towards this remarkable situation.*

I put in an open local telephone call to an unlisted number at the British Embassy in Moscow that Mrs Blyton had given me. There seemed to be some improvement in telecommunications these days compared to the *Kremlevka*, the old Soviet top security government phone system.

A young professional English accent at the *Angliyskoye Posolstvo* quickly came on the line, introducing herself as internal secretariat services. After I identified myself to her, I said, "Yes, Victoria, I need you to type a message to be sent through normal routing channels to a Mrs Ellen Blyton at SIS headquarters in London. An envelope in the pouch today will suffice. Message should read simply: 'I have made contact with Dr Molody in Moscow. Will be returning to California in four or five day's time. Nothing that may concern you. Everything that concerns the rest of us. Thanks for the introduction. Signed—Nicholas Anderson. PS: Need you to check the names of Linda Coughlin, date of birth is August 1966 in Armagh, Northern Ireland, believed to be living in the south; and Ursula Durance, in late-forties, she has either a German or French passport or both. A resident of Cannes, France. Claims to be married to a retired ambassador to the United Nations. Especially want to know if there is any remote connection between the two or not. I'll be in touch for the answers soon.'

The voice read it back to me word perfect with the spelling correct first time around. That should flummox the old lady's fluffy feathers no end, I pictured mischievously, when I hung up.

"At least I don't have to be answerable to them all the time," I murmured aloud to myself. Besides I needed to spend many more hours suspended in space heading back west, and to be in my own little world to catch up reading some of these damn files. I *wanted* to know their contents in its completeness. Yet my acquaintance with Ursula possessed a quirky brio that caused her to linger in the mind instead, at a time when I should be concentrating on more important matters.

My next call was to British Airways, it was no longer government-owned and had recently been privatised. My exact departure date was ascertained by their only seat availability in first class for the coming week, and so it was to be in three days from today, not the four or five I'd ideally wanted. Sheremetyevo-Heathrow-Los Angeles International—BA all the way, even changing planes at that stupendous Terminal Four shopping paradise in London. A sixth sense told me to resist an urge to reserve my return to Moscow, even though I still had them on the phone.

As I hung up, Mike called. "I've been trying to get through for ages. What's happening, Nick?" So I related everything that had transpired since I'd last seen him—not missing not one single iota—including the love connection. His odd response was to say, "Well, that way you'll probably get more reading done, *not* lying in bed." His voice was distracted momentarily and he barked some directions at his end, then it came back on. "I was just looking at my agenda... Seeing you're going to be gone for a week or so before coming back, Caterina and I may as well go and visit the family in Bratislava for a long weekend. We promised them we would come, so this is as good a time as any. By the way, book yourself back directly into Kiev, Ukraine, will you? There's something important I've been invited to see there, so you may as well come with me. It'll be educational for both of us. I'll be the one meeting you at the airport—with my shadows in tow, of course. Catty can have the extended holiday she wants back home in Slovakia. It's a long day and a half's drive from there to Kiev. Figure on being there for about a week, OK?" Then he was distracted again, so he quickly said he'd call later and to not schedule anything between him and I for tonight. "The woman in *my* life says we need more time together as husband and wife. Got to go. Happy reading, mate. *Mira.*"

I looked at the phone unit as I was hanging up, and grunted aloud, "Peace to you too, Mike. But that's what they all say: one week here, one week there, and before you know it, fifty-two of them have flown by." I chuckled to myself with the thought that at least I didn't live a boring life. Plus I knew there was a reason for not confirming flights with BA.

I sat staring out of the hotel window not really seeing, and not mentally ready to sit and read through the contents of the quartet of boxes. I didn't want to look at them even. I had already tried evaluating myself about my self delaying process—was it lethargy, fear, the past?—but no logical answers were upcoming. Though once I got switched on, I knew I'd plough through them all like a determined bulldozer with a tank full of high octane...

It was fourteen years ago on a similar day like today that I'd been given the final green light from London to proceed with getting the Molodys through a gap in the Iron Curtain to the West. They wanted him; they sounded like they wanted him badly and pronto. No way was I going fast for anybody. Everybody in the business knew what happened when you pushed too quickly; you made simple mistakes because you didn't give yourself time; time to think and plan it like a chess match. Every move counted. The only difference with the checkmated loser was you paid with your life. The statistic of death is a fact of life.

But I made it to my forties and I'm still here alive and well and reflecting on the annals of my perilous life. I must have been out of my mind to even think about doing those things then, you crazy bastard me. I sat in my Moscow flat then, as I did a second time now, shaking with incredulity at those vivid remembrances, wondering how many lives does a cat have, and how does that compare to mine?

The first thing I did back in that Cold War day was to spread a huge detailed map of the Soviet Union with its satellite states and next door neighbours, out on the floor. I stood over it like a General surveying the war fields. Obviously our already established dozen secret exit-entry points were to be considered—all of them initially land routes. Then there was the air, water and underground ways. I scratched out the latter on my pad. The problem was there would be at least four of us, that I definitely knew of, who would be in the party—plus limited carried items—the two Molodys, a trustworthy proven local guide and myself.

Another major issue was that Caterina Molody was a strong-willed yet panicky type. I'd considered her an aggressive-passive in psychology terms. She's good at creating a sort of a scream and a hush around herself depending on her mood of the moment. If things got perceived as a little hairy, she'd blow up and become a risk for us all. I could be wrong but I couldn't afford to be not right. Nothing saves us from us except our wits.

I hadn't yet gone over to their place to break the news, nor would I for a couple of days. First I had to figure out the time span, have all the spaces in my mind filled with facts, then I'd tell them what's what as total gospel. Think.

Fortunately I'd been involved in a military-style defection, a few years previously, of Major Irena Puchovskaya, a Russian, but the operation had been in next-door Poland. That too enmeshed four of us. It was codenamed GORA DOLINA…

* * * * * * * * *

I was part of a small team of three SIS men on an undercover mission. My mate Davy Brennan was one of them but he had an ongoing personality clash in the past with the other member of the party, I found myself in the middle of it the whole bloody time. Our minimal warfare crash course training included skiing and climbing up at Arisaig House near Lochailort in the Scottish Grampian mountain range. Boy, that tough instructor from SAS' crack 'G' Squadron really put us through our paces. I was the fittest bastard you ever saw when I got back from being under his care.

Our pre-departure instructions at the SIS' farm manor in Godmanchester, near Cambridge, had been pretty straightforward and run-of-the-mill. We were to assume the identities of summer holidaymakers on a one-week package trip organised by Orbis—the official Polish government tour operator—at the Polish alpine resort of Zakopane, which was up at the top of the hauntingly beautiful Tatra Mountains at the southernmost point of the communist country. Further instructions would be forthcoming on an ad hoc basis and depended on whether or not communications were established. But we had to be prepared as it pertained to physical involvement in a current red defection alert status.

We'd duly spent the week with the usual assortment of Operational Support department lads up from London, making ourselves familiar with the nuances of the mission, including memorising all the details provided by G/REP, SIS' forgery department. During that time we were informed that part of the reason we were handpicked for this task was our ability to think on our feet. Little did I understand the meaning of that understatement at the time.

As we were part of a diversified group of twenty British citizens, we were *not to know each other* prior to meeting all the other travellers in the departure lounge in Terminal Two at Heathrow Airport. We flew from London directly into Krakow on a rattling scheduled LOT Polish Airlines four-engine Ukrainian-made Antonov. Upon arrival at Zakopane we were assigned in groups of five persons to an old Swiss-style chalet, each with our own room. Needless to say, we three were acquainted in one of the wooden houses. The other two sharing the place were a middle-aged ex-patriot Polish miner from Wales who had become a naturalised Briton, with his Welsh wife, who was undertaking his first ever return to the land of his birth. Fortunately the duo spent the better part of their days being visited by various members of his family who were on day outings from the smoke belt of industrial cities a hundred miles or so to the north, and they were always smashed drunk and cold out in bed by 10:00 PM every night without fail.

The trip was becoming a standard overseas jaunt, one of many similar operations I'd been assigned whereupon absolutely nothing materialised. But your presence was required, in case. Other than enjoying day trips to tourist spots in tow with everybody else, it was getting tedious.

The big exception was the same day visits to the former concentration camps of Auschwitz and Treblinka, which remain vivid to this day. I don't think I'll ever forget the German words, *"Arbeit macht frei"*, which were inscribed on the gate at Auschwitz. "Work makes you free", was chilling enough given what happened to its inhabitants once they were in. To think that one and half million mostly Jews and gypsies never made it out, in the five years the camp was in operation. When the tour guide commented on that fact, Dave turned to me and said, "Crikes, that comes to over 800 people a day; day in and day out, all that time. That smaller figure has more impact than the larger one."

"You can still smell the stench on the surrounding trees on a bad day," the Polish innkeeper told us over beer after the tour had ended. The way he said it, so ordinarily, was pretty harrowing too.

Then one morning after breakfast, two days from the end of the holiday, our designated team leader, a British army Captain and former paratrooper, a dour, non-talkative Scot in his late thirties from Edinburgh called Ian McIntyre, casually strolled in where Dave and I were playing dominoes, and quietly said, "OK, boys, this is it, no larking about, file out. Grab your belongings. You won't be returning."

We stuffed what little we had in our bags and snatched our coats. Outside we jumped into an old Polish Fiat driven by an elderly but clearly sharp local wearing a worn black beret. He shook each of our hands firmly and then clattered off down the dusty road at a medium pace, so not to attract attention to ourselves. Mac, who was sitting in the front seat, turned around and calmly said, "OK, listen up, lads. We're heading towards a lake twenty miles from here called *Morskie Oko*, it means 'Eye of the Sea'. When we arrive at the destination, first, I want both of you to uncover the tarpaulin. You'll find three fully-loaded automatic weapons under there plus other survival equipment. Quickly go through the standard procedure to see if the equipment is in working order and then check the gun machinations too. Leave the 'on' switch on, ready for action. Second, Anderson, you are to find cover in the higher grounds. Brennan, you take the lower but do not leave the lake exposed to your back, lad. Each of you are to be prepared for possible exchange of fire. Third and last, pay close attention to detail here." Dave and I glanced quickly at each other.

"This is all I know so far. I admit it's not much but orders are orders and must be obeyed, OK? Within the hour a blonde woman will appear out of the forest walking in our direction. We are instructed to scour our surrounding environment for possible armed intruders. In any event, do *not* shoot at her. The specific objective is to take her into custody. She will not identify herself nor speak to us, except to raise her right hand in greeting when she becomes aware she is in our vicinity. Got it?"

"A question, sir?" piped in Dave with impunity. Ian nodded assent reluctantly. "What happens next, sir?" I must concede it came across a bit sarcastic. "I mean the woman. What do we do with her? Give her a lift home in the car all the way to Blighty? There's no room in here for her. Couldn't put her on the roof." His elbow digged me sideways gently. Frankly, I was surprised by his mucking about at a time like this but played along with him nevertheless.

McIntyre looked annoyed at both of us. But I could see the light beads of sweat on his forehead. The man was beyond serious and he raised his voice a digit, "Look here, you two, as much as I admit that my directives are not entirely clear, command centre tells me not to verbalise anything further. You will discover what we are to do in good time." He wiped away the perspiration. "We've been assured this is a very routine pick-up and no problems are to be expected whatsoever."

Finally I spoke, "Excuse me, sir. But didn't you say this is supposed to be a possible defection by a red? My immediate observations are as follows: A. Is the woman the asylum seeker? You haven't actually said. B. What if she is accompanied by anybody, no matter how many there are, are we to eliminate just that individual or all the individuals, even though they may outwardly appear friendly? And C. If she does have company, how are we going to know what to do next? Remember they're giving us firearms for a reason. Home office went through the trouble to provision weapons and I have to assume they thought we might need them. And what if you yourself are detached from us at a given point?

McIntyre and Brennan had both turned to look dumbly at me. To me, they were all obvious assumptions.

"Also what if she raises her left hand?" I added innocently.

After a few seconds of strained silence, Mac raised his voice and yelled at us, "Fuck it! Will you both just shut up for now! That's an order!"

His final command set an uneasy mood and we all twitched nervously in our seats in silence for what seemed like hours, but it was only maybe minutes.

As we bumped along the road, a lake could be seen in the distance. Brennan finally leaned forward to McIntyre in front of him, his voice hoarse. "Captain McIntyre, sir, with respect, your directive just now is hereby ruled as insufficient by Anderson and I. Furthermore, please be served notice that as of now we each are deemed in equal command of this operation, *with* you, of course, Captain. Rules say that if directives are on questionable grounds, especially on undercover assignment abroad, and with a situation presented with possible loss of company life, we are to serve such notice, plus it is to be respected."

Moments went by and McIntyre turned his head slowly and glared at Brennan who was leaning forward, both were inches from each other's noses. To cool this situation I rapidly interjected, "Look, why don't you just tell us Mac, make it easy on yourself, nobody will ever know except us and Polski here. Come on spill the beans, we're all in the same boat here behind enemy lines." He shifted his eyes from Dave to me, and held his maddening stare for what seemed like fifteen murderous seconds.

The car suddenly pulled to a stop in a clearing, feet away from the edge of the water. Without twisting his head, the driver said in perfect English, "Gentlemen, please! Please stop arguing among yourselves. Allow me to introduce myself. I am Dr Ralf Marczewski of *Bundesnachrichtendienst*, West German federal intelligence. I am also the cultural attaché at the West German embassy in Warsaw. I am an anthropologist by training. The subject is my contact. Her name is Irena Puchovskaya, a full Major in the Red Army. I have been developing her for three years now and she is finally ready to come over. Though she's really GRU—Army intelligence—in actuality, she is a head assistant to the chief of staff of the KGB's First Chief Directorate. Her reasons for being at *Morskie Oko* is for a well deserved weekend break, awarded by her superiors in Moscow Centre, due to completion of a month-long emergency project at the Warsaw embassy of the USSR. I have waited for this moment for weeks. Now, seeing you are obviously not satisfied with matters thus far, I trust this material is of initial acceptance?"

We three Brits stared at him, nodding approval ever so slightly, not really knowing whether to believe him or not. It was like saying this was a blue whale not a red minnow. "I should add," the German continued, "that as a child, I grew up between the two world wars in this very region. My grandparents raised me in the absence of my mother and father, and in 1938, when I was six, we emigrated to the Fatherland when they were realigning the boundaries around here. I am quite familiar with the territory. I've studied it for months, both from spending weekends here on the pretence of a holiday and from satellite photographs.

He pivoted his body around and smiled feebly. "Captain McIntyre could only tell you what he knew at this early stage. We only just met for the first time a few minutes before he came to get you from the chalet. However, I am glad you two young men had the presence of mind to question my seemingly obscure orders. You have good mettle and I see we will make a good team. It should be noted that the reason our friends from Great Britain are involved in this operation is because the tour company only brought in Britons to Poland. It would not have appeared correct, even to stupid Polish immigration officials, that three German men were in the group. Hence, your selection. We are all supposed to be under the auspices of NATO but I have absolutely no qualms with the graces of Her Majesty's Secret Intelligence Service. Which reminds me, why do the British Royal Family and the SIS both call themselves 'The Firm'? I find that odd."

Nobody bothered responding. I certainly had never thought about the coincidence up to that time. "No doubt they will realise that three British men did not make the return journey to their home, and then figure out it is connected to the disappearance of a Russian senior secretary in the area. Most probably they'll also discontinue the holiday tour soon afterwards to prevent similar occurrences. It was designed to be a hard currency money earner but it served a profitable purpose for us, at least.

"I do, however, grant you your request of equal command during the duration of this field exercise as there is an element here of having to play-it-by-ear. However, you do understand that only one person must be in charge until such time we depart company, and that individual is me. This is comprehended, yes?" Like a schoolteacher he started with looking into my eyes, then Brennan and McIntyre. Nobody spoke back to him for fear of a caning.

"Now gentlemen, as the Captain said, please uncover the tarpaulin over there. If you walk to that tree with the widest trunk, you will find it. One more thing…it is true that I am not anticipating a problem. The subject knows me personally. Once we ascertain she is alone, and when we have her in custody, we are then free to inflate the specially camouflaged covered life raft. When ready, two of you three will manually row five miles with the flow towards the south end of the lake. There is the beginning of a river which immediately becomes a rapid. The sweeping trip will leave you feeling queasy, believe me, as it will last four or five days, if weather and fate co-operate. Though at some 16 or so intervals along the way, according to the KH-9 satellite's high resolution photographs, the pass will narrow to a trickle and you will have to deflate, walk and inflate the raft for trips ranging from between 100 metres and up to three miles. I know the entire flow is downhill and topography is sloped continuously because I've personally timed it with a small low frequency radio transmitter placed on the lightest floating device available, and it was set on a timed interval beep at every 25 miles. It leads to the West German border near the town of Hof. The whole ride will be around 325 miles at an average altitude of 8,000 feet. If it were attempted in winter, I would say it was nigh impossible, but this is the height of summer and on a bad day it can still be near freezing at night. BND officials will be waiting to welcome you when you pass the East German-Czech border. Needless to state, this op is in EmCon status. [Short for Emergency Conduct, means no radio transmission whatsoever and hide your location and movement at all times.]

"Oh, as an aside, in case you were not aware of it, at my request, SIS also selected you three based on old training data related to response to seasickness and altitude sickness. In Germany we call it acute mountain sickness due to lower air pressure and thinner oxygen. We can't have you getting heart palpitations during intense exertion at 2,400 metres up." He brandished his dull smile again at us. "I will not and cannot at my age make such an arduous journey. Instead I will be back at my desk in Warsaw on Monday morning and I will be thinking of you all, believe me. Once I learn you are safe and sound, I will make arrangements to fly to Cologne, where I will spend the time necessary to interview the young lady. I am, fortunately, unlike yourselves, a *bad hat*." It was a reference to a spy under diplomatic cover abroad. He appeared impatient and checked his watch. "It is close to the expected rendezvous."

Brennan and I had our hands on the door handles. "Oh, the very *very* last item," intoned Marczewski. "To prevent radar devices picking up medium-strong electronic signals, the specially-fitted raft has had all objects with any amount of metal removed from it. I already know you do not wear glasses, rings or crosses on your necks but this also means you are to discard all your watches, belts...all except to remove your false tooth that has the GPS in it."

SIS men on deep cover foreign duty had built-it radio signals continuously emitting to within 300 yards of the exact position, monitored by 24 satellites equally divided among six orbits, 11,000 miles out in space, courtesy of the United States Air Force's Global Positioning System. The Russian system of GPS is called Glonass. They both worked under scrambled radio jamming too.

"Our guest does not have such a device on her either. I've already checked. Besides she's really an administration worker attached to the military, not designed for such strenuous errands." I thought he had said she was a military officer but didn't dare interrupt him. "If you are successful the West German government will be only too pleased to replace both regulation and personal items from our world famous department stores in Frankfort-am-Main. Needless to say, but this directive includes the removal of all metal-inclusive weapons too before leaving. When you are on board the raft, you are to return them to me. However, with participation from your clever scientists at the Forensic Explosives Laboratory unit in Sevenoaks, Kent, and using an invention by our friends over there," he pointed in the direction of Czechoslovakia, "you will be given a form of grenade made of Semtex-H with a special detonator implanted in it. It will explode within four seconds after being exposed to air just like a normal grenade."

Czechoslovakian-made Semtex was a high-powered compound, like PETN, Penta Tetro Ether Nitrate, which is mixed with a polymer that serves like a plasticiser. The putty-like substance, generally known as a plastic explosive could be moulded into any shape. It could be paper-thin and placed into envelopes, if need be. It could kill or maim the envelope opener when it blew up.

"There are 25 of them in the waterproof brown duffel bag you'll find under there. Everything understood? Then let's get on with it. Good luck."

Almost right on time a platinum blonde with her hair up in an officious bun and very white skin was strolling towards us slowly, alone. She looked like she was on a Sunday morning stroll, even though it was a Saturday, very relaxed, calm, almost too calm. *An iron maiden stopping to smell the flowers while fucking on the shoulders of giants.* I looked down at Brennan. He gave me a thumb's up. McIntyre and Marczewski were way back somewhere, where the car had been removed into denser bush to prevent it being spotted from the sky.

I scanned the higher ground above for anything—something, a sign of movement—indicating danger was present. Nothing.

From my prone sitting position, I looked behind. The same. I looked back again, a second time. McIntyre was camouflaged well and blended with a birch tree but he was noticeable to the experienced eye. Reminded me of a sitting duck. I couldn't see the old German anywhere but didn't dwell on it.

She came past the space between Brennan and I, humming a tune happily. Cool broad I was thinking. Good training to remain calm to pressure. Attractive, too, in that high-cheekbone Slavic way. Big blue eyes. Couldn't believe she was a Soviet army major in a million years; a college major in academics maybe. There goes the right hand in acknowledgement. Mac waved back motioning her to halt. I could see the older man come out of the shadows. The major and the Kraut diplomatic anthropologist were hugging.

McIntyre went through a thorough body search of her and then signalled us to come in. Davy was up in a second and looked up at me, stretching his legs. I too was about to jump up but I turned one more time. A spark of light caught my eye. I almost missed it and lurched into motion. Peripherally I saw Brennan crouch instantly in reaction to me. Something was out there moving. Suddenly I saw him. A black-haired, dark complexioned, small man with heavy metal glasses and a dark blue tracksuit was running along almost parallel to her chosen path. He appeared almost wimpy, definitely not the gait of a seasoned jogger. My finger grasped the trigger of the Heckler & Koch 9-mm MP5SD silenced machine gun. At 800 rounds a minute it could slice him in half at a single burst. As he came past Brennan's hideaway, the Northern Irish laddie gave him one sharp bonk to the back of the head. He laid there out cold but his legs quivered slightly.

An insect tangling itself after smacking into the web of a predacious spider. This action brought the other three running to where Brennan stood over the rumpled little man. I kept up my search up for others. That guy's doing was so out of the ordinary, it was almost far-fetched. Almost like he was running away, not towards. I went back to scanning the horizons. I could hear my adrenaline pumping.

I returned my gaze to the four standing over the one down there. I saw McIntyre handing the blonde Russian a pistol with a silencer. My knuckles whitened and I almost shot it out of her hand in fright. But I watched intently from my lofty position, my cross-hairs were trained on her heart, mesmerised at the sight. She bent briefly and shot the heap in the head. A sound of a single popcorn kernel hitting a pan of hot oil followed by a puff of smoke. Mac plied the pistol away from her hand. I went back to my surveillance routine then assumed my observation at the strange gathering beneath me. Brennan was telling me to come on down at once.

When I scrambled down the bank, I blurted, "What the fuck's going on?" Dr Ralf answered on behalf of the group winding its way away from the crumpled body. "He was part of the *rezidentura* at the Union of Soviet Socialist Republics' Embassy in Warsaw, that was to say the man's a member of the Polish station's Russian intelligence gathering team. An autodidact she bitterly despised. He was her forced lover, she says. We had no reason to disbelieve her. He had been left behind sleeping in the lakeside chalet they were sharing for the weekend. He was galloping after her like that for reasons unexplained, perhaps to catch her up. When I suggested she 'officially say good-bye to the Soviet Union,' she agreed to it. Don't worry; disposal of the body will be my duty only *after* you are gone. Besides it makes one less of the enemy to deal with."

As I contemplated his words, she had her back in front of us some ten yards away and I imagined she was weeping. But when she turned to face us she seemed almost gleeful. Backs towards each other, McIntyre and Brennan's deadpan expressions gave nothing away. I knew I felt uncomfortable with the unlikely situation but time was racing and we had to move on. *The only thing I've learned about war is you must try to keep a pretence of normalcy, no matter what happens around you.*

Within a quarter of an hour we were in the swollen RIB (rigid inflatable boat) waving good-byes to a disappearing elderly figure in his sixties standing on the shore.

The other two were rowing hard in silence and I looked across at Irena Puchovskaya slumped deflated in the corner, leaning against the hard rubber of the craft. She glimmered a flat smile at me, but I didn't feel like smiling back. It was around noon according to the glaring sun in the bruised heavens.

We reached the start of the drowning machine. The grinding noise of the waterfall was getting louder. We suddenly fell a steep three-story drop straight down, followed by a wild helter-skelter swinging and violent banging, hanging on like a carnival joy ride on a bucking horse. I don't know about the others, but my gut felt like it was in my mouth. The exhilaration was electrifying.

This went on for hours interspersed by trudging wearily on wobbly legs for snow-covered muddy miles at a time, either dragging the raft downhill or pushing it over ledges, only to quickly alight to slide down and splash heavily into the water below. Maybe for kids it would have been great fun but for adults it was a strain. The German doctor wasn't kidding; this was extreme mental as well as bodily exertion. Nobody spoke for hours at a time, just the sound of crunching on top of what there was left of the snow, plodding the earth, and heavy breathing. Our female guest was pleasingly uncomplaining. We all knew we had to preserve what energy we had. Mac referred constantly to the directions Dr Marczewski had given him as we boarded, using a specially-made non-ferrous miniature compass and a map temporarily tattooed on the underside of his wrist. The only statement during the first few hours was when McIntyre announced, "We are now entering *Ceskoslovensko*, comrades." Later he pointed eastwards, like a tour guide, at a triangular blip which was a blurred mix of clouds and rocky formation of the same colour. "Gerachovka. 8707 feet. Carpathian mountain range. No damn wonder this mission is called GORA DOLINA. It means mountains and valleys in Polish." We stared dully at the forever view seemingly on canvas, already tired. When on observation, Mac was a human camera for capturing detail. Clearly he had a knack for thinking in photographs. Puchovskaya never even raised her head to follow his finger; instead, she looked in the far opposite direction, almost in defiance, towards her future.

At our first camp, as we watched that mute bright illuminating eye in the sky on its planetary voyage, she huskily spoke to me for the first time in halting English. "I speak Russian," I offered at once. "No, I wish to speak in English, please. And I would like to speak to *you*. You have a pleasing face. Women lean to you." I glanced over at Brennan and then McIntyre. They appeared to be inconspicuously semi-dozing already from exhaustion.

It seemed she wanted to get a lot off her ample chest and at every night stop for three nights we routinely talked to each other, while the others remained obligingly reticent. Unlike her exterior image of hardness, she was an exuberant woman underneath. I'd put her at only a couple of years older than me, certainly late-twenties only. I'd imagined a prime body underneath the woollen padding. Her face was her best feature from what I could see. Clean lines, no freckles, and the whitest skin I'd seen, accented by extraordinary large indigo eyes with natural mascara lashes. When she let her white straight hair descend from the ugly knot above her brow, she transcended into heightened femininity. A twinge of desire came and went. But she retained an element of businesslike hardness about her, she had murdered her last paramour in cold blood. She was an object of sexual desire and I could see why the Soviet illuminati would utilise her. She had a sharp scalpel of a mind in there too. *A human preying mantis, a cold burning force—not an exercise in mystery but a study of power.*

Through the frosty vanishing traces of spoken breath, Irena educated me about her life.

She embarked on a whispered wishful tale—sound carried down the valleys at night—of already missing her daily strolls in Warsaw's Lazienkovwski Park, a few minutes from the Soviet Union's embassy on Ulica Belwederska. "I will cherish my frequent communion with the statue of Frédéric Chopin despite the music propaganda for Peter Ilyich. I always preferred his romantic piano symphonies over Tchaikovsky." A faraway dreamy look enveloped her.

Born and raised on the doorstep of Vnukovo-2, Moscow's domestic airport, being a natural communicator, the *moskvichka* had dreams of being an Aeroflot in-flight worker. Her parents, both now deceased from alcoholism, were staunch communists and insisted she enrol in the Red Army on the first day she became eligible. She became a *politruk*, a political indoctrination officer, responsible for preaching the party line to other soldiers in regular twice-weekly lectures. She never married, but had called off an inconceivable seven engagements in seven years. She explained that she didn't want children with the remarkably graphic, "I don't want any projectiles leaving my body," and, "There's no way I could have a bowel movement for any man." It was said without any hint of humour.

In her official capacity as GRU liaison at the KGB's First Chief Directorate foreign intelligence headquarters in Yasenevo, a Moscow suburb, she had access to all of its active measures files at Department A, so she was in a position to know what black propaganda means were in play to influence international events in favour of the Soviet Union and against the United States and its allies. (Active measures is a Russian military euphemism, which is called covert action in the UK and classified under psychological warfare-paramilitary operations. The "A" in Department A stood for America.) Most interesting of all to me was that she was also a highly trained specialist in prevention of defections.

Our colleagues, the BND, valued her knowledge to the point of all the trouble of getting her out because she unabashedly retained regular inter-course with three of her former fiancées and had done so for several years, and accompanied them on important business trips. These were the current bosses of Gosatomnadzor, Minatom, and the Kurchatov Institute. Respectively they were the Federal Nuclear & Radiation Safety Authority, the Ministry for Atomic Energy, and the premier facility where Soviet nuclear materials are stored. When I learned which organisations these much older *derzhavniki*—men of power—headed, I could see the logic in Germanic thinking. In her own time this communist broad was in essence a high-class whore with dangerously lofty capitalist ideals, and a big mound of deutschmarks and other hard currencies in her sights. It explained to me why she was neither an army girl nor an administrator.

In the Südeten mountain range, one night when we were hiding not too far from the stream that would elongate to become the Odra/Oder, the winding behemoth which separated Poland from East Germany, Irena said, almost as if to herself, "340,000 Red Army soldiers are stationed in the German Democratic Republic—a paradoxical name to the West, of course—but every year for the past three years about a hundred have deserted. I see it increasing, mind you. It carries a maximum sentence of seven years in the Motherland."

Her nearest condemnation of the eastern bloc she had just left so violently came with an off-hand remark, "Russians are starting to call their insensible, often contradictory, country Absurdistan."

I followed up on that statement and asked for one good example to explain her thoughts. After a child-like scratch of her chin, she referred to her Kurchatov Institute man again. He apparently had told her (between the sheets) that the Soviet Navy's Northern Fleet stored all its nuclear fuel—some 55 tons of enriched uranium—at Site 49 just outside its headquarters in Severomorsk and that the Soviet Union had 53 similar sites dotted throughout the country. To her having so many locations was total madness.

Other than that Irena appeared to me to be a true patriot with an unadulterated Russian disposition about her. A *russkost* she was. *You do too inspire lust, pure and simple; a savage sex in the mind.*

Every night the four of us would collapse fully-clothed, exhausted from the physical and psychological struggles of the trek. The raft had become a ball and chain around the ankles and a cross to bear on our backs. But every dawn for four days I awoke to a sensation of finding Irena curled up against me with her hand always strategically cupping my covered crotch. I'd remove it gently every morning without fail to go outside and take a cloud-filled pee.

It was half an hour after we'd rocketed down another sizzling whitewater rapids, past an area in the Erzgebirge ore mountains where the "pass on our starboard leads to the Zwickau-Mülde river, which means we are technically on West German territory"—another commentary courtesy of our resident travel agent Mac—that we saw our first other human in four long days. All we could do is stare at him, and he at us, as he stood upright from a squatting position on our right as we whizzed by in a cacophony of raging water. I observed him put a cellular device to his ear.

The racket was deafening out there in the watery maelstrom but in front and just above our rocking position, as we rounded a crevice spitting a resounding shower of water over us, there loomed a helicopter. We mouthed cheers but we couldn't hear each other's voices above the din. The grinning faces of airmen in helmets, with thumbs up, could be seen clearly along with the recognisable thin black cross and the letters MARINE broadside. All of a sudden the racket subsided, like somebody had hit a tone switch, and though we were still being propelled forward, the surrounding countryside was a mass of dense forests and no longer stark rock. We were on a deserted wide section of a river.

As I wiped my drenched face with both hands, the next thing I knew I was looking into the smooth open countenance of a blue-eyed young man wearing a helmet that had the black, red and yellow flag of West Germany in the centre front and on his overall's lapel *Bundesmarineflieger,* its Navy. He saluted smartly as I placed Irena in his care and one by one we climbed up the winch ladder to safety, while the raft rode towards another rapids.

Once we were ensconced aboard, a military-clad fellow with GSG-9 badge on his arm—I found out later it was a crack counter-terrorism unit—calmly in German said, *"bitte anschnallen"* (please fasten your seatbelts) then raised his rifle and took aim at the drifting raft and hit the duffel bag full of Semtex grenades with one shot. There was a prolonged roar as we swung away watching our home of four days sail burning into the Valhalla that would swallow it ahead.

Irena Puchovskaya? I only saw her once more. It was when I opened the window of a Hof country establishment to let the morning air in, feeling weary yet rejuvenated, having just showered and shaved after a good night's sleep. She was entering an open door to a black Mercedes in the cobblestone courtyard beneath me. All dressed up, she looked *brilliant*—which in Polish means a diamond. For some strange reason, she hesitated and looked up at topless me standing there and did a sweet hand wave and mouthed in Russian, *"Spasibo"*—thank you. I returned the gesture by miming goodbye in her tongue, *"Praschai"* and blew her a kiss which she graciously caught inside a clenched fist. I stood there naked with the towel around my waist as the car sped her for another ride to destiny.

Of course upon my return to London I'd immediately filed an after action review CX on my findings from her. Those two initials, which stands for Cummings Exclusive (after the first ever SIS chief, Mansfield Cummings), have always been an SIS acronym for classified top secret reports on agents. Hers was my first. (Up to then I had only filed YZ reports, which were marked under sensitive.)

I snapped to from sixteen years ago to the present, to find myself standing alone at another open window but in a Moscow hotel room just before a hazy dusk. Somewhere out there in this vast expanse of lights starting to flicker in their millions were some old men that knew Irena Puchovskaya intimately. I'm one of the few men who got to know her well too…well, vertically…

I locked the window and walked out.

Chapter Eight

Somewhere in both the left and the right brain of a god,
he or she managed to place me on both sides.
Sometimes they even change positions
but I'm still on both sides.

In the President lobby, the concierge was waving a wax-sealed A4 size envelope at me. It was marked British Embassy, Moscow. I sat down not far from where Ursula Durance and I had first acquainted ourselves.

Inside was a long original printout from Ellen Blyton in London. It read:

'Dear Nicholas,

Got an electronic message from Moscow today. Really, didn't you know we use double-transposition ciphered e-mail these days and not mail pouches? Welcome to the modern world, young man!

Regarding one Ursula Durance, the only bit of information we have on her—it must be the same person you ask about—is that she indeed is the current wife of the ex-Ambassador to the United Nations for France, Georges Durance, a career diplomat who retired from the French diplomatic service in 1982. They are permanent residents today of Cannes, France. I must say her dated file photo makes her out to be quite pretty when it was taken two decades ago. That's all there is on names listed under Durance, U. with the specs you gave. There are 115 others in France alone in our computer and 1,176 listed in the telephone directory nation-wide.

Regarding one Linda Coughlin—and this is my reason for responding immediately—instead of waiting for you to contact me at your own often lax leisure. It's because she's a known Irish Republican Army sympathiser who was born in Crossmaglen, County Armagh, Northern Ireland. (My, that's the export centre of Ulster's terrorism itself!) She mainly seems to be active in fundraising campaigns throughout ex-patriot Irish-Catholic communities in the United States, Canada and Australia, though there's a lone unsubstantiated report of her believed to be the assistant to the IRA Army Council's Head of Civilian Intelligence. She's also a graduate in international marketing and public relations from University College, Dublin, Republic of Ireland. According to the British Airport Authority data from yesterday, is that a Linda Coughlin has flown from London Heathrow to New York JFK by Air India, after arriving on BA from Belfast. She has a US resident alien Green Card. We are unsure if this individual is the same person as the Coughlin, L. you seek, as it is also a common name. Altogether we have 181 separate data entries under that name. Hundreds are listed in each of the British and Eireann telephone directories. We have no current file photo on record of her except a fuzzy bad copy of her driver's licence from our friends south of the border.

Seeing you are heading to the US very soon, I thought you may wish to know this information before you leave. In terms of them having any link to each other, I ran several crosschecks on them. As far as I can tell, there is no connection with each other. Neither has a criminal record of any kind anywhere in the western world though Coughlin has an unpaid ticket for drinking under influence, issued in The Bronx, USA, 14 months ago. I even checked against all the other Durance U.'s and Coughlin L.'s. Nothing significant came up.

Let me know if you want anything else.

Best—H-SEX

PS: Being me, I couldn't help to ask. Do you know these women? It's not cricket, not to know. I'll be fascinated to learn the answer over time. Behave yourself you handsome devil. Don't catch AIDS!.'

I smiled to myself about her curiosity. The H-SEX was a play on "C"'s personal secretary's real code name. Mrs Blyton was the big man's personal assistant.

I sat there tapping my fingers on the settee's upholstery. When I was looking out of the window earlier, I had an urge to travel around some of the old haunts in *Moskva*. 'Aye that's it, that's what I'm going to do, I'm going to take a look at Moscow's suburbs today,' I half said to myself.

As I came out of the President's grounds past the same gatekeeper, I wondered if he slept in the gatehouse. He was always there, without fail.

Across the street a man leaning and smoking on a Moskvitch car jumped to attention, signalling my attention. "Taxi, sir?" he called in English, though I could see that it had no green light for availability on it and wasn't a legal cab.

He looked quite presentable I thought, mid-forties, my age. "How much for a couple of hours just driving around town?" I asked him back in English. To cut a long story, once he found out I knew my way around and spoke Russian, the price came down by half that is if I paid in roubles and a further 25% if I paid in US dollars. He opened the back door but I got into the front passenger seat. He was a one-man gypsy cab operation and it soon became apparent he was moonlighting from his normal job as a policeman. His name was Yuri.

"Angleeski?" he enquired. *"Podrobnosti?"* I responded harshly, was he after details?

"No, sorry, sir," Yuri said, "I'm just trying to be polite. You speak excellent Russian, I must say. If I didn't know it, I would have thought you were from around Volvograd."

Interesting, I mulled, he's guessing Stalingrad—its old name—which is the next big city north of Rostov, my adopted home town. It was really Iosif Vissarionovich Dzhugashvili's hometown. I smiled friendship, "No I'm not from Joe Stalin-ville. Yes, I'm English. I'm sorry about that." I pointed to the Garden Ring Road entrance ahead. They called it *Sadovaya Spasskaya*.

There were still meandering human rivers flowing around the blocks of mountainous buildings. Its residents still have to queue for basic necessities in these days of supposed capitalism. Moscow, a bar chart of a city, where great expanses are suddenly interrupted by these stark various sized columns springing straight up as if on a white walled background.

We kept up our sombre solitude as we journeyed down the road. "Feel like a drink, Yuri?" I finally said. "I'll buy. Stop at the first bar we come to."

I wish I hadn't said that. The first one we came to was the nearest equivalent to the hard-nosed working men's clubs in the northeast of England which were full of coal miners, dockyard workers and local foundry labourers. This Russian version was a mix of Ivan's who looked largely like tough ex-armed forces men sprinkled with a few surly immigrants. Like in the cowboy movies, when Yuri and I made our entrance, the vocal din reduced discernibly and newspapers were lowered through the visible layer of smoke. They must think we're police, I thought, and they were half right. I put on a bad show of halting Russian to the bar man to let him think I was a tourist. "A shot each for my taxi driver and I please. Do you sell vodka here?" Somebody laughed along the bar somewhere and the noise resumed.

Yuri whispered in my ear, "That was a smart move, boss, I was ready to smash a few chairs over somebody's head there." We clinked glasses in salutation.

"Where is he from?" a man who looked older than his years asked Yuri, who looked at me first for permission before responding.

"England."

"Ah, yes, our allies in the world war," he exclaimed as he shook my hand. "I am an Afghan vet." He took a swig of drink as if to drown his sorrows. It was Soviet Russia's Vietnam and it was still smouldering. A nightmare in progress, like their advancing alcoholism. As if to himself he muttered, "Socialist countries like ours are like your mother. They're supposed to take care of you, teach you, feed you and take care of you. Fuck." He tumbled down off his stool and stumbled towards the loo. A bad limp indicated he had quarter of a leg missing.

As he made his way the man's drinking colleague nodded sombrely at me and volunteered, "I was in charge at the 40th Army's CPRDD post in Afghanistan, which is short for Central Point for the Reception and Dispatch of the Dead, a place where Soviet troop who die in war pass through in their body bags before transport home. Of course we were not permitted to actually use those words so instead the military code for those killed in action was 'Cargo 200', about how many we shipped each time a plane left and roughly the number of parts each man was in. What most of their families didn't know was that we had to regularly mutilate them even more to get what was left of the stiffs into the less than body-size zinc coffins…all in the name of saving space on the aircraft. That is to say what was little that was remaining of them after the *Dushman* had already hacked off their ears, noses, fingers, genitals and gouged their eyes out before sliced their guts and peeled their skin off while still alive." He downed a drink straight at his sorrowful conclusion. (Dushman in Russian is the Afghan mujahideen.)

In my shock over the last conversation I contemplated the tranquil contents of my glass and the rowdy occupants of the room. During the heyday of the Cold War, the military of the Soviet Union was five million active bodies. With the name change, it had been sweepingly reduced to 1.2 million on a budget cut to US$16 billion, according to Mrs Blyton's overview file I got. I marvelled at what the figures used to be at the height of escalation. I was overseeing the wretched results of that overwhelming overall overnight change. It saddened me to see my proud former enemy so pathetic in their defeat. History has a way of forgetting its victims.

I ordered a round of drinks for my new-found friends of ten minutes acquaintance. I raised my glass and proclaimed, *"Rodina,"* and gulped it down.

"To the Motherland!" the chorus came back. That made me immediately popular and more weather-beaten faces, looking older than their age, appeared to introduce themselves to me. It surprised me to see Yuri decline another re-fill. That impressed me but I never ever told him so.

A political discussion was soon underway. "It is said the President is a reflection of his nation. Well that's absolutely right. The man is forever sick." Everybody cackled. "Yeah, wasn't it him that said, 'I get my vision from you, the people. Your hopes are my goal, for you. Your dreams are my purpose, in life. Your cares are my cause, always.'" The speaker stopped his grand cavorting from his imaginary podium. "I've never heard of this kind of nonsense before. Now they're going to kill us with kindness." That brought a fresh round of laughter from his audience. Russians are like the Irish of the East.

The carcasses of the Cold War warriors were still lukewarm, kept so by the heat of vodka. In a sense *Rossija*—Russia—was now at war with itself. She had to reinvent herself pretty quickly or be stillborn. Either way its nationals' lifestyles were giving the new country heart disease and it may die young anyway.

I indicated subtly to Yuri to leave and we did so without our drinking companions noticing. An inebriated *sobor*. A sober ingathering it wasn't. Outside, to say we were in a bad neighbourhood was an understatement. A hostile looking crowd surrounded us, begging and pulling at our clothes.

That bar was a Soviet camp in the middle of enemy invaders. "Who are these people, Yuri?"

"Known petty criminals. Chechens. All bums, the lot of them. Racketeers mainly or panhandlers. They don't even say they are from Chechnya, if you talk to one. He'll describe himself from *Ichkeria*, the name they would call their country if they gained independence from us. As far as I'm concerned, we should just give it to them so they'll all leave Moscow and go back. It's like your Northern Ireland in Russia." He burped rudely as we got back in the car.

"I want to look at Patrice Lumumba University," I instructed him. "Then from there we can head back to the hotel." His last statement reminded me of my days at school there from ages 19-20, when I was first introduced to the pleasures of vodka. Just like he categorised the Chechens, the world's students at PLU widely regarded the Americans as only "interested in making profits received from war by the mass sale of armaments". Only an element of truth in both beliefs, which became fully blown fictitious facts, I thought sardonically. *Brennan's voice rang in my head, "The Russians and the Americans could not agree to build a bridge, so they dug a hole for all of us!"*

Yuri asked, "You going to apply for *propiska?*"

"No, not at all," I answered truthfully. It was the residency permit to live in Moscow, which you had to get from the police. When I'd arrived from Rostov before, I'd gone through that long-drawn out bureaucratic routine then. Discreetly slipping the morose clerk a few roubles to further me along the waiting governmentalism—*gosudarstvennost*—process had helped me considerably.

We headed due south in the direction of the Moscow suburb of Vorontsovo. Before long we were observing the campus, half way between Lenin Prospekt and the river. It brought back memories for me and we sat gazing at the closed buildings in stillness. I was thankful for Yuri's hush. It wouldn't take a genius to figure out I was a former student. A policeman like him could sense that. The only change, other than a couple of new houses, was the name—*Narodnyi Universtitet Druzhby* (People's Friendship University). A map of the world painted in colour on the side of a building was prominent. Its blazing torch burned a now empty hole from the middle.

The drive back to the city centre was a lost visit to my time back there.

As we neared Moscow city centre the *beriozka* stores were still open. We used to call them diploshops—classier retail outlets accepting foreign currency only. A decadent outpost among the starving.

Outside the President, Yuri and I shook hands. I paid him in *dollari* with a reasonable tip in roubles. He did the classic click of heels in respect, as he bowed forward in a brief jerk. Few words were spoken but he did ask me if I'd like his phone number at the police station and I duly accepted it. For some reason, he hugged me warmly and then jumped back into his jalopy and was gone.

* * * * * * * * * *

As I ambled up the President marble steps, the busboy I'd kept waiting once was pointing a white-haired emaciated man towards me. Two others were behind him who both had an official air about them followed. 'Oh-oh,' I enunciated silently to myself.

In accented but good English the man said, "Mr Anderson? I am Leonid Viser, a medical doctor working with Dr Molody. He asked me to drop in to see if you needed assistance with the files he gave you."

The pair were with us split seconds later. "Please allow me to introduce Mr Boris Kokorin and Mr Nikolai Leonov. *Chekisti.*" We all shook hands rather perfunctorily.

It was unusual that Mike would give this man my whereabouts without first asking me, I thought. I was equally surprised he would bring a person like Viser into his team; only for the fact that I disliked this man instantly. "These two gentlemen are from the competent organ I presume, Dr Viser?" His spat reference in street Russian after introducing them was noted by me. (*Chekisti* was a slur for men from the KGB while competent organ is the KGB's euphemism for itself.)

Before Viser responded, Kokorin, the visually outgoing of the two, smiled quickly at me and brightly declared, "Correct, sir. We are senior officers from the Federal Security Service. Yes, you are thinking right, we *were* KGB First Chief Directorate Line X officers in Department T, which was responsible for scientific and technical collection." A smart man, Kokorin, to know I'd picked up on that fact quickly. A hunter knows when the prey knows he's there but he told me more than I knew, purposefully or not. "We are detailed to escort Dr Viser on behalf of the state."

I pondered the words, "escort on behalf of the state". *Well, let's see what this is all about*, and directed them to the bar lounge. Let the games begin. I didn't let on that I knew that Line meant they were analysts and are not operational in the field.

Once the niceties were out of the way and the drinks were served, which I noted the oldest of the security detachment, a calm Leonov, signed for. He had to be close to retirement age. A receipt made it *very* official I ruminated. "To each according to his own taste," toasted Kokorin, the self-designated public relations man, in his perfect English. *"Nostrovia* (to your health),*"* I added somewhat sardonically. As I drank to that, I judged that the two security men were just doing their job. I had no problem with them at all. Maybe they had to stick around the shifty Viser, to make sure he didn't screw up something. I'll find out eventually, no matter what.

Right then, a portly man walked behind me, and Leonov and Kokorin jumped to attention like good military men do, even in plainclothes dress. Then they sat down again slowly. I looked to Kokorin for an explanation. "Vadim Medvedev, the President of Russia's chief bodyguard." I nodded understanding, another good reason why I chose to stay at the President Hotel.

Viser's speaking style evoked memories of a dentist drill. The kind of creature willing to pull the pin on a stink bomb and throw it. A complex man of contrasts.

Leonid Viser was sitting facing me, waiting until he had my full attention. It came like a boxing glove to the face. "I believe you are well aware that social realism demands optimism in the workers of the state."

I glanced over at the other two who were gazing lazily at the ceiling, as if they'd heard it before. "Actually I don't expect you to have read my project's files yet as Dr Molody probably put it at the end. He wants you to see his remarkable findings first, before mine. Any way, you'll know about it soon.

"The real reason I came is because I wanted to meet you; and you to meet me. I'd like you to know that I am a political dissident in whatever nation they choose to name this place I live in, and I am working with Dr Molody's project under protest. Fifteen years ago, like Solzhenitsyn, I did not adhere to the official principle of socialist realism and paid the price. So the Chief Administration of Corrective Labour Camps arbitrarily decided, despite my impeccable inventions to alleviate sickness, that my views were 'anti-Soviet behaviour'. Under Article 58-10 of the Soviet Union's legal system's criminal code, I was thrown into the punishment cells at Moscow's Lefortovo prison, without a trial. I was sentenced to the gulag indefinitely. It doesn't help that I am also a Jew."

His brooding silence now demanded an answer from me. Well, I wasn't going to give him the satisfaction. So I simply uttered sarcastically, "Don't cloud the issues with facts. Please go on."

He chose to ignore the jibe and resumed. "Even in your country, oligarchy rules in a different way but it's the same in the end." A good comeback, I smiled to myself.

"As I said at the beginning, Russians want the fruits of capitalism without the obligations of capitalism. *Glasnost,* openness, will not last. The *politburo* has been replaced by so-called free market forces which will make the country explode like a Molotov cocktail."

I rudely interrupted his ranting, "Will you please get to the point, Dr Viser. I am a busy man."

Leonov leaned over to put his empty glass on the table. "He's from Novokuybyshevsk, what do you expect." The city's name meant revolutionary hero.

Viser blurted, " I am not missing the point; I am merely making my own..."

"Let me take over, doctor. You have said your piece. Take a break will you," ordered Leonov firmly, as he cut in, putting his hand gently on his shoulder. Viser quickly appeared sullen. "Mr Anderson, Dr Viser here is a genius in electromagnetic therapy. He eats and dreams it all day long. To the state he is certifiably nuts, but we have slowly come to recognise that we need his knowledge. So Mr Kokorin next to me, how you say, is his handler. He is responsible for everything to do with the man."

It was Kokorin's turn, as he composed his face modestly to go with the part-compliment. "The Academy of Science and the Academy of Medical Science basically stole Viser's original ideas and projects when he was jailed but could not develop it further. At least not to the lofty exacting levels the Ministry of Science demanded. So it was suggested they get him back to Moscow. I was selected for the job and went to his labour camp in Solovetsky Islands—the most notorious in Siberia I may add—to interview him. As you can see he is slightly nutty but a world-class electromagnetic expert he is, I can assure you. Dr Viser's delayed project from 15 years ago has been officially reassigned under the auspices of Dr Molody's global health programme. You will find out all about his advances in electromagnetism under file number 100 which, I believe, is in your possession." I noticed he minded Viser almost in a loving way, like he was his grandfather.

Leonov and Kokorin were soon on their feet. Kokorin beckoned a still sulking Viser to stand up. "Come on Viser, man, you had your wish. You've met the guy. Now maybe you can go to work."

I looked up at them and said, "If he wasn't a prisoner of the state and could one day eventually be allowed to emigrate to Israel, do you think his production level would increase?" Dr Viser positively jumped alive at that remark, like a housedog expectantly about to go out for a walk.

Kokorin stared down at me, blankly, not responding. It seemed to me that nobody had addressed the taboo subject. "Well, Mr K," I reiterated, "I would appreciate a written answer from you within one month as to whether or not this is a possibility or probability. I think it would be fair to determine that Dr Viser could leave within a couple of years from now in return for his superb services. I'd like your card, if you don't mind. I will be following up on this matter, believe me. Thank you for your time, gentlemen." Kokorin duly obliged with his business card as they left.

On the way to the eatery inside the hotel, I informed reception to please forward any telephone calls upstairs to their restaurant. Right after I'd swallowed the main course, the expected incoming call came when the *maître d'hotel* brought a phone unit to my table. I knew it would be Michal Molody, MD.

I started the conversation. "I knew it would be you, we haven't talked since this morning. Your lady must be happy your home tonight. I wished you'd informed me about Viser and gang coming over, an interesting bunch."

"Oh, I'm very sorry about that. I got quite busy and by the time they said they would be there, it was already past. My apologies. Dr Viser, despite early reservations about you, actually liked you. In fact, you're the *only* person I've seen him warm too." I could hear Caterina singing in the background.

"He has good reasons to want to like me, Mike." Then I related the whole session to him.

Mike finally said, "Well, a brilliant talent he is. We'll see about his freedom part later. It has little to do with me really."

"Not so, Mike. If Viser is that good and he's happy, you could still be dealing with him in Israel. He can't get away from the world, no matter where he flees. So it's a long-term harvest," I countered.

The line was silent for a while, save for the lilting humming sounds. Then he said, "I never thought about it that way, to be honest with you." I expressed my gratitude to him making that simple humanistic concession.

In a way Dr Viser was right, people like to be frightened when they know there is no real danger. The world at large was approaching the perimeters of power in new ways, not all of it necessarily good. A sobering thought. *Niet sobornost.* No togetherness, anymore. All singular thinking, a basic form of modern capitalism. I detested it deep down but there was no other way available at the moment.

I'd awoken this morning with not much on my plate, other than a ton of reading to do, and it had turned out to be quite an eventful day and I hadn't yet started reading.

It was little after 11:00 PM and I was starting to feel a bit drowsy. I was slowly sipping a refill of coffee, lost in thought, observing in peace the various individuals who represented power chewing down their dinner. *You can learn a lot about a person from the way they eat, Nicholas, old chap. Some slice their butter while others scrape it. The aggressive and the timid…*

I'm glad I wasn't holding the cup at the time, as I'm sure I would have dropped it. My whole body went from parked to fifth gear overdrive in five seconds flat. Coming up the staircase together was Ursula Durance with Paddy O'Neill of the IRA. She was chatting gaily while he listened with typical Gaelic stoicism. I know I slunk down in my chair a fraction, I had nowhere else to hide. I was revving with deep-seated anger.

Entering the restaurant, Ursula saw me and beamed broadly waving her hand and broke into a stride directly to my table. O'Neill followed. I slowly stood up and she flung herself into my open arms and kissed me on both cheeks, then she cupped my face in her palms and smacked my lips forcefully. I was momentarily confused—trying to find time to suppress my ire—and it showed outwardly, while she creased her brows slightly puzzled at my facial tone. "Nicholas, please meet Mr Patrick O'Neill from Northern Ireland who lives in America. We have had a wonderful intelligent time together on the train from Estonia. Patrick please say hello to my English friend Nicholas Anderson, who also lives in America. You two have something in common in that you're both ex-patriots from the British Isles. It's a small world really." She had innocence written across her flushed face.

O'Neill was standing looking at me as if he'd seen me before somewhere, I imagined. Damn right he had, just the past weekend at the pub in Glenoe but only for a fleeting second. Could he really remember my face...we had a distorting glass and frame between us, with him standing outside and I sitting inside. We locked eyes on each other and we both hesitated, oh so briefly, before shaking hands in courteous greetings.

I invited them to sit down at my table. Ursula bubbled, "I had an opportunity to return earlier, so I did. Though I had a great time, I don't think I would have stayed a night at that foreboding monastery alone. Thank goodness, Patrick was sitting in my compartment. The dialogue made the day pass faster."

His eyes were still on me, no doubt wondering if his mind was playing tricks on him or not—at least to my mind. He had to *feel* that there was indeed something in common, but not exactly what Ursula had suggested. As we mature you instinctively knew that the other person knows something about your field of occupation; it comes with age. It was an unspoken feeling in the air.

"Tell Nicholas what you do, Patrick. I found it quite fascinating," intoned the effervescent Ursula, who was in sharp contrast to Paddy's outward melancholic personality. To prompt him she said, "Wasn't the Estonian company you work with called Kaitseliit or something like that?"

O'Neill leaned forward reluctantly, and openly started, "I'm sorry Ursula I'm extremely tired. My apologies to you. Yes, it's a non-profit voluntary organisation which exchanges information internationally in how to dispose of power engineering waste. Quite boring stuff really, let's talk about more interesting things. Ursula's travelling activities blow away my kind of work."

I'm not convinced of that, I told myself grimly. I couldn't believe my luck. He's sitting right here across from me at my table in a Russian hotel's restaurant. I first identified him in a photograph sitting in a jeep in Libya; I'd next witnessed him outside a British army camp in Cyprus which led to extreme dire straits for me; then just a few days ago in Northern Ireland after Brennan's funeral; and now. This is the closest I've ever been to him. I wanted to sit next to him, even closer. Perhaps even physically hurt him, somehow, someway. I tried to calm my exterior self, while my insides were being twisted slowly in knots. I hated him for what he had done to me—more than anybody else on the planet.

"I deal with Middle Eastern interests in a related field, specifically in the area of WMD," my voice warmly emitted. I couldn't believe myself. "I'm working in Moscow with the Kurchatov Institute. It's a prominent nuclear storage site for bomb-grade uranium and plutonium. There's a stockpile of over 70,000 small discs of the highly volatile material at its sister location at the Institute of Physics & Power Engineering in the former secret city of Obninsk." I was guessing that's how Irena Puchovskaya said it was fifteen years ago or so. "My Arab clients wish to acquire limited quantities of it. But there's plenty more where that came from. The reason they work with me, as you yourself may have encountered in dealing with them, is that the actual practice of verbally spoken literature, more often tells us that 'communication' between the Arab-speaking and the English is full of traps. That it is often based on misunderstandings and is perhaps ultimately impossible for them to deal with the vagaries of the English language. Thankfully I'm multi-lingual and I speak in their tongue which helps a lot. Just to give you an example, in the Chinese and Arabic worlds there are no words which literally mean the same in English, which creates miscommunications, and leads to friction in this specialised field." I was totally amazed at my chutzpah.

That seemed to have piqued his interest. His eyes lighted fractionally, as he relaxed a wee second. My unrehearsed lines were designed to fit into his gut reaction of me, hypothetically. I was lying through my teeth.

"It's not all plain sailing, mind you," I continued the pretence. Being British and speaking Arabic, sometimes I forget their customs. Islamic dates on the calendar are provisional and are subject to the visibility of the new moon at Mecca. I once made the mistake of phoning a customer of mine on a*l-hijra*, the Islamic New Year, on our 27th of April while I was at my daughter's birthday party."

I smiled to paused, finding time to retain a means between us—a hook—then picked up, "Patrick, I'd like to know more about the Estonian company, perhaps they'll be able to provide leads. There may be something in it for you, too. Better still, you should give me your card in the United States. I live close to Los Angeles and I'm flying there in a few days time, but I'll come and visit you, wherever you are."

I was thinking that last line, coupled with my speech, should make him put to bed his *feeling* on me, or greatly alarm him—either/or, or both. It was a gamble. Based on my story *to him*, I implied I had to be dealing with some major figures in the Arab world who wished to deal in nuclear, biological and chemical weapons of mass destruction, the WMD I'd mentioned so flippantly.

The Irish gentleman farmer from the border of the two Irelands chose the former. His eyebrows were raised and clearly he was interested in learning more about me. At the very least, I might be able to supply him with useful facts for his contact Moueen Mohammed Abu Farkh of Hamas. O'Neill probably chose to stay in the President Hotel for the same reasons I did. Its inhabitants had links to all kinds of power—political, explosive, or otherwise.

"I don't have a card on me...," he replied post-haste as I'd put him on the spot in front of Ursula, but his voice was steady, void of emotion. He patted his breast pocket. I thought he was really searching for his cigarettes.

Of course not, I brooded. *Your farm was on the south side and was found to have a tunnel under the border of Northern Ireland and the Irish Republic. You used it to illegally ferry IRA lads between the two countries. The British and Irish militaries closed it and you've on the run ever since. It was so nice of your boys to call us, using your name, to tell us of the whereabouts of the bombs about to blow us up. Were you aware that in order to differentiate between the cranks and you, SIS had to go through the trouble of giving your lot the code of the day, just so that we'd know it was the real thing? The first was 'Daffodil'. Fucker.*

O'Neill completed his sentence, "...but I'll write it down for you, if you give me yours too." He produced a pen and a notepad from his pocket and scribbled the pertinent information down, and then he handed me a torn-off piece of paper, to do likewise. *The invitation was made even though I had invited it.*

"New York City suburban number, I see. 718. Are you in The Bronx, Queens or Brooklyn?" I asked. I think I knew where.

"The Bronx," came the reply. "You're 714. That's Orange County, Southern California, right, where about?"

I had no problem telling him. "Newport Beach, actually the super wealthy liked to call it that to impress you. But I live in the artists community called Balboa, my place is on the beach on East Ocean Front." I thought to myself, *there's nobody there right now, thank goodness. Plus I'll tell my would-be lodger, when he moves in, to take messages, if any Irishmen call looking for me.*

"Balboa like in Panamanian money?" he'd asked then, as he held his gaze with mine for long seconds. That seemed to indicate he had been to Central America. He was truly warming to me, starting to throw in small talk. O'Neill scribbled Balboa on the paper with my phone number. I'd never heard of the money's name before and just nodded. Finally he broke right through the perceived wariness and queried, "So when would you like to come to see me?" Bingo, objective achieved! I punched my tensed fist under the table.

I instantaneously replied one week and that I'd call him from the area. O'Neill stood up, shook my hand, saying he had an early morning flight, on Delta direct to New York City. He bent to peck Ursula's cheek once, the American way, and then left the same way he came in his unhurried stroll.

Ursula was chuffed with herself for instigating a good contact for both. Forever the diplomatic high society liaison. As I was wondering how much of this game she really knew, she held my hand and whispered demurely, "I missed you, you know. Even for one day, I thought about you a lot." Then she added as an afterthought, "I didn't know all that about you, you know. I was introducing you two only because you both lived in America and were from the same country. You speak Russian and Arabic? That stuff on Arabs was interesting. You should come with me when I go to Egypt on holiday some time next year. You could come in handy." Her enlarged pupils imparted an unmistakable carnality that rocked my whole body.

I said calmly, "You mean *Misr*."

"*Misr*? What's that?," she replied in her captivating accent.

"It's what Egypt calls itself, silly."

She broke into a sexy grin, squeezing my hand tightly, then added, "You're going back to the US so early? I must cram more time with you or perhaps you may think of visiting me in France. It's nice and warm there right now. You know, for a second or two back there I thought maybe you weren't so happy to see me." I squeezed her hand back to eliminate that thought and she held it even tighter.

She clearly had designs on me; I couldn't help getting the hint. But I didn't take the cue, not yet. All I could think of to myself was an intelligence training directive, and kept repeating it in my head, 'Under no circumstances negotiate with terrorists, to talk to them is to surrender to them.'

Well, I just did with O'Neill and this lady's closeness was too good to be true. Almost a one in a million chance.

Fortunately, Ursula was a little hungry so she ordered something to peck on so I took the opportunity and went to make a phone call downstairs in the lobby. On the first ring it was answered. I spoke immediately, without introducing myself, "Kokorin, do you know a company in *Eesti* called Kaitseliit?" I was wearing my senior belligerent hat, just where I left off with him.

It took him a few seconds to think of who was calling. "Mr Anderson, I'm sorry. I thought maybe you were going to bawl me out about Dr Viser. No, Kaitseliit is not a company in Estonia, it is an underground paramilitary operation and we at the Federal Security Service's anti-terrorism centre have had many problems with them. It is reported that they are trading in arms from the stolen equipment from our former military barracks outside the towns of Parnu and Tartu. It is believed they are also brokering the liquid nerve gas VX and the nerve agent Sarin. As you might know VX is ten times more lethal than Sarin and causes death by paralysis. But we are still trying to find out how they got it. The type they have only comes either from Libya, Iran or Iraq. Why do you ask? I don't think there should be any connection between Viser and them."

I assured him that there wasn't any whatsoever and curtly thanked him for his information. My head was spinning with his abundance of detail. But before I could hang up, he had a quick query of his own, or rather it came over like a statement. "You got me thinking today about Viser, sir. You are right. This is perhaps the difference between the West and the East. I think you call it human rights. I must say I am in support of this for the old man."

Good, I thought but I didn't feel like talking anymore. I was shattered. After the shock of meeting O'Neill and hearing what I just heard I was badly in need of immediate light relief to amuse myself from the seriousness of the day.

Back at the table in the restaurant, Ursula had already finished her snack and was leaning over taking a couple of books out of her carrying bag. As I came behind her it was the first time I noticed her delicious neck. She was still excited about her trip to Pskov for the day and wanted to tell me more. "The best part of the day was when the monks led us down a candlelit sandstone corridor cave past more than 10,000 coffins. Spooky."

She put on her reading glasses while I observed her perfectly manicured clear nails then gazed into the chocolate pupils. "See this, by the Marquis de Custine in his book *'Russia in 1839'*, he wrote the following." She cleared her sweet throat gently. "'Everybody disguises what is bad and shows what is good before the master's eyes. There is a permanent conspiracy of smiles plotting against truth for the greater contentment of mind of the one who is supposed to want and act to the advantage of all.'"

She put the book down gently. "I have to say this *is* what I've seen on holiday in Russia so far. It's so true." I thought the statement applied to my mood of the moment actually.

I could only say back, "It seems to be the 'incurable darkness of the Russian soul.' It was Fyodor Dostoyevsky who said that." That quip got her thinking a bit.

I asked her more about her field trip and she rambled on excitedly at length. I wasn't really listening but found myself glancing down at her appealing knees and small feet instead.

There was a second book on the table with a rude leather tongue sticking out a quarter of the way down, so when she stopped prattling I interjected if that was what she was reading now. *"The True and Only Heaven: Progress and Its Critics,"* she stated as she picked it up. She seemed to like it that I was interested in her choice of literature. I was really watching her mouth opening and closing absentmindedly. My imagination danced crazily with her lips.

When it stopped, to be courteous I just enquired, "Well what is this one about, in one sentence, please?"

She stopped to think briefly and with that toothsome grin of hers, simply pronounced, "It's appropriate to where you're going to soon. 'Contemporary America is a culture obsessed with the pornography of Making It.'"

To which, I finally responded quietly to her pretty face, "And that's exactly what is appropriate for you right now, foxy woman. I am obsessed with making love to you. What do you say if we go upstairs now?" She grasped my hand without a word and we went upstairs to her room and we made a furious sweet love for the first time. I never detected any falsity in her nakedness. The passion for me was there though it had been almost 10 years since she had sex, so she said. It could have been that she read a lot of romance novels too.

Chapter Nine

Early-mornings and nights were more than satisfactorily spent with Ursula and lovemaking improved animalistically with practising regularity, despite her early rustiness. It always does with time, as the relationship building is still in its infancy. I was pleasantly surprised by her inexhaustible lust for sexual variety but wasn't complaining.

She had decided to depart Moscow with me and we rode to the international airport together at around six in the morning in another gypsy cab, at least a forty-minute cold drab ride from the city centre.

After much persistent badgering I'd promised to stop in the South of France for a couple of nights in seven days time on my way back from the United States to the Ukraine. So intent was she that she went ahead and purchased my return NYC-Nice-Paris-Kiev segment on her credit card at the Air France desk. I could have cashed it in anytime, as it was fully refundable.

Her own Air France flight left before my British Airways, so I had time to cruise the duty-free shop only to find the liquor prices far more expensive than on the streets. The caviar especially could be purchased at *four* times less at the local corner store in downtown Moscow; a cost which was at least *fourteen* times less than that in the West. The Russians were quickly learning the mores of capitalism.

After a prolonged de-icing by the ground crew of the jet and eventual take off to London, I began making some notes before settling into the first 75 manila files I had crammed into my carry-on. Reading is like flying—you spend a lot of time alone sitting in front of emptiness and living an adventure in your head.

Michal Molody had popped over the night before and we sat in my hotel room talking for an hour. The main gist of our dialogue was in and around his next statement, "If you are a good scientist, you should always be doing experiments to attempt to discredit your own theories, despite a western philosophy which encourages you not to." I liked that because it was my own non-medical attitude as well. When I'm on a job, I can never relax, and I find myself constantly giving talks only to myself and often write it down. I continue to question the question, if it didn't feel or look right.

I had only one dubiety for him at the time. I asked him, "At what point does a foetus begin to feel pain, Mike?"

Without missing a beat he said, "Between 24–26 weeks and beyond. We terminate well before 10 weeks when it has been factually determined there isn't any pain felt."

Given my recent liaisons, momentarily I contemplated how long it takes to create the biological process, a mere few minutes of pleasure?

No doubt he had come over to administer a pep talk to me, like a coach does to his key player before the game. "We have to pursue our responsibilities to humanity; a better life is just around the bend for all the sick. We can't find that elusive bend right now but I *know* you'll locate it somewhere, eventually." I was again reminded of how difficult the work is and how glorious the prize may be. We reached a gentlemen's agreement, on a handshake, and that I would at least be refunded my personal expenses—*if* I succeeded in getting him the publicity he needed. It was like taking on a commission-only job in a lifelong career position that may not pay dividends, ever. *I must dare to be heard or be ignored.*

Mike had also said something else which stuck in my head. "Too many physicians are taught the 'Big Science' of industrialised societies and dismiss other science traditions as unproven potions and practices, yet I have frequently found the latter has evolved over thousands of years and are effective. Open-mindedness is a friend of scientific investigation." Forget food for thought; it was a feast for the brain.

* * * * * * * * *

Centuries of systematic deception have shaped the way we think.
Big Brother marketed as Freedom and Democracy.

Music—the language of the body—constantly relieved the telepathic tension between the reading matter and me. I took off the airline headphones and looked thousands of feet down from my lounge chair in the air, rubbing my ears. My eyes ached too and they were going to ache more soon.

The vast expanse of Los Angeles loomed up. The smog had already settled in. As we began descent you could see the fumes escaping the trucks, their diesel engines emitting forty known toxins into our lungs. We landed in a country with the lowest price of petroleum in the Western world, where 4% of the planet's population create more than 25% of the globe's carbon-dioxide emissions. One hundred and ninety one other nations, speaking 6,800 languages, generate the rest.

I cleared immigration and customs quickly as I was used to the congested routine. The contradictions of California: No smoking signs everywhere yet it's one of the most polluted ozone zone within Generica, bar equally fume-filled Manhattan and Texas oil-soaked towns. I was again rudely reminded of the fatness of its people. In Africa it was a sign of the wealthy; but here it was a sign of being unhealthy. The right coast was a damn sight worse than the left around the middle of Americans bodies. One day they'll realise high disposable income doesn't earn happiness or health.

Again, the parade down the tunnel of strangers' eyes in the arrival hall. Ah, there was the unmistakable 6' 8" Ben Obertone, my buddy, with an unnecessary huge sign stating, "Rat Phink and Boo-Boo" held over his head. I had to laugh at the absurdity of his attempts at black comedy on the weekend of a major Hollywood release. It was a play on a "Batman" (and Robin) feature which was coming out soon. *The young of the world are uncritically fascinated by images from America, while ironically the East calls the cultural invasion by the West the pollution line, an intellectual enslavement to the US it was.*

Ben was a big human cuckoo clock whose tick clicked in and tock clocked out, depending on whom he was talking to. A man to watch, who timed his moves with precision, like the independent B-movie director he was. Within minutes he had manoeuvred through the metal monsters clogging the 405 freeway and we were in the car pool lane clacking south.

Fortunately he was talking business on his new cellular phone most of the trip so I didn't have to hear the latest woes of his wife's infidelity. Plus he knew me well enough to know when I was in a thinking mode.

Time flies by but I never managed to see the minute hand keep up with the seconds on my Longines. The medical data I read as I travelled halfway across the planet was mind-boggling. I had another seventy-five files to go. A Sisyphean thought crossed my mind. *We can't close the Establishment's eyes but can we, the people, open ours?* The rhythm of the road made me doze off.

Soon we drove past the Balboa Pier with fleeting specks of green sea between the houses on the right. My little grey home was still there, not bombed to smithereens by the IRA.

I packed my belongings quickly bar the bed frame, mattress, couch and phone unit, leaving the unlisted number for my friend's use. Ben had all his stuff ready to move in.

He had experienced the jarring jolt of catching his wife with his lifelong best friend. He had joined the ranks of those losing faith in humanity, except me at this moment in time. I never told him that I was currently the other man with a married woman too.

Later we went to Ruby's at the end of the Balboa Pier for the world's best hamburger and fries and I filled him in the best I could about what to do if Irishmen and whatnot came looking for me, without actually stating an Irishman per se. But I did disclose part of my past life to him. I'm not sure the dangers of what I was saying logged.

The rest of the week, I caught up with the remaining half of Molody's 150 files. The down time was filled by surfing the thundering rollers smashing the beachhead at The Wedge at the bottom of Balboa Peninsula. I went upside down a few times too as a result of mistiming the breakers, my head painfully smacking the bottom of the ocean.

Further up the shore, a tourist had drowned when the rip-tide undercurrent took him on an unexpected joy ride out to the unwelcoming sea. The death of that stranger left me with no doubt in my own mind about what can be if you mess up, and to go with the flow when the situation demands it.

In between staring at the sea, deep in thought, I read the last half of the files, and I got to learn all about what truly ails our world—medically-speaking. I present only select pieces of the wonderful data I had the privilege of accessing.

Almost as if he knew I would stop at #75 and begin from #76, the first of Dr Molody's hand-written critiques to me stated:

"Nicholas, logic is a many splendoured thing, but I always make sure I have sufficient data in my calculations to arrive at a conclusive result. *Logic fails when one has to fill in the blanks with politically correct platitudes.* Our food and water supply *is* the root cause of our crisis. Modern cities also have to worry about the air they breathe. They can't help themselves and are on a dedicated path to destruction with plenty of Man-induced cancers to come. Many international medical institutions, with some exceptions, strike at shadows while the problem is right there in front of them, yet remains invisible—more or less like the Emperor's clothes—because it suits them to ignore the obvious due to politics.

As an example, placebo—phantom pain or psychological anguish—is pain perceived in person's brains but lacking in physical cause. Most of the West uses this blind trial method on sick patients who do not know if it is the real medicine or a fake. In Russia *everybody* gets the medicine regardless as we believe everybody is entitled to it.

The biggest proponent of this incorrect international procedure is the US' Food and Drug Administration (FDA), an American federal agency who play a medical Russian roulette. FDA red tape kills their own countrymen—those who simply can't survive delays in clearing new treatments—in the name of making money. America spins nets of misinformation because cash is the single most important object of their human existence. This may well work in the short term, but when you pause: you may wonder where it is all leading to. In the real world, it is the survival of the fittest, to a quick and disastrous ending of a social experiment. Anyone foolhardy enough to believe the FDA's propaganda is definitely slated to die with it. And that is exactly what the vast majority of the developed world's citizens are doing. It is just Mother Nature's way to sieve out all the fools from the genetic pool, I guess. The American Way of Life is going a long way to accomplish just *that* objective. Politically correct thinking and nature just don't mix. That is the next lesson on human evolution that they will be learning—the hard way!

The very antithesis of the FDA, thank goodness, is Commission E, its German equivalent. Their policies are almost the exact opposite of the US' most of the time. The policies of Russia and Cuba are close behind the

Germans. I work closely with all three of their Ministry of Health's and have access to their information, by the way.

Their beliefs, in layman terms, are once you put the knife to anything and open it up to air, you compound the problem and what was not malignant cancer becomes malignant and spreads like wildfire. Quick and fast biopsies are not their answer. To give you an idea, 90% of prostrate cancers worldwide are not malignant, but once cut for a biopsy; it can become a potential death sentence.

You'll find a file of my communications with the FDA right at the very end.

In terms of the rest of the files you are about to read, we have extensive case studies on all patients, with slides and videos available for most—MM".

* * * * * * * * *

To learn more about a selection of these medical discoveries Internet search or library research of the following cross-references, applying variations, is suggested:

Ultraviolet Phototherapy-Photoluminescence + Blood Irradiation Therapy + Knott's technique

Microwave Resonance Therapy + high frequency low intensity electro-magnetic treatment

Electromagnetic Energetical Medicine + high frequency high intensity electromagnetic treatment

Microscopes 25,000-50,000 times magnification

Non-Surgical Treatment of Deep Burns + Cellcutana

Down's Syndrome + transplantation human foetal tissue

Insulin Dependent Diabetes Mellitus Type 1 (IDDM) + clinical pancreas transplants

Postcastration Syndrome (PS) + transplantation human foetal tissue

Parkinson's disease + foetal brain tissue + fruit fly

(Note: In North America foetal is spelt fetal.)

* * * * * * * * *

To receive an application from the US Federal Drug Administration (FDA) details on the following must be provided before filing for approval of the protocol is considered:

Pharmacology Studies, Acute Toxicity Studies, Subchronic/ Chronic/Carcinogenicity Studies, Special Toxicity Studies, Reproduction Studies, Mutagenicity Studies, Absorption, Distribution, Metabolism, Excretion (ADME) Studies, Multidose Toxicity/Carcinogenicity

Studies, Bulk Substance Profile, Container-Closure, Storage Conditions, Microbial Quality, Degradation Products, Biological Product Stability Studies, Pharmacodynamics, Clinical Laboratory Evaluation in Clinical Trials, Adverse Events, Laboratory Abnormalities, Early Clinical Experience, Animal Data, Drug Interactions, Potential Interactions, Concomitant Medication Profile, Drug-Demographic and Drug-Disease Interactions, Long Term Adverse Effects, Withdrawal Effects, Abuse and Overdose Information, Statistical Considerations.

Further information can be gleaned throughout this book.

Chapter Ten

The positive thinker sees the invisible,
feels the intangible
and achieves the impossible.

It was just before lunch time when I parked the rental car outside in front of the no parking sign at the Botanical Garden train station in the Bronx, the tough northern borough of New York City, and called Patrick "Paddy" O'Neill. After being screened by two concerned voices, Paddy finally came on the line. "You in town? Where are you?" I had no problem telling him my exact whereabouts, the railway tracks and numerous walls presented many hiding options if the IRA wanted to come and strafe the place with gunfire. "As you exit the station, with the Garden's entrance in front of you, turn right and walk across the bridge road, you'll see the Jolly Tinker public house on the corner in front of you. I'll meet you in there at the bar in five minutes."

Rather than walk the short distance I decided to drive the two hundred yards and survey the place he described.

When you haven't been there for a while there's a discernible streak of false narcissism on the streets of NYC that swamps you. I parked at a meter on Webster Avenue, sliding a quarter in the slot to give me twenty minutes and then jamming another coin in purposefully to make the time stay put.

I was dressed in blue denim jeans and a heavy blue denim jacket, with a red tartan scarf, over a black sweatshirt and white ankle sneakers—good for running, if I had to. I had my long hair let down, no ponytail today. No round John Lennon-style sunglasses were required this overcast day.

As I strolled into the bar, the strains of "Minstrel Boy", a song about a young Irishman who dies in a battle for freedom, was fading out. It was followed loudly on the jukebox by Van "The Man" Morrison's "Why Must I Explain" from the album "Hymns to the Silence". *"I never turned out to be the person you wanted me to be..."* For some reason I thought it fit what I happened to be doing. The louder the better to drown the singed nerves please.

O'Neill was already there standing sipping an early lunch-time pint of ale with another younger man perched on the stool next to him at the counter. The man near the door gave away who he was guarding, just from the way he looked at me. I nodded recognition at him, to let him know I knew.

O'Neill shook my hand, still somewhat stiffly, and introduced me to a slightly-built Feargal—no last name offered—and then asked me what I'd like to drink and eat from the home cooking menu. The bangers and mash with green peas were recommended and was to be their choice for the day, so I made it an order of three with the remark, "Aren't peas always green?" The Noraid or Irish Northern Aid standard green charity coin can, raising funds for the IRA, was sitting obligingly on the counter next to me.

Feargal, who ran the office, had been ominously scanning my face all the time, finally said in his Irish brogue, "Didn't you once play football for Shamrock in Queens, in midfield wasn't it, about ten years ago?"

It was true I had, amazingly, not by deceit but by chance, when a Brazilian friend called Engelmann had asked me to join the team he played for. He and I were the only non-Irish lads in the football club. "Aye, that's right I did, more like eight or nine years ago. I emigrated from England to America at the beginning of 1983 and married a local Italian-American lass. Unfortunately we're divorced now. We won the regional championship the only year I played for them."

Feargal clapped me on the back enthusiastically, "That's right, I always remember a face. I used to come and watch all the home games then at Downey Stadium, under the Triboro Bridge. You were a great goal scorer, man."

Well, that got off to a good start, even though he could probably have added, "that it was a pity I was English", something I heard more than a few times back then. I decided to really delve deeper, to blow them both away. So I took a deep breath and despite the overall negativity of my environment talked to them as if, in my initial ignorance, I didn't know whom they represented.

"Paddy, Feargal, I used to work for MI6 back home. Been retired from the intelligence service since the beginning of 1983. Was in the Royal Navy as a junior officer then they transferred me to the Secret Intelligence Service and worked my way up through the ranks over 12 years. When I got out, I decided to cash in and put my language abilities to good use. Over the years I've travelled back and forth to a couple of strategically selected Arab countries—'cos I figured they had the money, you know—and today, they trust me to deliver the goods. Pay me well, very well indeed."

I'd purposefully gob-smacked the pair of IRA men who were staring in disbelief at me. "Have I said something wrong?" I said innocently.

"No," exclaimed O'Neill, just a bit too hastily, "I never expected you to say that. You connected to London still, comrade?" His jaw was tensing.

I half-lied, "No, not at all." It was a safe bet that they didn't know about my continued access to Mrs Blyton. "My best friend in the Firm passed away a couple of weeks ago and I went to his wake, but that was about it. No nothing. His name was Dave Brennan, by the way, remember him?"

I would have died at that minute just to see a videotape of how my face came over. Their hardened faces gave it all away, about their apparent confusion and surprise at how candid I was. That was the idea.

Then I added, directing a cocktail of half-truths and half-lies at Paddy, "I saw you outside the pub in Glenoe after the funeral, you know. Never seen you before in my life. Danny O'Malley and another bloke got in your car. That same evening a sexy young Irish lady was asking me some very pertinent private questions that got me thinking. If she hadn't done so, I don't think I would have thought much more about it. So I did some homework at a London library on O'Malley, and in the course of researching, came across your own general description. It didn't take a genius to piece two-and-two together to make four. The fact we bumped into each other in Moscow last week was pure, I swear, a pure coincidence, even though I was inclined to think you were following me somehow. But I know for a fact now that you are the chieftain of the IRA, mate." That also produced a couple of gagged spits in the beer as their eyes hardened.

The food arrived and we spirited ourselves alone in the corner of the bar-cum-pub. It concurred with Linda Coughlin walking in the door and hesitantly heading towards us. Her prominent boobs seemed enlarged, but then she was sporting white this time. Her heavily made-up face was like an ashen Halloween mask as she gaped at me.

"Hello, Linda, love. How are you? It's a small world isn't it? Didn't we just spend a nice time together in the 'Province' after the funeral only a fortnight ago?" I stood up to take her limp hand. I enjoyed implanting disinformation among the enemy. The two already stunned men both glanced at each other suspiciously and then at her.

After that comment O'Neill called a time-out and excused the three of them, and they went into a huddle appropriately near the toilet doors. I scoffed my tasty pork sausages, creamy squashed potatoes and processed peas in apparent innocence. Two plates of food steamed, remaining untouched on the table. I could have sprinkled poison over it if I had some on me.

It had gone completely cold when they returned and Linda took the plates away (I imagined for heating in the microwave). They sat straddled on either side of me, leaning forward, facing me. O'Neill, stared into my face threateningly, as if suppressing anger. My stomach had fuelled my gutted brain, thankfully. I gazed calmly into his eyes. Good I thought, I've got him rattled. After almost a full minute of trying to psyche me, he printed in capitals on the paper napkin, 'YOU ALONE?'

Mock grinning, I showed him two empty spaces in the each side of my mouth where the molars used to be. When on active duty behind enemy lines, the left gap was fitted with either a tiny recording transmitter or a cyanide capsule, if you wished to bite the bullet; and the right space had a satellite finding device—when activated—within three-hundred yards of my location. Only one could burst if you retained hard pressure on it and counted to ten, even if you wrongly bit the right one.

He knew what it was and nodded.

'What about on your person?' was scribbled next. I stood up brazenly and took off my jacket, offering Feargal to search me. He did so thoroughly in full view of the bar's customers, who showed no outward interest whatsoever in the goings-on. It was probably a weekly procedure given the presence among them of regular ex-patriot Provisional Irish Republican Army soldiers in civilian uniform. Feargal missed my pen which I carried in my breast pocket. It would have beat against my heart to tell me if I was being recorded. I still kept it after all these years.

Coughlin returned with their warmed up lunch (I noticed the food had been completely replaced and even the plates were different—they took no chances this lot) and inadvertently broke the unspoken code by saying, "Brennan's wife, Mairead, according to Brennan himself, said he plays with a straight bat, you know." She covered her mouth jerkily in apology when the men chopped their hands sharply in the air in annoyance at her intrusion. I curved my lips at her innocent mistake and as a thank you for the compliment on my integrity, held her eyes directly as a form of acknowledgement before I blinked them both simultaneously. The cheeky lass actually did it back to me the next time I glanced over at her.

When the search was over I sat down again slowly and spoke up promptly, "Your food is getting cold, lads." O'Neill remained seated in deep thought for a second and finally the smell of the food penetrated and he joined Feargal in feasting. To me, it was halftime for now and I sipped on my lager. Coughlin remained at attention, hips and tits swaying slightly, like the fervent soldier of love she was. No words were said in the intermission. I listened to the music, humming tunes and tapping my fingers.

When the last man wiped his mouth with the paper serviette and leaned back contentedly, I inclined frontward, "What I want to know is did you order Dave Brennan to be killed?" If he had I am quite sure I would have punctured his Adam's Apple's and slain him right there. For what he had done to me alone I would have sent the other two with him, just for being there. I was fighting to retain my inner composure while hopefully retaining a calm exposure.

It was directed at the top dog's face and I wanted the mouth to respond right at me only. I couldn't find the correct answer by any other means and I had to know. David Brennan wasn't the type to commit suicide, even if he had legs that didn't function. He was much too positive an individual to let a little thing like that get into his head.

O'Neill's continued silence was maddening. It was his turn to play psychological games on me. He told Coughlin to leave. I snapped immediately that I wanted her to stay and hear the answer first. She had heard, third hand, the same as I had about Davy's demise. I could see O'Neill's veins dark purply-blue bulging on his neck; angry at the imposition on his authority.

Finally he forced himself to mumble, "I never knew the man, honestly, never met him. Though I knew he was Danny O'Malley's nephew."

It wasn't good enough for me and I snarled rudely at him, consciously raising my voice, "*That* is an insufficient answer and you know it. How the fuck don't you know. Are you in control or not?!"

He went off the subject. "Is this why you're here, the sole reason?"

"No," I growled, "it's the main fucking reason though." I steadied myself, then went on, "The man was a paraplegic, physically and mentally. He was out of the game. He posed no threat to you-know-what in Ireland."

Eventually he broke the deadlock by turning to Coughlin, who to my surprise, had tears welled in her eyes. "Get O'Malley on the phone now. Wherever he is, I want to talk to him now." As she wheeled away on her stilettos, he called after her, "And don't mention this to him either. I want to be the first to talk to him about it myself. Understand? I'll talk to Gerry and Martin later." They were the IRA's political wing leaders. She nodded back.

I glared back at him when he contemplated me again. A 3-D trick of photography suddenly replayed in slow motion in my head, of his face coming closer and closer, then blackness: Bulgaria was a total blank; him in Libya from afar; him in Cyprus a hundred yards away; him in Moscow across the table from me; and now his face in my face and coming back into focus, so close I could smell his beery-breath and cologne-tinged body odour.

"You want another drink?" he asked nicely, not looking into my eyes. I shook my head yes. O'Neill waved at the bar man with three fingers pointing at our empty pint glasses for a refill. Feargal who had not spoken the entire episode, gave me a nervous shrug. In a way I was glad he was present as he had an inkling of my personality, at least on a football field. I never deliberately fouled anybody.

This matter had nothing to do with Irishmen and Englishmen as such, everything to do with friendship for a fellow human being. And they recognised that, as much as it hurt them to admit it to the perceived enemy sitting in their midst.

O'Neill watched the back of Coughlin disappear out on to the street. "What was the other thing you wanted to talk about?"

"Arabs," I pronounced without hesitation.

"You know about Farkh then?" O'Neill blurted, and then knew instinctively he'd fucked up. His eyelids flickered a fraction.

"No," I lied, "who is he?" I was screaming inside myself, *I gotcha, I gotcha, I gotcha. I caught you lock, stock and barrel!*

His eyelids repeated the blink ever so slightly. "Oh, he's a guy we know. I thought you were checking on him. According to Linda you'd asked who he was." I rated it a good recovery.

Feigning ignorance, I quietly asked him back, "That's true. I saw him but his name still doesn't ring a bell. Should I know him? Will it help my esteemed clients?"

I let him off the hook and he took the bait and swam. "He may, he may not be. What kind of nuclear-related materials do you have access to, comrade?" From that, I got the impression he didn't deal in anything heavier than VX or Sarin, which I assumed he was being supplied quantities of from what had to be Libya via Estonia. Small rockets maybe, but nothing really big enough to obliterate the UK cities of Liverpool or Manchester, if fired from the Irish side of the Irish Sea.

I threw the ball back in his court. "Well what are you looking for?"

His response told me all I wanted to know, "We want RDX, lots of it." RDX is one of the components of the plastic explosive Semtex which was produced in the former Czechoslovakia. The IRA frequently uses it in their home-made bombs, when they are ready for free delivery to the public.

"You can't get that yourself?" I chided. "That's kind of small potatoes compared to what I'm into, Patrick. As I told you before, I acquire uranium and plutonium and the like for mass destruction purposes. *Allah Akbar—* God is Great-stuff. 'The removal of all Jews from this planet is the ultimate objective,' and I'm a working cog in the machine towards that goal," I chillingly lied, convincingly, with a dig below the belt for good measure. "I thought the IRA would have set its sights a little higher by now, like the Red Chinese who are willing to fry millions of their own kind in Formosa."

Feargal and Paddy both flinched visibly. Clearly this conversation was not in their league and it didn't appear to me that they'd thought about it either. Their target was for restoration of confiscated land, not to obliterate a whole country of Protestants who worshipped the same Christian god.

The Irish Catholics and the Prods even fervently supported Liverpool, Manchester United, Sunderland, Celtic and Rangers, English and Scottish football teams. The IRA had a more noble cause as it were, even if it amounted to the ritual murders of British and Irish citizens going about their normal daily lives.

For good measure I iterated, "You do have the same thing in common with the Palestinians regarding the desire for the return of occupied territory. But the difference between you and them is application. You have to understand Arab fundamentalists don't fear death. They *love* it and thirst after it. They're like the Japanese *kamikaze* Zero pilots in World War II. They believe they are beginning a new, much more beautiful life in paradise if they die in the name of Allah. A human bomber becomes a martyr."

I let that sink in. "I could get you Anthrax mind you, or do you have that already?" O'Neill must have decided that too much had been disclosed already and didn't answer my question. He was saved by Coughlin coming back through the pub door with a cellular phone in her hand. Their place must be right around the corner I surmised. She'd been gone for a total of five minutes of fast walking and back based on the faint beads of perspiration on her forehead.

A testy O'Neill snatched the phone from her hand, "Danny? Paddy here. Listen carefully, man. I want to know the truth about your sister's son. Yes, I'm damn well talking about Davy Brennan, fuck it! Was there a price put on his head? Anything you know of at all?"

He was listening to the response while he stared hard at me. Finally he handed the phone to me. My spine shuddered at that second. "Hello?" I said simply, "Nicholas Anderson."

The soft voice at the end had a slight echo from across the Atlantic in Andersonstown, West Belfast. "Hello, you sonofabitch," came O'Malley's lilting Irish accent, all businesslike, not enthusiastic at all. No introduction whatsoever. "When I heard you'd rolled into London unannounced and got together with my lad, I threw a fucking fit. Next thing I knew he'd done himself in. Yes, it's true we were talking to him about how the SIS works internally, inside stuff. No, he wasn't too forthcoming, I must admit. But to kill the kin of my own blood? Kind of ticks me off that you'd even suggest it, if that's what you're saying." You could feel the emotion stretching the senses. Every word carried meaning down the wire.

He wasn't finished, so I didn't say anything. It went static for a second, then his 51-year old voice cracking slightly, posed me a surprise angry question back. "You fucking playing blarney games with us, you git? Fishing around on our side to see what you catch? I should be asking you the same question, arsehole. Did you fuck him up, make him do that to himself...slip him something to drink that would screw him up and put himself out of pain? Even go so far as getting your mate by the hair and turning the oven gas on? Come on, tell me the truth, fucker. You were his best friend once but I wouldn't put it past Her Majesty's Service to do their own kind in, if it's going to effect the end result..."

I didn't even answer the question, but despondently handed the phone back to an on-looking O'Neill. "He's asking me if *I* did him in. I can't remotely figure why he could even think I would. He can sod off," I trailed off. *When you denounce the perceived perpetrator with extreme vehemence and bogus rhetoric, you weaken your own argument with a fair-minded listener.*

I stood up slowly to flex my legs while they ended their conversation. The same bodyguard at the door rose concurrently with me, hands behind his back, anticipatory. I patted myself on the back for calling him right.

Coughlin had the disconnected unit back in her hands. We all looked at each other with nothing to say. I sat back down.

O'Neill, now in the role of mediator, finally said, "O'Malley just told me that they are trying to get a copy of the autopsy. As soon as he does, I'll be able to tell you what we found out. I want you know that he doesn't really think that you would have done his Davy in, but he had to ask you back though." He reflected for a fraction, and then added, "I'd like you to know that I don't think you would have either. But Danny did mention something before he hung up, which I find quite unusual because I happen to damn well know otherwise."

I sensed a weird feeling, and injected, "Well what was that?"

O'Neill stared flatly at me and simply said, "According to our inside information at UKB, there is no record on file at SIS of either a David Brennan or yourself, nor was there ever since they started data entries in CCI."

"What a load of bollocks, you just found that out? There never was," I said sarcastically. "All orders were verbal. I thought you knew that decades ago." Then I added, "Well that's not exactly true about no files. Commands were spoken only but our personal records on our given codenames are still floating around somewhere. I still know what mine was. It's ingrained in my head, after all." *I was really thinking it's a damn lot easier getting into anything than getting out of it.*

The fact that he knew the correct acronym of SIS' Central Computer Index disturbed me. He also told me wittingly or unwittingly that they had a mole inside SIS. UKB was the section working against IRA ops outside the UK.

We left the Jolly Tinker and strolled to the office uphill from the Irish pub, turning left past a ramshackle small park. The lughead was still watching our backsides. He was more obvious than he thought. The location wasn't far away at all and our loyal follower remained at the foot of the steep staircase we climbed, a big ginger top bobbing in the sea of a darker Hispanic neighbourhood of smaller people.

Coughlin had opened the door with a key and gone in, taking her high heels off first. Clambering up the steps, O'Neill ahead of me had interrupted his own dialogue and volunteered to me that the main office was in Manhattan now. Most of the Irish men and women who worked there, who were involved in the joint administration of the US office of An Cumann Cabhrach and its American counterpart Irish Northern Aid Committee, commuted from this area of the Bronx though. It was decided to keep this older place in operation for other matters. He never elaborated.

To which I just casually said, "Everybody knows you're in Seventh Avenue in the city." Nearing the top it smelled a mix of detergent and perfume. *When entering into the lion's den it should come as no surprise that he bites you.*

Once inside, the stark walls didn't give away any clues, no photographs, no plaques. Salsa music could be faintly heard, played loudly across the rooftops in the distance.

The only give-away was the file on Feargal's almost naked desk. Upside down I could clearly read the acronym in a modernist font—WISE. To give Feargal credit he picked it up and put in the drawer, away from prying eyes.

O'Neill was more than obviously anti-English and while I had not paid full attention to his long-winded sermon all the way up from the street, he was coming to a breathless end. "...the idea of England's colonial oppression seemed like a kind of bad joke and they were never really seen as an oppressor because the local citizens permanently relegated themselves as second-class status and collaborated in their own oppression by denying the universal elements of their experiences." Feargal's expression told me he had heard it quite a few times before. When O'Neill finished he excused himself and went to take a pee in the lav.

Feargal looked at me and smiled apologetically, "Sorry about that. The old geezer has his moments, especially after having a few pints. Don't we all." I could only nod absentmindedly while I continued to search for an imaginary needle in the haystack of an office. There's not a hope in hell I'd ever see this place again so I may as well maximise the opportunity.

Coughlin popped her head round the door to say she was off for the rest of the day. I winked at her cheekily, and unseen by Feargal from where he sat she gave me a short tongue stuck out from behind the door. Sex was there, if you wanted to take it, despite our Glenoe-Larne bust up. We heard the outside door close and her starting to step down the wooden stairs.

Feargal kept talking the small talk while waiting for the boss to come back from the bog. "I think she suffers from Munchausen Syndrome by Proxy."

I looked at him for clarification. I didn't know what he meant by that.

"Linda Coughlin is hungry for attention all the time. I know a lot of blokes who have laid her. She's ruined a couple of marriages I know of. She's divorced herself, mind you. Billy, her husband of a few months in Blackburn went from bliss to blisters when he found out she was doing the horizontal boogie with her dance instructor."

I just had to laugh, and responded with a line from a song by the Beatles, "*Four thousand holes in Blackburn, Lancashire.* His name wasn't Billy Shears was it?" He didn't get it. It was an Irish name.

O'Neill came back in, still zipping himself up. "I was thinking about Davy Brennan again. They say that those that knew him were left with a scar on their hearts."

He sat down at his own nude desk, leaned back and looked at the ceiling in deep thought, then declared, "Arabs and Irishmen. I want to talk about Arabs, first. Tell me what you know. I'm searching for a good link from you on how we Irish may best work with them. A plan of action if you may." His hand swiftly went under the desk, as if he was balancing himself, and my pen started thumping on my heart. He was recording our conversation without telling me. A vindication of my previous sarcasm.

"Most parties involved in politics use double-speak—one, the art of oratory until coming to power; another one less effective, after acquiring power. By the way, are you recording this?" I must have looked a sweet angel when I asked it. The devil in O'Neill actually shook his head in denial, as I continued.

"Good. Well for starters you know our Islamic friends call the European Union the 'Christian Club' and that some Muslims view Christianity in the same way some Christians view Judaism—as yesterday's news…"

I shunted on down the track to goodness knows where. Each word part of a tracer's bullets to a distant horizon. *My goal was to remain in contact with him until I figured out what to do with him. I had no doubt he was thinking the exact same thing of me.*

O'Neill surprised me greatly when he articulated so elegantly in his rather posh Irish accent, "I want you to know that I've read the English-language version of the *Quar'an*. 'Fundamentalist' is a term which has no relevance in an Islamic context. 'Muslim fundamentalist' is an oxymoron. Muslim governments, however, rightly consider the term, 'Muslim fundamentalist' to be inaccurate and highly offensive, a product of ignorance and anti-Muslim bigotry. No Muslim, according to the *Quar'an*— or Koran—would identify himself as a 'fundamentalist.'

"So they say terrorism is incompatible with Islam. Though some demented individual who claims to be a Muslim might practice terrorism, he would *not* consider himself a terrorist. Your *kamikaze* related statement earlier in the pub, more or less covered that part, so I know it's true. Those who truly understand the meaning of the *Quar'an* and the teachings of Mohammed would never advocate terrorism and death since the *authentic* Islamic tradition is one based on love, understanding and devotion to praising Allah. So in many respects it's the same for Catholic Irish priests, many who have found their moral and professional impulses at war and are loath to condone the taking of any human life. To them life is sacred."

What a hypocritical piece of shit I thought, they don't do that, many are known to forgive killers deeds. But I was amazed at his knowledge. The head of the IRA has studied the way the mind of Arabic terrorists thinks. Who would have thought of it! He was making an effort to converse himself with me.

If it wasn't for the fact he was the ringleader of killers, I could have liked him for his intellectual insight. I had to smile at him. It even forced a glimmer back at me from him. When he did that, my calm hatred of him instantly returned. *Clash of Civ*

Of course, then I had to say, "Islam, which represents one billion people—almost one quarter of the planet's 5.6 billion people—are waging war against a few million Jews, most of which live in this nation and represent .019% or 5.4 million of America's 280 million. The couple of million Irish have a much bigger battle. Why do you try fighting against the British? You know, the Queen of England is the symbolic leader of 1.7 billion people—that's a second quarter of the world's population—through it's a exclusive global club called the Commonwealth of Britain? It's the biggest illuminati since they began monitoring history. The six foundations of the illuminati, or ruling entrenched élite, if you were, are: religion, the armed forces, rent, the stock market, the legal system and all their assorted bureaucracies like banks, currency exchange, etc. When the mechanism is put into motion, collectively they apply amnesia to wipe our memories off the slate and otherwise deduce the opposition to imply a distortion of untruth. They can play games all day with you and not lose, even if they do mismanage Northern Ireland forever.

"Just to prove a small point, the British prosecute IRA bombers under the Explosives Substance Act of 1883. They don't want to update it, just so they can keep you guys down. Another puny case in point is, what you just told me, that Brennan and I are no longer officially recognised at SIS even though you know we worked there for over a decade. I'm not surprised in the slightest, so why prolong a losing battle? Lastly—forget my teeth—their American cousins can hear us talking as we sit here, if they want. The Pentagon's own spy service, the National Security Agency, eavesdrops on global communications non-stop. The IRA is lucky the US doesn't have a crime of incitement to violence act like the UK so it's not against the law to be a member of a violent-leaning organisation. It only becomes a crime in America if it amounts to *complicity or conspiracy to commit a crime.* So hearsay is permissible but intent is not."

For good measure I added, "Approximately 75% of the world's armed forces continue to be concentrated in the hands of eight states, including the US, China, Russia, India, France, Britain, Japan and Germany—in that order of size. Between them they spend four-fifth of all military funds on the planet…"

"Yeah, and the Americans make 75% of the weaponry for all of them," chipped in Fergal. "Imagine how much money they make from war games."

Then there is the Almighty computer; an exact literate. 'Big Brother' makes lists of people who do not toe the government line and has software filters that kicks out relevant stuff. That's why I misspell on purpose."

My statements brought back the grimness to Paddy O'Neill's face, as he replied, "Listen smart-arse, I know you have a PhD in Social Intelligence, financed by the Royal Navy, but I have one from the university of hard knocks and practical experience. If I didn't think my effort would make a difference, I wouldn't have gone on my glorious path towards victory."

"Conceivable victory, please," I responded quickly, holding his gaze. "You haven't won by a long shot. I wish you luck but you're not even close."

O'Neill, his eyes bulging, all of a sudden started yelling, "Look here, you cunt, I could have you shot for what you just said to me. Fuck you! I was responsible for bumping off Mountbatten, you know, so don't think I couldn't take care of you too, you fucking little shit head. Don't talk to me about not making a fucking dent, motherfucker."

Lord Mountbatten, the Queen's first cousin, at 79, was assassinated in his twenty-nine-foot converted trawler, *Shadow V*, while fishing off the Irish Republic coast of Donegal on 27 August 1979. I knew quite a bit actually because Brennan had been assigned to the case afterwards and had told me all about it. Three others died when a fifty-pound bomb blew the boat out of the water. Later that same day, at Warrenpoint, just over the border in Northern Ireland, a one thousand 200-pounder extirpated a lorry full of British Army troops, killing eighteen instantly. Up to this day, it was the highest toll of life inflicted by the IRA on the British in one day.

I remained as calm as I could be, outwardly, "*You* said you were not making a dent, not me, arsehole."

O'Neill flew out his chair at me and accidentally tripped over a protruding piece of carpet and collapsed at my feet, all in one poorly performed action. I didn't flinch the whole time. My leg stayed crossed the whole time. It was a physical mismatch. Now the IRA leader, an unfit man in his mid-sixties, was huffing out of breath and in slight pain from hurting his knee from the fall at my feet. The lighter Feargal was up instantly, propping his much heavier boss up with his back against the wall. For a moment while they weren't looking at me I believe I could have had both their scalps at once. It was an opportunity but my eventual goal was much bigger than simply having two bad wigs.

You see, even the carpet in your office is probably Made in Britain," I said.

It must have been my dumb shit expression that did it. O'Neill suddenly broke into a pained laugh, to which Feargal mustered a forced grin. Good old, Irish humour even at times like this, I smirked to myself, while joining the tittering ensemble of unlikely lads. "Didn't mean to offend you there. I was just speaking my mind and, I guess, so was the down-trodden rug," I added.

"You're bonkers, Anderson. You know what, I think you're a fucking nutter. Either that or you've got massive balls," piped O'Neill. I ignored it.

I waited until the brief respite was over and they were seated again. Then offered, "Now that we got that out of the way, the precise road to work with the Arabs is as follows, so listen up."

For the next twenty minutes I spoke without being interrupted. It was all smoke and mirrors. I needed another chance to meet O'Neill. At the end, I concluded with the words, "Thank you for the honour of allowing me to live. But do we have a deal?"

O'Neill duly assented and we agreed to meet again. Mission accomplished. *I hadn't lost anything but I gained their respect.*

Chapter Eleven

The next morning across the street from where I stayed at a friend's cubby-hole of a flat on York Avenue whenever I was in New York City, I made a call to the British Embassy in Washington, DC. I identified myself and proceeded to dictate another message for the attention of Mrs Blyton in London. While I was rapidly plugging in the coins I was munching a buttered bagel, something I had promised myself in Moscow not so long ago.

The brief composition read:

'Dear Mrs Blyton,

I'm in NYC on my way back to Europe tonight. Got a few items you may be able to address for me:

1.) Following Brennan's passing, I was kind of wondering if you could update me on the whereabouts of Captain Ian McIntyre? (It would be nice to look him up.);

2.) Have you any idea what the acronym WISE stands for?; and

3.) I'd like some copies of my old SIS ID, if I may. Anything would be appreciated that has been declassified. Would look nice on the mantelpiece in my old age.

I'll try and call you from Europe when I get there tomorrow morning to see if you have any information for me. Written documentation should be sent for my pick up by the weekend at the Air France information desk in Paris' Charles De Gaulle's Terminal B.

Per Linda Coughlin, I've been looking around but I haven't seen her yet either in the flesh or otherwise...

Yours—Nicholas'

I had often wondered what had happened to Mac so maybe she could tell me something. The WISE thing intrigued me, whatever the hell it was. I did not realistically expect any give on my ID request but it was worth a try. The fact renegade Irishmen should even bring the subject up at all told me that there had been a disclosure made not long ago and that my name was active on the playing fields.

One thing was for certain, how on earth would Paddy O'Neill know I had taken a PhD thesis at all? The Admiralty's powers-that-be had thought it a good idea that I cram a couple years of studying a form of cultural anthropology, the theory behind human behaviour, while I juggled a minor first overseas posting in the quiet Copenhagen office of SIS' Danish operations. As far as I knew the Royal Navy, SIS and NATO were the *only* institutions that knew details of my education. Apparently it was not so.

I made another local call, and then I walked back to the tiny apartment to get my bags. Before long I was sitting reading the *New York Times* enduring a packed solid F train for an hour to Brooklyn. Wearing a New York Mets baseball cap, Bob Mendelsohn was there at the foot of the el—the stairway at the bottom of the elevated subway tracks—at the Coney Island terminus. I hadn't seen the lad in a couple of years. Had even fired him once from my thriving company before I got divorced, sold out, and relocated to the left coast. Hadn't changed much. Either way you looked at him, like the spelling of his first name front ways or backwards, he was pretty much the same. An unsophisticated streetwise cynical bastard, born in the ZZ-Top area of Jewish Brooklyn—Borough Park. Despite a trigger-happy image, he picked his fights with care and emerged unscathed. He had a form of drive-by management strategy, teetering between a kind of bullying and scare tactics. Always just tweaking through, surviving for another day. He was a Vietnam veteran and ex-Central Intelligence Agency operative who was fired for unauthorised killings in a fit of anger while on CIA field duty in Africa. At least that's what he told me. For all I knew he may not have been a real Bob at all but he was definitely an old spook.

Today he was a security alarm salesman whose lifestyle was more than his commissions, who when drunk would argue that rain falls upwards and American football—which I'd call rugby with helmets—is the world's most popular game. One just let things be in the name of peace, as wrong as he was, which was often.

Once in his nearby Ocean Parkway apartment and the customary Bud beer can in hands, I gave him a thorough breakdown on my recent events. Though he was labelled a failed operative; he was a successful secret keeper. No matter what, I needed somebody to know something about what I was doing; somebody who understood how these things work. There was no telling what the outcome would be, plus I had my daughter to think of nowadays, and I needed to have my arse covered somewhat. Until now, he never remotely knew of my past life at MI6. Strangely, he didn't seem surprised by my announcement and I didn't think he would be either. That's why I chose him.

Besides he was an expert at electronic bugging. His mid-fifties nasal Brooklynese confirmed that he was the old school type—an Office of Strategic Services-kind, the CIA forerunner—opposite of the archetypal young man who generally joined the agency today: The high school sports standout, Ivy League university graduate, destined for an overseas appointment as chief-of-station with administrative duties and a public relations role, rendering them out of touch with the nuances of universal practicality. Bob was a gutsy street fighter. The kind they needed more of nowadays despite his apparent failings.

"Things haven't changed much at the CIA since I left," Bob sounded bitter. "Their continued practice of paying large sums of money to friendly foreign leaders is in keeping with a morally defensible philosophy of covert political action, and that the First Amendment is only an amendment. The role of secret agencies in defending national security has evaporated even more with the disappearance of the Soviet Union."

All I could say back to this opening remark at the table was, "Well, the problem there, of course, was that it was usually the CIA's own perceptions and not realities that governed their thinking." He drank to that.

As a Briton, I thought I was getting anti-American in my old age: Bob already was. When he wasn't drinking himself into a stupor at home, he was a gregarious reader of on his home country's civil war history. Our dialogue consisted of long factual statements by him; followed by my answers, only to prove that I *was* listening. His favourite repetition was usually along the lines of, "Yo, you paying attention to me?"

"The American people are unknowingly trapped in a cancerous addiction of sorts, that their lives are controlled by 7,000 hyenas encircling them. Should an average yokel make an average honest mistake, then an attorney will make them pay dearly for it. They're like bankers and politicians, tools and keepers of the pigs' money, the chimera.

"Other keepers of da mon*aay* are my old employers. Though it's an official secret, it is believed, the annual CIA budget exceeds US$25 billion. They've been practically operating as a nation unto itself and start more warmongering than the majority of the world put together. The American people have experienced the distortion of the truth by intelligence officers in order to please existing policy, set beforehand. It's a serious problem when the lie takes over. If only the meeting rooms could speak. We'd learn more then what really goes on."

I could only respond to him in my best upper class English accent, "'Empirically groundless and, therefore, an analytically useless abstraction,' old chap. Mind you, we have identical problems in the UK believe it or not though our budget is not as high as that."

Bob needed to lighten up. To me he was *exactly* what New York City did to people who stayed too long. It made one too aggressive and too defensive.

He eventually heaved his shoulders, sighed, and ended on one more dig, "Well...the biggest problem in the good ol' US of A is those defence lawyers have access to the US government's evidence through the legal discovery process. My personal problem is that I'm caught inside Big Brother and I can't get out." He was one of millions who were trapped by the country's bureaucracy of minimum-wage bunglers. It was the final lid on a serious subject before we got into the lighter topic of baseball and why Englishman catch line-drives with their bare hands in the sissy's game of cricket. He did drive me to the airport afterwards despite our cultural differences and we did agree to stay in regular touch while I was away. And for that I was grateful.

* * * * * * * * *

That evening I was at the old PanAm circular spaceship terminal at New York City's John F. Kennedy International Airport, checking in on Delta Air Lines direct flight to Nice in the south of France, JFK-NCE. The plane was booked solid with many American executives attending an international television programming conference in Cannes, my destination on the French Riviera.

Following a five-hour nap, the sight of the snow white peaks of the Alps fully awoke me. The Mediterranean coast was always an awesome sight. While still only seven o'clock in the morning local time, the sun was shining brilliantly, fitting as this was the magnificent *Côte d'Azur*—the coast of blue—the playground of the élite, the rich and royalty. Monte Carlo, Principauté de Monaco, and its casinos with an evening dress code were a few miles down the road; in the opposite direction to Cannes' topless beaches.

"How was the land of extreme materialism?" Ursula laughed, after the kissing and hugging was over. I must say, I hadn't noticed how sexy she was before, now that she was in a much skimpier outfit than the fur coat attire of Moscow and its unsheathed blacked-out bedroom.

The purple convertible Porsche Carerra with the top down flew past the silver bullets of Renaults and faithful Simcas along the *autoroute* west towards her hometown. I found myself humming the signature tune to *"Un Homme et Une Femme"*. The half-hour ride over *les clics*—the kilometres—seemed only a few celluloid minutes, before we were pulling up to the Carlton Hotel. I whistled even more. This was *the* most luxurious hotel in Cannes, right on the promenade and facing the ocean. "I know the manager," was her only comment about getting a room on a busy convention week, while I wondered *how* well she knew the fellow.

As soon as the busboy was tipped off and the door to the suite closed, the inevitable intense sexual attack of each other took place. Then I slept again, exhausted. When I woke up, it was already late-morning and the room was empty. "Damn jet lag," I mumbled to nobody. I stumbled towards the *la salle de bain* and flicked the light on. As I stood there about to relieve myself, it was only then I noticed her brazen handwriting in red lipstick on the toilet seat's inside lid with a heart drawn expansively around it. "Before you get pissed off at me, let's have lunch! See you downstairs in the hotel gardens restaurant at noon, *chéri*. XXX."

Just before twelve, after showering and shaving, I got a table with a view of the jet set parading themselves like pheasants along La Croisette. The small town was littered with corporate global network suits with flunkies in tow and I actually received a useful business card or two from the next table. The lady showed up minutes later and we played out polite greetings on a more formal stage, in deference to her marital status. Despite her usual Latin-style gesticulations and protest to have a real meal, I *had* to have my favourite ham and butter sandwich inside a *baguette,* a *1664*—the local choice of beer, with a *café noir* after, which is something I did every time it was my first day in France. It was my first day back in England equivalent of fish 'n' chips or everything bagels in the States. The only thing which I did not miss was the stinking *Disque Bleu* cigarette smell.

Between there and a secluded dinner that night at a quaint restaurant in Cap d'Antibes, the next town over—again to avoid gossip—we went window night shopping along the exclusive fashion stores, no holding hands allowed. Then she went home alone while I hugged the hotel pillows instead. I was quite surprised I ached for her when she left.

Only at the end of second evening's dinner, when we were sipping *crème de menthe* outside on the hotel balcony, did we have our first serious conversation about anything. It was then that she learned what it was I was really trying to promote, the medical files I'd read, and the lofty goals Molody and I were striving for. There was no mention of SIS or IRA or the S-E-X we had just had. But her soft response was encouraging, "When you climb a mountain, you don't jump over it; you climb step-by-step, and you eventually climb the first mountain."

Over the last two days and nights I was in Cannes, I got to learn a couple of things about her. Or specifically about her ageing husband, who she still cared for but no longer loved. He is waiting to die." She appeared quite apologetic about her statement, that she would say that to her younger lover. It was then that I fully realised that it wasn't really me *per se* that she was so happy with, but the *idea* of me and what I represented in her mind. Whatever that was. Nevertheless I enjoyed her company tremendously.

One aspect about Georges Durance which really did appertain to me was that back in 1968 as a new diplomat he had been instrumental on forming the concept that information warfare is a permanent state of war. When the blueprint was approved he had worked with a unit that consisted of the French defence ministry, DGSE—the French secret service, and *Direction du renseignement militaire*—French military intelligence. The end result was the formation of *Centre d'électronique de l'armement*, known as CELAR, which was established outside the small town of Bruz, near Rennes in Brittany. Nicknamed the Trojan Horse by insiders, it was the electronic warfare centre of the country. "I understand CELAR today employs 750 and has a staff of 150 in Paris," shrugged Ursula. "CELAR monitors but does not operate spy satellites such as HELIOS and SYRACUSE. The next generation—HORUS, will be ready by the year 2005."

Even though I wasn't trying to find out information; it would still come at me. For as long as I knew Ursula Durance, I was never to know if that statement was planted deliberately or not. It was truly highly confidential material of national defence importance. Something I shouldn't get to hear lying in bed.

To get an inkling of how much wealth she enjoyed, when she drove me back to Nice Airport on the morning of the third day, there was an all-day strike by airport workers. No planes were taking off or landing and I knew I was going to miss my connection from Paris to Kiev. The woman seemed to be prepared for anything and produced an overnight bag from the back of her sports car, paid cash at the Air France counter and when the strike was over, boarded the Airbus with me. For each night I had stayed in town she had returned to her residence and now she decides this.

I found myself strongly attracted to the body language that accompanied her speech. Until then, I never realised that the art of words was so important in their translation by another form.

And so she paid for our night in Paris at a very nice hotel on the Left Bank overlooking the Seine River. On the expensive taxi ride from the airport into the city centre, she pointed at the *Quai d'Orsay*, the French parliament, where her husband used to work.

Much like New York City, I never truly enjoyed Paris. The materialistic atmospheres were much too alike.

When I kissed my sleeping beauty early the next morning, I promised her I would be meeting her in Egypt, whenever it was she was going to go. When I closed the door, I could hear a faint crying on the other side and it dug at my emotions greatly.

Back at the modern space age Air France terminal at CDG, after checking in I went immediately to the information desk. The envelope from Blyton was there waiting for me. It was only then that I remembered I hadn't called her as promised and didn't do it the night before either when I was here. Hopefully she would understand how distracted I was with a very pretty German lady.

I tore it open. She must have written it in a hurry because all it stated was:

'Nick,

1.) McIntyre: Certified with bipolar depression in 1980. Took early retirement with pension. Whereabouts unknown.

2.) WISE: Only entry we have is World and Islamic Studies Enterprise, Tampa, Florida, USA. A think tank off-campus at the University of South Florida used as a front to enable Middle Eastern terrorists masquerading as scholars to enter the United States. Also involved in fundraising for causes unknown. *(Note: Personally I could speculate there! "C" would like to know why you ask about WISE? Please elaborate on your findings forthwith. Thanking you in advance.)*

3.) Request for copies of your records declined per the last Security Service Act passed by law in the UK as well as normal Official Secrets regulations.

- EB'.

The blood rushed to my head. *"Request for copies of your records declined…"* I read the contents again, trying to find a hidden meaning or a clue. To hell with telling you about my findings my dear!

On the way to the departure gate, I bought this week's English-language *The European*. It carried a good review of the past seven days. But I didn't read it, as I was in retrospect all the way to Kiev about my own long week gone.

* * * * * * * * * *

After touchdown, as the blue and white 737 cruised along the ground towards the airport terminal in the distance, the day was heavily overcast with evidence of dirty ice sprinkled the ground. A sign at the top of the main building faintly read *"Kijev, Ukrainskaja* Soviet Socialist Republic" in an awkward attempt at Anglicised Russian. The Ukrainians still hadn't pressed forward their own identity after supposed freedom from Russification.

As I cleared passport control, Michal Molody was walking to me with a dark reddish-brown fur coat and a matching hat in his hands. He put the Russian bear's skin around my shoulders. It was a surprise gift from his wife and him to me.

I couldn't get much out of him regarding his holiday at home and the work he'd be conducting here in the Ukraine. About the only thing I squeezed out of him was that most of his family now liked to be known as the quiet velvet revolutionaries following the collapse of communism in Slovakia. Later, morosely, he added quietly, that whenever he left his homeland, it reminded him of that sad time before, when he thought he had left forever and that was when he had last seen his father alive. "It's a very terminal word, you know—good-bye. Caterina and I always sit on the settee at my mother's house in silence for several minutes before departing." I knew that it was a local custom to do so before commencing on a long journey.

A few days later, Mike asked me if I would be interested in driving all the way south to Armenia with them—an 800-mile trip as the crow flies—as he had a challenging medical study in progress there. The choice was being in Moscow for about a week by myself or coming with them. I chose the latter but I also had other reasons to stay in the upper regions of the Ukraine a wee bit longer.

Once I'd ascertained their route, it was agreed they would pick me up in two days time at the airport in Sevastopol in the Crimea Peninsula, a naval port city on the Black Sea. Besides I'd been there covertly before so felt no need to tour that dour deepwater hell again.

They then drove me back to Kiev Airport where I caught a clanking locally-manufactured Antonov turbo-prop flight to Lviv, a major city in the west of the country that the Russians liked calling Lvov.

At Lviv, the usual bored gypsy cab drivers were hanging around in a bunch outside the arrivals baggage area. Instead of them harassing me, I went towards them. They all jumped to attentiveness as only the police moved towards them like that apparently. Eventually I handpicked a wizened old hand who gave his name as Pavlo. Though he spoke Russian, he spoke Ukrainian fluently without a single Russianism, and I selected him as he could probably find what I was searching for. It was a shot in the dark I was prepared to take.

Once in the car, when he asked my destination. I simply said, "UNA or UNSO." He visibly hardened and looked at me in the back seat through the reverse mirror. I was waving a US$20 bill, "And this is for you on top of the fare."

He sat there thinking for a few seconds. "Sir," he said, "you are talking about a 50-mile trip one-way due west of Lviv, it's almost right on the Polish border. It'll cost you more than that, I'm afraid. Plus I've got to get back."

"Sire," I replied, "you *are* going to wait for me for at least one night too." After haggling for a while, in the end we agreed to sixty total—all paid in US dollars, half in cash immediately, and the balance upon our return to Lviv Airport. He would take care of the petrol, while I'd take care of his food and accommodation for the night. It was a great deal for him. He was making a week's wages in one day. I, on the other hand, didn't have to find the place, which made it an even better deal for me. I wasn't going to let him know it though.

Once in the vicinity Pavlo had to stop and ask directions a couple of times. The third pedestrian refused to give any information until we gave him some money. That cost me another fiver in American money.

Amazingly that likely lad must have felt obliged to tell me that UNA and UNSO were acronyms respectively for Ukrainian National Assembly and Ukrainian People's Self-Defence, adding, "Radical fascists organisations, though they'll claim they aren't. UNA was the political wing and UNSO it's storm troopers division. Be careful of those boys." Then the cheeky little bastard winked and sauntered off kissing the money in his hand as if he was a hooker.

Approaching the camp eventually, I heard the sound of a burp gun. So called as it sounds like a loud prolonged burp and not the usual rat-tat-tat. Had to be a Russian-made PPSH, supposedly the best machine gun in the world and far better than an Israeli Uzi. Fires a 6.72 in a bottlenecked 9-mm. shell. High velocity with little recoil and a muzzle brake. Extremely accurate with an eighty-one-round drum magazine, which fires 1,400 rounds a minute. A short pull of the trigger fires three rounds while people drop, swatted like flies.

When the car slowly came around the corner of the wet foreboding forest, we were forced to stop as there were three menacing black-clad characters with balaclavas in the middle of the road pointing SKS Russian rifles at us. Pavlo's eyes were as wide as the holes cut out of their facemasks.

Within minutes we were hauled in front of the fresh-faced company commander, obviously a Red Army dropout. These were all very young men. The oldest couldn't have been over 18. The elderly taxi driver was cowering and looked like he'd already wet his pants based on the dampness around his crotch.

"What do you want?" the uniformed leader barked at me.

"I wish to see Andry," I replied calmly, meeting his eyes.

"We have several," he screamed unnecessarily at me. "It's a common name around these parts." He tittered crazily at himself, proud of his authority.

I was thinking he was perhaps the slightly mental product of nearby Chernobyl and remained unflustered. I spoke quietly in return. "Yes, I know, comrade, but there is only *one* black man in the whole of the Ukraine called Andry and who speaks perfect Ukrainian. Tell him his good friend Nicholas Anderson from England is here."

That gummed him up quickly and I noticed the muzzles of the guns trained on us lowered. He snapped his fingers and a scrawny-necked twelve-year old obediently handed him an old radio-controlled mobile phone unit, another stolen relic of the recently dismantled Soviet army. Then as he turned away suspiciously, talking so I couldn't hear him, I looked around the base.

There was a badly done freshly painted sign that read, 'UNA into power, UNSO into the assault!' All of a sudden there was a sound of whacking. Another older boy was beating a younger one with a cane mercilessly, about 25 whacks in rapid succession. He was yelling like a madman, "Poverty! Vegetarianism! Abstention! No one is innocent! I'll teach you for sleeping, you lying dog!" The young soldier was scared stiff and stood to rigid attention, grimacing in pain as the swats were administered. Russian *dedovshina* was alive and well still even in the new Ukraine. It was the abuse that fresh conscripts to the army were expected to receive from senior soldiers that they called rule of the grandfathers.

The young commander was back, ignoring the beating just ten yards away. "We are taking you by car. The driver stays put." He still was shrieking like a lout, throwing his weight around.

I was slightly taller than him, and took a step towards him. My mouth was within inches of his flared nose and I said loud enough for everybody to hear, "*You* will look after my driver and feed him well. If not, I will come and beat you with a cane myself. Do you understand me?" His red-stained grey eyes drilled hard into me before quivering a fraction, and he finally slowly nodded. "Good," I lowered my voice, and directed my voice to his ear. "We understand each other. You may carry on with your duties. But try to relax, will you, you are annoying me with your uncouth manner. Even obedience has its limits." *It is almost a lack of respect not to take somebody at their word.*

Less than a ten-minute drive later I was getting out of the brand new lightweight Gazel truck in front of a large, modern building. It was set in the middle of a dense woods surrounded by an unwalked-on carpet of whiteness. As I stood there with the sunlight filtering through the over-hanging trees, I noticed a curtain on the top floor being pulled aside and a figure standing there looking down. The curtain closed.

Seconds later, a huge black man in army fatigues and soft slippers was clambering down the steps towards me with his arms outstretched. No words were spoken as we hugged each other warmly.

Minutes later I was sitting with my feet up in front of the fireplace. At his command the patrol that brought me had gone back to put the taxi driver in a room for a night. Andry came in with a bottle of blackberry-flavoured alcohol drink and two glasses. As he closed the door, he instructed everybody not to bother him for the rest of the night.

He was one year older than me, in his early-forties. He hadn't put on any discernible weight and looked very fit. Though not greying, his closely cropped forehead showed signs of an expanse. I had never ever asked him how he had ended up in the Ukraine. But I recalled once seeing a family photograph in his room, during the student days of PLU, a black boy with his white parents. I had to surmise his Ukrainian father, who had served in the forces of the Soviet Union, adopted him from either Angola or the Congo.

He had been a central defender in the university football team in Moscow and nobody messed with him. At PLU in the days of communism—much like my own political beliefs—I'd never thought of him as remotely *communista*. Despite our friendship, he leaned to the far right, and was his own brand of fascist. He was also a blatant homosexual but he respected my sexual preference. But we had a strange love for each other, which I could never explain. Andry and I were opposites in everything.

We talked far into the night. If food was served, I had a hard time remembering it. "Asceticism, obedience and meditation are the three sources and component parts of UNSO's philosophy," he'd said. "The Ukraine is still under Russian influence, even if they did give us independence. Ethnic Russians number 22% of our population. The facts remain they will control us economically. We will continue to owe them monetarily for the natural gas, the petroleum and all other industrial tools we need. After they've exhausted our scant resources and we have run up large bills, they will just walk right back in and take us over again. Monitor it closely in the years to come, Nicholas, you will see I am right. It could be easy to disregard this movement of mine, if it weren't for the queer twists and turns history takes from time to time."

Over the hours I learned that he and his supporters didn't trust the Russians one iota. "They've introduced western-style capitalism and all the decadent things that come with it, even allowing religions again, another form of mind control. They've installed their very own figurehead to run the Ukraine for them. Despite western thinking, the Russians are smart. They still have over twenty million of their people living in their former colonies around the world. They haven't returned home…they are ready to resume the expansion when the time is right. The Chinese follow the same game plan with many more expatriates overseas than that. Now the Americans will be coming in big numbers.

"To best explain it to you, UNSO is like the IRA and UNA is Sinn Fein—our own political party. It is said Sinn Fein modelled itself on the Hungarian resistance to the Hapsburgs, so I studied that era too. The purposes of our organisations are to be *ready* for when the next collapse comes. The last Ukrainian nationalists—the men from the forest—under General Stepan Bandera failed in their quest for a truly independent Ukraine after the last World War. This is a long-term plan and we know what we have to do to preserve *real* freedom for the Ukraine, and it starts with those young men you met at the camp."

I updated him on myself too on the two decades I hadn't seen him, and about my life in the British secret service, taking great care not to mention individuals names, only the groups they represented. It seemed he was particularly interested in an introduction to the IRA leaders I mentioned, to form a sort of joint venture. I told him I'd think about it. He understood that completely and kindly said to me, "I learned more about you when I looked in at you, not outside you. You have become the man I thought you would become. You are rare in that you know what you are about." I thanked him for that nice compliment and said he was the same.

He took me to my bed in the house and said he'd come and wake me in the morning, as a good big brother does.

As I lay down, looking at the full moon's light shining in, I was deep in thought. Well, it had been a hunch on my part, I couldn't remember Andry's surname to save my life. But the current mood of the nation fitted the mood of the man who had outlined his goals for his beloved country over twenty years ago. If he said he was going to do it, then it was a certainty. He was that way, like I was.

The strange thing was that I had managed to recall only the initials of his intended group even though I didn't know what they stood for. Little does he know that he had just triggered my own long-dormant idea. Not as remotely coercive or radical as his, it was nevertheless meant for the betterment of the world we lived in, especially those who were downtrodden and were from underdeveloped nations who never had a chance to educate themselves: *I would start logging information towards a book on my experiences.*

One could see that communism wasn't going to last, even when I was a student. I felt the same about capitalism today because of extreme materialism. There was a non-violent third way of the people taking the best of communism and capitalism: I believed it would be by the people deciding by vote on important issues and government following *our* directives, not elected politicians acting on what they think we need. Just like Andry, I must be proponent towards that yet unnamed fairer real democratic system.

At the breakfast table while eating *oseledsi* (pickled fish) and *holubtsi* (cabbage rolls) in the morning, a happy Pavlo joined me. He'd had a good evening with the youngsters and would now be forever promoting the cause of UNSO.

The first group discussion of the day had been in response to somebody's thought provoking statement, "I prefer to see us as guerrilla resistance fighters rather than a terrorist organisation." I sat and listened to their viewpoints with interest. It was really a propaganda get-together.

The best answer by an erstwhile youth had been, "Governments can always brand freedom fighters as 'terrorists' and televise their 'barbarism' lacking ideology, etcetera, while the so-called 'rebels' can't respond. These types of governments can't win on military terrain, they just win with their public relations campaigns." As has tried to solve this

Another simply put rhetoric had been, "The poor Ukrainians *were* the rope in the Russians versus the West tug-of-war." That drew a voracious toast of tea and coffee all around.

So when it was my turn I said, "I have studied this subject for most of my professional life. Certain events happen because of political considerations most people don't understand. Terrorists and/or freedom fighters have been compelled by circumstances into their current position. They no longer wish to be humiliated and denied their rights to a common living. Not doing anything is a choice too. But remember this: <u>Extremism does not win friends; it is the enemy of the people.</u>"

The room stayed silent as a sea of faces looked down the long table at me sitting at the end. After a muted minute Andry nodded and that was the signal that the breakfast's group discussion was over.

Before we left, Andry and I went for a nice long walk in the milky woods, which he said he usually did alone every morning after eating. We didn't talk too much but when we did, we spent most of the time discussing our former colleagues at Patrice Lumumba. I brought up Molody's name only in passing, but he didn't know the name or face. He had also mentioned how successful the Venezuelan student *El Gordo* had become— we'd once attended a party of his together where, ironically, I had first met Mike—but we didn't pursue that avenue as time was getting short and I had to leave for Lviv.

He did tell me, however, that he believed he was HIV positive. The news alarmed me and I promised I would be back in touch with him. Meanwhile I told him then what I knew, for him to maintain his health and combat it. It was a subject I was keenly interested in and had kept myself abreast of the problem since the day it was made public.

On the taxi ride back I perused the past 24 hours: Andry's strong ethnic identity enveloped the accident of his colour, so much that his hair was permanently dyed peroxide blonde. When he enters the hall of mirrors his reflection will match that of Guevara's in the public image—that is if he doesn't die of AIDS first or like the last ascendant, Bandera, get himself bumped off by the Russians. Despite his aims, I hadn't endorsed his movement. I preferred to wait and see, and had told him so. But I would lend my support to him where I could, within reason.

At the airport, the scheduled Air Ukraine flight to Sevastopol with a pit stop in Simferopol, was delayed four hours. So Pavlo at no charge had driven me proudly around a dismal Lviv for two of these hours. Nobody in their right mind would love to live here. It was a world of one bland colour grey. Plenty of large, unproductive factories and a lack of a proper financing were the twin evils of the communist economic system. It had to change to survive and now capitalism was following in its footsteps…

It was already dark when I arrived in Sevastopol on the Crimea Peninsula, *Krymski Poluostrov*. Mike and crew had got there earlier in the afternoon and had gone sunbathing, seeing it had been a rare sunny day there. All three of them appeared mildly tanned and happily refreshed on the Black Sea in the Ukraine in late-April.

The naval port was saturated with *praporschiks*, midshipmen on a few days leave, soliciting the sexy *natashas* for hire. I was stunned at the number of homeless—*bomzhi*—I witnessed. It was another sign of the current times.

Before long we were on the coastal route east to the Russian border. The town of Balaklava came and went and I momentarily thought of the initial dread of seeing those UNSO young men with their black hoods down over the heads. The road was sandwiched between *Krymskije Gory* and *Cernoje More*—the Crimean Mountains on the left and the Black Sea on the right. We stayed the night in Yalta, famous for as the place where the victors divided the spoils of World War II—only the conclusion resulted in initiating the Cold War as more money was to be made by the players.

The next day we had been detained at length at the Ukraine-Russia border post at Krym-Kavkaz and had to buy our way out. For the first time ever that I recalled, one of our guards, the driver, actually spoke without being spoken to. "All that for a few fucking *kopecks*," was all he muttered— a few coins of Russian money used for bribery. "Scavengers trying to find dirt." Then he apologised for his use of an obscenity, like the good obedient soldier he was.

His swear word seemed to trigger Dr Molody who then went on to give me his own long-thought out pessimistic opinion on the country we'd just left. "They are people steeped in negativity and the acceptance of failure. From my perspective, looking at them as an outsider, I can see their easiest solution is simply not to think about the problem at all, and hopefully, it'll just go away. Of course, it's a fatalistic attitude and it never really does go away. It is a classic hallmark of losers, which brings to mind the following slogan that I would love to shout from the rooftops at them, but will they even understand? 'Winners never quit and quitters never win.'"

I was jolted for a nano-second because that was Dave Brennan's favourite saying but I didn't want to interrupt him. "It is a sad conclusion on my part but I would love that special Ukrainian individual or two to prove me wrong tomorrow by accomplishing *something* worthwhile; something their countrymen can be proud about. And from this lead, others will carry the mantle to the next level of achievement. They've been under the thumb of Russia too long."

It was my cue. I looked at him and it was on the tip of my tongue to tell him about Andry and his ambitions. Instead I said, "I've got a Ukrainian guy that I've known, almost as long as I've known you, who thinks he is HIV-positive. You need to meet him because he may be the *something* you talked about. But I don't want you to charge him for your consultancy." Mike replied that it would be no problem and that he would like to meet whoever it was, before going back to gazing out of the windows at the scenery. He accepted my judgement, I was pleased to observe.

I sat looking at Michal's profile, as if for the first time, and thought about his encyclopaedic command of words. He does well with scenes painted large on canvas, and can vividly recall any event in minuscule detail from years before. Yet he does not claim to know everything nor pretends to fully understand what he says. He really deserves a Nobel for honesty as much as Andry does for his and should replace today's politicians on the podium.

Just a few hundred miles off to the left somewhere was Rostov-na-Donu, my Russian undercover home town for a couple of years. I'd never even been there and didn't have any inclination to either. Yet I knew its street map by heart.

Michal Molody wasn't wrong about the Ukraine, but what he said could have applied to Russia too. The Cold War had ended on the third week of December 1991. A fiscal quarter later, Russians still do not have the foggiest notion what democracy is all about and how it evolves around money. If they had an election right now, I doubt anybody would want to come. A nerve centre of capitalism they are not. It seems they have a willingness to fail too. Now that the curtain and the wall are down, they are putting up a wooden fence—around themselves.

Chapter Twelve

The grim reaper always escapes his prison to take you back.

Even though it's still not declassified, this is the story of Operation SEED. The story of my previous visit to Crimea.

On a wintry morning in late-January 1978 as it was bucketing down I dutifully turned up at the Special Boat Service's headquarters and training centre in the appropriately named town of Poole in Dorset, on the English south shore. The SBS are a unit of the Royal Marines, which in turn is part of the Royal Navy.

I was seconded at the time from the RN to the SIS' Sovbloc controllerate so I knew my next mission was going to be an infiltration to the Soviet Union or its satellite states. Whenever R3, SIS' in-house naval section, referred to anything as black you immediately knew that it was classified as dangerous. The pink dossier's evaluation page read: "Acceptable degree of risk—high. Avenue of escape—zero." I took a deep intake of breath when I read that. Very few ops got such an appraisal.

I knew I had been selected for this particular deep cover job for a number of reasons: That my trial on the black (illegal entry across another country's border) entry into the Soviet Union the first time was deemed a success and I had only just returned from the assignment four weeks prior;

that I spoke Russian fluently with the southern accent of a man from Rostov-na-Donu; that I was a former Royal Navy helicopter pilot who was used to extreme vertigo; and that I was a champion swimmer. All were key pointers as to why I was the right man for this job. And it wasn't going to be over ground but under water. Hence being at SBS now.

The reason this particular entry mode was chosen, the file stated, was because the KGB's Eighth Chief Directorate's satellite ELINT ops couldn't pick-up electronic sonar signals under sea level, nor could it use thermal imaging over water yet and because I had to bring in light cargo, too. There was a solitary by-line about rapid response killer dolphins but I didn't understand it, figuring I'd learn more about that in time.

During the medical examination soon after arrival, the military doctor had held my upper arm and intoned, almost to himself, "I see you have vaccination marks. I'll make an appointment with the dermatologist to have them removed immediately. I'm surprised nobody noticed that before. Here at SBS you will learn that we pay more attention to detail than most. In certain countries, where they don't have inoculation programmes, it would certainly mark you out as a foreigner. We wouldn't want all that unwanted attention over a stupid scar, would we, young man?" I knew then that this was a very serious mission and that if anything went wrong, I was going to bear the consequences alone. It's an unnerving feeling when you're an English lad of 26.

Plus for good measure, I was handed a coded telex that congratulated me on being internally upgraded at the Ministry of Defence to a couple of notches above top secret rating. I suppose that new standing was to make me feel important and more confident even though I still felt I could end up being a sacrificial lamb, no matter what words were used.

When the physical test was over, in the SBS mess hall, I was introduced to an unfriendly staff sergeant who shall remain unnamed because I can't recall his name nor his face. But I do remember the man resembled a turtle as his neck was sunken into his shoulders and he had a slight hunch. Though his body movements were slower than the average, it was his rapid fire speech that startled me. This concrete grey bloke was to exclusively train me—read that as bully me senseless—for the next fortnight in preparation for the coming sortie. His powerful handshake told me he was going to be a hard man and he was indeed. An SBS Arctic unit veteran who was formerly in 45 Commando Group Royal Marines and an experienced warfare frogman, he was my own live-in personal trainer.

My next full day in rainy Poole was taken up not with swimming but with reading various reports, including memorising the field (especially the Black Sea bathymetry's unique whirlpool currents). It also went into elaborate detail on how I would rendezvous in the Crimea with a Russian man called Such.

I was to undergo further acclimatising in Turkey; be dropped by plane as close to the Soviet Union as they may dare to fly; from that point on I was to proceed both over and underwater to the designated landing point in the bay halfway between the peninsula south of Feodosiya's More shipyard and the village of Ordzhonikidze; meet Such the next day; receive my Soviet ID papers from him; accompany him to a secret nuclear facility to undertake a limited surveillance op; and from that juncture on, we were to split...he returning to whence he came with the information we had jointly gathered, while I was to ensconce myself at a Moscow safe house to await further instructions on where to set-up shop to begin my life there as an NOC spy.

Day Three in Poole was completely taken up with the expected underwater fitness regimen that would have bordered on the insane for landlubbers, except for the fact I had been a water baby since birth, so actually lapped it up. Every other day for the next two weeks it was 10 hours a day being devoted to learning the basic skills of a diver and more. I particularly enjoyed the feeling of scaling ship's sides with the smooth sliding magnetic hands. But the worst part about it was getting used to the cottonmouth from breathing the 100% dehumidified air, not to mention constantly being refitted into the initially awkward Canadian-made White's dry suit (so that I would be free to operate in the flexible manner required and not freeze to death in the meantime).

At the end of his first week's course my lovely, unsmiling SBS technical expert informed me that the next week involved actual diving under the ice up in the Shetland Islands, north of Scotland, which would require special advance training, special equipment and special safety procedures...all of which were duly crammed into my overloaded skull and aching body. During the short time we were in that frozen outpost, which was supervised by the RN's own Section 16, which specialised in covert landings on Russian soil by sea entry, he repetitively told me how to protect against ice formation in the First and Second Stage; check the viz conditions underwater; how snow reduced the growth of microscopic life forms in the water; and how much clearer an object would be seen moving down there, i.e.: me. (Viz is diver slang for visibility.)

"Viz could only be 10-feet in the summer but in winter it can be up to 100-feet. However, as you near shore—passing into 154-foot maximum depth—the water will turn brown from the sediment reducing the viz to almost zero. Crimea is one of the few areas in the world where rivers can still clean themselves naturally. Also you must be made aware that the Soviets have reportedly trained dolphins to patrol sensitive security areas, so, *if* at any time one comes up to check you out….when you pat it, make sure you immediately attach the timed special magnetic limpet device like the one I'm holding here to its body somewhere. Then check it is more than 25-feet away before you to decide to detonate. No, I'm not pulling your leg. Quite serious. Upon its second run at an unknown (to it) human, the dolphin, we're told, is trained to blow itself up with its own attached underwater concussion grenades. So, lad, you have to get the damn thing before it gets you—understand that? If the situation is called for, the force of your own explosion will rock you off your feet if you're too close. If the dolphin beats you to the draw then it won the duel…you were killed by a fucking suicidal fish that was cleverer than you, that's all I can say. 'Death by drowning' is what it'll officially state on your demise report.

"Nevertheless, I'll give it to you straight in your favourite football terms: this route was chosen for the simple fact that the Russian goalkeeper has all the angles covered except for the space between his legs and that's where we're aiming to shoot…right through the only open space in its defence."

He let that sink in, smirked an ugly smile with a side tooth missing, before continuing.

"I will add, Flight Lieutenant Anderson, that we have no way of knowing if their killer dolphin story is true or part of their disinformation policy. But it is technically possible. It'll probably be too cold down there for them, especially the closer you are to shore and under ice. They can't come up for air. But out in the open sea, I don't know… You'll have to use your noddle, OK?"

I nodded, dumbfounded.

He too shook his head at his own words on the risk assessment, then carried on. "Upon submerging under the ice, in a worse case scenario, the ice is projected to increase steadily from 4" to 18" in thickness nearest to land. Mind you, keeping the killer dolphin strategy in mind, you'll be in trouble if a large slab breaks off from said explosion and falls on you, not to mention its own pressure wake."

His last statement was a poor miserable stab at a joke and it was the only time he ever cracked all his teeth in my presence. (I think I smiled back more in appreciation of his lack of wittiness rather than the humour. He scared me for a moment rather than make me laugh, and he knew it, which wasn't the idea.)

Then it dawned on me that ice floats!

"On a bad day at the landing spot it reportedly suffers up to minus 4°F (-12° C), which would reduce the time allowed in the water by half an hour, so that has to be accounted for. Maximum amount of time you can stay alive in the freezing water is three hours, and that's pretty damn good with all your gear. From late-November till late-March the ice in that area would be at its thinnest, which extends to two to three miles from shore to its edges and would be covering 50 to 100% of the visible surface of the sea. With luck its thickness will remain only 2-4 inches or roughly 5-10 centimetres, so presumably this will still give you sufficient cover."

I tried to see if he was joking again but this time his thin lips and colourless eyes didn't crease.

As my training and briefings proceeded with each passing day, it became clear that everything was being planned down to the second. In a nutshell, I was given two hours to penetrate Soviet Russia from the time I hit the water with an extra half-hour to an hour to allow for unanticipated delays. Anything beyond that and I was a dead man and I didn't need him to tell me so.

One psychological report I had read, soon before coming to SBS, had stated, "When you get there, you're not going to see the real picture. For the first few days everything is superficial. Eventually the real picture will emerge and you will see the reality of the assignment." (At that time I had even pencilled a note to myself in the margin: 'Poor attempt to pre-condition my thinking.')

But amazingly, suddenly then after two weeks, the snapshot really did start to slowly move off the celluloid inside the machinery of my brain and another level of human rationalisation came over me. I even noticed it myself. I had become the very 'thing' they wanted me to be and I was living and breathing it.

The old unhappy bastard's final words to me, with an emphasis, were, "No amount of planning can guarantee what the weather will be like when it's time to embark, Anderson, but the idea is *to stay alive.*"

At that, he shook my hand hard for the second and last time, turned on his heels and marched out. No good luck, no salute, no nothing, not even a goodbye kiss.

Sitting in a car for the next hour, on the way back up to London, that last statement was ringing in my ears until the chatty SBS driver next to me explained that 'to stay alive' was simply their jargon for 'beating the clock'.

I sighed with relief at that but wondered why he bothered to end on the apocalyptic. He must have been a psychotic, I supposed.

* * * * * * * * * *

Twenty-four hours later, after a pit stop for refuelling in Malta and discreetly entering civilian air lane Blue 21 just south of Sicily—to avoid being detected as a military plane—at sunset the RAF Hercules touched down at a nondescript air strip with no landing lights on the dusty Greek island of Rhodes. It taxied in the fading light alongside a extra small turbo-prop trainer aircraft painted in a camouflage grey that I'd never seen before. (I was to learn it was a Russian-made Yak, short for Yakovlev.) While both planes' engines were running, I sprinted from the bulky big one to the baby one carrying nothing but the clothes on my back.

Halfway over I stopped momentarily to pick up a tiny reddish item lying on the tarmac. As I boarded that screaming Yak (it bore no markings whatsoever), I noticed that the two-man crew were clearly wearing the insignias of the Turkish navy.

As we lifted into the darkening sky, with the RAF C-130 also preparing for take-off, I opened my clenched hand to see that I had snatched up a very long dead but beautifully preserved black-and-white striped moth with a red underbelly. I put that mummified article in my pocket for safekeeping. It was the only thing I owned then that was with me.

Less than two hours later we were landing in Gölcük, a naval station in Turkey, on the Sea of Marmara at the mouth of the Bosphorus—the thin strip of water that officially separates two continents (though the same country bordered both sides of it). You could see Istanbul glittering across the placid waters on the left as we were coming in to land. Romantically, I preferred to think of it as Byzantium, its original name, which somehow seemed appropriate as I was staring at the end of the West while arriving at the beginning of the East.

The next day soon after breakfast I reported, as instructed, to the windy harbour front where young chatty Turkish navy ensigns were carrying out the orders of a couple of senior midshipmen who wore badges of technicians.

They were testing a specially-designed, silent, underwater exhaust unit, the size of a watermelon, which they attached to the rear of a protruding metal cylinder that in turn was to be pulled by a motorised small inflatable Gemini boat. After several hours of frustration they got it to where they wanted it and we took it for a spin out in the *Marmara Denizi* (as the locals called the water there), while I stupidly clung on the back of it in a wet suit semi-submerged one-foot below sea level trying to master how to switch off the damn thing several times at speed.

The exercise reminded me of a kind of stupid water skiing manoeuvre except that I was horizontal half lying in and out of the whizzing water. The repeated practice was important, however.

That night, as expected, when I inspected the Yak's hold, a dark-blue, long-range DPV (Diver Propulsion Vehicle, torpedo-shaped, very fast, whisper-silent underwater transport) was patiently sitting there with that experimental motor device now securely attached to it. I had learnt to operate a similar DPV with my SBS handler minus the expensive miniature machinery. Everything else packed in the plane's hold looked brand new. They were obviously not sparing any pennies on this op.

The day of departure came much faster than I thought.

Two nights later the weather conditions in the Soviet Union across the nearby Black Sea were right. I quickly packed any belongings into a small hold-all that would be returned to SIS headquarters for my eventual collection, hopefully (or by my next-of-kin if not). The colourful moth was placed in a plastic bag right on top.

After the ATO (air tasking order, flight plan, "run") was completed, the same nondescript Yak with the same two pilots, took off low towards the moonlit curve of a thin crescent before turning away and levelling. It skimmed towards the Soviet Union at only 100 feet over the flat sea for several hours. It was small and low enough to evade radar as it wasn't carrying any overly-detectable heat-seeking machinery, while purposefully remaining hard to spot by any patrolling *PVO* (*Protivovozdushnoy Voyska Oboronystrany* or Air Defence Forces of the Soviet Air Force) interceptor birds looking down for prey. But within its innards it was loud enough for me to not to able to hear my rapid heartbeat.

This clearly wasn't going to be a RAS (re-supply at sea) op either so I spent the time reducing the nerves by just looking at the gaping hole below in the middle of the hold that I would freefall through, concentrating, then eventually sleeping to preserve energy.

Hours later, one of the crew tapped my shoulder, gave me a thumb up, which was the 10- and 11-minute warning to prepare the exit strategy. Assisted by one of them, first over the side went the DPV, with the timed special automatic drive attached to it. Due to sudden loss of weight the Yak almost touched the water as the DPV went overboard.

Then 60 seconds later, just at the moment the plane went into a sudden steep climb, I was manually pushed out…sitting inside a giant clear plastic man-size ball built with a gyroscope. It initially somersaulted several times then uprighted itself before settling into a fast skim, bouncing along the surface of the water with me just sitting there strapped-in wearing a heavy frogman suit and helmet. Whizzing along I glanced back and caught a glimpse of the plane's vertical stabiliser (tail) going away as it returned to home.

Approximately a mile later my bubble finally rolled to a stop and began to sink quickly, water seeping through the air holes, so I popped open the latch and climbed out into the foreboding deep.

It was colder than I thought even through the thickness of my layered exterior skin.

The timing was better than perfect though. Just as the bubble sank and I'd finished final adjustment of my bell helmet, while treading water, the DPV came chugging along just below sea level well within the expected 60 seconds wait time and I grabbed her tailfin.

Had we missed each other, it was designed to stop itself and float within a 100-yard radius of my projected final resting place, plus I carried a homing device to locate her. As I had no further use for the homing device I discarded it in the dark water and proceeded to switch off the mini motorised device that kept the DPV operating without a driver to steer it.

For the next 60 minutes the two of us cruised along in pitched blackness, me holding onto her, while sailing in a northerly direction. Like doing the breaststroke in swimming, submerged just inches below the surface, I would raise my head on a regularly timed count to stare ahead as the thin coastal line of a threadbare Iron Curtain loomed discernibly wider by the minute.

All the while I looked around ready for any surprises, as I was told to do.

Just as darkness died, droning along in the opposite direction portside, came a rusty Bulgarian-flagged freighter named clearly in Roman letters *Sipka*. The home port of Varna was under her name.

The rocking power of her wash surprised me and I wondered if my due north course was accidentally altered, but I had to keep sailing on by myself.

As the ship's echo slowly died, the starkness of the surroundings became visible as I delivered myself to the cracked edges of paper-thin ice.

The winking lights of a frowning Mother Russia was clearly up ahead over the bleached nothingness.

No dolphins had been sighted and I cursed whoever had speculated that they would swim in such adversely cold conditions. They damn well wouldn't. But they'd omitted to mention the solitary seaweed-encrusted, ancient mine that was the size of a car engine just below the surface. I had nearly rammed it while glancing back at the disappearing ship and had swerved at the last second. It's rope-like chain had all manner of waterborne trash snagged in it and snaked it's way into the faded hollowness beneath. I had no way of knowing if it was live or not but it must have been a relic from the Great Patriotic War—that's what the Russians call World War II.

Finally the time had come to go under and stay there.

It was the first and last time this atheist ever prayed, and in godless waters at that.

I found myself peeing into the mobile urinal receptacle just as I sank into the perceived claustrophobic hell of an upside down world.

With no one to hear me I was screaming maniacally in the silence of my head.

Suddenly a weird indescribable peace overcame me. Even though I had just passed a point of no return, I think I no longer cared about anything. Some may call it an insanity but to me it was an inexplicable calm, like dreaming with my eyes open. I would describe it as near to what heaven probably looked like, being under that blanket of increasing lightness. And way below me were welcoming faint hills of illuminated beige with hues of greenness waving its arms. The sun's few rays were beginning to glisten down to it in inviting multiple paths. The little fish and all sorts of plankton life came towards me and glanced by.

As time passed, the timeless ceiling and the smooth carpet began to narrow. My world was slowly getting murkier, blending into a flecked muddy ooze.

Ahead, to my amazement, what seemed like a sloped silver curtain loomed. The closer I got, it became a flowing glass-like gate in front of me, blocking progress.

I had to rub my visor to believe it.

I stopped the DPV, anchored her to the floor and like the man on the moon float-walked up to the phenomenon.

Upon closer inspection I realised it was loose nylon fishing lines, hundreds of them, like a watery cobweb. The results of snags from the summer and perhaps the decades of summers before, still disintegrating over time and swept by nature into this corner abyss that I had to by-pass to land on the beach of safety beyond. The lead weights, snarls of tangled blobs and the occasional bent brown hook hung every which way in front of me on various strings of faded pastels.

For seconds I was afraid to tackle it, in case I too would be sucked into the awful knotted mess. I looked around frantically in both directions as far as the eye could see, half expecting to see some crazed mechanical spider come scooting along. There was only one thing to do instead of channelling through this mad maze, it was to find and climb the stone pier walls that I knew were starboard somewhere.

A quick glance at the chronometer told me that I didn't have time to even be sweeping fallen leaves in a park, never mind cutting a path through this dazzling clutter. My clock had just ticked into the allotted overtime.

Restarting the DPV I weaved alongside the strange moving transparency for less than a minute heading east.

After a few minutes I could discern the depths of a different darkness in the far distance.

Reaching that sullen wall, I arrived at the end of the nylon nightmare, I cruised parallel now to it seeking a way up and out.

Popping in and out suddenly of a crack to my left, baring its razor smile, came a muscled eel thicker than my arm, making us both jump back in fright.

Finally above me I saw the bottom rung of a crusty rusted ladder that had stuck its feet through the ice.

Switching off, from a compartment I retrieved a small waterproof container of tricks with the enclosed standard floating knife that I needed plus civilian clothes.

Then I petted my DPV companion goodbye on her snout. When Spring came Nature's undersea ashes would have smothered her before peering eyes from above could think she was a dead seal.

Before swimming to the joyless overcast roof I spent a few seconds with my eyes closed, sinking in slime, helmet down against that crusted greenish barrier with the bag on my back. But instead of mute prayer all I could hear was the sarge's rebuke booming from behind me, "For every inch of sediment you disturb it can reduce normal viz of one foot to zero! Try not to do it as you'll be walking in circles in a square!"

Then I took a deep breath and dived directly upwards. Left hand gripping the lone metal rung with my body pressed against the twin corner of stone and ice like an upside down fly flapping, as I quickly proceeded to slice with my right hand through the several inches of hardness above.

Cubes of ice snapped in seconds, slithering under the pane, before skating slowly away beneath it and crumbling like salt particles into the water.

Four inches later I pushed my left hand up through the hole at sea level, gripping around the first slippery rung of icy metal. The cold air shocked me through my gloves as a feeling of relief washed over me.

Another long minute later of fast chopping and I stuck my head through the widened gap. Twisting to look around like a periscope, between myself and the wharf across the way, all I could see at my eye level were small abandoned pieces of industry that had fallen from above on to a clear plastic sheet.

I was in no doubt that I was peeking out over the outer edges of the More shipyard in Feodosiya, as the silent giant steel cranes in the grey sky seemed to bend down a fraction to see whether I was worth pecking.

Eventually I got my entire body through the widening gap, but did not switch off the oxygen as I began my dripping step-by-step ascent. I could not tell if I was creating a echo around the surroundings or not but the noise inside with my laborious breathing was certainly blaring.

I also didn't know if I would have to slide back through that open hatch down there to effect an emergency escape or not.

Half way up the exhausting cliff-like face I stopped to gaze around the harbour.

In the dry dock area yonder two small ships encased in frozen gauze were still being constructed. I hoped nobody was looking through the foggy windows at me from the low buildings, as I was just dangling stranded on a dike. Certainly there was no sign of life or lights on, and thank goodness, no dogs barking. Just the heavy metal rock concert within me in full maniacal flow.

Strangely, even though I was no longer water-bound all I could repetitively hear was that SBS man's voice again whispering as if pushing me up from below, "Seawater at 29.5 Fahrenheit sucks out body heat so fast that you could die within an hour even with your diving suit on…"

I slowly popped my helmet up over the parapet, and I found myself staring along the deck of an empty jetty.

Quickly and clumsily I hauled myself sideways over the edges. The suit of armour was heavy out of water and already starting to stiffen in the chill, adding more weight. The sound of scraping reverberated loudly from within my metal head as I held my breath. I didn't dare stand up and laid there quietly listening to my heart pounding, all the while looking around. Lying there, I felt like a hefty walrus at an empty zoo.

Then I decided to roll as fast as I could over to a high wooden fence with a roof over it, about 30-feet across the divide. There was no hardened sheath under there.

As I lay at the base of that hiding spot, I switched off my air supply then and slowly removed my bell hat. I could see my breath rising like clouds and tried to cover it with my gloved hands that were already starting to shiver violently, all the while I was trying to listen intently over and above the thundering orchestra in my head.

Then the shock of real oxygen smacked me hard, deep in my throat and I broke into a stifling cough. Fortunately for me, the gulls hadn't woken yet as they would have been squawking.

To survive frostbite I dressed speedily, taking off a layer piece by piece and shoving it in the bag I had, then replacing it with dry clothing from within.

After a few minutes my teeth began chattering insanely in the breeze, getting louder by each long second.

"Nyet razreshayetsa!", a voice shouted in the distance. "Not permitted!"

I froze to the spot. Heartbeat and teeth clacking stopping simultaneously.

But my hand was alive in the pouch, fingers scrambling feverishly through it searching for the unseen gun that was still inside its own bag.

All I could hear, as if coming from afar, was my blood's volume booming its bass in a slow approaching rhythm. Then damn it, I also started a slow hiccuping, which I couldn't halt as much as I tried with deep breaths while continuing to cover my mouth.

He *had* to know my location, he yelled in my direction. The walrus' slimy trail led right to me!

I couldn't tell how many phobias I suffered through in those drenched minutes, only that I did.

Finally my frantic fingers located the CZ Vzor 52 (a Czech-made 7.62-calibre long-barrelled automatic pistol, which fires eight bullets a second) and with one hand I clasped it tightly, hoping it wouldn't jam in the cold.

The voice behind me began a mumbling now, it sounded like an old man's. It seemed closer than before. He was repeating a word I couldn't understand followed by a clear *"...rechnoi vokzal."* "...river port." Then it was a question. "Police?"

Without showing myself I yelled quickly, *"Politsia? Nyet, militsia! Voyska spezialnoye naznachenia."* "Police? No, military! Special purpose troop."

It was maddening silent for long seconds.

I imagined he was thinking hard, like I was.

Why just one of me? Where was the rest? It didn't look right, feel right. What to do next? What made me say those stupid words?

The minute stretched to a numbing second one. I was slowly arcing into a frozen statue. I couldn't stand it anymore and decided to peek around at floor level. About 20 yards away, in a clearing at the foot of a crane, was a decidedly undecided elderly man with his hand in his pocket, a long night watchman's overcoat and matching hat. He was shifting his feet nervously on the spot in the snow.

Quickly he raised a small *samovar*, a Russian tea urn, to his mouth—I noticed that he hadn't shaved for days like me—and took a deep swig, face contorting, then burping.

He was obviously drunk and alone, but for how long? I don't think he knew my exact position. I turned away. Pieces of ice cracked off my sweating forehead when I rubbed it. Encouraged, back leaning on the fence, I started to slide up cautiously. I could feel my bones creaking with the action as blood flowed into crevices. When you haven't stood on your own two feet normally for a while, it's not as easy as it seems.

The drumstick rhythm of my hiccups were slowly reducing thankfully and a rush of adrenaline hit me.

I glanced back again. He was facing the other way now. I had no choice, I couldn't just stay there all day. I would freeze to death. For an unexplained reason I suddenly rushed out and blindly started running uncomfortably at the doddering old geezer. Halfway towards him, he turned to face me and his eyes widened, glued to the spot like a rabbit in fear.

As I skidded up to him with gun raised to hit him—close enough that I could see myself in the reflection of his pupils—…I didn't have to follow through…he toppled down in slow motion in front of me with his eyes stuck open.

Momentarily I thought he had fainted at the sight of me but instinctively knew from his oddly fixed face that he was gone before he hit the bleached dirt. I just stood there to see if our out-of-step dance union had caused any reaction elsewhere. I felt like an animal after a kill, my own nostrils wide, only I hadn't killed him—not directly. I had only intended to knock him out.

His hat had flipped under him revealing his empty bird nest thatch with curiously a dark yarmulke with a pin leaning against it.

Bending briefly to feel his motionless neck pulse I saw a tin-plated chain with a Star of David peeking over the collar.

I glanced up into his glassy stare: He had died either of fright or had a heart attack at seeing my bluing mask.

The fallen urn was gurgling vodka onto the floor burning a hole in the disturbed snow. When they buried the poor Jewish peasant, I thought peculiarly then, he was going to become a landowner at last in his final resting place inside state government-controlled property.

I jogged back clumsily to retrieve my pouch and finished changing into warmer clothes and donned a wool hat. I was feeling alive now despite his death. From the ladder to the fence and on my path back to him, I dragged and zigzagged that bag containing the wet suit behind me to smooth over the snow. I peered over the ledge quickly. I trusted the impending rain would soon shutter the drain hole I had crawled through down there. I picked up the old man's now empty urn, half deciding to use it as an item for future cover, but after sniffing it, the smell made me turn my nose away. I carefully put it back in its precise landing position again. The damn fool had been sucking down enough *samogon*, a home-made vodka that tastes and smells of paraffin, to blow his own bloody head off! I felt less guilty then and momentarily cheekily considered scratching an explanation on the canvas of the snow, *hatzofe shenirdam,* or the watchman fell asleep in Hebrew but thought better of it.

It was nearing seven o' clock in the morning, about the time local workers were usually due.

I started to run in and out of the high cranes' thin legs, through the crusted pools, towards the decaying row of buildings ahead whose windows grinned like broken teeth. The patter of my feet perforated the dirty chalk surface.

At the coiled, wire-topped wall, I stopped to catch my breath and to listen. There was a thudding and squishing sound outside becoming louder. Kneeling, I found a crack to look through. A split second later, a *tarantass* (a seven-foot-long horse-drawn, wooden sleigh) came flying past with a hefty bearded man driving it and a pretty Snow White-clad figurine in fur sitting in the back. They continued on their way. It grew silent again.

Finally the fourth or fifth door I tried, much to my surprise, was unlocked.

Creaking it open slightly, all that was out there on the milky floor was the freshly-made twin lines and hoofs marks.

I stepped out and followed the horse's path westwards towards the city of Yalta, taking care to adopt the unassuming unenthusiastic walk of a labourer on his way to work, pack on my back.

A dilapidated road sign for *Jalta* was right there over the first hill.

The beach that I was supposed to land on was away in the misty distance to the left somewhere. I had been instructed to bury my gear there but now I still carried it. I'd find somewhere else to dispose of it.

Walking, I had plenty of time to reflect: I obviously had an in-built psychological mechanism that didn't allow me to permit the possibility of failure. As a result, I kept progressing with that in mind. I had always fought against my limitations all the time and sometimes won.

Still, I was back in the land of the ferocious Russian bear again.

* * * * * * * * * *

Twenty miles up the Crimean hills inland, northwest of Yalta, not that far east of the strategic port of Sevastopol—home of the Soviet Navy's Black Sea fleet—is the palace of Bakhchisarai in the town of the same name. It was the inspiration for Pushkin's famous poem, *"The Fountain of Bakhchisarai"*, which later became the most famous ballet of the Soviet era.

It is also a main tourist attraction for northern big city folk, even though less people attended in cold February. In keeping with normal weather for that time of the year, a light precipitation was falling that day. In the courtyard leading to the military museum there is a T-70 World War II tank on a pedestal and an eternal flame to honour the Red Army dead.

It was where I was to rendezvous with a Russian Jew by the unlikely name of Such at approximately 12 PM to 12:15 PM. We had never met before but each of us had guidelines on how to introduce ourselves.

I was there early to check out the place and no longer had the demeanour of a working man but that of a student conducting research. I also carried several small new books and a notepad. I still had the hold-all with me.

The previous night in a hostel in Yalta I purchased used clothing plus a replacement hat at a market stall. Under cover of darkness, after wiping them down to remove fingerprints, the bell helmet and diver's equipment were dropped in a sack over a low bridge at a submarine canal where the deep black port water hadn't frozen. Later that morning I had shaved for the first time since I left England four days prior, as well as having a stand-up wash in a tin cubicle as the cheap hostel had no real baths to lie in, nor showers.

At a minute to the hour, I sat down on a bench in front of that iron monument and made notes. Actually the only words I wrote in Cyrillic were "Where is Nizhniy Tagil?" (which was inscribed on a small plate at the base of that tank and I later learned was the name of the factory where it was manufactured).

Nobody else occupied any of the surrounding other benches as everybody wisely headed directly to the museum's entrance, where it was warmer and drier.

Such's codename was Hilazon, the single word he was to state to me, plus he would doubly identify himself by wearing a sky blue scarf. My response would be the single word Argaman and to display the colour purple, not to be a part of clothing, so I had a purple leather bookmark sticking prominently out of a book, which had travelled with me from Britain. Additionally, he had to say it standing up and I had to receive and respond while sitting down. If any of those six criteria's were wrong or misplaced, then I was to depart straight for Moscow by train and make contact with others, provided I wasn't caught in an large animal trap here.

I had already fulfilled the part of being seated and for good measure pretended to read the book with the tongue poking rudely out. I would wait till 15 minutes past the hour and then no longer, effecting the second move (the fall back dispersal plan).

At 12:07 on the Cyrillic courtyard clock, from the corner of my eye, a diminutive, prematurely balding man with a clean-shaven round face, not that much older than me, was overtly staring at me. No casing of me this one, no checking out the target area discretely whatsoever.

Hatless and dressed in a nondescript overcoat that was too large for him, he was wearing the requisite sky blue scarf. Seconds later he shuffled up, looked around, and quite brazenly stood in front of my view of the retired combat vehicle, remaining stationary.

He appeared like Friar Tuck except thinner. With his bald spot, it looked like he was sporting a light pink yarmulke.

I glanced up at him, forced myself to look bored and then went back to reading.

He then took a single step forward, almost bowed and very calmly said in a low but perfect English, "My name is Such, short for Suchowljansky. I was born with the name Ehud. My wife's name is Ronit. We are 'rootless cosmopolitans', the descriptive term for Jews in the Soviet Union. Before you ask me why I use Such, it is only because in this language it sounds like I'm talking about something else and then they are always waiting for me to continue…while I'm waiting for them to tell me their name. You understand my mumbo-jumbo?"

I didn't utter a single word in response, remaining blank-faced. Instead I shrugged as if he were a dimwit talking to himself and kept on reading. I should have been alarmed but the air thankfully did not carry any tension in it and my own nerves had calmed somewhat. But why wasn't he following the established protocol?

He took a deep breath and then finally blurted the punch line, "Hilazon."

Closing my book I slowly put it back in the bag, then replied emphatically, "Argaman."

He nodded slowly once, almost as if to himself, and a thin film of perspiration had glistened on his forehead as I stood up. We clicked heels as we shook hands in a business-like manner. Neither of us smiled. He appeared quite tense suddenly then and I wanted to tell him to relax, but didn't say anything.

I also wanted to ask him why he had deviated from the plot, but didn't. Instead I walked in silence alongside him on the crunching frostiness before we entered a parked older model Uzhgorod, much to my initial consternation. (An Uzhgorod is a Russian-made jeep-like vehicle used by the police.)

Reaching under his seat he retrieved a *shofar*, tipped it upside down, shook it hard and out fell a neatly folded hard piece of paper. He handed it to me. From my short time in Israel I knew enough to know that in Hebrew, a *shofar* was a religious ram's horn trumpet blown by the ancient Jews in battle.

Opening it some eighteen ways, I saw it was my OVIR document, the Soviet Department of Visas and Permissions licence allowing travel outside Moscow, with half of my faded likeness officially stamped in the corner: Semen Yashin. Born in Rostov-na-Donu with the date of birth. The word Jew was quite prominent. A resident of Moscow. Occupation was as a researcher.

While memorising the DOB I was thinking: I'm in trouble if seen naked.

When he fired the engine, he volunteered, "I am very sorry about my little speech before. This is my first and probably last time I will be doing this. However, as I approached you, I just couldn't believe that you would be the person I was looking for. You appear so young, like an older teenager. As nobody in these parts speak English, I thought, let me communicate in that language, knowing that you were an Englishman. I must congratulate you on your response. You never showed that you understood my every word. You are a professional I see. Able to control your facial muscles. I am impressed with your ability."

I turned to look at him blandly and without raising my voice, muttered, "Right, and you were such a fucking twat that I was already thinking how I was to get myself to Moscow. You know that? I should punch you on the nose right now. But I won't. All I can assume from that performance is that we both seem to have the same sense of wonder in this crazy world we live in. If you are to be the right hand to my left and vice versa then perhaps we have the same genes." That brought a weak smile from him.

Then I deadpanned, "Now that I am known as Semen, it so happens I'm from the navy and like sex." Now he looked momentarily puzzled again.

Without getting my double pun, he shook his head in apparent agreement and said rather gallantly, "I will never know your real name, sir, but to me I will always know you as *Possev* or Seed, which I understand is the name of this operation. Hello Semen. And I am Such, OK. But please understand that had you not been you, I may already be terminated. A hole in my head. *Nosin smet tiranom.*" (It was the slogan at OGPU, the KGB's predecessor, which translated to: "We Bring Death To Traitors.")

Removing his hand from mine, he mimicked a gun to his temple then emitted a soft, "Boom." It was my turn to force a grim smile.

Minutes of silence passed as we wound our way slippery down to the rain-sodden main road to Sevastopol. I enquired, "So now that we have got the preliminaries out of the way, I have wanted to know this since the time I was told the passwords back in England: What does Hilazon and Argaman mean, and why do those colours have any significance? The words are not in my Russian vocabulary."

Grinning broadly for the first time, Such told me that Hilazon meant snail in modern Hebrew, which an ancient sky blue dye was derived from. Argaman was a biblical word for another dye in the colour purple that came from the same snail. Apparently this snail's glands had the ability to secrete and produce yellow, then purple, then sky blue after exposure to sunlight. Such had chosen those code words himself as he was a entomologist by profession.

It also turned out that he had purchased the vehicle from the police second-hand in his home region of Birobidzhan many years ago and had driven it thousands of miles and three weeks to the family's new residence in Sevastopol.

I'd never heard of such a far out place before and thought he was pulling my leg. He wasn't. However, the story of the Far Soviet Autonomous Region of Birobidzhan was quite fascinating. Such told me it was the official home of Jewry in the Soviet Union, which was on the country's northeast border with China. "If you do not believe me," he said, "It's precisely 48.48 north by 132.57 east. Check it one day and you will see it exists." (I did and it does.)

I can see now how his codename came into being...he never ever left a trail wherever we went and he did everything with extreme care, all very unlike my first ever impression of him as being extremely negligent.

* * * * * * * * * *

Seven hundred miles as the crow flies from Sevastopol (even though Such and I did it by locomotion, changing trains in Saratov) is Shikany. In military terms its exact co-ordinate is 52°N/47°E.

Actually it was two towns, three miles apart, imaginatively called Shikany-1 and Shikany-2.

Still, approximately 15,000 people worked there surrounded and protected by 60,000 Soviet armed forces. Nearby was the civilian city of Vol'sk, right on the river Volga, from which most of the outsiders commuted. The CPSU (Central Committee of the Politburo at the Kremlin), at a certain point early in the Cold War, combined the names of both Shikany's by classifying the place *zato*, a secret military city or installation, and thereafter identified it as Vol'sk-18 (from it's previous code name of Tomko). It was so named as it was simply 18 kilometres from Vol'sk. (At least that's what some bright spark at the British Ministry of Defence assumed.)

Specifically the non-combatant staff were research scientists of various denominations, in alphabetical order: chemical, bacteriological, biological, entomological, nuclear, organic, radiological. A strategic industrial complex of intellectual strangers.

Responsible for the facility's strict inner security was the Red Army's Troop Unit 61469. Needless to say that the whole area was a heavily restricted travel zone, an impregnable fortress, if force had been used to penetrate it.

Right in the heart of the enumerates was the small laboratory unit specialising in all matters relating to entomology, consisting of two personnel, which just happened to be Such's chosen trade. Ehud Suchowljansky, PhD. was the head scientist in charge and I was to be his temporary assistant while his other usual assistant was conveniently on a three-week seminar course in East Germany.

Vol'sk-18 was the Soviet Union's primary centre for the manufacture of weapons of mass destruction. The largest such closed nucleus in the world at that time.

Why had the SIS taken so much trouble to take advantage of a unique short-term employment opportunity that had risen only three weeks earlier, will be explained: For decades thousands of metric tons of the sodiumyttrium carbonate mineral called Adamsite, a rare colourless crystal, had been mined all over the Soviet Union and shipped to Vol'sk-18. There it was boiled in high temperatures with furfural and acetone. Thereafter its remaining solid yellowish toxic property was transformed into tear gas. The end result being an airborne incapacitant also known as adamsite that hugely irritated nasal passages and mucous membranes in humans, much like pepper does. The western military's terminology for Adamsite is Agent DM, short for the chemical abstract diphenylaminochloroarsine.

DM, has no odour and when sprayed stays in the air for only 10 minutes giving it a low persistency. But a low concentration can reduce large unprotected civilian populations to minor sensory disturbances like uncontrollable coughing and blinding headaches for half an hour. Higher doses caused violent spasms of breathing inability and vomiting for up to three hours, resulting in death to those with respiratory problems. Enough time for invading forces to gain a foothold on foreign territory or cause extensive damage in a targeted city.

However, Adamsite was found over the years to have no effect whatsoever on the environment of insects, who continued to survive in it while humans went down like flies around them. Later it was discovered that bugs resisted other chemical formulas too. As a result of those findings, soon after the end of World War Two, the entomology department was created to research this. But as the Cold War progressed, its long-term agenda was to develop the spread of non-conventional warfare by the use of swarms of mosquitoes, bees and other flying raiders, otherwise to be known as the Plague Programme. Snails were considered to be one of the most hardy insects of all. Maggots and beetles were next up on the list.

When I entered the lab with Such for the first time, equipped with my freshly-issued security-cleared photo ID, there were hundreds of specimens of snails going about their business inside dozens of smeared glass tanks.

I knew nothing about the subject but my unsupervised sole boss knew everything about it. He was to teach me enough to get by. But he had already succeeded in the objective of getting me on the inside.

No wonder he had selected the introductory code names of Hilazon and Argaman.

* * * * * * * * * *

For several days I had locked myself in that cramped lab while Such administered the basics. Small living quarters and army-style open plastic box showers were provided.

The most interesting development that Such's small unit had brought to light so far and already actively utilised by the Soviet military and intelligence-related directorates was: Female insects hormones could be discreetly wiped onto a designated target—a human's shoes or a box containing important paraphernalia—and when that marked person or item approached a security checkpoint, male insects of the same species inside a specially-designed box, would become so agitated they would immediately attract the attention of security guards.

Interestingly Such called it his safety smutch.

I made a mental note to remember to let my countrymen know of such a sexy idea. Kind of smaller, slower moving K9's.

Then I started venturing out in the pretence of going about my reasons for being there while the man got on with his real work. I was quite aware that he could have also smeared me with his invention in order to keep track of me.

The first time I ate in the canteen I found myself at the same table as a Spectrometer Expert, at least that's what his ID stated.

The very next day he nodded at me.

The third day we spoke.

I was to learn from this bearded man that his specific work task was to measure uranium enrichment that the spectrometer gave. I already knew that uranium was a key component in a nuclear bomb. By the end of the week in order to quench a young man's inquisitiveness on the subject this chap had actually given me some up-to-date documents to read from the nuclear department. Those sheets were duly micro-photocopied and hidden for eventual removal from the premises by Such.

More importantly, I had an intricate knowledge of the layout of the complex in my head. Much more detailed than any satellite could have photographed in those days. Even better still, on a daily basis I had logged the full names of all the department heads, their assistants and their assistants in turn. The material gained would be useful one day to others.

One petite young woman that looked like an assistant to an assistant smiled not that shyly at me too on that same day when I first went to the canteen.

By the fourth day we found ourselves sitting at a table alone.

Her name was Zhenya, only 22, reddish-blonde, green-eyed, classically beautiful and extremely feminine even with the unfashionable gold wire-rimmed glasses on her aquiline nose.

If I hadn't known better I would have thought she was an Irish colleen. No man in their right mind would say no to an attraction like her either. But she was strictly off limits to all and sundry because she was one of the local propaganda agents in training. Her employer was the regional KGB and she could move on to be an junior intelligence officer next if she performed well. She had been duly hand-picked from the *Komsomol*, (*Kommunisticheskii Soyuz Molodyozhi*—Communist League of Young People). [A *komsomol* was also one of its uniformed scout much like the West's own boy and girl scouts.]

So the local people avoided her for that reason while I swam against the tide as my instinct instructed me to.

Rather than pursue her as a normal red-blooded fellow given the opportunity would, and thus exposing my real intentions for being at Vol'sk-18, I let her dictate the course of action and played along with it.

Our mild flirting advanced quite quickly, with the desired effect on both of us. A kind of dangerous romance.

By the time the second weekend arrived I had received a complimentary invitation from her to attend a symphony orchestra concert in Vol'sk.

It was the first and only time I left that facility—Such was incredulous that I could be permitted to do so as a temporary worker but it was cleared by none other than the KGB themselves—and it certainly allowed me to observe how the security forces operated in person.

It was to be a priceless exercise in more ways than one.

On the day the worker-laden bus took me for a free tour through the interior red zone's various checkpoints and buffers. I took zoom lens pictures in my head, especially of the sophisticated microroentgen-reading radiation sensors and surveillance systems that trigger sirens—both the evacuation and immediately-locked-in-can't-get-out versions of high-pitch warning sound. At the perimeter wall I also observed vibration sensors, infrared cameras and what was surely an encrypted closed-circuit television mechanism. I even watched, without staring obviously, at a crew of technicians in the process of installing new magnetic detection devices. I never found out what the large hydraulic-looking crane-like system in the centre of this labyrinth did. Nor did I detect where all the communication command post was located and determined that perhaps it was in a centralised mobile unit.

Overall I somehow got the impression that the whole apparatus was to stop people getting out *en masse* as opposed to some outside party attacking by ground to get in there. The noticeable absence of a visibly active exterior canine unit told me so. An air offensive would be another story altogether. It clearly had not been factored into the equation, thus far.

The workers' car park, where most of the bus' occupants trudged out wearily, sadly also revealed that the Soviet Union's finest minds could only afford to drive Zaporozhets, a basic miniature car the size of an average iron settee on wheels. They deserved Jaguars and Mercedes'.

Upon arrival at the theatre in dreary central Vol'sk—I had borrowed Such's only suit, which was even more ill-fitting on me than him—the curtain opened and a tuxedoed amateurish band began the night. Not exactly a philharmonic of note, but still.

I knew Zhenya was going to be one of the main performers but I was completely unprepared for her above-average solo performance as a cellist. It gave me goose-bumps.

After the show I met her likeable parents briefly. Later I had walked her home a mile away in the cold evening and we had kissed lightly on the lips. I couldn't bring myself to tell her that I was leaving the next weekend. God and country forbade me too. And besides, a big deciding factor in the end was that I was supposed to be circumcised.

To this day, now as an older man writing his memoirs a quarter of a century later, I occasionally wonder about Zhenya. I hope she had a good life thereafter and feel that she did indeed. She must be a grandmother now and still doesn't know that she had a date with another kind of scout (for I was a *Razvyeadchik*, which is the Russian word meaning scout). [They do not use the words "intelligence officer" or "spy" in their vocabulary, they say "scout" instead.]

But I *had* to do what I did for far nobler reasons than loving feelings.

One of life's regrets is that we will never discover if certain acquaintances would have been a fleeting romance or true love. But when my fingers touched hers, a discernible electric current burned my senses, a most pleasing emotion. I am proud that I was able to override such a magnetic, almost hypnotic, effect within my entire body and mind.

I should add that, as I was instructed to do by Such, when I was finally alone outside Zhenya's small family dacha, I took a sample of soil and placed it in a tiny capsule he had provided. Such told me that the minute piece of earth I'd collected would eventually be evaluated in Britain to determine the exact power of an atomic test that had occurred in the region five months earlier.

When I heard that I wondered if that was the real scientific reason why I had experienced jolts of positron from Zhenya.

* * * * * * * * *

Job completed, I took the train to Moscow to start a new life. I left Such to return home to his wife Ronit on his next leave, taking the collated data and other dirt with him. It would ride its way through the underground network to the West. Pictures he had taken before meeting me of a secret military installation in Cape Onuk, at the east end of Crimea, also made the trip.

An hour after arrival in the Russian capital I found myself inside a run-down apartment building in a nondescript suburb, walking up the many flights of unlit dank stairs I stood in front of a door with crumbling paint that had a *mezuzah* good luck charm. I kissed and rubbed it as I knocked even though I was born a Christian Protestant.

A small dog had barked in response and a few seconds later I could feel eyes peering through the spy hole. Without further ado I bent to push a piece of paper under the door. It read confusingly in Roman block letters: HFXSLDOQZMHPB.

The briefing file in London had advised, 'Use only English written Atbash when meeting this contact and write his name.' Atbash was simple reversed letter substitution cipher, originally used by the Jews Before Christ whereupon the A became a Z and so forth throughout the 25-letter Roman alphabet with the median M remaining as is. It was safe to use in a land where most people only read Cyrillic but anybody not knowing what it really stated would have thought me to be illiterate. Besides the Russian alphabet has 33 letters in it.

The door quickly opened and I was beckoned in and then surprisingly hugged enthusiastically by the grinning stranger in a *yarmulke*, clearly a deaf mute. He looked familiar but wasn't when I realised he was obviously a SUCHOWLJANSKY as the door's tiny nameplate had announced in Hebrew and I had written it copied in backward English. He was expecting the note and as planned it was also my way of identifying myself to him.

After a short stay with another Jewish family in the same complex I was to await contact by an unidentified individual as I rode the metro in the morning rush hour, who would identify himself with something I would recognise.

Riding the underground every day to nowhere and back for the designated week, I was sitting there in boredom, looking out of the window at nothing as the crowded train was in a tunnel, when on my lap fell my Rhodes black, white and red moth still preserved in its original plastic bag.

I stared at it for a moment never once looking over at the person sitting next to me. Less than a minute later the subway halted at a major terminal, he got up and melded into the exiting mass, leaving a cheap cotton pouch on the seat that had been inserted between our bodies.

I determined that there was nobody watching in the now almost deserted compartment and I was the last to get off.

Instead of opening it at the Jewish family's flat and possibly endangering their lives (in case there was a monitoring device planted in it), I took it to the nearest park, which was just off Smolenskaya Square, and found a bench well surrounded by trees.

Using my tradecraft I had triple-checked that I wasn't being followed by Ivans doing their version of the same *konspiratsiia*.

It was a beautiful day and a little bit nippy but the sun was promising a new season ahead.

Appropriately peeking through the trees I could see the 100-plus floors of the tall building that was the Russian Foreign Ministry, which conducted the enemy's activities in my own country. To me Britain seemed so far away now as if it was another lifetime.

A quick going through of the contents revealed my new identity's paperwork, with coded instructions and plenty of roubles. My new life as a mole (little window in SIS jargon) had begun officially at that very moment.

I sat there reminiscing, reflecting on recent events while taking in the landscape before me, when a dry white snow flake fell onto my lips. I had almost inhaled it by accident.

Spring in Moscow is breathtaking as it rains summer snow. Seeds fallen from the thousands of female balsam trees that littered the city had covered the grass in white dust. The kids in front of me were excitedly building light piles of *pukh* (tuft) and their fussing parents were lighting each of them, only for the miniature pyre to flare briefly then fizzled out much to everybody's squealing delight.

But to me the silent karmic message, which had dropped out of the sky, spiritually meant that I should not to burn myself out too quickly. Indeed I was a seed myself, planted deep by Britain inside *Sovietsii Soyuz* (the Soviet Union) ready to blossom.

Chapter Thirteen

Ever wondered what it's like to exist
beyond the accepted frontiers of the mind?

When I was last in Moscow during these present times, I recalled I had said to Mike Molody, when he had first told me about what he was doing, 'Prove it to me first so I can venture forth with the power of my convictions.' He had truly taken that to heart.

The people and places he had lined up for me to visit, talk to, feel and touch were extraordinary. What really came across was *their* sincerity. They *believed* passionately in what they were doing. Many times I got goose bumps just from listening to them; forget what I was to witness later in their work. Of course, I couldn't medically verify it. I had to have it checked by other experts. Nobody had a problem with that and plied me with plenty of data, video and slides. I was to later pay for the translation and study of the information by *open*-minded outsiders in the West, both in the UK and USA, whose findings were, by and large, extremely favourable.

I had eventually phoned Yuri, the policeman-cum-moonlighting taxi driver that had taken me for a tour around Moscow and asked him to find me a reliable driver with his own decent car that would be available for hire 24 hours, seven days a week, if I so desired. Of course his remuneration would be consistent with that demand.

Within two days I had Smardz and his silver Zil. Ilya Smardz was exactly what I wanted—did as he was told; only spoke when spoken to; came when I asked him to; didn't get drunk; ran errands perfectly; kept his mouth shut when among others; and preferred his last name over the first. A stocky guy with bent legs he had a blondish-grey crew cut, was clean, medium height and my age. People moved out of his way when we went walking in the meadows. I had no doubt he was in the armed forces earlier in his life; in a sense he reminded me very much of those Afghan vets I'd met in that bar with Yuri not so long ago. With a name like that, I don't think he was even fully of Russian blood and was probably more Prussian. I never found out much about him and didn't care. What intrigued me most about Smardz was when I asked him to pick me up at, say, between 9:00 AM and 9:15 AM, he'd respond, "Tomorrow morning I'll be outside the hotel at exactly 9:02 AM"; or 9:07 AM the next day. Standing in the lobby I used to find myself timing him. Sure enough, right at the time when he said he'd be there, his car came around the bend into the hotel's driveway. In the fifteen months we were together, we never once had a meaty conversation and he never ever gave me a round number on the clock either: always an odd number. I suppose that's what Smardz was—odd. I'm not altogether convinced he ever slept because I never saw him do so. But a great driver to have around town he was and from now on whenever I go to Moscow, I want Smardz.

I opted not to stay at the President again, even if I could obtain an invitation to it. The less I had to depend on the British Embassy for anything, the better. A cheap suite at the Hotel Mezhdunarodnaya-1 was my permanent home, and I retained it even when I went out of the country on two trips of one week each. It came complete with availability of overseas phone calls and faxes. You have to understand access to communication is not something which everybody can have in many parts of the world. If you think the name of the hotel was long, its address was longer—it was at 12 Krasnopresnenskaya Naberezhnaya. Spelling it out to foreigners over the telephone became a drag, to say the least.

I spent most of my local car travel time divided between Molody's country research pad or the Barvikha Rehabilitation Centre, the latter which was also ten miles outside Moscow. When in town it was mainly at Kremlin-1, Ivanovsky Virological Institute, Sklifosovsky Research Institute or the Central Clinical Hospital, the last two located at 3B Kolkhoznaya and ulica Marshall Timoshenko 15 respectively. I know because I walked between them a lot as well when I gave Smardz the day off. I'd made one trip only to Sokolinaya Gora with Molody but didn't enjoy that morgue enough to want to return. I definitely prefer alive bodies to the dead.

Barvikha was peaceful, occupying one square mile of landscaped park. It had exactly a hundred beds, was equipped like a hospital minus operating rooms. The complex had all the luxuries and amenities of a western five-star hotel. It was the designated location for the treatment of the 50 Down's Syndrome children, and one of their parents stayed in-house with them the whole time. I don't care if anybody believes me, but the time spent there was the most rewarding in my life. Monitoring the tremendous progress of those children, aged 3-12, excited me. Their intelligence quotient was increased to a level their mothers couldn't believe and certainly none appear Mongol-like today. When I am elsewhere in the world and I come across kids with Down's, I have to bite my lips to prevent myself from giving those parents false hope because an effective treatment is currently labelled as not recognised in their home country.

The Central Clinical Hospital consisted of several modern buildings with a total capacity of one thousand five hundred beds. It is situated in a beautiful birch tree forest in a Moscow suburb. It was fully fenced with 24-hour security as this is where mentally retarded adults were housed. A lot of Molody's activities and surgical experiments with human and animal foetal tissue centred here.

At the Sklifosovsky Research Institute they specialised mainly in emergency medicine. It was also the base of Molody's Parkinson's disease programme. On several occasions I was present when patients were injected with the mix of human foetal tissue and of neural primordia of Notch *Drosophila melanogaster,* African fruit fly brain. The effects were so instant it was if somebody had just flipped a switch on the wall. This last word reminds me of the dark humour of its developer, Prof Dr Vyacheslav Vassilyevich Lebedev, whose frequent rather ignominious daily comment was, "Every day on the way to work, I wonder if I will find my patients on the ceiling (sic)." He's been thinking that for many years now and has been denied the credit for *the cure* for Parkinson's.

That leaves Dr Leonid Viser and his cronies. The Ivanovsky Virological Institute was the home of Electromagnetic Medicine. Again, I witnessed the direct destructive effect of EM on a wide range of dangerous viruses while non-infected cells actually increased their resistance. As an example, at one session a man with three cancerous tumours was facing the EM machine, which is the size of an average coffee table. They had already magnified and colourised each cell present in one of the tumours, and the cancerous cells were identified in purple. We were staring at a monitor. I was asked if I could see any cancer cells. I said there were three purples floating around, which was correct. They selected one of them, located its precise frequency within minutes by computer, and zapped it immediately. The purple cell disappeared from the screen in front of my eyes. They couldn't repeat the act for another three days as the human body can't take a hit like that until then. They are always playing catch up, as the purple cancer cells can replicate in the interim. However, many times they *have* caught up and the patient is subsequently declared cured. The problem is, not everybody is so lucky, but there are a lot of people walking around out there who did get cured of their particular problems. Since tumours absorb more light from laser light than healthy tissues, the last I heard, was they were studying the mechanism of the resistance of cells under the hypothesis that the exposure to EM altered the receptor apparatus of those cells.

At the very end of this subject, I now address Dr Molody's secret Kremlin-1 operation, which in general falls under the auspices of the Fourth Department of the Russian Ministry of Health [and is not connected to the Fourth Department (FD) of the General Staff—*Glavnoye Razvedyvatelnoye Upravlenya*—the former Soviet Military Intelligence]. This was the crown jewel of the Russian medical system and has served the 20 members of the Politburo and their families exclusively. It had every conceivable state-of-the-art amenity and was worth millions in any hard currency. This place contained two large presidential apartments, each with its own intensive care unit, equipped for cardiopulmonary resuscitation, plus a conference room full of the latest telecommunications. Kremlin-1 had 67 private and semi-private beds and was across Red Square from the Kremlin Wall, in the heart of Moscow. [Since my visit, the FD's name has been changed to the Medical Centre of the Government of the Russian Federation.]

Here was where the élite scientists in the former Soviet Union and now Russian Federation practised their medical crafts in relative anonymity. It was the nerve centre of the humane world objectives and programmes set by Dr Molody. Here they proved to me that they had developed a *sub-rosa* protocol consisting of biological, medical and electromagnetic methods for the effective treatment of several important diseases. The clinical experience, then and to this day, shows that this effective treatment will reverse pre-terminal and terminal stages of, for example, the AIDS virus back into the non-symptomatic stage. This means that the T-cell count will never regain the 947 T-cells of an average healthy person but, after two weeks of treatment, it will increase from even below ten to in excess of 400 T-cells. The latter number is the count designated as officially having AIDS. It is a predominantly foetal tissue-based treatment.

What is most intriguing about this is that in the West they market anti-HIV drugs known as NRTI's or nucleoside reverse transcriptase inhibitors. The NRTI's are proven to effectively slow the growth of the HIV disease, delaying the onset of AIDS and opportunistic infections, which was kind of one end of a pendulum. What the East had was a reversal of a different kind; it brought sufferers *back* to the centre, where they were before declining into the path towards their ultimate death, which was the other end of the pendulum. Depending where I was on the swinging motion in between the two ends is what I would try personally, that if I had ever contacted HIV/AIDS.

While not a cure, it is a promising giant step towards it. I wish the West would at least take a look at it without automatically denouncing it as a sham. It isn't. AIDS was one of many diseases they focused on at this particular location, along with Alzheimer's and Huntington's disease.

The aforesaid treatment is applicable to blood diseases too, such as sickle cell anaemia, thalassemias, aplastic anaemia, and other disorders.

As an interesting aside, once during a lunch break at Kremlin-1, a Russian evolutionary biologist, who shall remain anonymous due to the sensitivity of his work, but was attached to the space programme and responsible for exploring mismatch theory, said to me, "The regimentation of industrial society is proven to clash with genetic ancestry."

When I asked him for a further explanation the conversation quickly graduated to the origin of self-replicating macromolecular systems, the precursors of life.

The specific point he made was that the probability of something returning from out of space to Earth that could, say, destroy DNA-based life is low—but not zero. He said, "I don't know, nobody knows, what the odds are of life. However, our experiments indicate that the 'life phenomenon' is very robust and powerful and 'will find a way'. This fulfils our criteria of being a self-replicating species. What this means is that, given enough time, the chemical reactions, coupled with environmental conditions, chance mutations, and natural selection, could have replicated our world somewhere else in the universe, or vice versa. The ease by which we are finding organic molecules in outer space gets us at least one or two steps towards the fact that there is life elsewhere. What I am saying here is the probability of extraterrestrial life *is* optimistic."

Those brilliant scientists were right on the sharp cutting edge of our very existence in more ways than one. Sadly, whenever I brought up the practices and successes of the western medical Establishment, I got derisive looks and statements.

It was best summarised by a Russian doctor who wishes to remain anonymous, "Many self-righteous individuals maintain there is universal consensus on the need to prohibit the eventual cloning of human beings. In the meantime, until we get to that stage, they never asked the poor souls who have debilitating diseases what they think. Simply put, they are too indoctrinated—politically—in the West."

Then he added, "One major point is that ready-made embryos are about a quarter of the cost of ordering eggs-and-sperm from specially recruited donors for use for implanting. I think that says it all in a nutshell."

The last word as they say goes to Molody himself. I was thunderstruck when he said it as it was so obvious in its simplicity: "A part of medical training involves learning to overcome uncertainty. If a statistical study indicates there is a five per cent or less chance that two events—for example, inoculation of foetal tissue and a particular effective treatment—are linked purely by coincidence, then most physicians would accept the idea that the association between them has at least a 95% chance of being real and likely to repeat same, even if the nature of the link is not entirely understood."

He paused thoughtfully then added, "Theoretically I can never prove a damn thing but in practice I can."

* * * * * * * * *

Based on the AIDS treatment information I was armed with, I obviously thought of my Ukrainian friend Andry. There was no way I could just pick up the phone and call him. I went into a deep question-and-answer period with myself, giving Smardz a few days off in the middle of the week, as I stayed locked away in my hotel tower philosophising on the various consequences at hand.

Then I took a brief train ride out of Moscow on Fourth Department business, as scheduled, to Obolensk. There at the State Research Centre for Applied Microbiology, I learned all about Anthrax in animals through to its effects on humans and its manufacture for germ warfare, from Dr Pomerantsev. He even told me "one of the deadliest of a dozen strains of Anthrax was Vollum-B". What surprised me about some of the scientists at this institute was that they'd never heard of the 1972 United Nation's Biological and Toxin Weapons Convention, banning the development or stockpiling of biological weapons. They weren't the only ones though; Atlanta's US Centre for Disease Control did the same thing, all unofficially, mind you.

The result of that concentrated period of thought, and my one-day trip, was a one week to ten days on the road west as Smardz drove me to Andry's hideout, west of Lviv, in the Ukraine. The autumn weather was inspiring and I spent many hours mesmerised by the coloured presentation of the trees. It was nature in its entertaining prime.

My big Ukrainian friend looked the same, perhaps due to an excellent summer coupled with a new homosexual love in his life. The initial regimen I had given him of what *not* to do with his sexual life was apparently obeyed. After I'd gone over the Moscow AIDS treatment protocol with him, he was a willing guinea pig, based on my say-so that he'd benefit from a visit. He could sleep on my hotel couch if he wanted to. We set a date for him to come to Moscow during the upcoming winter.

His big thing of the moment was being invited to the next Europe-wide anti-NATO terrorist alliance in 1994. I'd never heard of such an unlikely gathering of happy scoundrels before, but apparently all the leaders of the banned organisations like France's *Action Directe*; Germany's Baader-Meinhof, also known as the Red Army Faction; Italy's *Brigate Rosse,* Red Brigade; Belgium's CCC, *Cellules Communistes Combattantes*—Fighting Communist Cells; and Spain's *Euskadi ta Askatasuna,* Freedom for the Basque Homeland—ETA; get together and have a meeting to pool their resources! "The notable exception from this group and absent from the last conference was the IRA, but their interests are ably represented by the ETA's political arm, *Herri Batasung,*" volunteered a proud Andry.

For him it meant an acceptance of all his dedicated hard work to date in over a decade of planning, particularly in lieu of the fact that his rebels hadn't killed anybody yet and didn't really intend to. He'd told me UNA-UNSO had adopted a non-violent resolve recently, thanks to my insistence.

"Who approached you about coming to this meeting?" I asked innocently, fishing for clues.

"Well, of course, I can't tell you this, but they were both French, an older man and a woman the same age. They said everybody had met before in Lisbon, Portugal, in late-1984. All in attendance had pledged to a 10-year anniversary assembly, to be continued until each and everybody's causes had been achieved, and this is the next one coming up. But I will disclose that they were starting to lend their expertise to Islamic revolutionaries and were going to some big meeting with them in Africa very soon, before the European one. I was invited to that too but declined. I mean what would they think of me there, some kind of freak: a big gay black man with blonde hair with a strange Ukrainian accent..." He sighed.

I think if I had pressed him more, I could have found out a lot more, but I shrugged it off. The news surprised me nevertheless that such communication existed among all the perceived bad guys. I'm assured the intelligence services must be aware of this congress of killers.

Though he did know that the CIS was the Commonwealth of Independent States—the old Soviet Union minus the Baltic states—Andry wasn't alone in his complete intellectual knowledge about NATO. The interesting aspect about him, and others, was that while they had heard of the organisation, they didn't know exactly what it's call letters stood for, nor *really* knew what NATO's real function was. So I educated him. This was something I knew a lot about.

The North Atlantic Treaty Organisation's original conception was to keep Germany in check after World War II; to keep the United States in Europe; and to keep the Soviet Union from expanding further westwards. NATO was a European Club based in Europe and policed by the US; while the United Nations was a World Club policed by the world and based in the US. Both are the policemen/goalkeepers in their respected designated territories. The problem was only *one* country had a foot in *both* camps, politically. Those that could follow the ball on the field objected to the same player being in goal for their club at each end. It meant one side would be scoring in an empty net depending which side the same American goalkeeper wanted to be at, at the time. The trouble is none of the outfielders actually took a shot on goal in forty-five years of playing the game at NATO's home ground to find out. That was probably a significant reason why the terrorists were ganging up as one collective team of all-stars to try and score, and in doing so, would test NATO's defensive mettle.

From a more democratic perspective; NATO was a product of old thinking. It needed to be revised drastically. The organisation is a military alliance; it is not set up to advise civilians what to do. Also somewhere along in the administrative mess it created for itself, like most overstaffed organisations, the policy paperwork got into a snafu. I am not in a position to say it was purposeful or accidental, but NATO's Article Five in its manifesto is a historical section which the US Senate refuses to debate with anybody. The article addresses an assumption that all will defend a attack on one NATO member. That is difficult to define, once again, when the players don't know where the US goalkeeper wants to be at the time of the attack. Just as in any team sports: if you're going to go forward; you better be ready to come back and recover, if and when you lose the ball. You have to have somebody dependable back there in defence in support of your efforts. But nobody at NATO knows which team the goalkeeper is on or wants to be on. I don't think the goalkeeper really knows either until the moment finally happens. It's a tricky situation with potential for disaster.

The first time somebody is successful in taking a good shot at the goal, we will all then know if it was saved or not. This whole concept is either very smart or very stupid. We will find out one day. Then it will go into blue as they say internally at both the UN and NATO, meaning official. Or the unofficial red…

Strategy is one thing; tactics is something else.

* * * * * * * * * *

When we entered the Czech Republic, I requested Smardz to take the high road to Prague instead of the low. I wanted to see the old escape route that McIntyre, Brennan and I had once taken—from this side, Eastern Bohemia. It looked just as beautiful as it ever was and the raging waters still bubbled energetically. It reminded me of real freedom.

In the city of a hundred spires, *Praha*, I met Bob Mendelsohn and Ben Obertone at Wenceslas Square, at the exact time and place we'd agreed upon. They were thrilled to be there. I had personally assumed the costs of their trip out from the US, as well as rooms at the Hilton. What was a bonus for them—and for me too—was that they were both temporarily unemployed. So I gave them a job to do with some foreign travel thrown in, all-expenses paid. They had brought their togs and equipment as I'd instructed them to.

As I was the boss and paying their wages, so to speak, I told the 5' 5" stocky Bob to discard his New York Mets cap immediately as he looked too American. I gave him money to go and buy a beret, like many of the locals his age had, and to take up shaving frequently. He appeared too surly and slovenly, and the spitting had to end. Of course, later he had to purchase an unusual blue and orange hat, the same colours as his favourite baseball club. He could be a central European now but he wouldn't be mistaken for Dutch. Still it looked OK on him. His bugging devices included personal on-the-body buttons and a listening handgun that recorded clearly from a half-a-mile; that is if there was no obstruction between him and the object.

Ben was so large and tall you couldn't hide him anywhere if you tried. His tan looked like he'd just stepped ashore, which he more or less just had as this was his first time out of the US. Still his personal camera had long-range lens attached and his old 16-mm video camera was still in working condition, even though Czech customs at the airport made him pay an import penalty, just in case he sold it for cash during his European holiday. Thank goodness he didn't come with his black and silver Raiders jacket this time. It was an American gridiron sports team he supported fervently. But he did advertise surfing brands on his caps and T-shirts at every given opportunity. Even if naked he wore all the hallmarks of a beach boy from California. I reluctantly left him to play the role in life he was used to.

Americans in general are strange hybrids abroad; each walking around alone seemingly in their own fish tank with wheels attached to the bottom of their structure, thinking they are inconspicuous while everybody around them knows what nationality they are. These two were like little and large sore thumbs. It was going to take some work to convince them to remain low key, but it was all I had to play with, and I was determined to make the most of their talents.

I carefully explained to them what I wanted; all they had to do was what they knew best—but subtly. After all one was a retired CIA spook from the old school; and the other was a young professional Hollywood movie director who was already a legend in his own mind. They had two days to prepare and check the field of operations I had meticulously mapped out. I was pleased to ascertain they were studiously serious about their tasks despite their obvious immaturity.

I met Paddy O'Neill on the first morning on the steam-engine ferry trip along the Vltava River and canals to Davle. We had compromised by meeting halfway between Ireland and Russia, where my base of operations were. He seemed to be able to commute between the US and Ireland at ease. Neither of us agreed to talk at each other's home ground. In his trilby, he looked to me like a well-to-do Irish country gentleman.

He asked me if I had come with anybody to Prague. I replied with the truth, "Only my Russian driver and I've given him the day off. I think he's gone sightseeing. He doesn't speak English anyway," I said. "What about you?"

He just shook his head. Frankly I didn't know if it was in denial or in admittance. I had already assumed he'd come with somebody to watch over the proceedings. I scanned the three-dozen or so tourists on the boat. I couldn't spot anybody that could fit the bill. My American stalwarts couldn't be seen anywhere either, thank goodness.

"Before we start," I iterated, "I want to ask you if you have any update on David Brennan's demise?"

"I do," he responded promptly, "in fact I personally spoke on the phone to the London policeman that found his body. He was face down in the oven, head leaning peacefully on the cooker's open door. Gassed himself, according to the bobby's account and the resulting post-mortem. It looks like that's final."

I nodded, disappointed. Right at that time I had a twinge of apprehension for a second. A young lady's inadvertent too hard gaze caught my eye as she turned to look away. She was almost too calm. I smiled satanically to myself at the thought, almost muttering under my breath, 'You lying fuck, O'Neill.' He must have mistaken my grimace as a reaction to the news of my best friend.

"I have a question for you too," said the Irish Republican Army chief. I hoped I could answer it. I held my breath. "Where do you want the deposit to go to?"

I handed him a typewritten copy. "It's all there," I said, "when Glenda Godfrey, my lawyer in Belize, sends me a fax to Moscow to confirm she's received the amount in full, at that numbered account, then I ship the Anthrax and the other stuff. You haven't told me to where yet."

Despite the steadiness in his voice, his eyes more or less gave the game away that this was new ground for him. "Well, that's what I want to talk to you about. Could you tell me more about the nuclear explosives?"

I nodded in agreement. I was amazed at my gall and calmness in bullshitting him. "We could go backwards and forwards on this one. Why don't you let me know *what kind* of nuclear-based explosives detection systems you are up against, and I'll tell you what works best, OK? For example, there are seven types of technology: Thermal Neutron Analysis; Fast Neutron Analysis; Pulsed Fast Neutron Analysis; Nuclear Resonance Absorption of Gamma Rays; Associated Particle Production; Nitrogen-13 Production-Position Emission Tomography; and Pulsed Neutron Backscatter."

I didn't let him dwell on that and embarrass himself with not knowing the answer, so I quickly enquired, *"You* are going to use it, aren't you? I hope you're not thinking of selling it to some of my esteemed Arab clients. Some of them know the nuclear material's source in Russia, even though the Russians tell them to deal directly with me. They're going to think I'm not being too forthcoming with them. It would put me in a bad light. Can you tell me *how much* you need at least?"

O'Neill dug a piece of folded paper out of his inside pocket in the tweed blazer with the suede elbow patches, and read it out, "One kiloton." I knew then it was new to him. You'd think he'd remember those two simple words for a huge order.

"That's about one-thirteenth the size of the Hiroshima bomb, if you dispose of it in one go. You must be planning to wipe out the entire suburb of Westminster in London. The tiny amount of germs you are ordering is a biological disaster, enough to infect a quarter of a million downwind in the Big Apple's Brooklyn over a couple of days, just from leaving a small box at Fulton Market on a weekend. A hundred pounds of Anthrax dispersed over a mile will kill or severely disable that many in a heavily populated city. If you want later, you could try smallpox, it's slower but just as effective. Victims that survived the attack would have to be administered three vaccinations in three days plus antibiotics for thirty days. I don't think the authorities are sufficiently equipped to handle it, to be honest. You'll either piss them off so much that you'll have major reprisals on the IRA or you'll get the desired effect, a united Ireland."

I finally succumbed to the urge to ask him about other matters that had troubled me. I wanted to know why the IRA claimed an elimination back in 1976, some two months after it happened. It was their usual practice to issue such immediately, if it was successful, which the answer was. "Oh that one?" he responded, after recalling the incident. "We didn't do it. It was a trade off with NATO. We have an arrangement with them sometimes. Don't like to do it much, but in this case we did. It goes against our policy obviously, but there are swings and roundabouts to negotiate sometimes. As long as we reach our desired destination ultimately, that's the main thing. They once got in touch with me to spy on other European freedom fighters at a convention of sorts. I adamantly refused and got around that by not going at all, seeing, at the time, they had nearly a dozen trailing me on surveillance. Got a written report later of it anyway. Heard, too, there's a special meeting with our Muslim brothers taking place soon."

I slowly nodded my head. I didn't bring up the fact it was probably in *Euskera*, the language of the Basques, if Andry was correct in his information.

The meeting was over as the boat was approaching its mooring back in the centre of captivating Prague. "So we'll be touch again soon. Heading back straight away?" I asked.

"Actually no, I came with my daughter and we're going to drive around central Europe for a month's vacation. She's standing over there watching us. She doesn't know anything about what I do and have done. I've kept her out of it deliberately ever since she was a child." He was waving at the attractive blonde lady in her mid-twenties, the one I spotted earlier looking at me. When she joined us, we weren't formally introduced.

I'd anticipated he may stick around longer and had planned for it, though my budget was tight. M&O, Mendelsohn and Obertone scurried after them. In the distance I saw Bob quickly and unobtrusively attach a tracking device to their car.

When I was back in Moscow I spent an awful amount of time poring over the more recently opened cleared *voyenniye arkhivi*, military archives, at the old KGB library I'd been to before. Winter was here in full force with several feet of snow on the ground, so I hibernated for months with my head burrowed in information. Not everything was available and I got some curt responses from the male receptionist. Either it was a gruff, "We have determined that the information you seek from our agency's files would not contribute significantly to the public understanding of the operations of the government of the Russian Federation." Or it was a laconic, "*Nevelel!* Not allowed! It has not been processed for declassification yet." I wanted to slap that guy so hard sometimes for his bad manners.

Perhaps the most disturbing report I found there at the library, among many others warranting equal consternation was, the fact that in 1964-1965 the United States government had deliberately released millions of germ warfare-developed bacteria in its own capital city of Washington, DC—on two hundred and thirty nine different occasions! They were *just* experimenting to determine whether travellers would carry the microbes across the country. They had, in fact, made this known to their own media in 1985, twenty years after the fact, claiming it was mere *Bacillus subtilis* they were using—enough to give its own citizens blood poisoning and respiratory problems. But what they didn't say was the important word "only", only because, according to the KGB, it was a whole host of much more dangerous chemical and biological viruses thrown into their experimentations—read that as manmade viruses; designed to induce cancer in humans—which were being produced in plentiful at that time at their laboratories in Fort Detrick, Maryland. [In the US it has now been re-named the National Institute of Health.]

Later, it was alleged the Fort Detrick scientists went to Uganda to try it out on equally unsuspecting human guinea pigs there. I noted no author's name, nor precise dates, were included on the pages in the file I read. The same Russian report went on to say: It should be noted that in 1975 a prominent guest speaker, one Jay Corbenson (no nationality known), at an international assembly of cancer researchers in Japan, advised everybody to prepare for a worldwide epidemic of a virus that causes cancer. The next thing we know, HIV had arrived out of nowhere, though seemingly not out of the blue—a deliberate contradiction of words.

There were a series of pages then that refuted the western allegations that the Soviets spread a disinformation campaign about AIDS, including a statement that "HIV doesn't cause cancer". But the KGB, in this document, denied any knowledge of this. To them AIDS was entirely an American synthetic creation, without any help from them. *If only society were advancing as effectively as AIDS has.*

Though in another file, on another day, I came across something where they *did* admit to planting one of their men in a prestigious position in the US medical Establishment. This fellow's name was Dr W. Szmuness. He arrived in America in 1969, four years after the KGB learned of Fort Detrick's US Army Medical Research Institute's for Infectious Disease's germ games. He was to rise through the ranks to become the head of the largest blood bank in New York City. Szmuness was almost single-handedly responsible for nearly one hundred per cent of hepatitis B (HB) vaccine receivers being infected with what was to become HIV in that country. One example of how he did it was by setting up the rules for the HB vaccine studies using *only* promiscuous gay men. At the time, at least in the Soviet Union, it was well known that HB was shed through blood, semen, vaginal secretions and saliva. Homosexual males frequently engage in sexual activities by inserting their tongues into the lower intestinal tract of their partner. This manoeuvre transmits any virus, which persists in the blood with devastating efficiency, even though there may be no virus present in either semen or saliva. Hepatitis B is now the ninth leading killer in the world and certainly the fastest spreading form of disease in the US in the nineties.

So it appears that the West came up with the number one hit among young men; and the East released another that reached number nine on the charts.

Thought has a disease and that disease is called information.

Chapter Fourteen

Andry came alone to Moscow for treatment. When he wasn't at the clinic, he slept on my settee in the hotel suite. Mike and Andry thought they remembered each other from somewhere. That surprised me—given Andry's skin colour, unusually dyed hair and size—you'd think that Mike have no problem remembering him. You don't see people like him in Moscow every day! *I recalled them both being at the Venezuelan's party in 1970...* Anyway, Molody undertook personal supervision of this special patient at my request at no charge.

Andry came for three weeks and went home to the Ukraine a much healthier person than when he arrived. Though Andry has had fully blown AIDS since 1992, he is living a pretty normal life. You would never know he was sick from looking at him. If there's a downside to his annual treatment of human foetal tissue, it is that this experience has made him less of a risk taker and more of a thinker, mellower. Time will tell. Aside to me, Dr Molody said Andry's positive thinking and avoidance of tobacco, dope and alcohol was the other half of the components imperative to his survival.

Andry disclosed that he'd given my NATO overview a lot of thought. "You'd said, 'the Americans will tell us it's a defensive alliance.' We cannot allow another nation who is not even on our continent—forgetting momentarily Russia—to dominate the final analyses of European national security interests. Is this correct?"

It was. For good measure, I threw in, "In between the end of World War II and the close of the Cold War, in and around Europe, every country was either in the Soviet Union's Iron Curtain, the Arab League, neutral (and there were only a handful), or NATO."

Andry digested that, "People say there's no place for private armies in a democracy, but they completely miss the point that we are *not* living in a democracy in the Ukraine. There are few real democracies. Britain is really a constitutional monarchy. Your royal family is one of the UK's largest landowners; they acquired the land from plunder over the centuries then charged rent for the privilege of living on the so-called property they kept. Land is there for everybody to use free of charge whether one believes it the will of a god or the intent of nature. Democracy is supposed to be a system where power is vested in the people, ruling through freely elected representatives and not inherently; but what really happens in these so-called democratic nations is those voted-in do as they wish and often contrary to the true wants of those that elected them. Real democracy is a non-hierarchical decision-making and decentralised organisation that does not compartmentalise the community into specific jobs but instead operates as a single movement to the benefit of all."

He stopped to mull for a moment. "Change is defined by the dynamics of the system being altered, but before change can be effected properly it is often prevented by the roadblocks installed by the political élite to stop encroachment into their cash production."

"That's what I call the illuminati or ruling entrenched élite, Andry, and the very same who impede Dr Molody and his medical discoveries and many other improvements I can think of," I injected.

Andry agreed with me.

I added as a summary, "The strategy for the future is one that has to be clearly better than the present equation and developed *three times over* before its initial introduction as a viable component of change. Success comes if the masses succeed with you and not where the few gain."

With those words ringing in his head, Andry departed home to hopefully begin developing just that for his nation.

* * * * * * * * *

Vladimir Nabokov wrote, "Read the tingle, the shiver up the spine."

My team of Bob and Ben called from Vienna. It had been seven weeks since I'd last seen them. Mendelsohn's voice said, without telling me who was calling, "Your subject has finally flown home. We have several hours of footage and recordings for your inspection. We will be in the café outdoors, one floor up, at Hundertwasser House at 3 Lowengasse, every day between nine and ten hundred hours for breakfast for the next seven days starting tomorrow morning, or until you come to *Wien*. Every taxi driver knows where it is. I think you should schedule a week here so you can go through it all with us. One last thing, boss, I have to report that agents are occasionally present. If you come through the door and see me wearing my wrong cap, bugger off and have breakfast somewhere else. OK? Then we'll find you." Then the phone clicked.

I had to think for a second about the ex-CIA man's use of the word "agent" and what it described, as I could be panicking for all the wrong reasons. The FBI's personnel are called "agents" and its informers and collaborators are "sources"; the CIA's personnel were "officers" and their sources were "agents" (it was the same at SIS). I wondered who and what he meant. Still it was a secure means of communication on his part, a way of confirming a clear connection.

I came through Mike's hometown of Bratislava, leaving Smardz behind in Slovakia to wait for me. I crossed by walking into Austria at the border post near Angern. From there I caught a bus into the capital of *Osterreich*, so named after Otto III created his eastern empire in the tenth-century.

As the Mercedes bus entered the centre of Vienna, coming across a bridge, I found myself humming Johann Strauss' waltzes. The first thing you notice about the city is how clean it is, and filled with an immensely attractive mixture of ancient and modern buildings.

From the bus terminal I caught a taxi to the meeting spot. Bob and Ben were sitting drinking coffee all alone outside on a sunny but very blustery and cold winter morning. Bob had his stupid Czech hat on, both were shivering. Apart from that you wouldn't think they were Americans anymore. They melded right into the scenery even though there was nobody else out there with them. After we shook hands we went inside immediately. "Sorry about that, boss, when we gave you that message, we didn't think it was going to be this chilly. Every morning for the past three days we've frozen our butts off for one hour every day, sitting there dumbly waiting for you. The waitress thinks we're crazies doing this for three mornings straight." Sure enough the lass did look at them strangely as she took my order of bacon and eggs; something you can't get in Moscow unless you queued for an hour at the McDonalds there.

This Viennese spot was a weird place to look at. Ben saw me looking around at the surroundings and volunteered, "Knowing your likes and dislikes we thought you'd find this place interesting. According to the principles of Friedensreich Hundertwasser, he built all his architectural structures without any use of plastics. As much as you have distaste for the Big Apple; he hated anything to do with plastic. I thought you might like to know that." He shrugged with a blank stupid face when I looked at him for a second longer than necessary.

Soon we were in their cheap three-star hotel room. A television monitor and videocassette recorder was ready to go. Ben switched them on as we all sat down on the edge of the bed to watch it. It was noon and you could hear the rhythms of the music played by a nearby clock coming from the direction of the square. It struck me that I was about to see and hear some timely information.

"What the hell is that ugly thing?" I said from the first image that popped up on the TV.

Bob said, pointing at the screen, "The Column of the Plague in Grabenstrasse. Shhh. Wait."

A clear likeness of Hamas' Moueen Mohammed Abu Farkh sprang to life. O'Neill was kissing the Hamas man on both cheeks in greetings. There was no sign of the Irishman's 'daughter'. I was to find out he'd been sharing a bed physically with the lady on the road all this time... Then you heard their voices talking.

I sat there in rapt attention for six hours solid. The quality of production and sound was just superb, but that was the Yanks' professions after all.

The lessons learned were many: O'Neill had purchased and arranged a shipment of "a ton of" Semtex plastic explosives while he was still in the Czech Republic capital of Prague, directly at the Omnipol arms company headquarters (which would actually be sent directly from the factory in Plzen, just over an hour away down the motorway, to its eventual destination in Ireland via Bilboa, Spain); Farkh also mentioned that he'd been in touch with a Dr Shahristani in Tehran, Iran, about manufacturing nuclear weapons for Islamic causes, but he had been rejected flat. The name seemed familiar to me. It was a name Molody had mentioned during his debriefing, I think. O'Neill brought up my name in response to that (hopefully it was because of the word 'nuclear' and not the thought of

Molody). Spelt out all of my available logistics and prices to the Palestinian, who had never heard of me. Clearly they had a consolidated arrangement to exchange merchandise between them, all kinds of materials from guns to bombs, and now—thanks to me—whatever biological and nuclear weaponry they could get their hands on. The ETA in northern Spain seemed to feature as part of both the drop-off and pick-up point men for each party, probably retaining a piece of the armaments in return for their distribution services.

It was an ambitious merger of bastards in more ways than one.

Due to static I couldn't make out who said it, but a voice intoned, "Well, my new chief bomb engineer, Yahya Ayyash, will take care of that. He's Hamas' 'yet to be unveiled secret weapon.'" It had to be Farkh, who went on to declare, "Our suicide operations are a message that our people love death. Our goal is to die for the sake of God, and if we live, we want to humiliate Jews and trample on their necks. Strangely, the Arab eerily half sang a tune for the benefit of his audience:

"We must fight the arrogance of power.
We must shame the agitators of hate into silence.
We must destroy the perpetrators of vitriol worldwide.
We must attack them strategically.
Principle is a weapon the powerless can never lose."

I shook my head at the ballad-form idiocy. Then they both talked all sweet and innocently, over a cup of tea, about quantities needed for improvised detonating fuses; timer-power units; booster tubes; and...adapted beer kegs as bombshells. Said O'Neill once, "When I was just in Plzen, I arranged and paid for a lorry shipment of Czech beer. We'll distribute it to our Belfast pubs but their empty casks are the best for what we need it to do." He was never in Plzen, at least not on this trip. From Prague he and his lady love drove their car completely in the opposite direction according to M&O.

They continued on to compare their methods of bomb-making; logging the chemical compositions of igniting mixtures. "Ethyl alcohol vapour can easily catch and explode, or spontaneous combustion could occur if mixed with another substance." "Wet-cell batteries contain sulphuric acid." "Nitric acid, a corrosive oxidising agent is susceptible to same and can explode."

"No, Hexa Composite is *like* Semtex, a high detonation velocity explosive."
"TATP (Triacetone Triperoxide) is the exclusive choice of explosive by our
bomb-makers." "We use discarded doorbells as detonators but remove
remote controls from the West's new decadent toys…" At the sound of a
chuckle I signalled to move the taped language of rage forward.

We three viewers started to switch positions to get comfortable for
another round. My neck was hurting me. Now they were exchanging the
best construction tools to use. Then O'Neill said, "I agree the best weight
of a pipe should be 12 ounces and that acetone should not be smelled, as it
alerts the unsuspecting."

"That's why we prefer the non-odour of Semtex because we can
conceal it in the lining of suitcases, beneath airplane seats and even as a
detonator in the tube of a tampon," volunteered the Arab.

All chilling stuff. O'Neill even corrected Farkh's knowledge at one
point, "A pipe bomb does not have a detonating cap." He went on to
explain about the IRA's patented expertise with making Mark 6 mortars,
"Measuring only 18" x 3"—since we made the first few in 1974—which
were built from drainpipes and ignited by car batteries. Quite effective."

Ben fast-forwarded on the remote. The whirr of the VCR stopped then
crackled alive. "…the only answer in New York City may be for an asteroid
to smash into the square block owned by the Jews, a intricate financial
matrix of control—Wall Street," came Farkh's mumbled voice. An Austrian
double-decker tourist bus had come between my two and those two, in
Mike-speak.

When the sound burst alive again, Farkh was spitting forth words of
hatred, "Israel, American Jewry's power vacuum abroad, which violates the
Geneva Convention at will, knowing the US will veto sanctions against it in
the United Nations. It's hypocrisy at its worst."

Bob patted my back with a good luck thumb in sarcasm at that last
remark we heard, as his Star of David was cradled in his other hand's
fidgeting fingers.

Farkh was still talking, "Revolutions that begin with promises of
redemption through the killing act, end up delivering nothing more than
just death, which in itself means nothing. The loaning of blood money by
international banks to developing countries should be categorised a crime.
This kind of investment rarely helps the poor of that nation. The
government loots it and it's the people who have to make the payments.

Fucking *shtetl.*" Can't say I didn't disagree with him, just the way he went correcting the problems.

Mendelsohn told me the unidentified word meant "life in a Hasidic community", and that the Palestinian was pissed off with the bankers funding of building homes for Israelis on traditionally recognised Arab lands.

Then the videotape cut out and all we heard was their ominous voices for another quarter of an hour, as the room loomed in opaque darkness. The most eyebrow-raising being from Farkh: "When we drink holy water from Mecca we are absolved from the sin of suicide, which is against Islam." I was thinking O'Neill should have mentioned there's a similar confessional in Catholicism for the IRA's killers…

Ben turned the light on when the voice taping ended. "Apologies about that, I didn't think they'd be talking that long. Couldn't recharge the camera out there."

I was tired so we went and had a quick meal. Of course I had to pay. Then we called it a day.

The next mid-morning we repeated the process. The learning curve just got better and better with each passing hour.

The third tape had a spooky beginning and I could appreciate how hard it became for my intrepid pair to accomplish their goals. O'Neill, Farkh and an unidentified third man were taped briefly from behind shakily walking into a place called *Seegrotte*. For good measure an obviously walking along Ben had the fortitude to film a sign in English, which read, "The Cave in the Lake". From the sounds of splashes and oars scraping, as the screen was temporarily "snowing" dark grey, I got the impression the three were getting on a boat. No words were being spoken.

After five minutes of nothing but water music which came and went, with black and cream shades interchanging on the monitor, they were speaking in hushed tones because of the echo carrying in the caves. Plus it was in a language I didn't know, of which dialogue was restricted to between Farkh and the new man. O'Neill remained strangely silent the whole time. If I had to bet, I would have said it was Urdu, the language of northern India. I hadn't heard it spoken since I was probably under ten years old when I lived in Bombay. I thought that because I heard a single word which resembled it. The stranger, I think, muttered rather forcefully at one point, what sounded like *"Azadi"*—freedom. I knew only five words

from any of the hundreds of Indian dialects but that was one which was in
my extensive vocabulary.

The two Americans were disappointed that I didn't know what was
being discussed, as they'd gone through a lot of trouble to get the scene and
tone to what it was right now.

This session of hard stress, coupled with my ability to speak fluently in
numerous languages made me feel like several persons at the same time.
Confusing but true and as a result of this, I always felt like a stranger. It was
at that moment that I resorted to never again learn to speak another
language. Frankly, it was just too much to know. I think the neuroscientists
would have said "that my software disc was getting overloaded". Actually
since that decision to end the study of language, my skill in writing English
has increased. Go figure.

I was stuck so I got Ben to rewind to the part where the three men
were walking from the cave backwards. He played it twice over then
stopped on freeze-frame. I stared at the rear ends of these human outlines,
thinking at length. At one stage I had my forehead pressed against the
flickering TV set from the strain. It must have sent me an electronic
message. Finally I said to Bob, "When you told me on the phone that you
had 'to report that agents are occasionally present' what exactly did that
mean?"

Bob looked perplexed for a few moments as to what I meant, then it
came to him, "Oh, yeah, yeah, that's right. I forgot. About two days before I
called you, this guy starts talking to me when I came out of the hotel to go
and have a drink. Ben was fast asleep upstairs that evening. Had a heavy
English accent. Knew I was an American. Anyway, I kind of ignored him
but he walked alongside me and sat himself next to me at the bar. Ended up
buying me a couple of beers while he only drank water. Pissed off the
barman somewhat, but in the end he got a good tip. I figured he was a
queer trying to pick me up. We were about the same age, in our late-fifties.
But then when he said he was in the diplomatic corps I got real wary and
kind of wound down on disclosing anything about myself."

I said, "What did he talk to you about, Bobby dear?"

He stopped talking momentarily to flash a glare at me, then kept on,
"Well, he was wondering what I was doing in Vienna, because he said he'd
seen me around the neighbourhood every day for the past three weeks. That
told me maybe he'd been watching us watching the other guys. Asked me if

I'd been in the US Army, which I have, but I didn't let on. Pretty observant guy. Kinda spooked me a bit. Added that he'd been here in Austria for a year now. Then he surprisingly gave me his card, saying I could call him for anything, and then left. I've got it here someplace. Hold on."

While he was searching through his jacket in the closet, I asked him if this happened before or after the cave recording. "After," Ben said, as Bob emerged from behind the door holding the business card. It read simply over four lines, "General Jafzar, KHAD; Government of Afghanistan; Uno City, Austria; and the local direct telephone number". No Christian name was stated.

"What is KHAD and Uno City?" asked Ben, who was leaning over my shoulder reading the card with me.

"Well," I said, "Uno City is the United Nations Organisation's building here in Vienna, it's their third headquarters in the world after NYC and Geneva. But KHAD I know for a fact is the Afghan secret police, because I met some Soviet war veterans in a Moscow bar not so long ago, who were telling me about them and their mutilating torture tactics on captured Russian soldiers.

I looked back at the screen and asked Bob, "Does that man on the right look like it might be him?" Mendelsohn gazed at the image and acknowledged, "Yup, now that you've mentioned it, that's him all right. I've kind of been concentrating on the sound up to now."

He wrung his hand nervously through his stubble of beard, "Fuck. Ben, we're in trouble, man. This is scary shit. The guy was sending us a message to back off by giving me his card. We just didn't know it in our ignorance."

They looked ashen-faced and I was worried too. It meant they knew our exact whereabouts. I went and turned off the closet light Bob had left on, and peeked behind the open curtain. "I should add," I communicated, "that the man in the cave made a derogatory remark about OMON, the Russian special forces, being sissies...in *Russian*. For me, that tells me Jafzar has met enough Soviets in the flesh, after he extracted the information he wanted from them, mind you." When I said it; I wished I hadn't. I scared myself.

Then we got a sudden jolt when the TV went blank with a loud fizz followed by a pop. There was a power cut. The three of us sat on the bed in waiting for the electricity to come back on. Dusk was settling and some light filtered in. It seemed it was just our building. I think they were thinking

I'd come up with something while we waited patiently in the semi-darkness. I was completely at a blank myself as to what to do.

The single knock on the door made us all jump in the eeriness. I went by the door and asked quietly who was there? "Smardrz," came the solemn reply. I opened the door slowly. I gagged loudly in fright—in unison with the two Americans standing behind me—as what resembled a swarthy man's body tumbled to the floor, pushed in by the Russian.

The dead dark face was horribly contorted into an agonised frozen look as his bloody innards flapped loosely out of a widely torn hole in his throat. I'd never smelled that kind of smell before, it was awful. All three of us were nauseated.

Smardrz simply said more words than I ever heard him say ever, without an ounce of emotion, "'Colombian neck-tie,' I owed this to the Afghans after what they did to my friends out there during the war with them. Their cruel practices used to sicken me. I've been watching this hotel building's entrance for two days while I lived in the car. The Afghans have been coming and going all this time. I'd know them anywhere, as I've seen enough of them close up in my life. I can even spot who's sucking *naswar* and who's not. Plus plenty of Pashto and Dari were being spoken. This man was the designated assassin who was going to demolish your bedroom door from the outside with an RPG; you'll see the launcher propped up outside the door. I followed him inside and eliminated him. Took a screwdriver I had to stab him and then pry his insides up and out. If I had time I would have bothered to peel his skin off too like they did to our boys while they were still alive… I think we should leave now before more come, Mr Anderson, sir."

Then he went back to his relative silent mode again, as much as I have tried to discuss anything with him since. He's just that way. (Though I did find out from him eventually that Afghans habitually place *naswah, an* opiate snuff, under their tongues in the belief it give them inspiration.)

Bob and Ben were scared shitless alright after that gory body hit the ground with a bang at their feet. Escorted by Smardz, with the grenade from the RPG inside the pocket of his long coat, we all piled into the ZIL that was parked down the street less than five minutes later, and headed out to *Flughafen Schwechat*, Vienna's airport as we all listened in silence to *"Radesky March"* on the car radio. M&0 caught the first flight back to their homeland from there via anywhere a plane was eventually heading to

America, they just didn't care where. Their mouths firmly slammed shut after their brief flirt with the brutal modern world of spying. I haven't seen them since, though I've talked to them once each on the phone. Ben apparently relinquished the lease he had on my California beach house immediately when he got back. Bob doesn't live in Brooklyn anymore. I think he moved west to Manhattan Beach, which is a few miles up the coast from Balboa. Maybe they still know each other, but they *are* lying low these days. Like I am.

The seven-digit wire transfer did come into the escrow account, amazingly, from the Bank of Ireland in the United States. With some finagling of my own I managed to debit 10%—and in the process reimbursed myself for all the monies I'd laid out during the twenty months of world adventure—before I instructed the attorney to return the funds to the sender. But my offshore lawyer in Belize turned out to be a sleaze bag. To the best of my understanding the Belizean never followed through with my instructions, instead she somehow "lost" the balance remaining (to fuel her cocaine addiction and buy a red Mercedes sports car). I know this because she did the same thing to two others, one had recommended me to her; and the other was somebody I'd given the same advice to in turn who had gone there to see her in person. But the IRA, Hamas and KHAD got a loud and clear message in response as to what happens if they come searching for me though, even though I had not planned that part.

As for the dozens of videocassettes and hours of recording spools, Smardz and I hand-delivered them anonymously to the British government representatives at Uno City that night.

They must have figured it out who did the good deed. My name is mentioned on the tape after all and a enthusiastic Mrs Blyton later told me on the telephone that the tapes were "down in Salisbury in the capable hands of Mr Pearson for analyses at the new Defence Evaluation and Research Agency, a research centre for chemical weaponry". I used to know it as the Ministry of Defence's top-secret General and Biological Defence Establishment at Porton Down in England's Wiltshire. I guess it isn't so hush hush any more.

She'd also mentioned that all other BL4 members would be accessing the materials I'd provided. Up to that point I'd never heard of BL4. I was to learn from her that they are five labs in the world that are certified to stock the highest containment level of dangerous microorganisms. I naïvely thought it was just Moscow and Atlanta who had it. Boy, was I wrong. Why so many? What do we need it for? Are we all mad?

"Mr Medusa" was heard to thud from the back of the car as we went around corners coming back into Vienna from the airport. He was making a mess of the back compartment and making a smell to boot. We stopped at a hardware store, which was about to close, and purchased a large new kitchen knife. The fearful proprietor couldn't wait to get us out of there as Smardz had a fair amount of splotches of different sizes of rouge all over him. The Russian was quite a sight and looked liked he'd run amok massacring people. I politely requested for a medium-sized empty cardboard box from the poor speechless retailer who complied without further ado.

The hideous head of the dead Afghan with the awful ghoulish mask was dropped off in that brown box at Uno City while we were there, for the eyes only of General Jafzar. The unexploded grenade was added for good measure.

Smardz had severed it from the rest of its bulk neatly without as much as a word and threw the headless body in the icy Danube that same night, complete with the screwdriver rammed dead centre into its cold heart. As I said before, Smardz was a great driver.

What little I have found out about Smardz since, and it was Yuri The Moscow Policeman who told me, was that during the Soviet-Afghan War he had been a Senior Lieutenant of the Armed Special Service's at the GRU's General Headquarters for Special Forces of the Soviet Union Overseas Division, and that he had been based in their Kabul station most of the time. He had been his job though to co-ordinate the return of the KIA (killed in action) on to the Black Tulips—specially-built large Soviet aircraft that carried home the dead in coffins—back to their loved ones so I suspect he saw an awful amount of butchered remains in his time. It may have made him what he is today. Though he nor I ever uses his first name, Ilya, I now respectfully call him to his face, *"Mstitel."* Pronounced like it's preceded by a "Mr" but in fact it means "Avenger".

And finally not so very long after this bizarre episode, according to Mrs Blyton, *the* most senior member of the IRA's Army Council voluntarily contacted the British government about how to peaceably bring the Troubles in Northern Ireland to an end.

Chapter Fifteen

If ever asked to describe the difference between heaven and hell,
my answer would be to say they were the same,
like here and now alone;
exactly wherever you are at the time
whenever the question was asked.

Back in the mid-seventies, five months after covertly arriving in Moscow via Crimea was when Dr Michal Molody said to me one evening, "What does your soul look like?"

The supreme flatness of the question jolted me. So I let it hang without responding, while I thought.

Slowly I uttered, almost under my breath, "If I talked about it, I'd get flattened by my own skeletons." Mike looked intently at me then and leaned forward saying quietly, "Here in the Soviet Union, the art of the leak is an unofficial pastime. Any drip of information is picked up."

We were only a foot apart from each other's noses for a few seconds I actually thought I would have to kill him and then eliminate Caterina asleep in the bedroom, making it look like a double suicide. I couldn't afford a slip on my cover as I would never survive another Bulgarian-type internment. *Damn*, I wondered to myself, *Imagine having to do away people you actually like.*

While I was still contemplating an answer, Mike, choosing his words carefully stuttered slightly, "I have watched you closely. For a man of 28 you are *the* most experienced person I have ever met. Certainly I don't think it was all learned in Rostov-on-the Don."

He sat waiting for me to speak, then he said quietly, "Please put a voice to the television." I took that to mean turn up the volume, which I leaned over to do. He got up and went to turn on the radio and came to sit down again, slightly skittish himself. "At a risk of having my lovely wife and I liquidated by 'jumping' from twenty floors up here to our deaths, together in a 'suicide pact', I want to say as a professional student of psychology that our individual sense of self-consciousness arises from the cerebral patterns permanently inscribed as a result of many of our life's experiences. What I am saying is that with your spiritualised background, it strikes me that you are very, *very* worldly."

His fingers were fidgeting. He cleared his throat nervously, then continued, "Are you spying against me for the KGB? If you are I would like to know now, please. For the sake of our continued friendship."

My eyelids fluttered at that, I'm sure, thus sending him the wrong signal. So I replied, "Are you serious? You really think I am a KGB agent spying on you?"

Then I held his gaze steadily, and he looked away momentarily, then shrugged. "Well, please answer the question at least."

"No, I'm not," I said immediately, meaning it. "I'm slightly offended you would think I was spying on you for Mother Russia. I wish to know why you assume this."

He relaxed visibly. "I...I thought perhaps I should ask you this because you are not an ordinary Russian. Believe me, I feel it in my gut. You are not the same person I met at Patrice Lumumba. In less than a decade no man I have studied under my personal microscope has such worldly views, unless of course he went through them first-hand. I have observed patients who have been to war in Afghanistan and Angola and seen appalling atrocities; others who have stomached severe cases of angst from genuinely abnormal circumstances; but both groups have lived to talk about it. You strike me as the same as such a person, on my life you do." He sipped his herbal tea. I noticed his hand jiggled ever so slightly. I let him continue talking.

"Whenever I have occasionally alluded to such awful places and mention some of the things that go on there or in my work, you don't respond. Yet I always get this gnawing impression that you *have* been there. Please fill in the spaces for me."

It was then that I took a gamble and spoke to him into the early hours about the fact I was a British former chopper pilot and MI6 intelligence officer who had seen various kinds of action in Libya and Poland. Then I informed him that I had been released from Bulgarian solitary confinement less than a year ago. Instead of agitating him, this news seemed to make him sleepy, as he stretched out on the settee. Only right at the end did I tell him of the British government's offer to help his wife and him defect to the West, if they wanted to.

He had accepted immediately. Caterina and he had wanted nothing else.

Little did he know that had his response been negative to my proposal or he wanted more time to think about it, I would have had no choice but to kill them, most likely the way he had already articulated.

As a result of that heart-to-heart talk, Operation KANTELE was born. More importantly something else had been established: Trust...in each other.

That same morning I had communicated to London that BENNY (Molody and his wife) was ready to go. As was with SIS policy, all departments were alerted and were ready to render assistance and information.

Prior to talking to the doctor, I had obviously thought about it at length. As I was to both organise and implement the task, I became busier than I had ever been in my life. The operation's duties consumed me twenty-four hours a day. Even in my sleep I realised I was thinking and re-thinking the enormity of what I was about to undertake. It became clear that I was travelling one-way only with the Molody's, and would not be returning to the Soviet Union. I would be leaving too many trails behind and common sense dictated I should not return under any circumstance. Too many knew of our friendship and it would take an idiot not to associate their disappearance with the music man from the south. London agreed with this conclusion too, which made matters easier.

Soon after the decision to defect was made, I found reasons to go on two business trips by car to explore the terrain. I had examined the extremely busy border crossing between the East German frontier town of Frankfurt-an-der-Oder and Slubice in Poland. One hundred and fifty thousand people at the time crossed there annually. Depending on the season, that calculated at over 400 bodies per day; of which one out of 10 were drivers steering heavy-goods lorries laden to the hilt. That came to 40 of these vehicles, on average, every day. At the time it wasn't open all hours of the day either. The clock that roughly a 100 East German and a 100 Polish customs officers worked on was from 7:00 AM to 5:00 PM, which meant they thoroughly checked four of these monstrous trucks each hour or only 15 minutes per—an impossible job.

Later on when I was having a cup of tea and a snack on the Polish side at a roadside mobile café, having cleared the long bureaucratic queues of passport control and completion of customs forms *twice*, going out and coming in, I stood trying to count the backlog of lorries waiting to clear the same paperwork rigmarole I'd just arduously gone through. That midweek day at the end of summer, at sunset, the vehicles stretched into the foggy distance as they sat parallel to the mist steaming off the smelly Oder River.

They were more than the 40 lorries that I'd previously estimated would be filed there on that particular day and I stopped counting as I passed by them in the opposite direction on the motorway due east to Poznan. If you missed the deadlines by the customs officials then you were expected to spend the night in your cabin. From observing the registration plates of the various nationalities—based on the West and East German, Polish, Russian and even one British and a Dutch—the parked tail-end lot appeared to be already asleep in their bunks behind the driver's compartment, I felt assured that the location provided a 95% chance of success of smuggling three people out. Though I'd heard rumours of the East Germans using a device that could monitor the heartbeat of a person hiding within the confines of a lorry, I never saw it in use. It was probably just a good propaganda deterrent.

A few weeks later I'd been granted approval for a business trip within the Motherland. A much easier application to get okayed, as it didn't effect my apparatchik upper class two international travel quotas in the year, which was itself restricted to within the enticing communist eastern countries at that.

The trip northwest from Moscow to Vyborg, the last major town before the Finnish border, was four hundred miles. The last seventy-five was a tarmac one-lane, wide enough for one lorry only; but from the capital to Leningrad it was a well-paved well-travelled monotonous two-lane motorway. The weather got noticeably colder the further north I drove.

Sankt-Peterburg was Leningrad's former name and its resident constantly referred to their city as such in defiance of the Soviet regime's then stipulation. Despite my disdain for Moscow—other than the sights of the Kremlin and Red Square's majesties—this melodious city was the opposite. If you wished to see art in galleries galore, you lived here.

On the first reconnaissance there, my own recollection of this hauntingly beautiful place centred instead around the Kazan cathedral at Piskarovskaye cemetery. I had parked my car across the street at the Stoyanka, as I was staying overnight at the Nevsky Palace. The view was so compelling, I just stood there admiring the inspired sensation for a full half-an-hour.

The next day I was on the road early and went straight past Vyborg and kept going. The closer to the *CCCP-Suomi* signs I got—the Soviet Union-Finland border—the heavier the concentration of Red Army troops and tanks.

I found a suitable spot overlooking the mainly flat dense forested area. Having spent a silent hour there, I was just preparing to leave when in the near distance, a half-a-mile below me, a Soviet platoon were piling out of an amphibious land-water vehicle.

The young faces and well-pressed uniforms of the dozen or so men told me these were new conscripts. I decided to stay a while longer and watch what their duties were to be out in the middle of nowhere. It didn't immediately hit me that *anything* was out here in the resplendence of this nippy autumn mid-morning.

The single officer was issuing orders to the soldiers. Through my Kombinat (brand of binocular) I could see their breaths rising. Of the many items they dismantled there was a piece of equipment I didn't recognise. It very much resembled an odd-looking bulky, camera-like object. It intrigued...I made a serious mental note to describe the gear to an expert along with the approximate area of exercise.

To cut a long story, I was to be informed by London that the troops were checking the general field with flir zoom lens, a forward looking IR (infra-red or heat) night sight with built in PAVE TACK radar. The machinery could be used in the super wide field of view and to detect an object miles away. It would automatically lock-on and provide magnification of up to 22.5 times, bringing the target in for quick and efficient identification. It was assumed they were going over the working order of the various warning devices that triggered the awareness of intruders before the onset of the severe Russian winter. Manned by the 220,000 Border Guards, throughout the Soviet Union's thousands of miles of boundaries with its neighbours, they had installed hundreds of elaborate *visirs*. These were normal and infra-red 24-hour surveillance stations with all modern long-range cameras, telescopes, plus other optical and sound amplification stratagems. They were staffed by heavily armed men supervised by the KGB itself.

The latter Finland exit, despite the presence of human corps and unseeing beams and sensors on the ground, was eventually selected over the aforementioned East German-Polish route for the simple reason that Caterina Molody suffered from claustrophobia. There was no way she could sustain even one full day in a false dark special compartment surrounded by goods being moved. No drug could be administered, even by her physician husband that could keep her knocked out for a maximum specified period of up to four days. The frequent jolting of the lorry could even make her assume a dangerous paranoid state, endangering everybody, including the unsuspecting Russian lorry driver whose vehicle's hull was to be selected. It should be added that it would have been another daunting job in itself to get through the second level of checkpoints further along the road, from East into West Berlin. Nevertheless London had ordered me to undertake the human-size container exercise anyway except to not put a real human body in there—as a dummy run so to speak. I did as I was told. I understood at a later date that a lot was learned from the trial as the stuffed cushions arrived untouched.

A third option via their Czechoslovak homeland into Austria was vetoed completely for four good reasons: (a) They had already used up their foreign visits quota issued by the authorities; (b) Even if specially approved, it would compromise their respective innocent families in Bratislava, which was right on the countries' border; (c) Plus the added emotional conflict of knowingly saying good-bye forever to their parents would be too much; and, lastly (d) Caterina's general state of slightly leaning to passive regressive acts were to be reckoned with…or, looking at it differently, control of "a free spirit" was not a option.

Despite this, at no time did I ever consider leaving her behind. She was the fuel that kept the enigmatic fine engine of Dr Molody functioning. Without her the whole idea of getting him out was defunct.

However, in investigating the idea of Austria as a way out, it resulted in the bulky delivery of a top-notch kayak and winter water sports equipment being smuggled in to me via the Moscow underground connections I had. SIS reimbursed me after I purchased it on my real Grindlay's Bank credit card, while at the flagship store of Kastner & Ohler in Vienna, during my last but one illegal trip out of the Soviet Union. (SIS personnel's monthly salaries are paid by standing order by the Foreign & Commonwealth Office through Hambro's Bank, which included a predetermined stipend for all out-of-pocket expenses, whether it was spent or not.)

Without further disclosing this proven elusive channel to the West at the future disadvantage of other exfiltrations, even in these days of supposed friendship between Russia and the NATO allies, I can only write that there is a Russian-born man who has lived in Finland most of his adult life; who still undertakes the occasional dangerous mission of guiding the likes of us out to freedom. I shall call him "Tuomo" as he has become a naturalised Finn; a take on his real Russian name.

The reason Tuomo continued to do this, when requested through the highest diplomatic avenues even then in his very fit late-sixties, was that the Stalinists butchered his entire family when he was a child.

After we had penetrated the heavily patrolled twenty-mile no man's land security zone, we three men walked took turns towing a woman in the kayak across the border between the Soviet village of Vysock and Virojoki in Finland.

But we didn't do it the traditional way, over recognised land where the barbed wire, electric fences, monitoring towers and unseen devices were. We did it on top of ice in the dead of winter where the lasers beams couldn't cover movement.

But the mines and underwater microphones were still there, sitting on the sea bottom waiting to explode when they detected magnetic field or sound of a target coming by overhead. So before our arrival it had been Tuomo's job, using a basic Russian-made superconductivity magnet he'd obtained, to check the route. Just the day before, he told me he had also played a "silent fun game of bowls on the ice by sliding a heavy object ahead of himself", and by doing so he made a note of the clear zones with the use of a special non-magnetic sextant (a compass which checks position by observing the sun and the stars). I also saw the starlight scope (a hand-held infra-red detector with a range of 1.5 kilometres) he had in his possession, a gift from the British Army.

He'd been doing this brave, dangerous work for nearly forty years and had been on British payroll for half of it. He knew the area like the back of his hand, yet to avoid suspicion he still hadn't learned to speak fluent Russian—so he could claim he was accidentally lost after ice fishing, a common occurrence in those parts. The fishing tackle, rod, bait and even freshly caught fish were duly part of his repertoire.

What I will repeat are the vivid statements which each one of us involved did say during that extremely cold journey across the *Finski zaliv* or *Suomen lahti*, depending on which language you preferred to call the Gulf of Finland, in Russian or in Finnish. A trip which entailed bellowing winds, snow flurries and frostbite. It was the nearest I could imagine to what the North Pole was like with plenty of flowing water to boot as I could feel it rumbling underneath sometimes when the ice thickness was only a tingling foot deep, though the average density was twice that out on the open sea.

For the exhaustive eighteen hours it took to encircle the mapped infrared and mine sections, we were instructed not to speak to each other. I could see the dripping ice freeze and envelope my colleague's entire bodies, and I must have appeared identical. From time to time I would crack the white hardness off to prevent immolation build-up and preserve mobility.

At some point during that trip I pretty much made up my mind I intensely hated snow and ice. Later in life I was to be diagnosed with mild Seasonal Affective Disorder (SAD), a form of winter depression. Psychologically, it may be because I'd crammed in enough of it already to last a lifetime.

When the self-imposed silent period was over, Tuomo, our guide who will forever remain anonymous, stated, "Over the past year, a wink in ecological terms, we've seen strange things we can scarcely believe in the tundra. Elk huddling in huge groups; bears fighting wolves; wolves killing coyotes; wolves forcing coyotes to den in hiding places where they are running into and awakening hibernating brown bears. The natural balance of predator and prey has been disrupted and now predator preys on predator." *His statement reminded me that the spy business was exactly the same.*

Even after having endured the severity of the bitter cold and making it to Finland, it was well known that the local jurisdiction would hand escapees back to the Soviet Union where they would most certainly face the firing squads. They didn't wish to upset their powerful neighbour as the country had a thriving business from the Russian Bear. So we were to have to watch out carefully too for Finland's armed security forces. Finlandisation in the Cold War was a euphemism for enforced submissiveness.

It didn't help that before departure from Moscow, SIS had informed me that they were *not* going to let their erstwhile colleagues at the Finnish protection police unit, *Etsiväkeskus*, know of our plans either. There had been a spate of intelligence data somehow getting back into the Soviet's hands, reportedly to a double agent inside OSZ. *Otdel Spetsialnikhi Zadanii*, were the Special Task Branch of the Soviet military intelligence organisation called GRU, the armed forces own version of the KGB. So we were the lone actors in the play.

What did help was that Finland was the most densely forested land in Europe. Lakes and bogs cover ten per cent of the country and it contained a staggering ninety-eight thousand islands.

In the haunted darkness of pre-dawn, strolling through the munching rhythm of leaves and twigs, the four of us trampled on the crunchy snow, Tuomo had actually spoken for a second time offering an interesting titbit in English. "There is an ingredient discovered in Finland from which chewing gum was made from birch tree sap. It's called xylitol and it prevents tooth decay." Nobody had said anything as we were digesting the information looking around at the thousands of black and white sticks of birch trees which engulfed us.

At dawn the bullets scream ahead of thought, before its target's brain can react, ahead of its sound's impact...and then loud silence...a nothingness, a life slammed into eerie deadness, and the very end has come and gone.

The sound of the shot was audible from 100 yards away: a cannon ball smacking the skull. Tuomo and I both hit the deck instantly while Mike and Caterina stood glued to the spot, aghast looks on their faces.

Seconds later the Finn was up on his feet—it was the first time I'd seen him laugh—and I got up slowly and followed him. We walked towards a bear of a man, a hunter friend of our guide, who had just killed a stag. As the two Finns chatted, I stared agape at that antlered creature with the dripping red blob which replaced its nose. It reminded me of Rudolf the Red-Nosed Reindeer…dead. I looked away to see the Molodys making their way to us, the scared expressions still painted there. Minutes later we were on our way again.

We came out at a clearing at a *laavu*, a sheltered bay on a lake. There was music drifting across the water before dawn. I knew that it was the 6th of December, Independence Day in Finland, which marks their freedom from Russia in 1917, and was celebrated with parades, blue and white candles and much Finlandia vodka. They were getting an early start.

Still crunching through the forest towards freedom for the Molodys, at first light the full orchestra of dawn's chorus struck up fortissimo, with the ducks and fowl singing their praise for us. The opera of the birds stirred the senses.

Hours later we were taking off our outer clothing in a deserted cabin on the outskirts of a village just east outside Virojoki. Then Tuomo shook hands with everybody and bade us *kippis!* "Cheers! I'm going to have a drink now!" He got to the door and chirped then flapped his arms wildly like an albatross, smiled, then flew out.

A quarter of an hour afterwards we followed, in his exact same empty footsteps in the deep snow, then mingled with the small crowd already out and about. I made a quick collect phone call at a *puhelinkoppi*, an outdoor phone booth. As I was waiting for the connection, I could hear a wonderful harp-like sound in the distance. I broke out into a wide grin just to myself in satisfaction, all alone in my own tired cheerfulness.

The instrument was called a *kantele* played to a Finnish folklore to promote the well being of a tribe—I'd heard it before—it was the descriptive for which I had named Operation KANTELE* after.

* * * * * * * * * *

We slept like logs on the three-hour all-stops bus ride west from Kotka towards Helsinki, the capital of Finland. I woke up before the other two, and watched in silence out of the window as we entered the centre of the city in the late afternoon-early evening. We had unintentionally missed a few stops previously for Helsinki Airport and were going right into *Helsingin Linja-Autoasema*, Helsinki bus station. The festive season's decorations were beginning to burst as the coach was turning the last couple of streets into the terminus.

An attractive young lady sitting across from us, who introduced herself as Kirsi, in perfect English told me a story why Helsinki was illuminated by

---

* Unlike other NATO countries the UK does not use words for its operations' titles that describe what the objectives are.

the twenty-light installations of the Festival of Light. "It was to brighten up our dark and cold winter days," she had smiled brilliantly. When she stood up at the terminal, like the furniture from Finland, she was an all-embracing design culture of functional practicality. I reminded myself guiltily I had a Danish version of this waiting for me in Switzerland.

The red Swissair DC-9 with the white cross thundered into the night sky over Helsinki bound for Zürich. I will never ever forget Caterina and Michal crying freely as they held hands together with mine. All I could think of to say, at a time no words would suffice, was merely, "That tomorrow is finally here today." To say it was an emotional moment was a massive understatement.

Though I never told them, we were joined at the Swissair check-in counter by a male officer and a female officer from SIS who had slipped me the Molody's British false passports and tickets, and who also joined us as the security detail for the flight. I'd called them earlier to confirm our arrival in Finland.

The plane landed late at night in Zürich and we flew on a small Crossair commuter jet to Lugano, in the Alpine mountain region of southern Switzerland. Still accompanying us were the inconspicuous British duo, all the while appearing to be on separate business trips. The Molody's were too elated and too tired to notice them. Their taxi followed ours from the airport to the house where they were all finally introduced before heading to our own bedrooms.

I woke up the next morning to a magnificent setting. We were some 2,500 feet up in the white-tipped Alps. Sloped below us was *Lage di Lugano*, an invitingly romantic lake. If you stayed on the nearby main road driving south around it, you would come to the Italian border inside a quarter of an hour.

I was also to be Dr Molody's controller and at the breakfast meeting I met the other fourth member of our team, a British male officer who had already been in Switzerland for a few days. He'd set up this location for us and brought the recording equipment in with another SIS officer who had since left. The latter had installed all matters of technology, including voice stress analysers and oscilloscope to compare voice patterns and speech. I thought it looked like an electronic jury.

After the SIS crew had a good hearty morning meal, the Molody's were still sound asleep in their room, so I slipped a note under the door telling them why we were locking it from the outside for half an hour.

The four of us—all now armed—went for an investigative walk around the one acre of overgrown bush to inspect the fence and literally test the grounds for ways to get over and under it. The homes on either side of us were unseen over half a mile away, while the house below was three hundred yards down the slope, half way down to the edge of the lake. Nothing was above us, just nature and the sky beyond that. As a group of six we were under strict instructions not to leave the place collectively under any circumstance, unless it was approved by London. Food and other necessities would be brought in by the single individual assigned to go out once on the weekend. After a while, we took turns doing this, if only to get a change of scene for an hour or so. There were to be no days off.

It was going to be our home until the exercise was deemed over, certainly a couple of months at least. Our names for the purposes of being heard on tape were A, B, C and D. I selected "C" for the hell of it, after the esteemed overall leader of SIS. "A" was the young woman officer, fluent in German, who would be quietly spending time with Caterina Molody, who also herself spoke German and English well, depending on her mood. (In time, the diplomatic English lady was to go on to hold the post of First Secretary at the Foreign Office.); "B" was a graduate student of the same man that debriefed me upon my release from Bulgaria and an expert in psychology; and "D" was the resident physician who was supposed to know everything Michal Molody might refer to in medical terms. All lone wolves in the human connection business. All of us trained MI6 intelligence officers in differing specialised fields.

Headquarters in London had sent a list of topics to cover, in any order. I elected to go chronologically, as it was easier to remember as I already knew basically what had happened in his life, all of it medical-related: it was to be Space, Sports, Research and His Contacts. The how, who and where part would be learned by real medical doctors working from the transcripts we generated. Mike would be spending many months in Britain with them after Switzerland was over in a kind of show-and-tell.

I knew there would be other matters not on the list of "must do" topics; it always did in any walk of life. I already had one foot inside his head; now we had to get the other foot in to kick out the rest of the information. We were mentally ready.

But they were not. As bad luck would have it Mrs Molody was understandably sick from the strenuous and emotional rigours of the previous few days. So collectively—the Molody's included—we made the decision to take three days off and to commence on the coming Monday, when the working week usually started. With permission granted from London, I had immediately taken this opportunity to fly back from Lugano's Agno airport to Zürich and gone home to Berne for the weekend to see my Danish award-winning sculpture of flesh. With exemplary timing Vibeke was off every day too.

By nine o'clock on Monday I was back, fully rejuvenated having driven from the Swiss capital in my firm's faithful Audi. Now we had two cars at our disposal in the driveway, the other being a big Mercedes.

Michal had appeared all relaxed too and we started straight away. I never got to see Cat for two full days after I got back, as she was still resting. I already knew a lot of the earlier stuff we covered, but we had to record it for posterity.

After graduation from the University of Bratislava Medical School, he had been drafted to work in Moscow in January 1961. At twenty-one he was a Soviet government protégé, already certified a probable genius in his time.

His first job was at an unnamed secret city outside Moscow. It was later to be named Star City. The Soviet Space Agency programme there had started the year before his arrival. With a team of top medical physicians, a fresh-faced Dr Molody was assigned by the chief designer, Sergei Korolev, to work on human body research with Cesar Solovyov, the chief rocket engineer and instructors to the first cosmonauts. Vostock-1, the first flight with a man as passenger, had been four months after his commencement there, on the 12th of April, when the young Czechoslovak was sent to Dropping Region 306 in the uninhabited part of the mountains of Gorno-Altai where sections of spacecraft were designed to drop after lift-off from Baikonur. While there he discovered the poisonous effects of the fuel called heptyl was a total disaster to human health.

Whether it was of any significance or not, Michal also relayed a story to us on how the Soviet Air Force's Lieutenant Yuri Gagarin was three pounds overweight and Solovyov ordered him to be replaced by German Titov, his backup. But the Kremlin, for unknown political reasons, had ordered them be switched despite the weight problem. Mike's own opinion for it was "perhaps for future Soviet public relations as Gagarin was handsome and charismatic."

Despite the nation's leader Nikita Khrushchev's assertion that Vostock-1 "reflected the heroic accomplishments of the Soviet people", Molody's was the first revelation that Gagarin's flight into orbit was far from the seamless triumph that the Kremlin publicised for so many decades.

Altogether Dr Molody disclosed the names of three other closed cities that he had worked at in the Soviet Union: Oblensk (near Moscow); Arzamas-16 (southeast of Moscow); and Krasnoyarsk-26 (northeast of the real city of Krasnoyarsk). Each previously unknown place produced nuclear warheads.

He told us of the existence of a space launch pad it turned out neither London nor I had ever heard of, at Pleseck in the Archangel region, 400 miles north of Moscow.

We were also to learn, amazingly, that this gregarious physician's second love after medicine was mechanical science. In fact, Michal Molody disclosed in great technical details that "Man's first voyage beyond the planet was nearly a disaster", helping to illuminate this hidden crisis of communist history.

Having a sense of humour of his own, Molody had a few quips here and there. Two I recall were, "I bet you didn't know astronauts have trouble burping in space" and "Nobody can hear you scream in space."

My favourite was, "Khrushchev had really sent Gagarin and Titov to check on the Russian Orthodoxy's Patriarch Alexei of Moscow & All Russia's claim about heaven being up there and that had they looked and had found nothing."

Dr Molody also had access to the old and new data from both Sputnik, which had flown in 1957, and the secretive N-1 moon rocket, which went four times around the moon between February 1969 and November 1972.

The latter spacecraft was 34 stories tall and had 30 NK-33 engines with an incredible 10 million pounds of thrust. I was later to learn that it compared to only 7.6 million pounds for Saturn-5, the US' moon rocket. During the Cold War thus far, the Russians perfected ten times more liquid-fuel rocket engines than the Americans.

The success was news to us as the Americans had claimed all four of N1's flights were failures, while Saturn's were the opposite...

Molody was later transferred along with Valentin Glushko, the top designer of rocket engines, to GUCOS, the Soviet Space Warfare Programme, which was under the directive of the Chief Department of Space Affairs, an independent body of the Soviet Strategic Rocket Forces. While there he also got further interested, almost as a hobby, in the obsolete 1957 R-7 intercontinental ballistic missile project and was able to tell us many of its design components in great detail. While it was a subject long put into mothballs by the Soviets, it was of interest to the West to learn of its functioning parts nevertheless.

GUCOS was in charge of everything connected with space warfare and eventually the entire Soviet space programme fell under its auspices, including Mir, the space station. The Space Warfare Centre's offices were located in Bolsheevo, a 30-minute train ride from Yaroslavsky Station in Moscow. It took another 15-minute bus ride from the station to the location. I knew this irrelevant fact when I was a student at Patrice Lumumba University. He had told me of his long commute then, when I talked to him for the first time at the party near the Moscow Dynamo sports complex.

From the Bolsheevo office he had dealt with the aircraft maker Tupolev's plant in Zhukovsky. "From 1968 until 1973, they tried seventeen times to build a supersonic jet commercial plane, then they disbanded production. Though I can't prove it, I *know* the designs were stolen. Because after that there was a British-French built Concorde. On my life it was the exact same design."

I seemed to recall an opposite account of that...then I shook my head, I wasn't the one who was going to analyse all this information...

He claimed that the Russians had *sovershenno seketno*, top secret information, from the fledging thirteen-nation European Space Agency's intentions from the beginning. They knew of Kourou, in French Guinea, on the northeast shoulder of South America, being a would-be launch site well before it was built, including the fact their rockets would be named Ariane...for the Greek goddess of mythology.

Dr Michal Molody worked in space programmes on and off for 12 years.

His memory for detail was excellent and needed little or no prompting. I was slowly beginning to see how Molody was of value to the Soviet Union and to us.

At this stage, so far, we had been taping for almost a month and sending a duplicate reel every week via the British consulate in Geneva to SIS in London for transcription and dissemination. The fact that we hadn't heard anything back was a good sign in that they were happy with the contents. We were on a roll and had worked every day straight through Christmas and the New Year celebrations without a break; though on both occasions we'd drank the best champagne at our employer's expense. *A calm, masterful consensus builder with powerful conviction goes far, especially if able to bring people together positively.*

"A" reported Caterina was getting itchy feet. Around this time Michal also wasn't so forthcoming and we had to pry certain details out of him. Over dinner one evening, I had suggested we all take the weekend off, and go into town for a few hours tomorrow.

Everybody initially had been all for it, although "B" had brought up that it was breaking the rules. We were!

Despite personally looking forward to the half-day out before he went to sleep, I was surprised to find "B" a little nervous again the next morning, and he whispered to me, "What if the enemy have located us and have been waiting our group's exit? I'm volunteering to stay and mind 'home' while you all go." So he stayed put to mind the store.

I had added that I disagreed with his assumption but it was better we be sorry than not have somebody mind the fort at all. He had two spare cars if he changed his mind. He knew where he could find us. He probably slept the entire time we were out instead.

Once the five of us had walked down the slope and were excitedly aboard one of the two regular ferries that churned around the clock. On our way to Lugano town surrounded by white-covered plunging mountains over us, I hugged Caterina Molody suddenly and exclaimed, "Happy Grandfather Frost Day!" It was Russian Christmas, 7th of January. It was really her reward for being a good girl so far. If she was happy, Mike was. A psychological move on my part and I decided to concentrate my attention on her today, when I subtly could.

It was to be an exceptional outing that became all day and *half* of the next day. So much for a few hours of rest. In fact we took off a third day to recover from our exhaustive tours.

Switzerland only has seven million people and between them they speak five languages, one of the minority being English. By far the most popular was German, followed by French, Italian, (then English) and Romanisch; the last only one per cent spoke.

We were very obviously in the zest for life Italian-speaking sector. *La dolce vita*-style Lugano is in the canton of Ticino. They were also more banks per square mile in this glitzy little town than in any European capital.

The landlocked Swiss, always proud of their country's wartime status as a neutral island in a sea of fascism, were the same Swiss dealers who were suspected of being fences for the loot from Holocaust victims. They were practised in the art of hypocrisy that many of them freely admitted it. They changed money at will around the world on both sides of the law; and both them and the world knew it.

We docked at the Old Quarter and immediately found ourselves on the main square. Piazza Riforma was saturated with appealing cafés so naturally that was the first thing we all sat down to experience. It was then that I picked a moment to explain to Caterina that, regrettably, Mike and she *had* to have the three of us along as security. It was still conceivable that her husband could be killed this day, as our sojourn into town perhaps presented an opportunity to execute him. It was highly unlikely, of course, but that had done the trick and saved the days to come of any unnecessary complaints. She hadn't let go of her husband's hands after that little chat either.

As we sat inside the Tango café-restaurant watching the world go by, we could smell the pizzeria upstairs, that wondrous American invention the Italians imported. At the suggestion of Mrs Molody we went to eat first then she was to choose a museum to visit after. She was temporarily back in her element and nobody wanted to suggest alternatives.

As with the local custom we ate Italian but not in a pizzeria. We did so at one of the numerous *grotti,* the traditional eating houses, with beamed ceilings and open fireplaces. So welcoming was the place that everybody was *very* content to let Caterina be the boss for the rest of the day and especially after she chose the region's favoured Merlot wine.

I had learned a couple of things too from her that day. The first was, "Wine kept the doctor away and was good for health." The first time I ever heard that and now it's common knowledge.

We went to *two* museums after that, though the best gallery was closed for the winter months.

As I knew my lady was home that day, I'd resisted making a telephone call to her in Berne. It was against the rules and my call may have been traced to Lugano. Then I'd treated my brief disappointment by gorging on chocolate samples at the highly unusual museum, which had an overhead walk over the actual real chocolate production area. Then it was back to the house after that.

The next day when we returned to town, still minus "B", we took the funicular train ride to the village of Monte Bre for a head-spinning view of the towering Alps, with the Matterhorn peak very prominent in the distance. Up there we had walked for an hour or two in the head-clearing mountain cold. The air had a most effervescing feel to it.

A stranger would have observed five people walking around more closely than normal...with the Molody's always securely in the middle. Down in Lugano centre itself we were lost in the crowd but up here we were a most conspicuous strange group indeed as we bunched far too near—a moving knot.

On the spare day, ensconced back in our warm chalet, a supremely satisfied Caterina's happy voice stirred the air. I wheezed a sigh of relief that my game plan had worked to perfection.

For the next month we breezed through the rest of the debriefing of Dr Molody, albeit in a lighter mood, without one person in the team projecting negative energy over the rest of us.

On that first day back at work, about the only item I recalled him saying about the subject of Sports was, "Steroid-abusers' bodies simply give up and die. They wear down the liver, kidneys and heart, and the body simply just says, "I've had it." After athletes stop taking steroids, the effects remain. The damage, like social drugs, is irreversible.

"Of course it was a decade ago, prior to the Tokyo Olympic Games in 1964 that many of the Soviet Union's younger female athletes were ordered to have sex with their coaches. When they became pregnant shortly before the big competitions it toughened up their bodies, which profited from the resulting hormonal change. Naturally the state took care of their abortions but this practice was extremely successful and enhanced their performances 30%. It gave the country many gold medals. That was when I was brought in to figure out what to do with the human foetuses."

With all the extremely complicated dialogue he disclosed under Research, I was happy "D" had taken over the helm for that week. I was getting jaded myself and returned to Berne for a few days, once again. After all I was the team leader, and I was also the one who stayed up into the early hours with him when the others had turned in to bed. I deserved a break too.

I had thought then, however, that one of his statements on the latest theme merits a mention. "Most scientists have come to accept the evolutionary theory, based on DNA and RNA—deoxyribonucleic acid and ribonucleic acid—evidence, that Homo Sapiens originated in equatorial Africa about two hundred thousand years ago. Mongoloid, Caucasoid or Negroid; we are all kin under the skin. Biologically, scientifically, genetically, whatever." Nobody present had a response to that and sat there nodding dumbly.

"B" was a black man by the way. He'd later disclosed to me privately, that the reason he didn't want to come into town with us a few weeks before was because of his colour. He felt it would draw attention to us. As he was the expert in the science of the mind, there wasn't anything I could add to the conversation, except, "Well, you missed having a good time, mate."

But I did appreciate his concern, and he had a good point, because he would have stuck out like a sore thumb that day admittedly. When I thought about it, I never saw other than white people all that day in Lugano.

Mike's personal Contacts were extensive. To this day SIS still utilises the non-disclosed names which were experts in cybernetics, artificial intelligence and weapons designers. While many should remain anonymous, I can mention Andrei Gromyko, the archdeacon of apparatchiks was one of them. Another was a Raisa Maksimovna, who turned out to be Mrs Gorby. Also the future director-general of the new Russian Space Agency, Yury Koptev, showed up as a pal of his.

As too was one Dr Hossein Shahristani, a Canadian-trained Iraqi, who was Saddam Hussein's chief scientific advisor. In the future he would refuse to make thermonuclear weaponry—H-bombs—for the despot and defected to neighbouring Iran.

Molody also revealed the previously unknown name of Vladimir Pasechnik but his job title was of great interest: Director of the Research Institute for Especially Pure Biological Preparations. The Leningrad-based outfit was part of an organisation called Biopreparat. "Pasechnik would very much like to leave like I did," the doctor volunteered. I understand that statement instigated the boys back in London to approach said individual with a proposal to "come over" too.

On communism he had been both critical and defensive, then doubtful of himself. "I can sense there is a buried factor of self-doubt among the Soviet Supreme leaders. The confrontation for me personally, on my Hippocratic Oath, was that the success of Man and his family was the constant factor; the dominating compulsion."

There had been a brief pause...nobody thought to prompt him, then he added, "My painful detachment is, of course, a mask. I am simply too unsure of my own gifts to make the fullest use of them in Soviet Russia."

Again there had been only the hissing of the tape on the reel, then another comment, "That place was the shame of the world." He had wiped a tear from his face then and sniffed. We remained silent in respect. It was the voice of an ideologue without an ideology.

He had perked up pretty quickly after that and continued with an attack on organised dogma. It came across as if he was discussing religion or politics or maybe it was viewpoints in general. "According to a psychologist I once knew, the problem with true believers of all stripes is that their faith tends to waiver when they can't convince others. Hence, their mad will to proselytise sometimes nefarious non-believers to their cause. The mental gymnastics involved in their defence of sometimes absurd beliefs are often something to behold. There is no known cure because the belief has become a part of their brains and nervous systems." It sounded more like heresy to me this time around.

The wildest thing from this episode is left for the very last because I only found it out many years later, in fact just a year before I retired from SIS. When I was told the information by Gordy Bassett of SIS' Intelligence Branch—the very same person to whom all of Molody's Swiss recordings and files were originally sent—I will admit to being absolutely flabbergasted.

The German cultural attaché, Dr Ralf Marczewski, the BND West German federal intelligence man whom I worked with on the defection of Irena Puchovskaya—was found to have been a long-time spy for China! His motivation was not ideology but pure greed for money, lots of it.

It took various intelligence communities years to figure it out but it was all because Dr Molody had mentioned in his dozens of uncelebrated Contacts that one of them had been a Pakistani called Farooq Ahmed. It hadn't made any sense to the SIS transcription evaluation experts that Mike would even have remote communication with a Pakistani in Moscow because there was no record of a Farooq Ahmed ever having visited the city. But they kept checking and rechecking the visas approved for Pakistani nationals arriving by air at the Soviet capital, which had been secretly procured, but they still drew a blank. One day they even went and had a special meeting with the doctor in Scotland where he was working just to ask him (among many other items) where, when and how he had met this fellow from Pakistan, including what they discussed. It was fairly routine to follow up constantly on defector's information that didn't add up. Detecting disinformation was paramount.

Mike had truthfully responded that it wasn't in Moscow that they had met. It was in Turkmenistan in the Soviet Near East at a hotel function near the top secret space installation called Baikonor. Then he happened to also recall that the Pakistani had said that he was employed at a enterprise called Institute of Nuclear Science and Technology. Adding that he thought the town it was based in was called Kahuta. Both the company and the location turned out to be correct.

Further investigation revealed that the Pakistani had been the frequent world travelling flunky for Pakistan's N-Plan chief nuclear weapons designer, Abdul Qadeer Khan. Simultaneously it came to light that that the West German counter-intelligence unit, BfV, had arrested one Farooq Ahmed under suspicion of spying in their country on some other unrelated matter. As a bargaining tool to try and obtain his own release he had panicked and confessed that he had once obtained a blueprint on how to manufacture Chinese-designed nuclear bombs from a West German national many years previously. The person he said who sold it to him was the enterprising Dr Ralf, who had since returned home from his posting in Poland but had been AWOL for some time.

Up to that point it was known that Pakistan had secured the knowledge on how to make a Chinese designed nuclear bomb but not from who. It was known too that the deal was not originally conducted *directly* with China but through an unknown middle man.

To illustrate: The little guy who had been running after Puchovskaya in the forests in Poland had *not* been the *rezident*, the senior intelligence officer, at the USSR Embassy in Warsaw, as we had been made to believe. He was in fact an Iranian who Dr Ralf had originally routed the transaction to. However, at the last minute the Pakistanis had come up with a better offer than their hated Iranian neighbours, but the problem was the payment and delivery had already been effected. So the West German had quickly introduced Puchovskaya—somebody whom he had been in the process of developing anyway—to the Iranian to lure him out into the Polish countryside, have sex, then drug him, whereupon she could repossess the blueprint's capsule for Dr Ralf. In return for succeeding he rewarded her with defection to the West and he used NATO to achieve the quest (who in turn assigned SIS to the task). Seeing too that she did not do a very good job of drugging the Iranian and that he had awoken to find the receptacle missing from his person (actually his rectum) and that he had chased after her like he did, it became her responsibility to eliminate the poor bastard with a shot to the head. McIntyre, Brennan and I did not question the West German's directives (and his and her motives). However, I vividly remembered that it hadn't seemed right to me at the time and that I was puzzled, especially by Puchovskaya's delighted facial reaction.

Using the usual Chinese-style tricks to throw a false trail and have us all thinking a Russian army woman was defecting to the West—plus having the Iranians and then the Pakistanis think they were buying nuclear knowledge from a Chinese source—he had used both the dead man, her and us to obtain the documents somewhat free of charge *twice*. Subsequently he doubled his millions.

It was complicated, but typical of the way the spy business can sometimes entangle into a snarled clutter. Dr Ralf was equally tripped up because the same Farooq Ahmed, on a different trip to Tashkent (also in the Soviet Union) well before his arrest in West Germany, had contacted an unsuspecting Michal Molody a second time about the exact meaning of a complex technical translation. As a result of having met a couple of times in person, the Pakistani had fashioned a relationship with the doctor and continued to cultivate it by requesting further information over the years by telex and telephone. Mike had only mentioned his name during debriefing in passing to us because he thought he may have been somebody important, and indeed he was.

Funny how sometimes things can unravel over time.

The Dr & Mrs Michal Molody double exfiltration was worth its weight in gold bars many times over.

Chapter Sixteen

It is safer not to know,
for what you don't know
nobody can get you to talk about.

The dangerous moments of my life as a Secret Intelligence Service officer had been relived in my mind once again, one more to the thousand times. Back in the present, the fact that I was retired now didn't seem to make a blip of difference. I was mentally back on the same wired wavelength. Even the Moskovskoye vodka I drank for breakfast rang true in the Russian good-bye for "have a nice day". I hadn't downed that private toast for over a decade.

The Aeroflot Solo jet from Moscow was descending to Narita, Tokyo's spanking new spacious airport. Coming down, even from the air on my right, I could see silver *shinkansen*, the bullet trains, moving along the ground like mercury rises on a temperature gauge left on the floor. (The policy of most intelligence services are for its staff, even on overt operations, to not schedule direct flights to destinations—and so it was the same in this instance.)

The transfer had gone swiftly. Before long I was crunching *osembei* rice crackers on the All-Nippon Airlines flight to Shanghai. They handed out yesterday's copy of the communist government-owned *China Daily* along with this morning's sovereign Japanese newspapers. I took the Chinese *ribao* or daily. I was back in Asia, time to begin figuring out what's behind what is said and meant. I mused as I munched, as vague as their predictions, even fortune cookies are not a Chinese invention but another American marketing idea.

It was a proletarian democracy now. I didn't care what the anti-communism West's politicians labelled it with their hogwash. But it was still a *renzhi* system and not a *fazhi* system. Ruled by man and not ruled by law. I studied history plus I grew up here. It was always so from the moment Chairman Mao implemented the "Mandate Made in Heaven" in 1949, a policy of promoting *heping juegi* (peaceful rise). From the moment he declared it; the commandment disappeared in a puff of smoke. It was similar to a typical Chinese general's war strategy to get everybody focused on the wrong place for an attack elsewhere.

In the same year that Mao Zedong formed the People's Republic of China, the population exploded in over forty years from five hundred and fifty-five million to 1.2 billion—so much for the one baby per family lie. Though in accomplishing the production revolution, by moving the people towards the factories in the cities, he had to eliminate the loss-generating, immovable peasant masses to the tune of thirty million and did so by launching a deliberate famine. When I travelled with my father in China with his entourage, between the late-fifties and early-sixties—I was only around the ten-age mark—my servant told me they were "looking at me so because I looked like a good plump goose to them". He watched me like a hawk all the time. He knew my Dad didn't want me cooked and eaten. The servant, Liang, had an iron rice bowl with us—a job for life.

In those days, Mao's political distraction to the world media was the three million-strong People's Liberation Army invasion of Tibet in 1950, which they now call the province of *Xizang Zizhiqu*. He smartly kept everybody focused on the domestic Buddhist problem for a whole decade, while the other internal alignments needed time to take place. If you were read the "Art of War" in bed, as I did as a kid, instead of fables, you would understand it as an all-normal everyday Chinese philosophy. My personal servant Liang, he who had the same name as the "old standard of weight since the Tang dynasty", must be long dead now. That guy was my sole prophet of influence when I was a child for he had once said to me:

"The key to understanding is to see the mind and brain as inseparable; one way of looking at the same thing."

Once I understood that, there was only one way to look at life after that. His favourite proverb was to often proclaim, *"Si liang bo qian jin."* Academics in China like to argue what it means but I understand it as "four ounces can repel a thousand pounds." When things are going against me I think of his saying.

Shanghai was the single fish out of water in the whole Chinese aquarium, perhaps because it always was the seat of enterprise in a sea of poverty, until that defining line of 1949. It was the New York City of China, and by far and away its largest populated city, as well as in the whole of Asia.

As I came out of the airport arrivals hall, as expected I saw my name printed on a placard in Roman letters. My driver-cum-guide-cum-bodyguard while I was here was to be Pan, my PA—Personal Assistant—and a former Red Guard. He looked like a she, certainly not a hairy demigod as his name suggested. We bowed greetings to each other.

Pan spoke very good English. But for no explicit reason, I never told him I spoke *putonghua*, Mandarin, as spoken by 70% of the country, especially in the north. It literally meant the common language. (The other main language, Cantonese, is called *yue*.) Besides when I heard him speaking to the locals I didn't understand his words completely either and it wasn't the dialect that was confusing me. I later learned that in Shanghai they spoke their own slang—*wu*—which is like their version of Cockney, or Geordie, or Brooklynese.

Not unlike Peter Pan, Pan was a smiling effeminate pixie of a man, my age. He would have made a beautiful woman without makeup. But he was also an 11th dan degree black belt in judo and knew how to kill a man without the victim even feeling it. Whenever an esteemed Russian government visitor came to China, they hired this guy, even though he never understood Russian. I came to discover that he was in fact very much *tong*, Chinese Mafia. I was also the first person he had worked with from this source that wasn't a Russian. I was the first real Westerner he had ever come in personal contact with. It was like I was a trophy for him to show around.

The airport was west; a way out from the city, and the traffic was the worst I'd ever seen in my life. I was so jet-lagged that I fell asleep in the back seat amid the flood of humanity.

Eventually we arrived at the all-purpose penthouse in a skyscraper that the Russians kept for their guests, including a computer and facsimile unit. This place was clearly for entertaining—it had all the mods and cons—and so it should be nice: for China accounted for at least 70% of Russian arms exports totalling over US$3.5 billion for the past few years, or so the documents in front of me stated in Cyrillic.

I knew that fact because, within minutes of unpacking, I was flipping through a revised version of a major proposal for China to buy advanced Su-37 and Su-30 warplanes from the Russians. I shook my head in wonder at what people leave around for strangers to read.

As time went by in that place I would come across other bids by the Russians to the Chinese. For instance I found tenders for purchase of: S-300 PMU01 air defence missiles; Mi-26 Halo helicopters; MiG-AT (for Attack) planes; and just one only Ilyushin IL-76 transport plane (codenamed Candid by NATO), the biggest aircraft ever built.

Travel itineraries to Zhuhai were also strewn in the waste-paper basket. It was a port city, between Hong Kong and Macau, where an aerospace exhibition had taken place recently.

Pan told me to sleep as long as I wished because the first of our three appointments throughout the coming week was just outside Nanking tomorrow, a hundred miles past the same airport we'd just came from. I rolled my eyes at the thought of repeating that journey on the same road.

When I awoke, Pan was still there. He slept in the next room all the time whenever the suite was used. Rather than keep snacking on the salty roasted watermelon seeds on the kitchen table—which required a knack of opening the nuts with your teeth and spitting out the inedible parts—at his suggestion, we went out to eat. It was then I discovered we were located in the recognised heart of the city, in its northern sector, in the old foreign section of Bund, which was on the waterfront at the intersection of Nanjing Road.

Walking along I noticed the billboards for Tsingtao beer and Hongtashan cigarettes had no disclaimers that they were health hazards. On the contrary they professed an extension of a happy life.

I agreed to have a street vendor's meal of sumptuous grain. One part of a food I hadn't tasted before was Tiger Lily buds. Standing there eating and watching the world pass by I felt like a single fig leaf among marauding worker ants, a slightly overwhelming feeling.

From our stationary curb-side spot, I was surprised to see a number of fake Jeep Cherokees and a number of gay men holding hands without a hint of fear or shame in the dense crowds. Pan himself was a self-admitted homosexual. Despite that he had asked if I wanted a female prostitute for the night, but I declined the offer explaining the dangers of AIDS. I was even more surprised he knew little about it. Much like religion in China, sex *was* publicly discouraged but not banned altogether. It had to be remembered that in the old days—and I was informed of this fact regularly as a child by my master Liang and my Dad—a father could legally kill his children if they disobeyed him. Such was still the mentality of the Chinese culture and an equalising rationale as to why I was such a good boy in my youth. *So much so that I think it structured me to be the way I am.*

Early the next morning I joined Pan working out on the balcony and did my exercises. It was then that I observed his practised moves were martial arts-related and I was informed of his prowess at judo. From our lofty vantage point, as many as a hundred people below us could be seen doing *taijiquan*, what the West prefers to call tai-chi now. My own morning habits were a combination of everything I'd been taught, mentally and physically. I made it up myself over the years to suit my own particular time-restricted requirements.

Soon we were out of downtown Shanghai and past the airport quickly. The bulk of cars and lorries were going in the opposite direction. The elongated Da Yunhe Grand Canal stretched beside us on the left almost the whole way on the two-hour fast motorway ride to Nanking. We came alongside the wide very busy yellow-coloured river, the Yangtze, *Chang Jiang*, on the right, with its dozens of laden cargo ships heading to and from the East China Sea and on to the world by way of the North Pacific. Just before the city, we turned off and were soon outside the imposing gates of what appeared to be a walled prison.

Efficiently we were herded into a meeting with the Commissioner and five of his head wardens. Tea was served and we sat cross-legged, low at the small table in his office. The constant smiling told me they were serious. Pan acted as translator.

They quickly asked me how many body parts I wanted. I produced a sheet of paper provided by Dr Molody. As they each leaned to read it I watched their faces. It was the first time these men from the Chinese forced-labour system had discussed the subject of their *laogai* with a foreigner, and exported deliveries of fresh human organs harvested from their prisoners. For them it was a bonus way to cull the flow of criminals and a further detriment to prevent them breaking the law. The Chinese, however, chill at the thought of their chopped beings ending up inside another country's citizens; though it's not so bad and certainly acceptable for their own kind to receive.

Surgeon Mike needed the parts for experiments and transplantation replacements, mainly livers and kidneys. The latter were at US$20,000 each in quantities of one dozen. Corneas from eyes were cheap at US$5,000 a pair. Lungs were guaranteed to come from non-smokers. It was like we were discussing parts at a car factory. Samples were going to be needed for analyses and they had no problem with that, except we were going to have to pay the costs of refrigeration and air freight. In this case, it was to be shipped to Molody's Moscow clinic.

For the next hour we haggled over prices. I was intrigued they would argue in not *renminbi* only but *yuan*, *chiao* and *yen*—it was like discussing English pounds, shillings, pence *and* farthings—but the price came down if we could barter for some medical equipment they needed from Russia, and was lowered even more if payment was made in either Hong Kong dollars, US dollars, or Swiss francs.

The Japanese yen was factually the most advantageous currency for them to trade in at that moment; yet I noticed the rate they offered for the money was extremely unfavourable. They chose to play the same undermining, tit-for-tat game back as their hated neighbours did to them.

At lunchtime we walked among the potential living organs inside moving bodies. Two hundred in this particular location were to be publicly executed on the next national holiday. "Altogether around 6,000 each year are conducted nationally", I was told.

The tour was fascinating in a morbid sense; that the cruelty imposed on these enslaved criminals was beyond what was acceptable for animal life in the West. Their crimes ranged from forgery to robbery and murder. A lot of these bad guys looked bad and the women looked worse.

My experience of prisons was limited to Northern Ireland on the outside and Bulgaria on the inside. China was neither. It was akin to the southern US' chain gangs, the prisoners virtually naked and flogged mercilessly while they *were* working in hard labour conditions. Afterwards they were over-crowded into cells far worse than anything I had seen or heard of. There were dead left over when the cells were emptied out every morning. These were not being used for their organ harvesting programmes, they were donated for minced animal feed instead. Wait till the human and animal rights activists get their hands on that in the West, I thought, it'll be the first time they agreed on the same issue.

We promised to meet the boss again at another site nearer to Shanghai in two days time. It turned out he was the Commissioner of all of Jiangsu province's labour camps. Just as we bade each other farewell, I heard one of his wardens say in Mandarin to another one, "Pan thinks he's so cool escorting an Englishman working for the Russians, doesn't he? When we eat the 'Rice Flag' soon, Yellowbird will be out of a job in our 'five-star Cantonese restaurant.'" I had smiled widely at the fool out of apparent ignorance. Little did he know I understood his every word. Chinese called the British flag—the Union Jack—that because the criss-crossing design resembled the Chinese character for rice, which itself looked like a big asterisk. Their own national red and gold banner was nicknamed the "Five-Star Flag". He was making reference to China's take-over of Hong Kong in 1997, which by then would have been under British rule for one hundred and fifty-six years. Cantonese was the Hong Kong dialect. The part about Yellowbird I assumed was his nickname.

Pan didn't respond, nor look at the man, but did acknowledge hearing him.

As we drove away I got to thinking that China *is* the East's Wild West—the new frontier.

We headed towards the centre of *Nanjing* and I even noticed one sign state *Nan-ching*. Either way, it was the capital of Jiansu province—even though it was three times smaller than Shanghai—itself once capital of all of China. Nanking meant southern capital; while Peking, *Beijing*, meant northern capital.

It was a little known fact that China does not call itself China. The Chinese like to call their country *Zhongguo*, as it literally means middle country, for they once thought they were the geographical centre of the world. Though the full name for the People's Republic of China was another tongue twister: *Zhonghua Renmin Gongheguo.*

We never went right into Nanking, because just east of it, at the top of a steep hill we climbed called paradoxically Zijen *Mountain*, we stopped at the local tourist attraction, the tomb of Sun-Yat-sen. The plaque read that "Sun established the Republic of China in 1912." It was absolutely a gorgeous place to be buried, surrounded by a variety of trees, and we strolled around for a while playing the tourist then left as it was getting dark.

On the long drive back I sat in the front next to my driver. He was pensive and we didn't speak for a long time. Finally I asked him, "Pan, have you ever been to Hong Kong?"

He kept staring into the distance, headlight beams shining on his face. Then he turned warily to look at me. "Yes, many times. Why do you ask?"

"Oh," I said innocently. "That's unusual. Not many Chinese have passports nor have the opportunity to travel there. You must be well connected."

He didn't say anything for a full five minutes, but I could feel it fermenting in him. I waited until the foam wanted to pop the cork. "You know the Chinese language, don't you?" he finally said, as he looked over again. I nodded, holding his gaze.

He smiled fractionally, "I thought so, not only did you hear that last idiotic remark, I was already thinking your responses for translation indicated an understanding of words I certainly never said to you. I do think it was a good idea for you not to tell them you knew. That way you can check their integrity for doing business. Besides, I don't trust state workers and they certainly do not like entrepreneurs like me. In a way I empathise because putting naked capitalism against the social-market economy destroys a nation's confidence and it does create job losses. Theirs not mine, however."

"What happens in Hong Kong that you go there so much," I queried him. "That is, if you do not have a problem telling me." Again that half-smile from him. His nearest eyebrow arched a fraction.

It didn't take him long to tell me. He was a philosopher of sorts, like me. "Logic had already joined the chickens and flown the coop," Pan finally cackled. I was puzzled with his statement and begged an explanation.

"Have you ever heard of Yellowbird?" He was serious when he said it.

"No," I replied, truthfully. "What's that?" Obviously it wasn't him then.

All the way back to Shanghai he told me that he was a tong soldier, a recognised worker for the Chinese underworld. It was generally reputed to those in the know that he was associated with the extraction team that arranged the escape to Hong Kong of dozens of Chinese political dissidents. This Chinese "undragon" unit had smuggled a couple of hundred people through their underground railway.

Somebody had to be the contact man, and he was it. At times, he feared for his life but he was compensated well for his high profile. Besides, he had a fatalistic attitude and it reflected in his lifestyle. He wore noticeably loud western clothing and expensive gold trinkets in defiance of the communist dress code.

The fancy name—Yellowbird—wasn't a person at all but instead derived from a Chinese proverb: "The mantis stalks the cicada, unaware of the yellow bird behind". Operation Yellowbird was the Chinese gentility's secret response to the 1989 Beijing massacre in Tiananmen Square when Chinese troops fired on dissenters, even though the world media didn't point out that demonstrating was a counter-revolutionary crime in China and culturally considered an ugly act.

Operation Yellowbird was an odd political alliance of human rights activists wanting "out"; and western diplomats wanting to pay for their "out". The Hong Kong Mafia were the brokers, represented by the bravado types like Pan operating on the wrong side of the fence, and advanced both the noble political and self-serving capitalistic causes. Pan himself was confident that when it became too hot for him one day, he would simply escape to Hong Kong. His problem was that when 1997 came around, he wouldn't know where to go from there. That's why he was nurturing the only other avenue he knew of, and that was the opportunity with the Russians and perhaps anything I might be able to offer him. Hopefully if he played his cards right, somebody could learn to trust him and see his value. It was a long-term game plan. "Mind you, I'm so bent, screwing around and getting drunk with the money I'm making. I might just die of a stupid venereal or kidney disease before 1997. Or even that AIDS thing you told me about," he laughed crazily like the swashbuckler he was.

The reason the prison official, Ma, had made a sarcastic reference to Yellowbird was because he too may take advantage of the opportunity it presented, but Pan and he were ex-lovers and on acrimonious terms. "He is a fucking hypocrite and goes along with the system which serves his desire when he feels like it. Ma screws the young boys in jail and if they talk, he singles them out for human harvesting to shut them up. All they do is anaesthetise the victim, surgically remove the parts they want and their life is terminated without pain as the body ceases to function naturally with the relevant organ missing. Barbaric, but it saves them bags of money that way and its clean. Being sympathetic does not make them sympathisers."

He chewed on his thoughts then added, "Ma has the same problem as me though, in that if he decides to go to Hong Kong now, what happens in 1997? He's jealous to see me developing a relationship with the Russians and yourself. I bet you didn't know the Soviets and the French used the same underground railway going the other way to get their spies *into* China." I shook my head.

Pan concluded on Yellowbird with, "The tong knew it was going to be a good source of income. The going rate for a want-to-be refugee to be smuggled out of China is US$27,500 each. I do okay from my cut." It was amazing information and I sat chewing on the French connection.

After a few minutes of silence, Pan asked me, "How about going to a discotheque tonight? We have nothing to do tomorrow."

I agreed, "OK, as long as it's not an all-gay club, Pan."

He giggled mischievously, "Don't worry, we all frequent the same place. Some of the beautiful 'girls' are really men too. You won't be able to tell, believe me. Once one of the Russians picked up a 'woman' prostitute only to discover 'she' was a man."

"Ugh," I injected, "he must have thrown him out on his ear straight away!"

"Oh, no," said Pan, flatly. "He'd already paid 'him' so he went the whole way anyway. He was sufficiently turned-on and blind drunk!"

We both laughed.

When we got home we changed quickly. I put on my jeans and a T-shirt but Pan reappeared dressed as a beautiful woman and if I hadn't known I'm quite sure I would have been physically attracted.

Within minutes of walking from the flat we were in a deafening nightclub packed solid by swarming humanity, and not one foreigner in sight except me. I could see my purple self everywhere in the neon reflecting multiple mirrors and revolving glass balls. Whatever he had ordered for a drink—"*Mantei*, a powerful Chinese spirit served with turtles blood"—was taking its effect quickly on me.

He was right about the boys and girls and "half-an-halves both ways", there were plenty of women I thought maybe were "men" too. It was hard to believe this was communist China, it could well have been the risqué West Berlin's Ku'damm Eck area at the height of its sexual infamy even during the Cold War. It was the decadent West German version of London's Piccadilly or Times Square in New York City.

The atmosphere in the Shanghai club was synthetic and hung in the stale air like one of those mini-jukeboxes draped at a western 24-hour downtown diner.

Fuck, I thought, *all the ideology fighting against Chinese communism resulted in this. All those secret trips I took into the world's most repressive regime, Albania, to prevent it becoming "Little China" in Europe, for what?*

I had a key to the penthouse and left Pan gyrating doggie-style with another "man-woman". Jet lag was also an excuse to depart.

The next morning a bleary-eyed Pan awakened me. I figured that the drink at the club must've contained a drug. I hadn't slept that long since I was a baby. He had a fax from Dr Molody in his hands.

It was from Moscow advising me of a trip that he was making to Milan in Italy. Similar to my reasons for being in China, it stated that he was going to the notoriously overcrowded San Vittore jail but he didn't say why. For the life of me, I couldn't imagine the Italians were into the same body parts scheme as the Chinese. He also wrote that Kokorin had called him to say Leonid Viser *would* be granted emigration to Israel within two years. Good, he'll get his asylum as I fisted the air in paper victory for him. The rest of the facsimile spelt out when and where he and I were to meet in Zaire in a fortnight's time. I thought instantaneously about Ursula Durance's plans to visit Egypt one day. This was the opportunity for us to enjoy at least a week together in North Africa before I headed down to the former Congo Republic. After all, the Russians were paying for my travel so why not take full advantage of it…and I missed her.

An hour later while eating breakfast, with Pan playing tunes from a set of handmade reed pipes in the next room, I sent three faxes from the machine in the flat's kitchen. Personal first, to Ursula: I told her about what a good idea it would be to meet in Cairo. The second was for Mike Molody: updating him about the trip to the forced labour camp outside Nanking and the one I was to make to Shanghai, with another out of town later. The last was the longest and was to be received in London:

'Dear Mrs Blyton,

Sorry about not keeping in touch during the past year or less. Yes, I'm a bad boy for disappearing off the face of the earth. You know how it is, the usual ordinary madness.

Thanks for your last communication which I picked up as scheduled in Paris. I bet you're surprised to see this fax is coming from China! Yes, I'm having a great time on the beach and my suntan is improving. Wish you were here in your, er, um, bikini and all that.

To answer your ages old last question first: Tell "C" I simply saw an Irishman reading a file with WISE on it, that's all. So it's an Arab school in the US? Big deal. I have no further details for you regarding the subject. If I did I would have told you already.

Bummer about my SIS file. It's *that* bad that they can't let me see it!?

To update you on what Dr Molody wanted me to do: It's that he is seriously claiming cures to major diseases! I'm not sure it's true but I'm still checking on it. Will let you know when I know, OK? Hold tight, sounds very interesting indeed and it consumes me to the point that time flies by so quickly.

I just received a communication asking me to meet him in Kinshasa, Zaire, in two weeks time. I don't know what tricks he's got up his sleeve there in Africa but, if things go according to plan, I *will* be meeting that lovely German lady from France again there in Cairo for a hol. Sand, sun and more sand!

Got a couple of questions for you of my own:

What do you have on Operation Yellowbird?

Also while not related to the former, is there anything currently open on the blackboard about "anything going on" in this part of the world I'm in? Just like to be aware of matters. May be able to "kill two birds with one stone" so to speak.

Luv,

Nicholas Anderson'

She couldn't know I hadn't written for so long because I was irate at their inability to provide some cleared information on myself. Surely something was available. I really didn't care for SIS still trying to control my life and it showed in my prolonged absence of communication. I had served them honourably and didn't think I deserved a shafting in return. I half expected her not to reply.

I must have fallen asleep again because the next thing I knew Pan was shaking me gently waving another very long faxed sheet in front of me. Amazingly it was from Mrs Blyton and I could tell that she was mostly in her business mode. It read:

'Dear Nick,

You're lucky I was staying late in the office when your fax came in. You wanted to know what Operation Yellowbird is?: It's the underground system through which the Chinese government's most wanted person, a student leader called Wuer Kaixi, was the first to escape from China to Hong Kong. The French government bankrolled it. (See next for the current list of Chinese individuals to have found freedom through this remarkable route.)

Is there a link between your lovely lady in France and Operation Yellowbird? According to our 1990 records, there was a French delegation in Hong Kong at the time of that first successful escapee's arrival. Ursula Durance and her retired husband Georges were there along with France's new Ambassador to the European Union. Wuer Kaixi lives in Paris now. Might be a coincidence but you never know.

Two related matters are in the hopper right now. Neither is NOT For-Your-Eyes-Only status...so here it is:

1.) *Hua Ren Jituan* is otherwise known as the China Resources Holding Company, based in Hong Kong. Their vice president is a Red Chinese Military Intelligence Department top officer operating under their cover. Has been there for a year now. Their recently appointed commercial case officer is another top-ranking military case officer recently transferred from Guangzhou. Something must be cooking in Hong Kong but we don't know what is at the moment. Keep your eyes and ears open to anything, however remote it may seem.

2.) A decision-maker from the Riady family who own the Lippo empire in Indonesia is presently in Shanghai. Lippo Group is a front for the Red Chinese communist government. Again, be on the lookout for any snippets of info.

Now we have a favour to ask you, young man, before you disappear off again. Seeing you say you will be in Egypt and be on your way to Zaire, exactly in between the two countries...is the Sudan. We have a simple no-skin-off-your-nose missive for you there. It will only take a couple of days to check it out. When you arrive in Cairo, the resident attaché there will be expecting you to contact him forthwith. It is imperative to us that you carry the task out. Naturally Her Majesty's government will foot the bill to ensure the delivery of this assignment.

That's it for now. I'm going home to bed. Will be thinking of you.

Sincere regards,

Ellen Blyton'

Damn, it was finally going to be payback time for all the free info I was getting from SIS. Another reason why I'd deliberately avoided being in contact with them for almost a whole year. Interestingly she had contradicted herself a bit in her wording in that whatever it was going down wasn't important to me but it was important to them. She may have been tired after a long day but I was sufficiently seduced to know what was up.

I gave Pan the list of Chinese names who had used the Operation Yellowbird escape route. Pan read it and looked back at me in wonder, "No matter what, Yellowbird's tunnel must remain *bao mi*, kept secret. You must be well connected yourself. I can put a face to each name. Who *are* you?"

I thought I would let him read everything I'd received by facsimile in my presence. The chances are he had read it already, while I was sleeping, but I wanted to watch his face for any clues. His Chinese expression gave nothing away though his mouth did.

The first thing he said was, "I swear I haven't read this before. I would never do that to you." Which told me he probably had. I never responded, just kept gazing idly at his face while he skimmed down the faxes.

He looked quizzical at one point and looked up saying, "The Riady man, he's always here, screwing all the S&M women. Lippo is an Indonesia-based conglomerate which acquires major institutions throughout Asia for the general purposes of *both* capitalising and socially; the 'ultimate goal' of the new China as it expands beyond its shores."

"You obviously know something about the subtle change of Chinese governmental direction, how did it came about?" I asked. "Because what I am seeing isn't what the West thinks is happening."

"Oh, yes, I do know a lot, very much so," he exclaimed, looking proud of himself. "After I got out of the army, I went back to school to study New Economics. The transformation of Chinese government-owned enterprises to private or joint government-private ownership is only just the beginning. I think the main reason lies in that it is almost entirely through transfers of stock to the employees, something the greedy few in the West don't generally permit. We call it 'the third way', one that mixes the market incentives of capitalism with a more equitable distribution of ownership than most western societies can claim. It's the true real definition of socialism actually…"

The fax unit rang. It was Ursula's hand-written note telling me that based on my fax to her; she had already reserved her flights and hotel. Her schedule was included. I resisted writing back asking her if she knew anything about Operation Yellowbird. I may ask her in person later though.

I spent the rest of the day alone. I was thankful when Pan went out for several hours to give me my space. He had not asked me again who I was. I watched television for a while. Still that message of mixed signals comes across in China, Communism seems to be promoted but when you go outside and look for it you find nothing but capitalism.

In round figures, forty years ago "The Maoist Strategy" was a prolonged war with the then nationalist government, prompting its final collapse. Then thirty years ago, he turned the country on its head with the "Cultural Revolution", but didn't tell the rest of the world how he was doing it. His successor Deng Xiaoping had kept up the same tactics some twenty years ago by introducing the "Four Modernisations" programme. Historians hadn't given this successful shift a label yet but will in time. Even revolutions evolved.

One thing that did remain a total constant throughout in China was that nothing was middle ground. Either they turned the tap completely off or they turned it all the way on but they didn't have to mention they did anything, and generally didn't. It was up to each individual to find out for themselves.

The small library in the apartment contained literary works in Russian, Chinese, French, German and English. The main volume I spent time reading was on medicine in China written in Russian. Sitting outside on the balcony, overlooking other high-rises in Shanghai, I re-capped on what I already knew about Chinese medicine.

What the West calls "alternative medicine" is traditional medicine for 80% of the world, and what is called "traditional medicine" is only a few centuries old. Western physicians are not the alpha and omega after all in this Eastern part of the world: not the beginning and the end of the ailment process.

Chinese medicine is based on the belief that a life force or *qi* flows through 12 to 14 channels in the body, which has up to 365 acupuncture points. Half of the channels were on the right male side of the body called *yang;* while the left female side was *ying.* When there is a slight blockage stemming the energy, needles stimulated these human strategic points to re-establish the natural circulation. It was believed a person's energy field extends beyond the skin and into the air around them.

I'd always known that, and credited old man Liang for making me aware. He had also taught me *tan-juan*, a method of breathing introduced by Buddhist monks, which had helped me considerably throughout my life, especially when relaxing, like I was now.

I subconsciously heard my master talking to me again. "You are crying, child? Go and stand on one leg in the corner there. When you are quiet I'll call you and then you can change to the other leg. Learn to breathe while you are there for the hour." As I had grown older it had been lessons in discipline about "Finding a healing place of my own where you can think"; and "Grow plants, be around positive people, laugh a lot, find a person or something to love who can blossom like a flower with you, and enjoy music and art."

As an adult, I'd pretty much stuck to the game-plan he laid out for me as my parents weren't around enough to do it. I had nodded to the heavens then to thank him for his wisdom. I felt he had passed on by now. I miss him. *Gratitude is the heart's memory.*

Some of my Dad's Asia-based foreign associates' faces next came into vivid focus. I was surprised I could recall their names now so readily. Were they in the same business of spying? I don't know... The American Wes Pedersen; Tom Maloney from Ireland; and the Swiss George Jaeggi, were all just my "uncles". The latter had died when his small plane he was piloting crashed. I wondered if the others were still alive.

I thought of Molody. He had once told me "double-blind, placebo-controlled studies are traditional medicine's gold standards, yet half of its acceptable practices had never been subjected to it." A contradiction of current-day policies. The operators in the olden days had more integrity.

I heard Pan coming back in and I closed the leather-bound book, kissing it as if it was Liang's skin—it felt warm. I was beyond grateful to be so close to him once again even for a few seconds.

The next morning Pan and I were heading directly north out of the city going parallel with the canal. It eventually ran into the intersection of the Yangtze, one of the world's longest rivers at 3,900 miles.

Another mile along there and we ground to a halt with a huge oil-based blaze raging. The traffic was jammed solid in both directions. The fire brigade had arrived right after us.

Pan had impressed me with his knowledge then as we sat with a grandstand view of the drama for two hours. "The Yangtze River is one of the world's lungs, you know. Despite western environmentalists lying in fundraising matters and saying the rainforest trees provide the amount of oxygen in the atmosphere, when it is in fact determined by the oceans."

Despite the high number of vehicles stuck on the road, Pan also told me that only 5% of the 1.2 million passenger cars on the road in China were privately owned, a rate of one car for every 20,000 citizens. It seemed more than that...as we were surrounded by a few thousand of them right here.

When the fire was subdued we continued on and drove past Wuhu air force base. The medium-range H-6 bombers with nuclear capacity were parked on the tarmac. We witnessed the exciting spectacle of a squadron of Sukhoi SU-27 (Flankers) fighter planes in Chinese camouflage livery scream into the sky one after another, like a stream of slow smoky tracers fired at a distant target.

We finally reached the village where we were aiming for. The men there were seen to be reading the wall posters as they did in the old days. You were allowed to express a personal verbal opinion in the parks and public areas about anything but you could not criticise the government at all, the official newspapers did that part for you.

At our unfortunately late appointment, the same amiable Commissioner we'd met two days ago was there to greet us and introduced us to a group of sombre white-clad physicians.

I wasn't purchasing adult body parts today. I was in the market for bulk aborted embryos and foetuses. In China an embryo is classified a foetus at eight weeks. More bargaining pursued at around the US$2 mark each and we were discussing a couple of thousand for an opening order. The prices were supposedly cheaper here than anywhere else in China, only because the city of Shanghai provided a quarter of the country's abortions, they told me they had a bumper 70,000 terminations at this site alone last year.

Nowhere were there examples of foetal tissue banks where women bred for the purposes of paid supply and demand. It simply didn't exist here or in Russia, nor were they aborting as a means of birth control. The main reason, according to Chinese data, was that they wouldn't be able to maintain the child financially. The same reason why they couldn't afford billions of birth-control pills and condoms, despite millions sold. Besides some didn't know who the father was and there was a social stigma attached to that, the exact same problem as in the more decadent West—which was itself gradually changing to standardised acceptance of single mothers. According to their research these doctors told me that most pregnancies in Shanghai were mainly the results of illicit affairs stemming from dancing unions at the hundreds of old-fashioned ballrooms in the city. The statistics, apparently, did not include the younger generation's discotheques and nightclubs where the liaisons were more forthright.

The day after Pan and I flew from Shanghai to Qingdao on the north coast changing planes at Beijing's Capital airport. The distance from the capital to our ultimate destination was almost a third of the way back to Shanghai. Go figure the airline timetables.

It was a one-day trip and back to inspect a high-security women's prison. Our hosts wanted me to at least see it and funded the trip. It was like a leisurely day out to the zoo. The brutish male guards here surprised me by carrying what only could be described as the *lupera*, shorn-off shotguns, as favoured by the Sicilian Mafia, and naturally I thought Mike must be seeing a similar thing right now in the Land of Machiavelli—as I liked to call Italy.

At the brief melancholic meeting, after the tour we had around the jail, they wanted to discuss the possibility of commencing a programme for the use of the fresh body parts of healthy pregnant women, complete with an untouched foetus. They proposed to deliberately impregnate the prisoners and then ship them like slaves one-way to wherever I wished—within reasonable distance of China—say to clinics in the nearby Russian Far East regions. A future project being developed was for the children of these violent Chinese women prisoners. They were becoming an expensive burden on the state. The medical professor in charge was thinking of selling them at US$35,000 each for research experiments. Every year they had 1,000 kids available, all under-12... I should have been aghast.

My own personal inclination was to walk out, I didn't. I promised them they would be directly hearing from Dr Michal Molody himself about their proposals... I knew instinctively that he would decline their offers.

I realised once again I was void of emotion and no longer shocked at hearing these statements. The same reason why I had quit SIS in 1983. Had I become desensitised to such horrors? Back then I would think cynically, *The truth of politics is that it is a cocktail of economics and populism, and I want no further part in the accomplishment of that manipulation.* That is about all I calmly felt about this sick new concept too. *There is never any indication that any amount of words translates into action.*

By that night we were back in Shanghai and a few days later I bade Pan good-bye.

It had been a productive week.

The night before leaving, Pan had offered to buy me dinner. "This nutritious food will make your skin smoother and your body stronger, it's also good for your kidneys," he said. The delicate aroma of noodle soup with paper-thin sliced vegetable had come, and I was soon chewing thumb-size pieces of pork flavour with ginger. Using bone chopsticks and a ceramic spoon, I slurped the savoury broth down enthusiastically. I loved Chinese food. After I swallowed the entire bowl, which contained some half-dozen tasty bits of meat, he told me I had been eating boiled human embryos.

"In China we eat them as a delicacy. The males from younger mothers are best."

* * * * * * * * * *

The view coming down into Cairo at night is breathtaking. Thousands of lights blinking like fireflies up against the dark wall in the garden.

At the packed airport arrivals terminal I had noticed many SSI details, the domestic state security service, who looked like the *Mukhabarat el-Aam*, the Egyptian General Intelligence Agency—the international division—mingling with the hundreds of foreigners flooding the country. Despite the influx of tourists, the local authorities appeared concerned, at least to my trained eye. The happy North American, European and Asian throngs were unaware of whatever dangers the Egyptians knew of.

At the hotel Ursula almost mauled me in the lobby. I couldn't get a word in edge ways in her enthusiasm to tell me what she had planned for the next seven days.

Five of those were taken up with a cruise down the Nile River from *Al-Qahirah*, the Egyptian capital's local name, to the famed Aswan Dam. In the space of a few days I'd had the rare privilege of experiencing the third and now the longest river in the world. The pyramids and the desert dunes from the aft of the ship at sunset had naturally been spectacular, as had Ursula's performances in our bunk.

It had taken me all of three days to ask her if she had ever been to Hong Kong. Her prompt open response puzzled me. "When we went there a couple of years ago we were the guests for one week of the alumni of École Nationale d'Administration, an elite education institute in France. It is not a unit of the government of France. My husband graduated there. I don't know about him, but I had a good time. When *we* landed in Hong

Kong it was like dropping out of the sky into some woman's laundry basket…"

"But why where you there, for what purpose?" I asked.

She stopped staring out at the banks of the river and turned her concerned face to me, her hand on my waist, "Why so much interest, Nicholas?"

"For the hell of it, let me be more specific. In Hong Kong did you ever hear of Operation Yellowbird?" I asked point blank, trying not to sound anxious.

She seemed to be thinking hard, slightly schoolgirl-ish by having a finger on her chin and eyes looking up. Finally an idea hit. "Well, firstly, I never went to the many seminar meetings they had. But you know they think of themselves as a kind of French establishment, controllers of the world's affairs. I don't know. Who cares? What's so important? It was all political bullshit to me."

She seemed so innocent I wanted to hug her. But I didn't know enough about her really. I was discovering a prudish side of me. The "we" wasn't her and me; there was a third person I had to factor into our "we". In a way seeing her with the Irish Republican Army's Patrick O'Neill had always remained in my consciousness too, whether it was a genuine accident or not, I had yet to find out.

"I'm curious what your political affiliation is, Ursula. We've now spent a couple of weeks with each other closely, and I've known you altogether for well over a year, but I've never asked you. Though it seems we have an animalistic attraction for each other, it's about time I explored inside your head."

She responded with a frank speech, "Didn't you already guess, silly. I'm married into the upper echelons of European society, but as I'm getting older, I find them more and more disgusting with their addiction to money and profit. I'm a pure convert to the aims of socialism. That does not, in any way, mean communism as the Americans mistakenly seem to think it is." She did not elaborate any further than that.

I decided then to tell her about my MI6 past, seeing that I told O'Neill and his cronies already to their faces, *if* they indeed did maintain contact with her. In a way I was fishing and not gambling.

Her big brown eyes widened more at the beginning, then she appeared relaxed. When I'd finished summarising about the medical projects without actually mentioning Molody, the first words out of her mouth was, "My millionairess friend, Nicole Bru, would probably like to meet you. She's going to spend lots of money on trying to find cures, especially for AIDS and cancer. Her husband Jean is dying of cancer right now. I'll introduce you to her."

I shrugged the offer aside. "So you cannot shed any light on Operation Yellowbird at all?" I asked again. Ursula just stood there shaking her head.

I decided to drop the subject as it wasn't going anywhere. Furthermore I had made no mention of anything to do with the "government of France", that was her own volunteered statement. I was intrigued. My gut was activated by that clue, but like the residentura story in Poland, which wasn't, I figured it would clear itself up eventually no matter how big or small it was.

It wasn't quite the same for me after that. My defence mechanism was being put up, brick-by-brick. Time would tell.

When we got back to the Cairo Marriott, I left her there while I went to the British Embassy. I had to sit in reception for one hour before the resident attaché appeared. He seemed ticked off and the first words he said, without introduction, were, "You were supposed to be in touch with me nearly a week ago. London got worried and had me waste time checking on your whereabouts. You simply disappeared off the face of the Earth after it was confirmed you had arrived in Egypt. Finally a Mrs Blyton informed me by phone you were probably playing around with some damn European woman. Still, you're here now, old chap. Step into my office."

I resented him wiggling his finger to follow as if I was some croupier. The most dangerous thing he'd probably done was ignite a flaming gold lighter with his initials engraved on it at the blackjack table.

In his spacious lounge, the bloke was uppity the whole time. These haughty upper class English fellows, with their Cranwell or Sandhurst backgrounds, tend to look down upon we northern British lads who are perceived as less sophisticated. To him the topic of conversation was very serious stuff in the Sudan. To me it was a piece of cake, certainly not life threatening. Reading upside down I could tell he was briefing me from a file prepared by SIS' old friends from the British Ministry of Defence's in-house information arm, DIS. I even asked him if Air Chief Marshal Mick Hermitage was still in charge there. I got no bites. When I finally left I felt like a one-armed bandit.

Ursula was upset. "Ooh, la la. Nicholas, *mon filou*! My bad boy, you've been gone for five hours, please tell me where you have been?" For reasons that went against reasoning, based on my current feelings for her, I really *did* tell her what had transpired at the British Embassy—and then some. I felt like I had nothing to lose by slotting a coin in her, so to speak.

She sat there, slumped, looking slightly dejectedly at me, not talking and thinking. "OK, as much as I hate to do this, because my husband may find out about our relationship, I'll make a telephone call to him later tonight. I just have to think how I'm structuring the question of obtaining a copy of your British SIS file through the French government via the NATO alliance."

She never did tell me what she drummed up for her old man, but on our last day together, he called back early in the morning, and I happened to answer the phone too. We had a formal chat—he sounded old—and then I handed the phone to his much younger wife. I watched her piquant face for clues but it stayed pretty much pensive, while she wrote down some notes on the hotel mini-pad.

When she hung up, she simply said, "Well he knows about us being here together. Amazingly, he isn't mad at me, more understanding than anything. Georges confessed just now to having an affair once, and he puts mine down to us being level on that."

Ursula wiped a tear, "Anyway, he's going to try and get you a copy of your file from Belgium someplace and then he'll forward it to you somehow, wherever you want to receive it. I'll be back in Cannes by the time it comes, if it comes. Also, of course, there's a small price to pay. In return for this favour, the same French hierarchy I despise want you to repay them one day. More detailed information about what you are going to do in the Sudan will suffice, he said. Our family's good name is on the line here."

I'd hugged her then but the mutual reciprocation was lacking for the rest of the day. I think it was the "our family" part for me. The wave of desire returned the next morning though when we naturally found ourselves naked in bed.

We had already done the tourist attractions in Cairo and undertaken a half-day trip to Port Said. There I vividly recalled standing alone on the desert at age eleven, in a blue and grey British school uniform, watching the white P&O liner from the Orient sliding along the top of the golden sand towards me. It was half-term and my parents were returning from Asia to England for a holiday, but I flew to meet them in Egypt, then called the United Arab Republic. The huge ship was sailing through the Suez Canal from the Red Sea into the Mediterranean. A driver from my Dad's firm had picked me up at Cairo airport and taken me there.

Now over three decades later, Ursula and I had kissed feverishly at the same airport, despite the local frowns at the custom. She said she loved me but I remained non-committal. She had requested I tell her if I meet anybody else that looked like developing into a serious relationship. I said I would. Her big thing was the want to travel the world with me when her husband passes away, and *that* was the problem—when. But she made me promise to keep in touch with her whether I received the SIS file copy or not. Left to my own devises, of course, I would I had replied, I liked her more than a hell of a lot.

Just like Moscow, we were departing to different points. Her Egypt Air jumbo jet took off for Paris and my Egypt Air small plane flew south, concurrent with the Nile I'd sailed down a few days prior, towards the world capital of terrorism—*Al Khartum*. The many Bedouin wagon trains could be seen romantically winding along with us down there, white patches riding on a brown magic carpet.

* * * * * * * * *

When the pigs were looking,
but not close enough to see clearly that they were wrong;
I understand why the extremists react the way they do.
But it does not mean I agree with either side:
They are both wrong to do what they did.
Neither is the "road to Damascus".

A few miles from Khartoum airport, in a dusty suburban area on Africa Road, I saw him walking along the street. As the taxi came level with him, I stuck my head out. In Russian I said, "You are Dr Abdullah Bakarat from Lebanon. Remember me, old chap? Try peeling the moustache off my face." His grey eyes stared at me, visibly taken aback with shock. I knew my smiling face sparked his interest as he stared quizzically without an air of being in danger.

Finally I said, "Think of Novogorsk." It was Moscow Dynamo football club's training ground next to the tavern where we had first met. He looked relieved and broke into a rare broad grin, leaning over enthusiastically to hug my shoulders through the cab window. His face now bore the hallmarks of a heavy drinker along with his usual faint pockmarks and generally pale complexion that flustered easily, while his overall physical appearance amply displayed the pleasures of both the table and the bottle. Almost absentmindedly to himself he blurted in his soft high-pitched voice, "Imagine they won 11 Soviet championships and nothing since 1976!"

His flat was only a few yards further down. Inside it was modern and airy. Old copies of the liberal Russian-language newspapers *Sevodnya* and *Nezavisimaya Gazeta* were stacked on the floor neatly with plenty of magazines from around the world in different languages. I knew he spoke fluent Spanish, obviously, and his English, Russian, Arabic, French and German were accented but otherwise very good. With a Tuborg beer each in hand, my friend was much heavier than he was 23 years ago when I'd last seen him during Moscow university days at Patrice Lumumba. It was at his birthday party in that bar where Molody the Czechoslovak and I had first met, with Ukrainian Andry present.

He was Venezuelan. I'd followed his international travails with interest. Always in the news but not in a nice way. Even when I was in the Secret Intelligence Service I'd kept my mouth shut about knowing him. To admit I knew him may have subjected me to unwanted pressure and scrutiny. I hadn't done anything wrong, other than happen to go to the same Russian university. He was a rabid reactionary; I believed that negotiation and mutual understanding must replace war. We had a friendly bet long ago on that very first day we met, and we both knew instinctively at this moment that time proved I was finally the winner.

Not speaking, we raised our foaming cans and clinked to that. With a forlorn look on his face, he was gracious to even say it: "I lost the battle! I tried everything within my power to prove otherwise but I failed. It's too late for me to change now, comrade, so I won't even try. However, it doesn't mean that you won the struggle. That continues on."

I knew him as Ilich Ramirez Sánchez and he was one year old older than me. The global public knew him as "the most wanted terrorist in the world" still at large. He was otherwise known as "Carlos the Jackal".

Our lives had taken entirely different paths. I was on one side of the fence quietly making a difference the long way round. He was on the other track killing and maiming innocents on the shortest route. I won't go so far as to say I went right and he went left; for I was more left-minded than he, and he was extra-ultraconservative-right-wing-thinking in my opinion. There's a right and wrong too, but I won't say I'm morally completely right either.

Ilich had believed passionately in the Palestinian cause and was an anti-Semite, in particular towards the Israelis. He didn't have to tell this to me again as I'd heard him say it enough times when we were in Moscow—twice to be exact.

But even after the lessons of the commandments and parables of the Old and New testaments, the British and the French, following the end of World War II, really screwed up royally by repeating the modern version of the same biblical mistakes when they arbitrarily allocated Philistine—Palestine—to the Israelites; the latter again in search of a land to call their own.

My own take on this, admittedly with ample hindsight, is those in power then—the second coming of the Pharaohs and Romans—did not anticipate the consequences of their rash move. They should have given it more thought. It was a time of bad judgement and Britain and France are to blame for the sorry continued state of affairs in the split lands of Samaria and Judea today.

I sympathised but I understood there were two sides to every coin. He didn't. He argued that United Nations resolutions recognised the right of armed resistance to military occupation, in this case—Palestinian over Israeli.

There was some truth to that. If you read the clauses, it did in fact allude to that, but it was all in the semantics of *how* one read the messages. It was a bit like how certain fundamentalist Muslims interpreted the Koran violently and certain Catholics believe they are granted forgiveness for murder. Both go out again to kill with a cleansed soul in the belief they are doing the right thing.

But you couldn't discuss the two sides of an issue with those with a one-track fanatical mind. Only proof of time could clarify it for them as they matured—as it had in his case. Getting them to admit it is something else.

He still verbally stuck to his guns regarding the crime against the Palestinian people: "Since the failed Holocaust, it has been clearly proved that Zionism is an imperialist movement in its development, aggressive and expansionist in its aims, racist and extremist in its formation, and fascist in its means." Then he stated the fact that the Jews had already built settlements on disputed territory. I had responded with the fact that his same descriptive terms would have applied in reverse too, had Zionism been replaced with Islam. They would have done the same thing, given the identical situation and opportunity. It was basic human nature to do so.

The fire momentarily flashed in his eyes but it was quenched with a swig of cool brew. Holding his angry fixed glare back, while his ageing emotional circuitry fizzed and unplugged itself, I added calmly, "You are still trying to squeeze through the static form of verbal and written words, Ilich, and *still* thinking of resolving it with violent actions."

The staring persisted for creeping seconds. He finally laughed, burped, and stood up and went to get another couple of beers from the fridge. On the way out he said, "You should have been on my side, Anderson. You're a great putschist." I didn't let him see me exhale with relief.

I looked around the living room. It certainly looked like a female lovingly maintained it. He was divorced from his German wife Magdalena Kopp. But he always managed to attract brash trashy women into his life despite his ugliness.

"How is your daughter?" I asked. I didn't know her name but I'd heard he'd become a father.

"Rosa is fine, just fine. She is named after her grandmother, Rosina. Her mother—I call her Lilly—and her are living happily in my country, near Maracaibo," he beamed, as he returned with two more chilled cans in his hands. "I am officially 'attached' to a beautiful Jordanian dentistry student now." He winked at me. Lots of sex with multiple feminine partners was what drove him, even when he was married. "Polar beer from there is better than this stuff too."

When we sat down and I had his full attention again, I told him that the British government had selected me to come and see him. It was partly my own fault because I didn't realise Dr Michal Molody would list him as one of His Contacts during debriefing in Switzerland. I'd let that one go at the time as it was already recorded. But I was kicking myself when he had said it.

Later some bright spark at SIS had followed up on a rumour and smartly asked Molody in person, if Nicholas Anderson had really known Carlos the Jackal. Mike had stated the truth about where we all had met each other in Moscow in 1969. According to that particular transcription which the Cairo-based British attaché had read to me a few days ago, Molody had said that as far as he knew we were not in contact with each other. That part was true, thankfully. Until now. But from then on SIS and NATO knew they had somebody in their ranks that could identify the wanted man when the time came, and it had.

"Ilich, my specific instructions are to inform you that your cover is blown. You can either give yourself up or they will come and get you. You see, the British government are the only ones who know exactly where you are here in the Sudan. Apparently a belly dancer turned you in after another one of your affairs turned sour. They have not yet approached the Sudanese government about their knowledge of them hiding you, preferring instead to have the likes of me chat to you first. The Yemenites are on the block, too, for allocating you a false passport. Once the Sudanese know we know, their price for you goes up in all sorts of economic and trade bargaining. I hope you realise this. You, in a sense, are trapped in this country and will be held for ransom, much like I've been forced to come and see you against my wishes.

"I am in the same boat as you because my own countrymen have just informed me that my SIS records don't exist anymore, *until* I correct the problem of allegedly lying to them about our acquaintance. In this instance, my job is to persuade you to give yourself up without too much of a hassle. But even after that, the British will always have me over a barrel backwards and use me whenever they want. I'm a victim of my own circumstances of having been non-official cover for them."

Ilich sat there not saying anything to begin with, not focusing on me. Absent-mindedly he said, "Just the other day I heard a journalist was temporarily kidnapped for exposing a drug baron. They permanently tattooed the woman on each of her breasts with the two initials of the subject of her recent article. Then five men forced oral copulation on her. That message was clear too."

Then his glazed gaze came back to me. "I had heard you had gone into the British Royal Navy, but not SIS. We can be proud we each did what we did for ideological reasons and not purely for the cause of money. At least *I* should get a prize for ambition." He spat out of the open window in disgust. When he did that I wished Bob Mendelsohn was taping this session...but he wasn't.

"No doubt the fucking Sudanese too will try and concoct up a famine to get more foreign aid. Using me as a gauge as to how much they get. You see, every time your governments try to attack me, the mud splatters and soils them even more," he added, chuckling.

His ego was going to be the problem, I judged. He's suspicious of everybody and doesn't follow his own logic.

"Well, *El Gordo'*, while I'm here in the Sudan, let me know what your answer is," I offered, standing up to prepare to leave.

At that, the bulky "Fatso" insisted I stay and sleep on his settee, even though I had a hotel room reserved for me in town. That way we could talk further about the wide-ranging implications. So I did accept, except it was for three nights and days.

The subject matter varied. We only left once—for a long walk to see some heavies—all that time. At most we slept five hours then talked an exhausting ten. I'd awake from sleeping to find him at the typewriter copying from badly scrawled hand-written notes. Nobody even telephoned him the whole time. I even checked the unit was working once when he went to the john, and the dial tone was on. Whatever happened to the Jordanian woman he claimed he had?

"I try to write about whatever comes to my mind," he muttered, as he never looked up from the machine. "It helps me put things into a broader perspective, as bad as a typist I am. If it's ever published, it would be a memoir." I could only wonder back. Here was a man who invented the blowing up of passenger aircraft as the *crème-de-la-crème* of terrorist tactics, yet admits a foible such as that.

He was in search of an answer for me to take back. There was no easy straightforward one. He had to work it out for himself but with a little help from his guest. He was lonely too, I could tell, and he'd only been in the Sudan a month. He had reportedly, according to the British brief I'd got, regularly paid prostitutes for sex here. If he did, it was in the hope of loneliness going away. A woman's body wouldn't satisfy his needs, but an old school friend—who knew he was a killer and who could call him without fear by his degrading nickname—might. At least that was the game plan.

He was surprisingly very well aware of the problems of the Sudan and its neighbours' economic woes. I think he was trying to repay some of his violent deeds in a way the impoverished could benefit, kind of like Robin Hood. So he was talking out loud to whoever would listen. In this case, me.

He had the insight to say, "The black African countries' burden of debt is today's slavery. They have not been able to escape from the perversity of servitude. In continuing to accept white men's money, Africa evades the solution in controlling its own destiny. A bit like you and me, isn't it?"

"Who are you now, an old overweight Ché Guevara?" He'd looked at me seriously, and then laughed at his own ramblings, toasting me with his empty beer can upside down.

But he was quite sedate on the topic, and had a view of the local strife torn problems. "I see the rebels on TV here sometimes," he said. "The ones at the heart of the central African crises proudly wear *Interahamwe* embroidered on their shirts or carved into their rifle butts. It means 'we kill together.'

"You know, in return for their safe haven, the Sudanese had me sell American-made landmines to Ugandan rebels last week. I met that crazy Lord's Resistance Army leader who thinks he's God's messenger, Joseph Kony. He came to the meeting on the border between the two countries wearing a woman's dress and dreadlocks, would you believe it! He even gave me the choice of any one of his 50 or so wives to fuck and paraded them in front of me to choose. It was a different kind of screw I have to admit. One day I saw him instruct one of his men to cut a man's nose off just because he was riding a bicycle. He thinks bikes allow the people in his three-quarters of a million tribe to alert government soldiers. Meanwhile he's fighting them with young girls under 14 with AK-47's. It's a sorry sight really.

"Kony is going to be worse than the Derg, the Ethiopian 'Red Terror' Marxist military junta who murdered tens of thousands of their own in Stalinist purges during the late-70's. The killers' reasons were that they spoke a language called Amharic, which the rulers declared was no longer the official national tongue. They were finally overthrown the year before last.

"Before that I met a large Iranian government delegation who came here. That was a heavy duty crowd seeking to implement deeper Islamic causes into cash poor Sudan. Then we all attended the largest ever gathering of Islamist freedom fighters that they sponsored. I was pleasantly surprised at all the Europeans present, like the IRA's representatives the ETA, coming all this way to Khartoum to listen."

He chuckled, "The Arab warriors from *Mahktab al-Kiddiyah*, the Afghan

Services Bureau, fresh from victory over the Soviets, acted as security for the so-called terrorists. We'll go over and see them at some point while you're here."* A prolonged smile stayed painted on his face at some secret thought. I was thinking it's a small world.

The next morning Ilich exclaimed, "You have to understand I've done a lot in the four weeks I've been here and I'm worth it." He flashed a few used pay stubs in my face. Luckily I memorised the Arabic lettering. Later I would get it translated. [It read: Military Industrial, a Sudanese government company. More free info.]

The conference he referred to earlier must have been the same one Andry was telling me about. Further proof that revolutionaries all help each other as much as they can.

I was getting exasperated with his verbal traipsing and interrupted him, "I do not believe the developing nations have a monopoly on ethnic hatred and intolerance. But, Ilich, what's your point?"

He glanced at me as if I'd slapped him. He sounded vexed, "My point is that these crimes go unreported in the western press, while they fight for the *exact* same reason why I fought my cause for the Palestinians. I'm far nobler than the men I've talked about. Some are so bad their nationalities' names should be re-titled 'Xenophobians.'

"So?" I said. "So what. You murdered many innocents in cold blood too. Don't deny that. Then you became a fugitive once more, unlike them."

"Yes, but the Jewish fence, the *eruv* had to be steamrollered down, don't you understand? You can't compare my responsibility for a couple of dozen

---

* [* On the second night we got dressed up a bit. Ilich insisted that I wear socks like he did, no bare ankles, and to button up my long-sleeved shirt to the top, no T-shirt. "To be respectful to our hosts." We walked at length in the warm poorly lit evening on the dusty streets to another neighbourhood, a district named Riyadh, the same as the Saudi capital. He knocked on the high metal gate and upon hearing a voice responded in Arabic. There was a rattling of chains and two sentries trained cocked machine guns at us while a third bodily searched us. These boys looked hard and wore full Arab robes. After waiting in a ground floor room where we were served water and fresh fruit, we were finally escorted upstairs by a fourth armed guard to a man standing at the top of the steps who introduced himself in perfect Americanised English as Wadih El-Hage. He had the keys to the locked door we went through. (Ilich later said the man was Lebanese.) There was a lot of cleaning going on everywhere one looked, almost all silent Arab men who I thought were not Egyptians as I had just been there and who are rather loud by comparison to the much quieter Gulf Arabs. Sprinkled among them were clearly Afghans in their distinctly different Farsi dialect and dress. Apparently this bunch of mujahideen's collective supreme leader was coming next month from Afghanistan to live permanently in this building. One young mujahid kept loudly repeating, "*Marg, marg bar Russkis*". When I asked El-Hage what it meant he blandly said, "Death, death to Russians. They lost 300,000 fighters in the 10-year war between 1979 and 1989. He thinks you are Russian." Ilich apparently met Osama bin Laden's 12-man Shuria Council regularly at this location, from where Holy War was planned worldwide. A learning curve of solid intel it was.]

deaths to their tens of thousands!" *It is interesting how many people wage a battle within themselves with their own survival being the only goal.*

Faulty memory can be a way of selective forgetting too. At that moment I knew he was in complete denial of everything. Whenever he got close to anything resembling remorse, he'd do a flip and negate. You better size up, Mr Sánchez, I thought to myself, because while the moment had not yet arrived, it is coming with a climactic bang—woman or no woman to help you get off. Yet you can't even acknowledge the end is nigh, evidenced by my very presence in front of you. Very clearly he was psychotic.

Forty-eight hours after first putting it to him, I asked him one more time, "Are you going to turn yourself in or not, Ilich?"

"Well, put it like this. I want to do one more thing. I've been working on it for a year now. Now I'm where I want to be to do it while all this time I've been working with other people's money, never my own. If I pull this deal off, I'll have my own money to do what I want. If I fail, I'll turn myself in then because it will truly be the end for me."

"OK," I asserted. "Tell me what it is."

He held his hand up flat, "Fuck, no. I don't trust anybody." He didn't sound so convincing when he said it. He didn't have anybody to trust at all. There was only me and he'd let me harvest usable data.

"Not even a clue about time-wise?" I could feel my own anger rising. "You realise the clock is running here, don't you?"

He smiled brazenly at me like an unpunished little bad boy, non-committal. I abruptly stood up and went to the balcony for a change of scene. Sánchez joined me out there after a few minutes.

I finally uttered, "Ili, I'm leaving tomorrow. I have to tell them something. Not for you, for my sake. I've given you some time to respond and I take it you just have given me your answer. It's that you are not going to turn yourself in."

A jet plane flew noisily overhead and I took the opportunity to lean into his ear, "I'm not sure I'm going to tell London the precise outcome of our conversation. I have to think about it too. If they know you're here, they must be recording our dialogue from miles away anyway. This is perfect wide open space to point their listening devices at." He looked into my eyes from inches away and his head lurched forward a fraction in comprehension. I could intuit waves of tension between us. It was down to him or me now. He had made that clear.

I had to be leaving anyway. I had no idea how I was going to meet Mike Molody in Zaire in four days time. It was only the next country south but Kinshasa was 2,000 miles away from where I was. I wasn't exactly going to use the return half of the airline ticket the British Embassy had given me so they could monitor me at will. I had to break that control over me. Obviously they had an "in" with the authorities at Cairo airport to know I'd arrived before. Who knows even what the French—via Georges Durance—could have quickly galvanised, knowing I was coming to this country to reportedly see Ilich Ramirez Sánchez.

Little did Carlos the Jackal care if I was very much in a trap like him. He only addressed his side of it. I must do the same now.

Well, that last night with Ilich unexpectedly revealed three insights rolled into one, including half-answering a previously unanswered question.

I'd asked him innocently how he'd ended up here of all countries. He didn't want to tell me at first...then all of a sudden his floodgates opened and he told me everything...and more!

His response to the question was that a Palestinian sympathiser called Ali Abu invested in his scheme to steal a shipment of 330 pounds of gold bars worth US$1 million, which was soon to be air freighted by Lufthansa from Sudan to Germany. Ten per cent of the profits would be given to the investor, whose real investment, from what I could gather, was simply paying for the broke Venezuelan's air fare to get to the Sudan. Sánchez balance, $900,000, was to be used to start a new wave of terror.

What he told me about the western Arab man was doubling interesting. He was a minor financier of an American education outfit in Florida called WISE and that a large portion of Arab militant groups monies are transmitted out of the US via a Brooklyn ice cream shop owner's bank accounts. It's a small world again, I mused, once it dawned on me the acronym was the same one I saw on the IRA file in The Bronx, proving to me that they are all linked intricately somehow or other. They attend the same conferences after all. The New York City ice cream fellow was a worthy lead and would be followed up on.

He even went on to elaborate on who got him into the terrorist game. "Vladmir Yemifovich Semichastny, it's all your fault," he once toasted in jest. "You knew he approached a group of us at Patrice Lumumba in 1969 don't you? He was already a former head of the KGB at the time and still a young man himself, and he persuaded other young men like me to think of fighting against the West's legal genocide of Palestinians. It was the first time I had the impetus, the urge, to want to do anything with my life. He gave me that goal. Once anybody verbalised an interest, Vladmir Yemifovich put us in contact with the Palestinians directly. I wonder what the man is doing with himself now?" His habit of switching subjects returned.

He once, almost as if I was a silent immigration officer standing in his kitchen, took out a dark green Syrian passport from his trouser pocket that was marked *corp diplomatique*. He opened it on the photograph identification page, raised it to my face so I could observe it and see his likeness staring at me, and then flipped it shut. No words were exchanged then except that the name loudly inscribed there was clearly KHOURI, M. He was like a kid sometimes.

"You know my team once told me they knocked on SIS's door at its West Berlin office in the old Olympic Stadium to ask for directions. Just for bravado I understand. Mind you they did the same thing in Karlshorst at the KGB regional headquarters in East Berlin too, to relieve the boredom..." He smiled sadly to himself at the images in his head. He looked more and more resigned to me as time passed.

As I suspected, he had nobody to talk to. The so-called fiancée had also flown the coop a few days before I'd come. He was truly alone.

We had hugged and kissed each other on the cheeks and mouth quasi-Russian and Arab-style when I left. I gave him an address in Moscow where he could get in touch with me if he wanted to. I don't know if his mind was coherent enough to know, but I instantly knew I would never see him again. I don't think he fully understood *I* was the one who was going to seal his fate, not Britain's or Sudan's governments, nor France's maybe.

Ilich Ramirez Sánchez' thought nothing could happen to him ever. He was invincible because nothing really bad had happened to him so far. He was always the opposite of me. I'd always thought anything could happen to me, because it had all through my life, at any given moment.

I was going to continue my forward motion all the way to the end. It wasn't just Ilich. I was beginning to see that nowadays truth isn't as important as what people *think* happened. It was a realisation that others'— not just individuals but also governments—motives cannot be figured out and are often complicated affairs, especially if you are in the middle of their mess. I had to divorce myself completely from all of them.

The taxi came and the driver headed towards the airport based on Ilich's assumed directions. Half way there I had him do a U-turn and take me into the heart of Khartoum, capital of the Sudan. It was time to become invisible for a while myself. I didn't like being blackmailed by my own kind to do jobs for them I didn't want to do.

Sudan translated meant Sahara, as good as any a place to disappear in, and to cover up in this vast Everest of the sand.

When we reflect and the threads of our lives all come together; what we are left with are tangled paradoxes. How ravelled we each insist upon making what is so profoundly and uniquely simple.

Chapter Seventeen

Hunger is the devil that drives the people to strive.

It seems that every time I was in the blackest part of Africa, there was a civil war going on. Here in the Sudan in early-September 1993, it had been going on for 10 *long* years. According to the standard British government culture booklet, the attaché in Cairo had given me, it stated, 'the Sudan was Africa's largest and poorest country and that since 1983 more than one million had been killed in fighting, famine and disease, more than the combined number in Bosnia and Rwanda'—the latter two which had perplexedly been given much more world media coverage. The British explorer, David Livingstone, had called the Sudan an "open sore on the world" over a century before. I could see how. It still was such a horrible mess.

Ilich Ramirez Sánchez hadn't wished to discuss the problems of the Sudan itself, only its neighbours. I took that to mean a psychological transference, as he was more than indebted to the Sudanese government. Sometimes, again, it was what wasn't said that was the actual situation. I was disappointed to discover that, under his façade, the man was an adult adolescent who excused his behaviour because he childishly opined, "others were worse."

The thing that got me about him was his obvious self-interest. If only he had delivered his lines with less righteous bluster and more admittance of the truth—cutting the whiff of hypocrisy—then I may have wholly endorsed his goals. I'd always preferred lack of pretension to one's intellectuality.

He could never factor in that the Jews lost six million people during the last world war. Because of *his* attitude, I too wouldn't concede *to him* that what the suffering Israelis have experienced over their short history is being played by them on the Palestinians today. That would give him more fodder for hatred, and to use in the argument against me. The crux of the matter was the Arabs were entitled to the same rights that were once demanded by Jews and granted. It was fast becoming a holocaust of *both* races.

Focusing on the motorist's rear mirror, I had looked at the reflection of my taxi driver's face for the first time. I'd been in another world in the back seat from Sánchez' flat in the half-an-hour I'd sat back staring up at the folded roof top of the cabriolet. The cabbie was black among mainly Arabs, outnumbered by a thousand to one, from what I could see. In the city's daytime hours it was packed with *muhaggabbat*, veiled Arabic women, in their roomy white or light blue cotton garments called *niqab*. At least I assumed they weren't all black-skinned underneath.

I asked him who was *his* real leader in pidgin Arabic. From that seemingly innocuous question, by that evening I was being whisked out of Khartoum in a goods train driven by a elderly black driver south to a town called Malakal.

I spent the night in his noisy, rattling, smelly, unclean compartment just behind the black rusty steam engine he operated. I tried screaming at the old man in English and French, and later quietly in written Arabic—a declaration of muteness—once I realised he was tone deaf. Only in the tortuous latter could we communicate, and even then his reading ability was severely limited. Even I had a problem trying to read what I'd shakily written in the flapping wind. But we did relate to each other in our own way, and managed to laugh a lot at goodness knows what. What I did learn from our scribbles was that the wide-ranging river we travelled alongside was still not *The* Nile singular but the name had now elongated to the White Nile, *Al-Bahr al-Abyad*. And after our destination, it was to become *Al-Bahr al-Jabal*, the Mountain Nile.

I stood for hours in the loud vibrating moonlit night in the open doorway of the moving truck and gazed at the wonder of that beautiful glittering water mass rolling in the other direction. Standing there I wore my T-shirt over my head and ears to block the deafening chugging noise, while my torso stayed bare.

At one point, standing there, I lapsed into vertigo and had to hold on to the sliding door as I thought I was stationary and the river was rocketing past. I related the unbalanced feeling to the fact I was going against the flow myself. *I have a sharper sense of existential dread than most, reasonable enough given my experiences and that taut emotional tug of survival.*

Just as dawn's light crept in, I opened my eyes to see a dark robed figure swing into the compartment. I shot out of the bunk and grabbed the first thing I could, a metal stick of some kind, while my stance was pure martial arts. The man was black but I could see the whites of his eyes and his teeth grinning, hands half way up in the air in captured innocence.

The mouth moved and said in a clear bass accented English, "Mr Anderson, I have come to get you before the train reaches the terminal at Malakal. Please allow me to introduce myself. My name is Makol."

His mid-thirties face came to the beam of light shining through the gaps in the wooden moving structure. He was as handsome and as coal black as they came, and I liked him instantaneously. We shook hands warmly. He especially liked my makeshift cotton head-dress, which had fallen across over one eye, in my rush to jump up. I must have looked a senseless idiot to him.

We both waved good-bye to the soot-faced train engineer, who only smiled toothlessly back at us, and turned to face the direction his machine was rocking in. Another strapping young black man in flowing robes came galloping along the train with two free horses. My fairly heavy bag was thrown to him but he caught it comfortably with one hand. Standing behind me, Makol told me to jump broadside at the count of three on to the first stallion, and this I did, successfully landing—painfully—in its clothed midriff where there was no leather saddle. I grabbed its flowing mane to stay on. When I turned to see where Makol was, he had already mounted the other horse, coming level with me, and was leaning over towards mine to hand me the loose reins.

I'd never ridden a horse before and found it most uncomfortable yet wildly exciting. As we rode away from the train winding with the river down below us the train whistled at us in its own farewell as we went over a rocky ledge out of sight.

Fifteen aching minutes later, all perspiring profusely, we dismounted at a lone dingy jeep parked in a dusty clearing. The other horseman dropped my bag in the back of the vehicle and took off with our two steeds. Makol gunned the ignition as I sat down aching next to him.

For two hours I held on to that metal rocking horse's hard seat while my Sudanese driver caromed over bumps and gullies. I found myself closing my eyes, to equally stop the muck getting in and the tears getting out.

We passed what seemed to be abandoned farm sites. Makol yelled over, pointing at them, "Overgrown coffee and tea plantations." He smashed over a few mangoes that had fallen from the trees onto what could be described as a road.

Suddenly we were entering a camp of some one dozen small green tents spread like a swarm of locusts in front of us. There was nobody there. For a moment I thought the thousands of insects, which bugged us incessantly, had eaten them.

Makol poured me some warm water to drink and sat down cross-legged jovially, inviting me to plop next to him. I was so bloody sore I remained standing, feeling lobotomised.

Chat we did, just him and I alone in a thick-forested area not far from the sandy banks of the river. Apparently we had skirted around the town of Malakal and were now south of it. We were on the northern fringe of a 200-mile war zone of which the centre was the southern Sudanese town of Juba. I was going to have to encircle it or pass right through the middle of it to get to the Zairian border on the other side. The religious fight was between the north and the south of the country. Arab Muslims calling themselves the Popular Defence Forces, who were the government, dominated the north. The Christian black rebels were the south, itself represented by different warring factions of the same colour.

The outpost we were in belonged to the Sudan People's Liberation Army, the same popular PLA the Chinese called themselves, I mused. This unit was far beyond their natural habitat, but seeing they were already out of their way, were instructed to take me to their SPLA leader by the less dangerous circular route.

In Khartoum the day before, I'd mentioned to a group of wary black men—a sort of wise men's secret council—what my background had been and what my travelling problem was. They had finally thought it a good idea to help me in return for meeting their revolution's chieftain. It wasn't everyday these impoverished Africans got an Englishman on their doorstep asking for help. Simply stated, but here I was in the middle of nowhere less than 18 hours later. An ulterior motive had crossed my mind, however, in that I was good kidnap material who could be held to ransom in return for certain concessions from the West. But these were not the government troops so it wouldn't serve their best interests to get bad publicity. Or maybe it would be perceived as good to them, who knows? Basically for me, in the end, it was the lesser of two evils to pick from and I was willing to roll with the punches. But savouring it I indeed was, as my poor aching body and punched rotten behind had attested to.

What perpetuated the civil war, according to Makol, was the slave trade. "The Arabs think they can just come down here and take our people to clean their homes, wash their horses and have sex with, whenever they feel like it. We do not tolerate it anymore. So our brothers, the United Salvation Front, and ourselves fight them. We have no choice. It's *Rassenschande.*"

"Excuse me," I cut him off. "What's that mean?"

Makol smirked blandly, "German for race defilement."

"How come you speak such good English and know German words," I asked him. I was more than curious.

Makol exclaimed at great length how he had been the long-term employee of a German family who were owners of a coffee plantation but the language of choice for business reasons had been English. He had ended on, "But you are the first Englishman I have met."

Then he changed the subject back. "We at PLA are open to any help you can bring to us. We will get you to where you want to go, never fear. But we hope you will remember our good deeds. I told my leaders to trust Europeans more than Arabs. If you talk to others about us it will spread the word. The world does not know about us and what horrors we experience. Arabs abducted my sister when she was ten. A charitable group from Switzerland bought her freedom only a few months ago. At 20 she already looks like an old woman. But she was one of the few lucky ones. When they are used up or sick, they usually throw them away. The Arabs know they can go and get a cheaper replacement. In her case, they beat her daily to make her practice their heathen religion...I can't even say it out loud. So I have sworn to get revenge for her and all of the others they've taken. Likewise I have nothing else to do anyway as there is no work for pay."

The sound of approaching men made him reach for his rifle suddenly, but it was his own accomplices returning to base. Makol stood up to introduce me to this group's leader. "Mr Nicholas Anderson I am proud to present my cousin Paul Malong Awan."

I shook hands with a lion of a man dressed in army fatigues. It wasn't his size at all that impressed me, for we were the same height and build, it was more the way he carried himself. If I hadn't been presaged I would have thought he was the headman to talk to anyway, just from his demeanour.

He spoke fairly good English too but let Makol do most of the talking to me. About the only memorable statement Mr Awan said was, "The Arabs have stolen our children and strangled our very lives for centuries while the rest of the world watches. It is time we must do something. This war is not about money or religion for me. It's about preserving our futures. We are being choked slowly to death as our numbers decrease over decades."

"I can see *Weltschmerz* at work," I uttered to them, while Makol was nodding in agreement and my use of German. "Disenchantment with the world. I can only repay you with what I know and I will teach you both in the theorems of war."

As the regional commander and his shabby group on several horses, a camel, one jeep and a mule, with the rest walking, travelled south back towards more familiar terrain and to their headquarters, I spent time sweating in the open air jalopy steered by a fourth person…talking to my attentive pair of African rebels, while mopping my brow profusely.

I taught them what I had learned as a child from the Chinese and what I had put into practice in my adult life in order to survive it. Amazingly they produced a child's small blackboard and chalk so I could write and draw on it. Going backwards in motion, I would be standing closest to the sun in the mid-section of the vehicle like a professor in a classroom with my two pupils with their legs dangling airily over the sides. The jovial driver Kameri even joined in the learning sometimes though he didn't understand English at all, just distractedly repeated words every now and again when he liked the sound.

A day and a half later, I could safely say they had absorbed their lessons well. They could repeat back to me the principles of: tactical manoeuvring, the critical objective, selected policies of attack, preparing surprise, economy of force, rules of mass, the five essentials for victory, simplicity in calculation, and retaining secrecy. In front of my eyes, they were children in their respective thirties who became grown men with their new-found knowledge.

My teaching was, "Tactics is the art of using available means to reach an end and that end is strategy: the careful plan for achieving the end. You only win if you translate your tactical gains into some strategic objective; you go nowhere if you are all tactics and no strategy."

As we had some time to spare, I also threw in a quick lecture on the five sub-disciplines of philosophy. I thought they had potential for wisdom. Soon they were reciting words related to epistemology, logic, metaphysics, aesthetics and ethics. They were quick learners and I was proud of my pupils' progress.

We were going around the eastern route close to the Ethiopian border, which was ten miles further to the east. The others were constantly on the alert with their ancient fighting equipment, but I imagined the richer Arabs had far more modern machinery. Their only way to succeed against the odds was what I had drummed into them. "Now you two must spread your recent lessons learned to your brethren," I repeated a few times. They did agree, enthusiastically. I felt slightly absurd saying it, mind you, as I felt like a Euro-Jesus Christ, with my thin white tanned body, long dark hair and a unkempt week-old beard.

The two-day trip went without mishap although twice we could hear the sound of rat-tat-tat and a boom, echoing maybe about five miles away. In two instances I observed many occupants of villages dozed off in bunches in broad daylight with sleeping sickness.

We had gone level with the Sobat River, a Nile subsidiary, and passed through the rebel-stronghold village of Kit where we spent the next night. There I had slept on a mat on the floor of a bamboo-style hut with all the creepy-crawlies climbing over me. I scratched myself more than I had ever done in my life that night.

When I awoke I was lumpily tattooed! My hosts apologised for the behaviour of their bugs and had a topless, pretty, teenage girl come and bathe me in an smoothing ointment, which she rubbed all over my bare body, including my genitals. She never stopped giggling the whole time.

I asked both the much older Sudanese consorts what gives with seeing so many children here, some two hundred unattended by parents and between eight and fourteen years old. Many were begging pitifully for food.

Makol responded that all the juveniles I was looking at wandering around were in fact child soldiers.

"But," I exclaimed. "They lack the moral judgement to refrain from committing serious abuses, Makol!"

He contemplated me for a second and simply said, "Well, Mr Anderson, that's exactly *why* we favour them." *Something about severe poverty and automatic weapons together bothers me; an uneasy combination in the annals of my mind and in the pit of my stomach.*

The further we went inside that wide radius of Juba the cacophony of war could be heard closer in the distance, a disconcerting constant feeling of being on the tottering edge.

A messenger came out of nowhere from Juba where their Dinka tribe was based. The SPLA head man, John Garang, could not meet me after all as the fighting was getting heavier. But Paul and Makol were being summoned to go there immediately. We shook hands quickly, hugged and they quickly left. I only knew them for two days but I will never forget them.

Young Kameri was to take me alone to the Zairian border a hundred miles away, another one full day on horseback. I cringed at the thought of it as my bottom and the animal assigned were clearly not compatible. Plus the Sudanese fellow and I were separated by the gap of age and language.

At one stage he pointed to a peak in the distance. "Kinyeti. Kinyeti," he repeated excitedly. I got the impression it had a religious connotation to it.

Later Kameri patted the ground we walked on, saying, "Uganda. Uganda." After a while I couldn't help but notice he said everything twice, to make certain I understood. Here illegally on Ugandan soil I thought of only one person: Vibeke Brink. Uganda had a particular potent bearing on her life and I wept uncontrollably in remembrance as the teardrops mixed with my sweat in the heat, even in the shade under the protection of the trees. I visualised her double standing on top of Kinyeti staring down at us; like an angel guiding. Thankfully, Kameri remained void of chatter during this poignant period.

We waded across a river. I was astounded to hear Kameri say, "Albert Nile. Albert Nile." As if it was a person. We were still on the Nile? How many thousands of miles is this damn river? I was later to learn the Nile commenced from the Lake Albert further south of where we walked over.

A few times my guide alternated between exclaiming, "Sudan. Sudan," and "Uganda. Uganda," then all of a sudden it became, "Congo. Zaire." It's old and new name together. He never ever said, "Congo. Congo" or "Zaire. Zaire" interestingly enough. The nuances of our geography's, I shrugged.

Despite me thinking we were almost at our destination, it was still another two sticky bumpy hours of nothing but dense green land to go as we continued to criss-cross the borders of the Sudan and Zaire or Congo, depending on what my companion wished to call it.

Through the view of the basic binoculars we had, one village we skirted around also appeared to have a lot of the natives sleeping at mid-morning. Kameri's mime for me, with his hands clasped together next to the side of his tilted head, was indicating so too. But he had peculiarly added a vomiting motion. I'd assumed from that action of his, they had all been drinking and partying the night before in celebration of a victory.

One hour later the chirpy talking head of Kameri suddenly became a face of a ghost. Following his silent gape, two hundred yards north to our right, walking down a hill beneath us, were five *Janjaweed*, Arab horsemen, dragging a dozen or so naked black young girls with chains around their necks. A sickening sight just by itself and worse with the occasional whipping action that was going on. I'm grateful for not being subjected to the sounds of cries and snaps. But I am haunted by those scared faces I could see close-up with the field glasses.

They hadn't seen or felt our presence as the breeze was drifting towards us. Kameri and I, despite our language differences, spent tense seconds staring at each other wondering what to do. We did nothing but dismount and spy for ten pathetically long and electrifying minutes, until they disappeared out of view. We had one antiquated hunting rifle between us against a rapid deployment unit of five armed men with semi-automatic Kalashnikov AK-47 guns. It would have been like throwing damp blunderbuss in defence against the side of a raiding pirate's galleon.

Slavery and justice are completely incompatible and mutually exclusive of each other. The unforgettable scene captured a depraved rule of force that the Germans call *Machtpolitik*—and it is stamped in my head forever.

I spent the remaining hour on flashbacks on what I'd seen. At times speech and thoughts are hard to duplicate on a page, especially when utterly helpless. So strangely I thought of a poem I had once memorised by an unknown Arab refugee. I repeated it in numbness to myself.

"You can uproot the trees
from my village mountain
which embraces the moon.
You can plough my village houses under,
leaving no trace of their walls.
You can confiscate my rebec,
rip away the chords and burn the wood,
but you cannot suffocate my tunes
for I am the lover of this land
and the singer of wind and rain".

Poetry, the soundtrack of memory, which can be replayed by the mind.

For the last half-mile this white man walked with his bag strung over his back alone along the jungle path towards the mud huts representing the Yei-Aba border crossing. Kameri had preferred to stay behind hiding in the bush. I was a fish out of water as I proceeded through the passport controls from the Sudan into Zaire officially, both predominantly black nationalities gawked at my presence among them. For many of them I must have been the first fair-skinned person they'd seen.

* * * * * * * * * *

Never depend on someone else's understanding
if you are to live your own life.

After all the zigzagging, my first real taste of Zaire, the former Belgian Congo, which was also scrapping in a long civil war of its own, was at the height of the shimmering mirage on that taut quivering rubber band around the middle of the world—the Equator.

Mike explained the purpose of why we were there. "When I was a plastic surgeon in America, I tried to use the natural way to enlarge women's breasts instead of toxic-prone transplants. There's a plant root from the jungles of northern Thailand called *pueraria*, a natural estrogen booster that grew female breasts by one inch in five days. But I faced so much hostility due to my success then that I stopped using it. A pity because it really worked. Anyway, ever since then, I've been inclined from time to time to go on medical fact finding trips into nature like this one."

The first meal we had together was of a delicious unknown serpent and pulped with something or other, plus *fufu*. A bit like African boiled mutton sausages and mashed potatoes with the local bread, which was a tasteless mix from corn and manioc. The snake was great eating though. Moreover I'd wondered if it was a male or female, young or old...in deference to my first and last embryonic meal in China. When I asked the Zairian cook looked at me as if I was stupid.

The very next day, four of us with four animals for transport, found ourselves south of the old Stanleyville—Kisangani—purportedly to be where in 1871 the British journalist-discoverer, Henry Stanley, said to another Briton, a long-missing missionary-cum-explorer, "Dr Livingstone I presume."

While sitting astride a mule, one of our two appointed guides, Kimoto Simba—*simba* meant lions in Swahili—frightened me by starting to yell frantically at me to "gallop away from this spot!" He and I were next to each other idly watching Mike and the other Zairian man standing talking in the near distance by a river. Kimoto and his steed then took off in an ungainly spurt. But my mount would not budge, as much as I blindly followed his screaming orders and dug my heels in. The half-ass had previously obediently slowly followed its counterparts, wherever they went it followed, but not now naturally.

Kimoto was now shrieking at me to run. As I scrambled off the half-horse I saw what Mr Simba's concern was. A large but thin twelve-foot long jet-black snake was coming right at me through the riotous greenery at considerable speed! I had always been passionately afraid of them and sprinted towards where he stood, now about a fifty yards away...like a hare at a greyhound track.

That black mamba, one hundred thousand times smaller than that dumb stationery herbivorous mammal, hit it broadside like a torpedo smacking a ship below deck. The mule screeched in its death throes as the toxin from the angry bite took its poisonous hold. It staggered momentarily as the tangled affair of shivering coiled rope wrapped itself in strangulation around brawn and pulled its target down like a wrestler.

"Animal dead," was Kimoto's limited brusque summary of the attack.

Mike and the other guy caught up breathlessly with us. Bluntly the doc said, "Shit, those all-muscle black mambas will come at you if you are on their territory. One of the world's most aggressive and venomous vipers."

Then it was back to work, all forgotten. In the gratifying after-chill of fear I rode tandem with Ekanza Ndama, the other man. The experience shook my hinges no end.

Snapping out of my world of anxiety, Mike's voice in a monotone mode invaded my senses. "...I believe that in evolutionary terms, we've swung down from the trees, and that one of the things that made us human was the relationship with certain plants that tripped us into consciousness.

"Scientists theorise that environmental damage to previously pristine forest areas brought about the emergence of HIV-AIDS and Ebola as a major health threat. The theory is that these viruses were dormant until its environs was so severely disrupted by man," Dr Molody mumbled, almost talking to himself. "The forests' treasure is fast becoming green gold."

We had returned further downstream to a lake adjoining the same river. I was wondering if this too was a subsidiary of the Nile but, when asked, Kimoto told me it was the Congo. Shoals of dead fish floated on the surface like a carpet, not edible even to the dancing birds swooping to check.

Ekanza Ndama was in reality a medical research assistant attached to Dr Molody. They were collecting samples from nature and sealing them in glass phials. The government-appointed tour guide was Kimoto Simba.

Mike was still nattering on low-key, "Eutrophication is a process whereby the rate of growth of microbial aquatic organisms increase and their metabolic rate also increases. It is stimulated from an increase in water temperature and the concentration of nutrients in the water as well as other factors. The results in increased reactions that deplete the oxygen in the water causing the fish to die."

"Mike, are you talking to me?" I finally said. He appeared thunderstruck for a second.

"I'm talking to myself, aren't I? Well, I do that when I'm bothered about things. This is awful what we're seeing here, really it is. There's no explanation for all this hardship in nature. There' something terribly wrong around this region. It's like a sewage gutter."

I watched him potter around a bit more, a frown on his face, then he spoke more forcefully, "I don't know if you know, but HIV-1 was first discovered in this country twenty years before the medical Establishment announced it to the media. They found it in a Bantu tribesman in 1959, who had lived in Kinshasa, when it was called Leopoldsville. They've since learned that chimpanzees have a similar strain in them and, well, people in Africa eat monkeys. As a result, it would be reasonable to assume that all you have to do to get it is digest a cooked one which has the virus—who knows? But I *do know* for a fact you can't get HIV from eating it...it would be degraded as it is a fragile virus.

"But HIV is the body version of *kuru*, a neurological virus disorder that plagued islanders from New Guinea, which was transmitted through ritual cannibalism. We know *who* and we know *when,* but we still don't know *how* humans were first infected with HIV. As you know there's no cure yet. That's why Mr Ndama and I are collecting nature samples for me to take back to Moscow to investigate it thoroughly. I can already tell from my naked eye that the overall prognosis looks grim. I'm shocked. This country is the white lab mouse for all sorts of experiments by the world."

Ironically that night we did have the choice of monkey for dinner but Mike declined on our behalf, so we ate vegetarian instead. I couldn't tell you if the cooked leaves we had were well done or not either, to save my life.

Like the Sudan, there were noticeably high numbers of individuals apparently fast asleep at all the wrong times and places. One man was laying prone among the ripe rot of percolating rubbish bins. In the West, one would have thought he was a drunk. Finally I asked Mike about it, but Ekanza responded, "It's called *African trypanosomiasis*; sleeping sickness. Just to give you an idea how bad it is, in medical terms an epidemic is defined when prevalence of a disease in the population is two per cent or greater. Well, we've got 20% to 40% of entire villages down with it. It is curable but without treatment, those that have it will die, mainly from coronary failure."

"Yes, but, how do you get it and what gets rid of it?" I blurted, selfishly thinking about myself among all these sick people.

Mike took up the mantle. "How, is by bugs, like a lot of other diseases. But to cure it involves an initial screening with the CATT blood test, whereupon positive patients are examined for parasites in their blood and lymph fluid. If they have them, lumbar punctures are used to see if the disease has spread into the central nervous system. Treatment is effective but the two drugs required, pentamidine and melarsoprol, are very expensive.

"Pentamidine, used to treat patients at an earlier phase of sleeping sickness, costs US$20 per person for a full course, if supplies come from the World Health Organisation. The price sky rockets up when it is bought on the commercial market because the drug is used to treat complications from AIDS too. Another rampant problem here.

"Melarsoprol is highly toxic and used only for patients whose central nervous system are affected. The dosage, based on a patient's weight, has to be measured daily, requiring intensive training of local staff who have to be taught from scratch, adds up to a huge expense. It costs about US$8 a vial and a full course for a patient is US$80."

"I heard that the rebels in the Sudan, where you just came from, have their own way of joining the battle against the disease. Anybody who did not come for the screening would be put in prison for six months," added Ekanza, grinning. "Die here or die there, you actually have a choice."

I must have appeared vexed. Mike smiled and went on. "Nicholas, in the end the way I deal with the unfairness of life is to put it down to Mother Nature's selection process. You must understand the lack of drinking water often kills as many people with fatal diseases like cholera, typhoid and dysentery—dehydration also—than bombs and bullets do. Certainly far more than sleeping sickness, HIV-AIDS and Ebola does, in total numbers."

"OK, alright" I said, raising my hand in finality. "What's the real reason you wanted me to come here, Mike?"

"I'm glad you asked," he responded. "It's more *reasons*, plural. I needed you to see first-hand the worst and then the best the world has to offer. This is the worst—generally-speaking—and the best country is the one known to those who were in the Soviet Union during the Cold War as 'our aircraft carrier'—you know where I mean—which is where we are flying to next week, all-expenses paid. I can tell you this now though, that what western propaganda will have everybody believe *is* the truth...is really the opposite of the truth. Too many in the press re-write the facts to suit their governments' game plans. The fact is just one per cent, only 12 of the 1,200-odd new therapies patented between 1975 and now—1993—were for infectious diseases. Yet typical third world diseases like tuberculosis and malaria claims millions of lives annually while first world pharmaceutical companies *do not* bother focusing on the problem as this is not where the money is for them."

The next day we became more mobile with the availability of a Land Rover. We drove many hours north of Kisangani.

Eventually we stopped in a place where nothing seemed alive. Not even the sound of bugs and bees; they didn't even come to be swatted. A deadness prevailed and my neck hairs were standing. There was no wind. I honestly thought that perhaps a god had turned off a switch in this country.

Mike and Ekanza did their usual thing in the bush while I wandered over to the edge. The bad karma was definitely perceptible and I was curious. There below me thirty feet down in the pit were bloated, chopped remains of what once were living persons drifting in the shallow water. Victims of unimaginable violence. I'd seen similar dead masses of bodies before but whatever that was beneath me had been hacked repeatedly into pieces. A faint acrid smell like sweaty football boots after a game in the heat rose from the mangled depths. It is an abstract picture that remains framed with permanent residence on the mantelpiece in my memory's living quarters: A horrible pottage of rotting tripe.

It was my turn to yell at Kimoto and as I wheeled to do so, some half-a-dozen camouflaged gun-totting white men confronted me and one vaguely familiar face was beaming broadly at me with his arms open in greeting.

Captain Ian McIntyre, still continuing to smile indulgently, said in his broad Scottish accent, "Nicholas Anderson I presume?! Welcome to Ebola-land, where we assume it kills 90% of its victims and we do the rest...you bloody Sassenach!" He clasped me roughly. "What the fuck are you doing here, you cunt? Even with the poof ponytail I'd recognise you anywhere. I've been watching you through the binoculars for a full five minutes, arsehole." He clapped me on the back not for the first time.

These blokes were clearly mercenaries; soldiers for pay. Didn't take an idiot to figure out that they were "Mikes", out here in the middle of nowhere. "First, we've got to get the fuck out of here right now," urged Mac promptly. "Come along for a ride to our friendly headquarters. What you've done is walk into a local forbidden zone here. We'll go and have a cup of tea and talk there." He sounded like a local helpful tour guide in Poland and Czechoslovakia once again.

We rounded up the doctor and a strangely rigid mummified pair of Africans. While riding to their base in a South African-made Scout, which I knew were purposefully built to withstand a direct hit if it drove over a landmine, I had to ask Mac what happened to those shockingly mutilated bodies. "Hell man, these blacks do it to their own kind. That was a *vodou* area back there. In the African language of *fon,* voodoo means sacred. They don't just kill them themselves, you know. Instead the serpents do it for them, when they shove them down the victims' throats alive. See a body a week butchered apart for the *sangomas,* the witch doctors. These motherfuckers in the capital will pay good money for body parts for worshipping. "How's it go Mick?" he turned to one of the others sitting behind us.

"Mick Reeves, Sergeant, retired, ex-Special Air Service, UK, stationed at Stirling Lines, pleased to meet you sir," said the Welshman professionally, as we shook hands. "As I understand it every week they sacrifice some unfortunate soul from another tribe for a variety of uses. I hope you're not too squeamish, sir, with what I'm going to say: Female genitals and placentas are used for infertility and good luck; hands burned to ash and mixed into paste are 'cures' for strokes; blood is drained for vitality; brains for political power and business success. In Kinshasa they'll pay US$400 for a heart for uses against heart disease; $200 for a kidney; and about $80 for a testicle or gall bladder. So on and so forth, a lot of the smaller bits and pieces are believed for aphrodisiac uses."

"Didn't work sweet fuck all for me," a heavily-tanned serious-faced man pitched in. "I tried some of it. I still can only get it up once a day. Guinness, egg yoke and milk blended together is much better."

Everybody laughed. The speaker was Wines. "Just Wines," he called himself. He was a tough looking Belgian and a former French Foreign Legionnaire. His lapels advertised both his country's flag and the Legion's insignia of a small red grenade sprouting seven flames.

"That's nothing," piped in the clearly French-Canadian next to him with a distinct accent. His worn beret displayed a metal pin with the distinctive blue and white arc of Quebec on it. "Last month the nice little black secret programme our next-door neighbours from the Pentagon were trying out was worse. A bunch of them from the US Army Medical Research Institute of Infectious Diseases set up their monitoring equipment a few miles away from here. We got to understand that they were supposed to be trying out germ warfare devices on the natives. Unbeknown to them we were sequestered watching them too, under their neat guise of testing biological weaponry. But that laser they utilised for target practice was so miniature it was fitted on the end of a rifle. They had a lot of fun shining it into unsuspecting rebels faces from a discreet mile distance and blinding the subjects for life. A step towards non-lethal war, I guess. Then they packed up and left. I took a platoon with me to permanently put out the lights of those casualties. Put them down humanely—in a way. Piece of cake when they don't know where you are. Actually I can see it being good for torture though."

They were more than pleased to learn that Molody was a real doctor of medicine. It was requested he look at a few soldiers injured in a skirmish the previous day. Of course the doc couldn't say no, even though he didn't have his kit bag with him.

Wines and Quebecois were mates, I was to discover the Belgian and French-Canadian had been through thick and thin together, having first met in 1961 when they were 17 at *Legion Étagère's* 17-week basic training course in Sidi bel Abbes in Algeria. Each had saved each other's life once. Such fine Philistine chaps I thought, looking at them. Every time Quebecois spoke his voice sent instant chills down my back, for some reason.

At HQ, which encompassed a tablecloth of green camouflaged tents, the other white mercenaries were formally introduced. All, bar one, were over fifty years old at the time. Altogether there were seven of these well-paid fighting machines, leading and advising a hundred or so government troops who were in this makeshift cotton-clad fortress. Two Brits, a Belgian, a French-Canadian, a Zimbabwean-South African, an Israeli and a Yank.

The American immediately gave me his business card printed on both sides, which I retained, and it read: "Paul Michael Mason, PhD, Gunnery Sergeant, United States Marine Corp, retired. World Traveler, Adventurer, Marine, Casual Hero. Soldier of Fortune and Foreign Wars. No War Too Small or Too Big. Specializing in Jungle Fighting and Bar Room Brawls. Indo-China Experience from Korea (Member of Seoul Chapter) and Vietnam (Member of Danang Chapter). Plenty of Fruit Salad." On the other side the US Marines' *Semper Fidelis* (Always Faithful) motto was printed. There were no contact numbers or an address on the red and yellow card. His "PhD" in slang was for Purple Heart Donor—wounded in combat. "Fruit Salad" meant that he'd been awarded a lot of medals and it served as a public résumé for him.

Frankly, I thought there were plenty of cracked nuts thrown in his bowl too, probably from the exposure to the defoliant Dow-made chemical Agent Orange. The herbicide was supposed to be used to uproot trees and shrubbery but in war it ruptured the human brain's mechanism and caused a wide range of cancers.

As I took my leave from the American I fake saluted him and said to him in mock seriousness, "I will never forget you." It was a take on his a US

Marine saying, 'We will never forget you.' My attempt at dry humour was unfruitful and wide off the mark as he replied earnestly, "Thank you for the commendation, sir."

Later the quiet reserved Israeli, Yaron Cohen, who was the darkest émigré present, told me unasked while he was exercising topless that he was from Rimon. I didn't know what it meant. "It's the Israeli army's undercover death squads whose speciality was to kill Palestinians. It means pomegranate." He added almost too calmly, "Now instead I kill black men all day." I got the distinct feeling he was *ra*, evil in Hebrew.

At least Cohen seemed impressed, in a glassy-eyed way—as I was attempting to try and make small talk with him—in my knowing that his name came from Cohanim which meant the Jewish high priests that predated rabbis and that he was practising *capoeira*, Afro-Brazilian martial arts. He claimed he didn't know either of those facts until I educated him, strangely. When I walked away from him he bowed slowly and low like a moonstruck monk might do. I was thinking that depression was a job injury and that I would not want to meet him on a dark alleyway at night.

This alphabet of characters was more representative of reversal of fortune rather than soldier of fortune.

I came across Mike grinning after tending to a soldier's wound. "They give us enough diseases. It was time we took something advantageous they offered us. Fly larvae—maggots—dissolve dead and infected wounds yet leave healthy tissue alone. They also secrete enzymes that kill bacteria."

The lone white man keenly interested in Molody's activities was Eddie van der Boer, the leader of this for-hire troupe. Mac was his second-in-command. Being the paterfamilias; van der Boer was the youngest too. He was about mid-thirties, told me he was born in Rhodesia (as he insisted "not Zimbabwe please"), clearly boarding school educated like me, and a former intelligence officer for BOSS, the South African Burcan of State Security to boot. The naturalised *Suid Afrikaan* was spooning out of a bowl and kindly offered Mike and I some, "Have some pap, men. I make it myself. It's really corn mash. You could eat all day and slowly starve the body to death if there's no nutrition in the intake. Hey, I'm very up on this kind of bush treatment, doc. I don't know if you noticed, but we have a lot of other naturally blind bastards out here too, *not* the targets of lasers. Care to teach me a thing or two on how to prep against that? I'd appreciate it. Nice to help them out, you know."

Mike seemed to appreciate the genuine interest, and quickly injected, "Well, unfortunately, that's now the opposite side of what I just said about larvae and is commonly called river blindness in these parts, *onchocerciasis*. Millions have it here. It's a debilitating disease, which is transmitted when a female blackfly bites a person and deposits the larvae of a parasitic worm in the human's body. The larvae reproduce, and blindness sets in when the tiny worms migrate to the victim's eyes. I hear there's something in the works to prevent it but I doubt it'll help those that are already blind."

I shuddered at the thought of worms crawling inside human bodies that were still alive and left them deep in intimate dialogue.

Finally I was alone with Ian McIntyre in his tent. "Marks & Spencer's tea bags," he said proudly. "Always carry them with me." We raised the steaming canned mugs in a toast. "*Binti*. Daughter of Sunshine," he said in half-Swahili. "Click clink, up yours, you git," I said in acceptable obnoxious English to the Scotsman.

McIntyre was watching Mike and Eddie across the way with his African men. He had some put-down observations about the troops, which weren't Zairian at all, which I originally assumed, but black South Africans. "This is just an LIC to us white men. You know, low-intensity conflict, below the level of conventional combat between regular armies."

It was an attitude of superiority I detested. I wanted to get off that subject. "So who pays your salary, Ian?" I asked politely after sipping.

"Ultimately, I guess Elf Aquitaine and De Beers do, the French major oil producer and South African diamonds mining group which have the monopoly in Zaire, only after President Mobuto Sese Seko has taken his cut, mind you. But Eddie van der Boer's man, Henderson, at his Johannesburg-based company is the cheque writer," he responded blithely, not obviously keen to say any more than that.

I looked out at the chain-smoking van der Boer, still keenly interested in what Mike Molody had to say. Long blonde hair, thinning and as thin as his frame. Unusual man and noticeable with one eye green and the other blue. An attack pit bull version of David Bowie.

I returned my gaze to a pent-up looking Ian McIntyre. He seemed broody, wanting to get something off his chest. We were never quite buddies, really more business acquaintances thrown together by circumstance. We'd always had somewhat of a strained relationship and would never have invited each other down to the pub. The spectre of Lt.

Cmdr. David D. Brennan, RN (ret.) had always separated us. Every time I had been in his company it seemed my mate from Northern Ireland was present. This was the first time he wasn't with us.

"You know your best pal Brennan was a grass, don't you?" was his next remark. That rocked me aback on my heels. I didn't say anything. "Lying fuck, Fred (turncoat), tout (informer), hellion, ock aye he was all, and a Lundy—a traitor—to our country," spat a bitter McIntyre. I remained silent and still, my jaw grinding, waiting for him to spill his guts. *This* was the reason I had asked Mrs Blyton of his whereabouts. I wanted to know why Brennan and he had this on-going animosity for each other. I'd experienced it in Poland during the Puchovskaya defection and I was beginning to learn there was more going on then than met the eye. It was time to get to the bottom of it and it was kindly presenting itself to me.

"Worked for the IRA, deserved everything he got coming to him." Mac wasn't meeting my eye, but wiping a thin film off his forehead in controlled anger.

He didn't continue for a second or two, so I interjected, "Did you know he's dead?"

Seemed like he didn't hear that. He was reliving something in his head, excavating the past. All he uttered was, "They should enact a law that exculpated anyone who had not obeyed the orders of a superior officer, no matter how atrocious their deeds may have been. We didn't have a choice. He did."

"Do you mind being more forthcoming," I said. I was completely in the dark about this matter.

He stared at me as if he'd just seen me for the first time. I repeated the question for the present, thinking he'd switched back from before.

"I heard you the first time," McIntyre snapped at me, his Scottish brogue more pronounced. "You really don't have an idea do you?"

"No, I don't," I blurted. I really didn't. I found myself breathing heavily. "Why don't you tell me?"

* * * * * * * * *

Captain Ian McIntyre took me back 17 years and a few months to Dublin, Republic of Ireland, on Tuesday, 20 July 1976:

I had been sitting in the corner near the bar in The Brian Boru, an un-sophisticated working man's public house overlooking the canal just north of downtown in the Irish capital at late-lunchtime, having a peaceful pint of Guinness and a delicious meat pie with a bag of crisps, minding my own business, reading the *Irish Times* quietly. I'd come down on the spur of the moment from Belfast on the first flight of the day to follow up on a lead, and already dropped my overnight belongings at a nearby bed and breakfast. The morning interviews with two Irish political prisoners had gone well at nearby Mountjoy prison and I'd gone and taken a peek at the IRA's newspaper's legally operating editorial offices too, which was walking distance.

For some impetus I looked up when this familiar face strolled in, it was Davy Brennan. Though we had talked on the phone a few times I hadn't seen him for at least six months, since we were both at a fortnight's SIS training course in Cheltenham, England. I raised my hand absent-mindedly to get his attention, and as quickly as I did, I started to brush the side of my hair as if I was bored. I realised immediately he was working on an undercover assignment for his stony gaze told me, 'Don't even think about it.'

Intrigued, I went back to perusing my newspaper for another minute while still paying lazy attention. Face on Dave was ordering a Smithwick's pale ale at the far end of the nearby bar counter. As the drink was getting poured I distinctly lip-read him to ask the barmaid, "Where is the bog?", meaning the men's toilet. She pointed at the door just to my left. I calmly folded the newsprint, placed it under my pint, and stood up to walk next door first. There was nobody in there, no stalls even. As I was standing there taking a piss, Davy boy came along side me and said straight to the wall in front of him, "'The Pale' stands for *that* part of Ireland colonised by the English."

I quickly asked the wall in my fake Scottish brogue, "Come again, mick?" I was thinking about him ordering that pale ale for some reason.

His quick response was, "'Beyond the Pale' is the wild world beyond the enclosed stalked-out area around your home..."

Right at that moment then another visitor walked in behind us, as I zipped up and turned away, and the other bloke conveniently took my spot. I walked out through the door back to my table without even looking at my friend and resumed reading. Less than a minute later Brennan ambled out and I saw a matchbox fall out of his near-side pocket on to the sawdust-laden wood floorboards. He went back to his place by the bar, his back to me this time.

I slowly stretched my whole body out of boredom and yawned as my heels cupped the object. I took a good long look around the pub floor to see if anybody noticed. No eyes were on me that I could see. The place was thinning out as the second shift's lunch crowd of men in overalls and office workers of the drinking class were heading back to work. Brennan still had his back to me chatting to the fair bonny lass working the bar but kept pointing animatedly and repeatedly at the street beyond him with a sharp left with his hand, as if getting directions from her, which I took to be all for my benefit.

Still reading the paper, my hand scratched at some imaginary itch on my foot and the matchbox was swiftly inside my pocket. I looked around again. Nobody seemed particularly interested in me still. So I opened it and there was a single car key placed inside. I was puzzled, but it was obvious there was a car outside the pub *to the left* that he wanted me to either drive or get into.

I gulped down the dregs of my black drink and headed out straight away. Once outside I glanced again at the key and noticed a Ford insignia on the new key's plastic head but no registration plate number inscribed. A quick scan told me that there were at least one dozen Ford vehicles parked around the small square to the left where a lot of cars were parked. It was an impossible task to figure out what he expected of me.

So I crossed the way to the other side and wandered further down before leaning against the gated entrance to the tiny green park, all the while looking at the single two-way road that led into the enclosed area, as if I was waiting for somebody to drive in and around and pick me up curb-side and drive back out again. Brennan eventually came out of the pub and walked up towards my location at a medium pace. I walked parallel with him stopping across from the small garden lots. As he entered the passage he stopped at the very first Ford, a two-door four-seat pale blue Cortina, and opened the passenger curb-side door before leaning in to get something on the far side driver's seat. He was in there for what seemed like a whole 60 seconds, before shuffling back on his feet again on the pavement. He looked around as if he was searching for a phone booth and walked back again in the general direction of the pub around to a row of them further away on the other side of the rectangle.

When I got to the side of the car. I glanced down inside. On the seat was a piece of paper clearly written in block letters, 'GET IN THE BACK SEAT, STUPID.' I went for a brief walk and a few minutes later I used the spare key I had and was huddled against the back seat on the car floor.

Within a minute I heard somebody get in, start the engine and drive off. I was hoping it *was* Dave because I was going to look pretty stupid hiding in the back of a stranger's car. What would I say?

After precisely two minutes, Dave's familiar voice said, "OK, Nick, you can come in the front now. It was a pure piece of Irish luck I saw you, man. I'm so grateful to God to have you here with me. Sorry about the precautions. I'll explain why in a sec."

When I climbed over the seat and was next to him, what I quickly learned was that the day before when he was in London he had been instructed by SIS' Requirements & Production section to report immediately to an office at the army camp in Aldershot, southwest of the capital. When he entered the room at the base he found it staffed by officers representing Army Intelligence, British Services Security Organisation and Irish Joint Section—a unit jointly operated by both MI5 (domestic) and MI6 (international). A silent driver in a fast unmarked car with commercial plates had then specially delivered him six hours one-way from Aldershot to the port of Holyhead in Wales, where he stayed overnight in a b&b.

The next early-morning, this same day, as pre-arranged, he had picked up the car we were in, which had Irish plates, that was parked just down the street at the ferry terminal, and had arrived in the Irish Republic this same late-morning. Before starting the car he said he checked to see it wasn't rigged with some electronic devices and/or booby-trapped. He had done so because everything had been tight-lipped plus his specific instructions were vague: to stay and follow an assigned marked car in Dublin; observe and do nothing, no matter what. According to Brennan, the lot in Aldershot had requested a natural-looking Irishman and he'd been tasked the job. As he said that, I was thinking again to myself, what exactly is a natural-looking mick?

"Fucking barmy kind of command, if you ask me. I don't like it. So when the occupants of the car in question went to have a two-hour business lunch, I thought—fuck it—I'd go and have a break myself. Then when I saw you in there, I blessed the heavens."

He'd parked the car again, had switched off and we were sitting talking. It wasn't like him to be nervous. So I tried bringing him back to the beginning of his assignment. "Pure poppycock balderdash twaddle," he said, not really following my behest. He was already starting the engine again. We'd been stationary for only five minutes. "Good timing! " he said to himself. "See that dark blue Jaguar XJ6 coming out now from the restaurant driveway ahead? I've been told to follow that car for the next twenty-four hours and I've been at it since eleven this morning. I've got to sleep in here too until 11:00 AM tomorrow. What kind of stupid directive is that? As I've been sitting here, I've been seeing and hearing the craziest things."

As I was about to ask a question he leaned down and turned on the special one-way radio, and we were now listening to the occupants of the top-of-the-line Jag in front of us talking to each other. Obviously it had been bugged and a radio transmission set up between the vehicles and I instinctively thought that it was possible he and I were being one-way monitored in turn.

Some joker in the car ahead was heard to say in his Irish accent, "It is believed that God created alcohol specifically to prevent the Irish from ruling the world!" I smiled.

"The posh bloke talking now is the new British ambassador to Eire," Dave said pointing at the box. "Transferred from Paris. Just appointed a couple of weeks ago. Boy, is he a sharp geezer. Appears like he intends to stop the Troubles at once. Good for him."

We could only keep tuned to the airwaves. It was all business and politics. The main speaker's accent was posh clipped English and he was a very direct get-it-done type with a definite follow-up attitude, conducted in a proper public relations style. "When I spoke at Nuffield College in Oxford last week, the Secretary of the Joint Intelligence Committee was in attendance and was duty-bound to report that I publicly announced that we are working towards having them throwing rubber rocks at us, at which point we will then be willing to fire rubber bullets back." Interesting bloke, I thought, with an unusual concept.

The best line we heard that afternoon on that radio was from that same distinctive ruling-class English voice, "The Irish people are caught between an entrenched ruling class called the British and Irish political extremists, some operating under Protestant and Catholic religious flags of convenience. The answer is that the every day ordinary folks of Northern Ireland must again be governed by themselves."

He'd got that right I thought as Dave muttered under his breath and punched the steering wheel, "Bingo. Hit the nail on the head."

We got to see the ambassador twice when he got out of and in the car at the British Embassy. A tall, bald, PG Wodehouse-look-a-like with a dark patch over one eye and a monocle on the other. He didn't stay in the building very long and soon we were on his car's trail again. He was a busy chap.

Hours later, we were still tailing the car and were now on the Enniskerry Road heading south out of Dublin. About seven miles later, we turned off somewhere near a pavilion named Marlay Park in Sandyford. It was quite scenic as we were at the foot of the Dublin mountains, appropriately called the Wicklow Hills, clearly overlooking the distant city. Three miles of curving under high hedges along the back lanes, we finally passed a discreet street sign which read Murphystown Road.

The Jag pulled into a gravel driveway with a high wrought iron Gothic gate. You could see a rare laurel lawn, a reminder of Victoriana. A single uniformed Irish bobby saluted the car as we passed the entrance to the mansion. We heard the upper crust voice say, "O'Driscoll, that'll be all for the day. I will be entertaining some journalists later. Please advise the staff to make sandwiches and tea, some biscuits perhaps, old boy. Enough for say half a dozen guests. Put the fireplace on too to make them feel cosy. Extra hand towels in the lavatory and all that. Thank you." The double door locks in the limousine were heard clicking shut.

Dave and I sat peering down at the crackling void in front of us as we pulled in the first available lay-by, surrounded by light woodland. "So?" I finally piped up. "What's so unusual about this?"

My Irish buddy was staring mesmerised in the direction of the mansion. "I'm telling you. I don't like it. There's something fishy going on. Since when have you seen *one* security detail policing an enemy ambassador's residence? We are supposed to be at war up in the Province, remember? Also no armed escort. No nothing, except you and I, and I've been told not to be involved if anything happens...not until tomorrow morning, that is, *if* something happens. If that's not odd, I don't know what is. Something *is* going to happen, that's what."

He had a point. "Well what do you want me to do, Dave? I've got a few things to do myself back in the city, and then I'm heading up to Belfast tomorrow. Came down at the last minute today. I've kept you company most of the afternoon while we chatted about old times."

Brennan was characteristically promptly straight to the point and quite specific. "Well, seeing God dropped you out of the sky at a time when I was feeling like a pigeon waiting for a hungry kite to swoop, I figure you're here to help me, Nicholas. What I want you to do is stay the night in the car with me. Help keep watch, that's what."

"You're fucking kidding me!" I said right back in my best sarcastic accent. "Gor blimey me old China, me stay here in this country lane keeping lonely you company, while you snore and fart your brains out? I've done that once before with you. Never again, if I can help it. Anyway I've not been authorised so. You know, I'll have to report it too. What am I going to say, 'I came across Brennan and he was out of his depth in a 'Publin' car park puddle shaped like a harp and I rescued him from drowning?' Besides I've already paid for a nice bed in town."

Brennan never spoke but sat there looking at me, like a wet puppy, pleading. A Northern Ireland-registered car with two men passed us. They looked lost. A few minutes later, the same car came by again in the opposite direction, going slower. We saw the amber indicator light come on as it turned into the ambassador's compound.

"They must be some of the reporters the man mentioned," I said out loud to myself.

Brennan was getting out of the car and looking in the boot. There was plenty of food and drink in the back—the usual provisions for a planned stakeout. I couldn't help but notice a Walther PPK pistol inside the basket placed on top of the cloth serviette. "Seemed like they expect you to defend yourself though," I muttered as I picked up the gun. The magazine was full loaded, well oiled, in good condition.

"That's yet another nail in the coffin," intoned Brennan flatly. His face was still pensive. "It's not a standard regulation issue, as you can see. The registration number has been scratched out too, if you want to see for yourself. I feel like I'm being set up for something, and it's not all good."

"Alright, OK," I replied. "You owe me one for this. I agree it doesn't seem quite right. A bit odd. But if I don't have to hear about this from you for the rest of our service, I'll be happy." He grinned a wee bit with relief at last as I slapped him on the back. It was already nearly evening, getting close to six. We broke open two lukewarm bottles of fruit juice and mumbled to each other *"slainté"*—cheers—while we munched on a ripped in half roll of roast lamb.

"By the way," I asked my close friend, "what exactly did you mean by 'the Pale' in the pub before?"

He finished chewing his food, looked bashful, and said, "Well, when I first saw you there, I was warily ecstatic to see you...initially. Then when I was drinking at the bar, I had a brief thought that perhaps you were assigned to clandestinely meet up with me, so I thought I'd test you with the assignment code I'd been given, just so you could identify yourself with something I'd recognise. Based on your answer, you hadn't a bloody clue what I was saying at all, which tells me you being here is my fortune. 'The Pale', by the way, was the 14th century border around Dublin that represented the land controlled by the Anglo-Normans. The rest of the country at the time was Gaelic. An ominous password to have, to say the least."

Later we found an ideal parking spot a quarter of a mile on the other side of the entrance on the way back to town, in a clearing where we could see better. We figured if anything happened we could best see it from there. We were to alternate on two-hour watch duty commencing from twenty-two hundred hours.

On my two boring reconnaissances I only heard owls hooting. Each time I set off into the foreboding gloom, I swore at my own uncomfortable predicament as my back was getting sore and my neck ached.

Sometime before dawn, Dave rolled up during his sally and was shaking me awake. My watch told me I had only slept for twenty minutes. When I looked at his blurred face properly in the car's interior with the weak door light on, I knew instantly he'd seen something out there. I switched on the adrenaline in my head. 6:20 AM.

"I think it's the same van that came through a few hours ago, I can't be sure. But two blokes dressed in electricity board uniforms rolled up then to do some emergency job in a ditch between the house and us. Only stayed a couple of minutes then left. They didn't see me that time. Now it's four of them but this time I walked by them briskly moments ago...as if I was some local simpleton heading to work early, I nodded, 'morning' to them but nobody even looked at me, nor spoke, nor even turned their flashlights around on to me. It was dark enough as two were down in the same trench area and two had their backs to me, but in the time it took me to walk on over to here, I got the distinct impression those blokes weren't real electricity lads." 6:22 AM.

"How so?" I was still rubbing my eyes. "Well, if I didn't know better, I got the feeling they were foreigners, as in not European at all. Originally I'd thought maybe they were Black Irish, dark-haired lads from around Cork whose descendants were from Brittany in France, but Irishmen always at least nod back at this time of the day, you know… Look, you're the language expert. You'd know by just glancing at them. Come take a look-see with me, will you? They're only about a hundred and fifty yards down the road. It doesn't smell right besides. Whatever it is they're in a hurry to do can't wait till morning?" 6:24 AM.

I jumped out of the car right away with the PPK in my hand, which he'd dropped on the front seat next to me, and started walking ahead of him down the eerie winding country lane, quietly but fast. His scepticism was beginning to get on my nerves somewhat. I needed something to allay his fears. Neither of us had a damn torch to see well. The air was slightly nippy and Dave was right behind me breathing down my neck, like a giant grey leprechaun. 6:25 AM.

We hadn't gone the whole way before we came across one of them taking a leak on a tree behind a gap in the hedges, off the road. Steam rose on the early morning dew near his feet. You could see the other three further down, slightly hidden around a sharp bend in the road. Two were still knee deep in a gutter digging with the third standing looking down as if inspecting their work, his back to us. Dawn was breaking. 6:27 AM.

We saw the man zip himself up, stretch and walk lazily back towards his colleagues. Fair Irish he certainly wasn't. His complexion was more of a Moor, if anything. One of them down the road hollered something indecipherable urgently at him, obviously pissed-off at the man taking his time. It sounded much like, *"l'enmerdeur"* —"the pain in the neck." Our slacker, still within listening distance of us, clearly and in a guttural accent called back in sarcastic French, *"C'est Dieu et mon droit,* fucker." It was a brazen reference to the motto of the British crown's "God and my right," while his right hand cupped his genitals rudely. The statement stopped me dead in my tracks as I dragged the following Brennan down by his sleeve into a crouching position. Alarm bells were tolling in my head. 6:28 AM.

"What did he say?" Dave whispered. "Doesn't matter what he said," I said, "You're right all along. There is something *really* fishy going on." I was trying to think what to do next. It was 6:30 AM.

Their van's engine was heard starting and Davy standing quickly, peeked through the shrub, "Damn, they're all getting in it too. They stayed exactly a quarter of an hour. Get back to the car fast!" 6:31 AM.

We scrambled alongside the rough wrong side of the high hedge, half-hunching and slipping as we ran. Just as their van came level with us, we both slammed to the damp earth. As soon as their vehicle went round the first bend, we scampered across the narrow country lane and dived into the waiting Ford Cortina that was hidden from view. 6:32 AM.

Brennan had that car's ignition on immediately, and like a true pro came out of our blind hidden clearing *slowly*. The car picked up speed enough that, within two minutes, we were only 100 yards behind the van carrying the *agent provocateurs*, or whoever they were. We could see the rooftop of it over the bramble clearly winding its way in front of us. 6:35 AM.

Amazingly two police cars passed us, one behind the other, going in the opposite direction. "Always too late," mused Brennan. "Where were they all day yesterday of all days?" 6:38 AM.

The road seemed to encircle all the way round and we saw the van pull into an abandoned old side lane which had become an empty lay-by. It was within sight of council estate houses a few hundred yards across a recently ploughed brown field. We couldn't exactly go and park behind them, so we drove on past them staying on the parallel newer section of road. Trying not to stare at them I noticed the three that had exited had changed out of their workingmen's overalls into what would be best described as hunting gear. 6:40 AM.

Looking in the adjusted side mirror now, the van was speeding off again. Within half-a-minute it was right behind us, almost bumper-to-bumper, for a whole mile before turning off. Dave and I had spent those frustrating few minutes trying to read the number plates in reverse in the rear view mirrors but failed as it was too close up and hidden from view. On a couple of corners the van driver swerved out as if he urgently wanted to pass us, but I still couldn't see the plates as the angle was off. We were swearing to ourselves about our predicament being in *front* of the subject under surveillance, and had reacted with typical public annoyance by turning our heads sideways to the discourteous in-your-face driving so early in the morning. As the van came along side to finally overtake on a straight stretch of road it never fully completed the manoeuvre, instead it screeched off suddenly at an angle down a side lane. 6:43 AM.

Dave had immediately braked and reversed at speed back to the corner of the T-junction where the van had turned right. I shouted at him to quickly let me jump out and for him to meet me back at that old lay-by a half a mile down the road. He took off tyres squealing after the van. I found myself sprinting at a good pace down the completely empty road. I still had the gun tucked in my back belt so I grabbed it and ran with it clenched in my hand. There was still no other traffic at this early time. I slowed down when I finally got near the lay-by and tried walking to appear normal as well as regulate my breathing, despite streams of smoke escaping from my mouth. It was precisely 7:00 AM.

Which way to run? I managed to climb an oak tree and spent a few minutes on lookout as I regained my composure. I figured, whatever they were doing near the ambassador's residence, it must be somewhere back in that westerly direction over there. I spent minutes staring at the estimated spot where I thought the mansion was. It was still misty. Everything looked the same from every which way up here, all trees and country fields, except for the terraced houses behind me. I wondered how Dave was doing. 7:10 AM.

Then I saw a slight movement in one of the fields several hundred yards in the distance. A disturbed partridge was getting away from something there. There was no sign of a hawk above, nor a fox running after it. 7:12 AM.

My eyes watered as I continued my fixed gaze on that particular point. Then I swear I saw the earth move ever so slightly. I was convinced that's where the three were holed up. It was about time Brennan lad had rolled up too. Maybe he'd gone to call for help. A few inconspicuous cars and a lorry came rolling by. People going to work. 7:30 AM.

I decided to make my way to the location in the distance. I had to check it out for real to be sure that it wasn't my imagination playing tricks. The problem was the only angle to approach them was from behind, which meant a walk through those thickets and dense dark trees. I kept looking at my watch. If Davy turned up, he was going to have to know where I was. There was nothing I could leave him to indicate my current position. I left at 7:41 AM.

I got lost in the thorny bush a bit but I began to sense human company. The usually squawking ravens and crows had flown the coop this morning. The only sound was my own breathing and the occasional crispy twig I stood on. I was standing right out in the open like a stork on one leg for long seconds. 8:00 AM.

Cigarette smoke hazily escaped to the sky over there. It breezed slightly my way. I recognised the smell straight away, it was the unmistakable fart-smell of the French-made brand, Disque Bleu. They must have been 10 or 15 feet away from me. They were jabbering in French at times but mixed in with another language. I couldn't make it out. "Kassaman?" "Polasario?" Were these their names? Then in accented English one of them clearly said, "I thought today was our last day of shame. Then it was..." A car horn honked once as I went down on my knees. I looked back finally and could make out a pale blue car parked way back in the distance. I used profanity not for the first time that day. 8:03 AM.

I didn't move from there for a whole two minutes. I was cursing under my breath so much at my stupid circumstance standing out there alone in the middle of the creepy woods, not knowing what I was doing even. 8:05 AM.

I started off moving backwards, not taking my eyes off where those men were. Upon closer inspection I could make out what appeared to be a well concealed tarpaulin. So that's what had made my eyes think the ground was moving before. Mobility was slow and painful, and I winced every time I could feel rotted wood crumpling under my weight. When I finally got to the parked car, Dave was by now another 100 yards further down the lane with his back to me searching. I whistled a couple of times and he turned around eventually. He ran to me like a whippet. 8:19 AM.

"So did you track the van?" I asked. Davy shook his head, breathlessly, "No, it just disappeared into thin air. I can't believe it. Has to be holed up around here still. I went up and down the houses several times. I think he may have gone into one of the garages there. I must have stared into the faces of everybody who came out on their way to work, trying to sense any telltale their actions could tell me. Besides the milkman, almost all of them were women strolling to the bus stop. Fuck, what the hell is going on Nick? Any luck finding them either?" 8:20 AM.

"They are over there, about 300 yards away, the other side of that clump of trees." I pointed to the area. "They're using plenty of French and English words between them, and I think perhaps an Arabic language, which I can't place. Certainly not Middle East lingo. I'd recognise that easily enough. Did you call anybody while you were at it?" 8:21 AM.

"Aye, of course I did. I could only think of the police. The lass' voice said, 'well, there's a patrol there in the area already.' But she wanted to know my name, and then I hung up. I thought to myself, I don't know what's going on, but I'm not incriminating myself by leaving my name on a recording tape. No sir. An insignificant sunlight starved youth as I am, who wants to be invisible in this instance." 8:22 AM.

We both simultaneously looked at our watches. Two dumbstruck young Britons stuck in the Irish Republic with one pistol between us at 8:23 AM.

I made the decision and he went along with it. I was to remain and make my way back to the vicinity of the three suspects. He was to go in the car and alert those two cop cars the police dispatcher said were in the area and have them look at the... We both instinctively looked skywards as we thought we heard the sound of a helicopter. 8:30 AM.

On the ground only when a heli is headed in your direction can you hear it coming, not when it's going away. We spent a couple of silent minutes still gazing up at the murky blue but we never saw it. "Hey, maybe it was a police chopper sent over after my phone call," Dave surmised confidently as he gunned the car again. I smiled. I hoped it was because I felt we were sitting ducks at an amusement arcade if it wasn't. 8:32 AM.

As he took off I cursed as I never finished telling him about having the cops look in that ditch the four foreigners spent time at… Shit! I re-traced my steps arduously, moving much slower this second time, and was in due time back in almost the same position near their hideout. They were chatting less frequently. That helicopter was up there again too, you could definitely hear it scouring the heavens. 8:55 AM.

Then the clattering hum subsided as it faded away. Time stood still and hushed. No more words emitted from these men anymore. I too became frozen. I kept hoping the Irish police or army would finally show up. If that 'copter came over us I kept picturing what I looked like standing motionless in a clearing in the middle of a woodland, gun cocked in my hand pointing at nothing discernible to onlookers. I must look like a sitting Chinese Peking duck. I looked at my watch again. It had been 33 minutes of zilch. 9:28 AM.

9:30 AM. Suddenly there was a loud sharp click. I looked down immediately at my feet to see what I'd inadvertently stood on, as both my hands remained gripped around the PPK. One of the men hidden in front of me was heard to say sarcastically and quite loudly in French, *"Fais-moi l'amour, branleur!"* ("Make love to me, wanker!") Then a tremendous roar rocked the airwaves as I fell instinctively to the ground. As I hit the dirt, half a mile away over the field, a black object could be seen falling from the air.

That car had been blown up! Fucking hell! I had no time to think about that because three armed men some 20 yards to my left were already sprinting towards the lay-by. I don't know what really happened next but I started scrambling to my feet, screaming in rage at them and firing at their mobile figures. I was running flat out towards them and shooting wildly. I just didn't care at the time—I was so mad! One even had hanging wires and whatnot sensor activation devices still in his hands, which made it difficult for him to run. The other two started to drop on their knees to fire back at me.

The deafening din of a military helicopter that lacked any national insignia and was unpainted—a typical NATO stratagem—whined over and started firing at *all* of us, and I took cover in the bush. Thuds and whizzes were heard all around me. To expunge anger, I started crazily puncturing the air back at the whirly-bird knowing I couldn't hit it. I was yelling at them, "I'm on your side!" A waste of hot air and metal.

Those men were still running away, escaping. The air relaxed for seconds as the chopper encircled again. I got up and started my wild spree again. I was sure I hit the nearest gunman in the leg because he staggered at one stage. His accomplice came back to help him. Then the bullets ran out. It was just empty clicking and a barrage of swear words as I could see them galloping along the road now...

In the corridor of life there are many unlocked doors which sometimes have to be opened... I was standing back at the present day in 1993 at an entrance to a tent in Africa. McIntyre was saying, "We'd been called in from Quebec barracks in Osnabruck, Germany, the day before, and spent the night at South Armagh's Bessbrook camp. During the next morning's brief we were told they'd been a tip off that a man with a gun would appear in the vicinity immediately following the possible detonation of an IRA incendiary device. We were also informed that a three-man team of ours were already on the ground trying to locate and prevent the discharge of said contraption. My platoon's snipers and I were in this unmarked chopper and our specific orders were to shoot the lone assassin upon sight. The resulting explosion blew the Jaguar 30-feet up in the air and left a 10-foot crater on this thin remote Irish country lane, just 150 yards from the ambassador's residence. Two escorting police cars were right behind it. When I looked down through the binoculars, who was standing not far from the scene— Brennan! I'd first met him at an indoctrination course only the year before. But he was one of us! I immediately called control and iterated that I knew the man in the sights and were they sure? He was just standing there holding his head, leaning on a car, while all this pandemonium was going on. It didn't look right at all. But the bastard did nothing he was supposed to be doing. Meanwhile a fucking huge 200-pound landmine had just blown a carload of people to smithereens within 100 yards of him on the other side of the trees!

"Then suddenly the answer came back over the tannoy, 'He's working with the IRA bombers. Kill him.' It confused me. But by that time the three blokes we were supposed to be protecting were being shot at by some player (terrorist) down there. They were radioing us frantically to come and help them. The bird's pilot was already heading over to the shooting scene, seconds away. We fired warning shots at all of them to begin with, then I made the decision to stop. I mean, we didn't know who was who and they were all running and firing at each other. They all had black hair and they all looked the same to us from up there. They were all within the same rough circle. Whoever that odd man out was fucked it all up for us. We were instructed to get out by then anyway. Get the hell out of the place before others came. It was a top secret job, we had no choice."

I was thinking then about what Dave had once mentioned about Mac, something about his instincts never being democratic to begin with. "You have to understand he is unstable. It's all window dressing and it's not going to change what's in his head," he'd said in his brogue. Then he'd added later that McIntyre also had triskaidekaphobia, fear of the number 13, and would even refuse jobs that fell on dates starting on those days.

Mac went on, "Brennan and I later faced separate internal inquests as to what happened. He vehemently denied all knowledge to SIB of any other person being near there with him. As you know, Special Investigations Branch is the British armed forces internal investigation service. There was supposed to be a weapon for his use in the car he had collected but he said he never saw it, nor did they find one. Unbelievably he stuck to the fact that the blast that destroyed the ambassador's car rendered him incapacitated and unable to respond but he was apparently OK again when the medics tested him. I was there looking across at him at the tribunal and I never believed a word of it. He fucking chickened-out, that's what happened. Then off-the-record it was reiterated to me privately that he was suspected of having connections to the IRA and I always watched him like a hawk after that. *He was Irish after all.* Then you and I and him got that defection job in Poland that came up—remember?—I never turned my back on him once, not once. I always took the rear position throughout. Though he was a pal of yours, I'll admit to you, I never could trust him after that. Even the ERU–the Irish police, the Garda's, own élite Emergency Response Unit— could find nothing, which also turned out to be the biggest manhunt in Irish history. That fucking killer got clean away, amazingly. Soon after the investigating committee ruled the whole case closed."

I noted McIntyre never expressed remorse for the ambassador and his secretary who were blown to bits, and he took the lies for granted about his Irish team-mate. "But you were primed to kill Brennan as the so-called hit man anyway?" I said.

"Well, yeah, *if* he was holding a gun and active at the designated setting, not standing there doing nowt sweet fuck all as it was. The game plan was to catch the attacker in action at the scene of the crime. When Brennan stayed motionless, just sucking wind, it confused everybody involved. As it turned out anyway we were misinformed, it wasn't him who was the killer, it was the dark-haired man who was in a gunfight with the three in our team down there. The one that got away. Fuck."

It was all so pathetic and I found myself with tears welling in my eyes, as I looked at Mac and said quietly, "I know who that odd-man out was who was doing the shooting. The one that got away as you say. The so-called assassin."

"Oh yeah, you do? Who?" He seemed genuinely taken aback by my statement.

I waited a fraction, then sighed, "It was me. I was your villain."

He stared aghast at me. His mouth had dropped open, eyes blinking. He plonked down on his bunk shaking his head. "Why where you there, for God's sake? Are you telling me you were 'in the frame' (associated with a suspect), betrayed our country too?"

"No," I replied, "on the contrary Dave Brennan and I loved our country so much that we were probably too nationalistic in our beliefs. It never occurred to us until that time that these things could go on. Being set up. Ambassador Christopher Ewart-Biggs and the unfortunate woman who was murdered with him on 21 July 1976 were nothing but extras on a big stage, like Dave was supposed to be. Victims of some hierarchy intent on stopping a diplomat who most likely would have solved the Irish conflict single-handedly had he lived. Of that I am convinced. They just didn't want the problem solved. Whoever *they* were. Meanwhile they left it to miserable psychotic bastards like you to carry out the orders, who wouldn't question their motives and be prepared to shoot dead a face you actually knew. Asking ourselves, 'what have we been told to do here?' was something David Brennan did all his life and I have continued to do. What happened to us in Ireland that day became the wind which fanned our flames. It was all wrong Mac, so *very* wrong."

I didn't tell him that I knew it wasn't the IRA all along because since 1971-72 their strategy had always been to warn the police that their bombs were about to blow. Why they didn't do it on this one particular instance...if that wasn't a bloody clue I don't know what was. Nor did I mention that in the confines of my Dublin bed and breakfast lodge, when I had returned to pick up my overnight bag I had checked the aim gauge on the Walther PPK because as a qualified marksman I'd wondered why I could only hit my targets in the knee from 25 yards. It was clearly tampered with and had undergone subtle changes in the trigger and the gun-sight, enough to effect missing its intended target.

A future landslide of reasons hide in the dormant mind awaiting the ticking alarm clock to ring true, to re-experience the exile today.

I was frothing inside. Then I added, angrily, "You are now a tyrant of absolutes. What happened to you, Mac? You have built a nonsensical case on emotional bedrock. I'd go so far as to say you are quite mad. You've even surrounded yourself here with some of the same.

"Davy Brennan, admittedly, was a man who sought the exhilaration of toying with adventure, who would dive off a cliff down into the dark waters below just to feel what it was like to be a bird for a few seconds. *You* may think he was slightly retarded for doing so but he wasn't hurting anybody. He was also an academically brilliant soul who dared anybody to match his experiences, but few accepted. I loved the guy for that. We need more like him. Yet this kind of experience just grounded him. It deflated him that his countrymen would participate in assassination of their own and set him up to take the fall. I knew he was still mentally down when we were in Poland

and he had expressed that he had a desire to push you down a mountain peak but he never wanted to tell me why you of all people and, besides, I dissuaded him from doing so. But I never thought he meant you *per se*. I thought it was the idea of you at the time as you were supposed to be our CO. All he had said was, 'If you go down the tube we all get to move up the pecking order a bit!'. And all I had thought at the time was, 'As always he was beyond the intellectual vision of most of us mere mortals!' Both puns. I guess in his way he was protecting me in the end, but I never actually knew it was you in that helicopter until just now. Just that you also know how noble and honouring of the Official Secrets Act he was, all he ever told me following that tribunal was (quote): 'NATO is able to restrict SIS on information used at inquiries and in British court as well as conduct hearings behind closed doors. It's a big conspiracy of silence, Nick.' That was it. Full stop." I could not think of anything more to say...

Then under my breath added, "...so it was an inside job after all and you were part of the system I've slowly come to hate, you fucking hypocritical piece of shit..."

I couldn't speak anymore with anger and I could feel my bile rising. I didn't want to hear his answer after that, whatever it was. I turned and stormed out in disgust, leaving the former British Army's Captain Ian McIntyre beginning to weep as he clasped his head, rocking on the side of his violently quivering bunk. I never saw him again, nor had any desire to.

Chapter Eighteen

When was the last time you did something for the first time?

As luck, unfortunately for some, would have it, 12 men including the two flight crew, the six white mercenaries—with the thankful exception of McIntyre—Molody and I plus our two African assistants, were to travel to Cabinda, Angola, together. We shared a 2,000-mile ride south in two helicopters, stopping to refuel several times. They flew at ground level the whole way—not that I thought there was radar in existence in this part of the world—and it took all day. At least I had a seat facing forward; I disliked going backwards.

I thought that the reason Mac did not embark was because he was avoiding me. It wasn't until we made our first stop and re-boarding that I realised we counted as a dozen travellers, and then it dawned on me that he would have made it 13, the number Brennan said he was afraid of. I shook my head, no wonder he cried off feeling sick.

Molody and van der Boer were inseparable. I had to smile to myself when Eddie was heard to exclaim once above the noise of the whirlybird, "So this is a kind of medical 'dada' then?" I learned something about the South African from that off-hand remark because *dada* was a movement in art and literature based on deliberate irrationality and negation of traditional artistic values. He must have been a man knowledgeable in that to use the word in his vocabulary. I liked him despite his eccentricity. In a way, we were the same modern-day product of the British colonial system.

There was a lot of money behind this operation. The Russian-made Mi-24 helicopter-gunship I was in smelled fairly new, all equipment was up-to-date, and more interestingly, no soldiers had complained about the pay so far—normally a traditional pastime among those on the front row of death.

Suddenly, to my right, I thought I glimpsed a US$40 million British-made Harrier jet flit above us at three o'clock high on the horizon. I was scanning the sky silently trying to pick it up again. When I finally turned my head to look at the others in the loud cabin they were all staring to port pointing at a single toy-like Sukhoi SU-17 (NATO dubbed it Fitter, the best all-purpose fighter plane the Russians had made) that was gliding down along side us. It bore the red and black marks of the Angolan Air Force, with a look-a-like gold hammer and sickle smack in the middle of the insignia. I could see the red helmeted black pilot through the clamshell canopy wave greetings as he whiligigged past, as our chopper rocked in the jet's wind tunnel momentarily. We had been cleared to enter air space over Angola.

Quebecois and Wines were sitting together directly across from me. Judging from my lip reading, they were chatting low-key in French. It was too thunderous in the cabin to hear much of anything they were saying and I was just looking at them out of boredom if anything, and what else they were pointing at below.

Wines kept rubbing his knee at regular intervals, like some guys scratch their irritating crotches frequently. From what I could gather they were talking about Morocco and how they were in some fight for control of the Western Sahara years ago. The ground below us in Angola reminded them of the same place apparently, as they kept making some geographical reference to it. In their conversation they both brought up somebody called Mohammed Abdel-Aziz. They had repeated it quite a few times so I could get the name right. It seemed the man was President of something or other.

Then Quebecois said "Polasario Front" and repeated "Polasario" again in another statement. They stopped talking as van der Boer was giving them directives. We were coming down to land.

The back of my hair was standing on end. Polasario? Before that car bomb exploded in the Irish Republic, that same voice had uttered that 17 years ago. I was sure of it.

We were starting to stand up in the cabin to stretch our legs before disembarking. The engine was switched off and the blades were whining to a stop. I was going to be the last to file off as the far side door swung open. I flippantly said to Quebecois, whose back was right in front of me, "Hey, you two lads ever been to the Emerald Isle at any time?"

"Ireland? *Mais oui, baise-moi*—but yes, fuck me," he said, "That was where I saved Wines' buttock when he was shot by some *branleur*, a wanker, in the knee cap, it's why he limps now if you noticed."

He clambered down and I was standing there by myself in the open doorway as everybody was walking away in a group from the silent helicopter, joined by the squad from the other bird. My head was spinning and I couldn't hear anything but thunder in my ears. *That swear word confirmed it, I'd heard that exact same pronunciation before!* They both had dark hair still under the greying. Younger versions of their aged faces flashed through my mind. My own legs had turned to jelly as I supported myself by holding the sides of the hatch.

Mike Molody was suddenly standing there looking up at me. He was mouthing, "I said are you OK, Nicholas?" He sounded as if he was at the far end of a tunnel.

"Yes, yes," I responded, "just a bit of cramp." Everything was echoing.

He shrugged, "You looked like you just saw a ghost."

The vertigo ended abruptly. As I jumped to the floor next to him, I said, "You know, I keep meaning to ask you, what did you do with the serums you were collecting before we met this lot?"

As we were walking towards the distant hangar, he pulled a handful of small bottles and plastic zip bags out his large carry-on bag, waving them as he peered into the contents against the sunlight. "The bottles contain zootoxins. Pure venomous poison extracted from spines, stingers and fangs, not from just the usual group of animals but plants as well as marine vertebrae. No two the same either, except I've doubled up on some by oversight. Each is a unique brew of chemical constituents but all lead to circulatory collapse. Nice little time bomb of a magic box I have here." The look on his face told me he was proud of all his hard work thus far.

Trying not to sound too enthusiastic to hear that, I asked, "What happens if you are the accidental recipient of some of that stuff, delivered free by its original owner, Mike?"

Dr Molody didn't miss a beat in responding, "Oh, neurotoxic components cause nervous excitation, leading to muscle cramps, vomiting and convulsions, or nervous depression, producing symptoms ranging from local numbness to systematic paralysis, respiratory failure, cardiac arrest, and—in some instances—a painfully slow death."

"But what are you going to do with it?" I mumbled as I stared at Quebecois and Wines' cocksure swagger from behind.

"Nicholas, nature holds so many treasures waiting to be put to beneficial use. I already know the green-capped liquid serums are good for research, and the red are lethal, while I'm unsure about the blue. All other non-liquid samples are inside the bags."

He was placing them back carefully in his pouch and talking to himself, muttering exactly what I wanted to hear, "I've got too many of the same, I think I'll discard the 'two-sies' while were here. I know I'm going to collect more, so I may as well make space for them."

I could barely contain my thoughts and tried not to look at anybody in the eye while we cleared the Angolan military's customs entry procedures. We were only going to be here two nights before Mike and I were moving on. I didn't know when the others were going their separate ways.

I knew the doc well enough by now. When he said he was going to do something, he usually did it within a few hours of saying so. So I paid close attention to his whereabouts, making sure I was stationed in the room next to his.

Lo and behold, he did the sorting through his precious cargo within the hour. Thirteen bottles and bags were ejected altogether: two had red caps. When I came into his quarters, he was instructing a medic in Russian on the phone to come and dispose of them, telling him they could all be found on the dresser table, without mentioning exactly how many.

Then he grabbed his towel and a toiletry case, and set off in search of the shower rooms. Seconds later both the red bottles were in my pocket.

In the corridor an Angolan army orderly with a medical badge passed me and entered Mike's room to take the remaining bottles for discarding.

I had to check one more thing with my two ex-Legionnaires. I saw them in the far corner when I entered the huge hangar-like canteen for dinner. They were actually beckoning, so I waved that I would join them at their table, as I went and got myself a can of fruit juice from the counter. I was trying hard not to smirk too much. I was so excited to get this opportunity.

They were still eating. After we did our gang-style fist greetings and I had sat down across from them, fortunately, Wines opened the dialogue just the way I wanted. "Ever been to *Al-Jumhuriyah al-Jaziriyah ad Dimuqratiyah wa ash-shabiyah?*"

"No, where's that, sounds Arabic?" I played dumb.

"It's Algeria, Democratic and Popular Republic of," Wines said with his mouth stuffed.

I kept shaking my head in denial. I'd never been there. "Why, do you ask?" I asked.

Quebecois spoke, "He thought you'd been there at some point, you look familiar to him."

"No, I must look like a Frenchman you knew in the FFL," I replied, trying not to be too conceited.

Wines who had swallowed his food, mouthed, "Frenchmen are forbidden in the French Foreign Legion. You didn't know that?"

I didn't for real. So I chuckled, "Then I must look like an Algerian you knew."

They didn't laugh. I was beginning to think they knew something I didn't. I tried not to appear nervous about it as I clenched my fists under the table. "We were only in Algeria for our first year, then in 1962 they declared independence and they moved the headquarters from near Algiers to Aubagne, outside Marseille. We completed our training course in Castelnaudary," Quebecois responded.

"Where's that, in France too?" I said. They both looked up from their food at me as I was a stupid imbecile and I must have looked suitably idiotic, so Wines just nodded affirmation and shrugged. Quebecois put down his knife and fork, meal completed, and was wiping his mouth leaning back. I was damning myself. I was not getting my third chance as I'd hoped for. Everything was on hold. I was cursing internally.

He said, "So why are you so interested if we've been to Ireland? Why did you ask us about there, of all places?"

My mind was racing. I needed time to think, so I stood up and said, "Look, I'll be glad to answer that. It's a really interesting project I'm involved in. They are looking for a few guys to do a job there with good pay. Stay here, while I go and get my food before they close up, OK? I'll be back in a minute. Anybody want some more to drink? Beer, Coke, Pepsi, fruit juice?"

They both wanted another beer each. I got my tray laden with food fairly fast and put it on the table in front of them. As I was turning to go back to get the drinks, which were from another area in the Angolan army canteen, where cash was accepted, I quickly injected, "By the way, what does 'Kassaman' mean? I heard it once."

"'We pledge,'" they both said, almost in unison.

Quebecois continued, "It's the Algerian national anthem. It's also a sort of macho cry before battle."

I must have looked studious, "And what's the Polasario Front? I thought I heard you talking about that on the bird over."

Wines looked bored, "Yeah, we were talking about that a while ago. It's a small war between Algeria and Morocco where the borders with the country of Western Sahara meet. Nothing important, except we were there once."

Oh, righto," I bowed, as I left to get the drinks. Even though the troops were beginning to empty from the large room, the two mercenaries were watching me wherever I went; curious object I was to them. I couldn't do what I really wanted to do. They were clearly suspicious, but I was upbeat about this exercise I was conducting.

I got back to the table and was standing directly in front of them holding the top of a plastic cup of beer each in either hand, as I held my arms straight down beside me. I tried to act as if I was suddenly thinking about something I'd forgotten to ask. I said, "I thought today was the last day of shame...in Ireland?" It's the 12th of September today, isn't it?" They both looked down at their watches for the date and indicated yes.

As they did so, by manipulating my thumbs against my thighs, I discreetly dropped the serum from each tiny bottle into both the beers. "Of course it is the 12th," intoned Wines, starting to get annoyed with my dumb questions, as I tried to soundlessly drop the plastic containers on the floor via my boots' uppers. Thank goodness for the echoing going on in this unused aircraft hangar I thought.

I gave them their drinks and picked up my unopened can of fruit juice. I raised it to wish them "bottoms up." While I was popping the tab, they gulped down half their drinks straight away. Both emitted slight burps. Quebecois even mentioned the Portuguese beer tasted good and I smiled cheerfully at that. They looked quizzical at me and drank some more. They must have thought I was unusually buoyant. I was.

"So tell us what you were going to say about the job in Ireland?" croaked Wines, rubbing the middle of his chest as if he had indigestion.

"Ah, yes," I said, appearing forgetful. "Are you both familiar with the British Ambassador to Eire, his name was Christopher Ewart-Biggs?" I was surprised that got no reaction from them. Maybe their minds were elsewhere. I added, "A car bomb killed him in a small village near Dublin, in a place called Sandyford."

Quebecois gave a start and was quivering slightly, sluggishly distracted looking down at and flexing his stiffening fingers. But his eyes showed wary recognition as to what I was talking about, "Yeah, I was there." I think Wines was already dead. He sat there with a stony look on his face, not moving like a frozen statue. His head had lurched slowly to the side, his tongue slightly visible with a watery sludge oozing down the side of his open mouth.

Quebecois clearly understood what was happening and he looked over at his colleague almost as if he was bored with the proceedings, dully felt the side of his pal's neck, and then turned slowly back to me, with that voice I had hated for almost two decades. "You poisoned us why?" He was gasping for air, like a fish out of water does, while gripping the table tightly in front of him with both hands steadying himself. He was dying and he knew it with each passing second.

"Well," I said calmly, holding his hardening gaze, "you two and a third ruined my life and that of my best friend, not to mention the anguish you put so many others through, arsehole. Who paid you to do it?"

"No...nobody that I knew," he replied at once, "we were following orders." I believed him. They say dying men don't lie.

"Where can the third and fourth men you assisted be found?"

He was shaking his head, convoluting in slow motion, "I don't know. One man was Algerian, he was the bomb expert. Wines was only the button pusher. The other one, the driver, I can't even picture his face anymore. I don't know his name now. All of us were from the French Foreign Legion."

As he said his last three words, he puffed his chest in pride and died, coming to a shuddering end at the full stop with his pupils wide. I swore under my breath that life hadn't given him a few more minutes.

I too never had time to ask him about McIntyre's involvement with them. Oh well. Damn.

I was strangely very relaxed after exacting revenge on the two men sitting like dead frogs in front of me, legs slightly astray at odd angles.

As the last group of Angolan government soldiers were exiting the massive room, going back to their war with the UNITA rebels, I sat there and started to eat my food, pretending I was still in quiet conversation with my relaxed colleagues. The troops could say they watched three white men deep in conversation at the opposite end—some 25 yards away in a noisy converted hangar—two with their backs to them and the one facing more animated than the others.

So comfortable, in fact, was I that I sat peacefully for a full five minutes with them. I really didn't care if I was found out. Actually I was really re-enacting Dave Brennan's funeral in my mind. I will admit to joy and sadness as I sat there with tears in my eyes, grinning somewhat insanely. *Everybody is entitled to a moment of madness and this was mine—a madrigal to call my own.*

Fait accompli, finally I stood up in the faint darkness, as dusk was settling. As I checked their pulses, I couldn't find any remorse in my heart at all, just none. All I could think of to say coldly to these two, as I saluted them slowly was, "Pain is weakness leaving the body, men."

Then I walked to the door and turned the lights *on* so they could be found. Such was my controlled merriment. I even called back to the deceased loud enough, "What goes around, comes around, I'm sorry to say gentlemen."

I wasn't proud of myself but I wasn't feeling guilty either. No complicated psychology was attached to my deed. Now I am a killer of killers…in the name of what…no question mark.

The next morning, Eddie van der Boer matter-of-factly declared to his troops that the foreigners Wines and Quebecois had left the company suddenly and were on their way to Kinshasa's Mama Yemo Hospital with an unidentifiable food poisoning. Nobody seemed surprised, least of all Dr Molody.

I could understand de Boer's tact as he didn't want to demoralise his South African and Angolan teams with such frivolities as death. They probably truly were going to that hospital too...but in body bags. According to Mike, it was a unique hospital as it had the city's only morgue and that they understood French very well in Zaire as opposed to Angola's Portuguese.

Then Eddie indicated me to follow him outside, while everybody ate breakfast inside at the same canteen. I was sure he was going to bring up that I had been seen last with them, so in my nervousness I jokingly dropped in, "Are you sure they didn't get Legionnaire's disease?"

He seemed slightly perplexed and didn't bite at that at all as he handed me a slip of paper, "Sorry, there's a lot going on today. I got this telegram a few minutes ago. Apparently my men up there say your old mate Mac wanted you to be proud of his actions, then he did this. It doesn't make sense." It was my turn to be a bit bewildered as I glanced down to read the note in my palm. It read:

"Kisangani, Zaire. It is with great regret this day, Monday, 13 September 1993, that we announce that Captain Ian McIntyre (retired), died at 0:13 AM when he walked off a cliff to his death. His last words were to tell Mr Anderson that he was going outside to hug a Mr Big's (spelling?) but several eye witnesses said it looked like an attempt to hug the full moon just before he went over the top. We are still trying to retrieve his body."

I looked at the man's concerned face in front of me and said to nobody in particular, "I guess his bi-polar depression got the better of him finally."

"That's 13 men I've lost since this fucking mission started," replied the South African absent-mindedly. "There must be hex on us."

* * * * * * * * * *

En route from Angola's capital Luanda to Havana, the CUBANA Aviaciòn jet made a scheduled smooth landing at the barren Cape Verde Islands, a former Portuguese colony off Senegal. We taxied to a halt for a refuelling stop in the middle of the Atlantic Ocean on the only rock between West Africa and South America.

No passengers were allowed to disembark but after five minutes the pilot had asked, "if there was a doctor on board" and Mike Molody had dutifully responded. I was permitted to go with him, when he said, I was his assistant. I guess there was some truth to that. In fact the sick man on the ground happened to be the only medical physician at this remote airport site and a snake had bitten him.

We were in and out of that sprinkling crumbs of a country—as the volcanic nation appeared from the air—inside the hour, back on the blue, red and white Russian-made aircraft shooting up to the sunset drama of the sky.

"He didn't have a zapper handy nor an anti-venom in stock," summarised my intrepid travelling companion placed next to me. I looked at him for further explanation, "Zapper?"

He nodded. "Yes, it's a stun-gun. Not scientifically proven to work. When a viper bites you lethally, normally you have six hours to get help. Had he been bitten in the vein, I would have given him ten minutes. His heart was superexcited nevertheless. He was lucky I fell out of the heavens. You have to understand four out of five snakebites are not lethal though. Still his training helped treat the poisonous area properly until help dropped by."

"Yes, but what exactly does a zapper do, Mike?" I asked.

He sounded bored when he said it, as if he was reciting a passage from a volume. "A high-voltage electroshock treatment of poisoning by vipera. It seals the area around the fang marks and relieves pain as its shuts down the vessels by electrospasm. It confines the venom locally long enough for it to become inactive. You see, snake venoms contain enzymes that cause extensive tissue damage, almost looks like being badly burnt on the skin."

He mused a bit and got out his pen to write a note. "Even though I doubt it will ever be integrated into western medicine, I will try and get Dr Viser focused on this area for treatment by electromagnetic efficacies. It's worth scientific investigation. Mind you, no zapper would have saved that mule you were astride in Zaire under any circumstances, or you for that matter."

I was still intrigued. "So what did you do for him in the absence of anti-venom?"

Mike was smiling to himself and turned to face me. "Well, that's why he was so fortunate, because I happened to inject an anti-venom agent into his muscle from a plant we collected in Africa. It's called *Peschiera fuchsiaefolia*—I'd filed it among my green category bags—and it worked just fine."

I never volunteered to him how well his red version worked nor ask how would he deal with it if it was consumed. I already knew the answer to the last.

Based on the minute incident on that speck of an island, the pilots had invited us to join them up front. Dr Molody declined this request in polite halting Spanish, saying to me mockingly in English, "They might want me to land the plane next." He stuck to his notepad deep in thought.

I'd gone alone to the cockpit. I hadn't sat at the helm for nearly two decades. It was exciting and I was still feeling remarkably exuberant from events in Cabinda. Approaching Cuba we had flown down the furthermost western air traffic corridor south to north. The engineer told me it was called Giròn and it was eighty-nine nautical miles long. The port of Cuidad de La Havana, once the sexiest city in the world, was at the end of it.

In October 1492, Christopher Columbus had described it as the "most beautiful land human eyes have seen." In October 1993, Nicholas Anderson agreed with him.

Once back on the floor at José Marti Airport, I was inclined to add that the island's women were incredibly sexy and beautiful too.

Ernesto "Ché" Guevara de la Serna's likeness was one of two that dominated everywhere. An outsize portrait of the fallen guerrilla warrior loomed large over the Plaza de la Revoluciòn, the main square in Havana. His allure stemmed from the nostalgic longing for the pure, uncompromising ideals of the past. In this age of ferocious competition and bland consumerism, humanity will always seek a hero with values. In the Argentine rebel of yesteryear, the people had a paradigm. The image the Cubans had of him was of a stand-up guy who was honest, completely selfless and who was constantly perfecting his personality. An intellectual rebel who came to realise that much of the world hated such frowned upon conduct, and paid the price for it. But the man was no angel either.

The other frequent image on display was of the country's Maximum Leader or Commander-in-Chief of the Revolutionary Armed Forces, naturally. Again, the western media painted Dr. Fidel Castro Ruz as a baddie. Little attention is given to the fact that its previous despot, General Fulgencio Batista, was a hell of a lot worse. Under Batista's Cuba it was one of the most repressive dictatorships in the world for nearly seven long years in the 1950's, until Castro came along with his lovely brother.

We didn't waste much time in the city and headed out east into Provincia Havana. Before long Mike and I were at Sanatorio Santiago de Las Vegas. Despite the allusion to casinos, it was a gated scheme of a different kind. This was one of two official government-operated HIV-AIDS camps in Cuba. They called the disease SIDA here, for its Spanish call letters. We stayed the few nights in comfortable quarters for guests.

Despite another misnomer by the western press, the inmates were committed there for having the disease…but weren't stopped from leaving when they wished to. But by remaining inside, the patients had food and lodging on the house. Not bad for a country where the average monthly salary was around US$10. What could you buy with that?

All health and education was paid for in this socialist system. The best available in the world, according to Molody. The downside was everybody was "metalised", the local slang for having to find money somehow, some-way, for other necessities. So many men and women used their bodies in the *zonas de tolerancias*, the red-light districts. Instead of pushing a hard rock up hills, they spent it on their backs.

One obvious ex-prostitute, who still wore glitter and heavy rouge on her once pretty face, sat down next to me and spoke at length. She was my age but appeared to be in her sixties. She was with her adult son. He remained mute while her English was excellent. "I have finally found that faith does not heal disease. My grown son, who could not accept my impending death, now has AIDS also."

She hunched her shoulders expressively and continued, "I did go to church regularly, but He never listened. I know I wasn't heard because we wouldn't have got this sick from the joys of sex had He existed."

It was a moment pregnant with meaning. As we stood up she leaned on my chest to cry. I could only hug her skinny frame gently in sympathy. As her son was about to lead her away, the little black woman smiled bravely up at me and said, "It's almost unreasonable to be reasonable for I selfishly mourn only myself. Now like my customers; my own grief satisfies myself."

In admiration of her inner strength and way with words, I stood watching in awe as the pair slipped away in their flip-flops down a long dark corridor.

After a few days, we went on to the other SIDA camp in the central province of Villa Clara for a quick inspection. Among others there I met a skeletal young white man, a former homosexual gigolo. He was a bad stutterer and he died of heart failure the next day.

Instead of living in the camp, we were ensconced at a great man-made lake in the mountains called Hanabanilla, south of Santa Clara. It was the abundant fauna there that had attracted Mike Molody for more research. "Wild plants and animals are potential sources of live-saving medicines. They provide genetic diversity that could increase resistance in crops and livestock, because a varied landscape is more stable and better able to recover from fire and flood," he had said. "I don't know if you knew the plant life of the oceans makes up about 85% of all greenery on the planet."

I didn't. But for me it was the best place in the world for freshwater boat fishing as I landed numerous fighting largemouth bass. The best was a 10-pounder.

The following morning Dr Molody formally introduced me to a genial Maximiliano Garcia, a slick Cuban in his late-30s. Purportedly he was a technical advisor for a company called Servimed and he was to show me around the nation's *turismo de salud,* its burgeoning health tourism industry. The idea, said Mike, was that "more countries should adopt to this national programme and the Cubans were only too willing to be consultants."

Unbelievably, before Garcia could say anything, Mike found it necessary to go into a long-ish recital first, like a medical school lecturer. "Following the revolution, more than fifty hospitals were built in remote rural areas, like the one we are in now. The nation also built dental clinics, hygiene and epidemiology laboratories, blood banks and other health facilities in the provincial capitals.

"The medical measures implemented to eradicate or reduce infectious diseases have eliminated polio, malaria, diphtheria, tetanus and tuberculosis. Cuba has one of the lowest infant mortality rates in the world and the one of the longest life expectancies for both sexes.

"The island has achieved significant development in the field of biotechnology, the medical pharmaceutical industry and in the design, development and manufacture of medical equipment. It is one of the very few countries in the world that produces interferon; 'Epidermal Growth Factor'—medication that stimulates normal skin growth which is very effective against all kinds of burns; a vaccine against hepatitis B; an anti-menincogoccal type B vaccine—the only kind in the world; and recombinant streptokinase—a fast-acting drug used in cases of myocardial infarct.

"Both the meningitis vaccine and the streptokinase were developed exclusively here. The Cuban medical industry also produces drugs against thrombo-embolisms, drops in the immune system, high blood pressure, cholesterol and some forms of cancer.

"Cuba is *the* leader in the world of genetic engineering. While the Soviet Union used to subsidise Cuba for US$4 billion a year, what they've done here is a better job of what the Russians themselves were trying to do." Fortunately, at that point somebody interrupted and he headed off abruptly to take a phone call, just like that.

Both we younger men stood there dumbly like obedient pupils when he had completed his speech, saying nothing. Once Molody had got out of earshot, the very first thing Max said was in impeccable English, "Cuba is free of *all* the diseases as listed on the world's official health regulations, as well as others subject to international epidemiological monitoring. The only problem is that it was written in disappearing ink by foreigners."

He peered closely at me to see if I was a person who understood a wisecrack or not. "Was it written legibly?" I asked straight-faced. He started to laugh. We were like pals who sat at the back of the classroom after that. "Likely lads" we'd be described as back in Britain: at each other's throats but still buddies. A Spanish version of an Irishman I once knew. However, my biggest problem with him was that he fumed like a chimney and smelled like an ashtray on fire.

Garcia was not only a great tour guide, he was constantly funny and seriously insightful to boot. I spent five days gunning around the countryside with him in his old, smoke-emitting Lada, another product made to hopefully outlast itself outside Russia. He made me think as well as be on my toes every last second of the day much like David Brennan used to.

Max Garcia was from the very mountainous south or easternmost province, Guantanamo. "Home is where the sun paints the sea in a thousand hues of red and yellow and purple," he announced dramatically one evening when we were down there witnessing it on the beach at Baracoa, his birth place.

"On the other side of the island, at Bahia de Guantanamo is where the American naval base is parked on our precious soil," he sounded somewhat remorseful. "Fourteen thousand landmines and seventeen and a half miles of fencing separate us. In the eyes of the Cuban people and in the words of Henry Kissinger, *that* outpost 'represents America's perpetual antagonism towards Cuba'. But we know what they are up to and won't permit them another inch of our land. We know our country is regarded by the United States government as within its 'sphere of influence' and that is the core of the problem. They need to get real. It only proves today's imperialism *is* a legacy of the US' own czarist statism, which they have the nerve to call it a democracy. That is why Cuba permits American tourists in and doesn't stamp their passports so they don't get in trouble upon return to their own country…plus they will spread the truth among the people when they get home."

Of course Max omitted to say why the United States has an embargo in the first place. In case it's forgotten, it was due to the confiscation of US\$800 million of American property without compensation. A drop in the bucket of water by Yankee standards of living though. (I wondered too about the word's largest eavesdropping station that was based here in Cuba—Russia's 28-square mile site at Lourdes that captured intelligence from the US off the airwaves.)

Added Max wistfully, "Since 1975 we have sent military forces and/or advisors to Angola, Mozambique, South Yemen, Congo, Ghana, Mali, Guinea-Bissau, Grenada and Nicaragua, always freely admitting we charge for our services. The *Yanquis* don't directly charge but also do it for personal gain in a different way. Always after coming to 'help for humanitarian reasons' they then imperialistically manage to 'stay on' in the territories for further exploitation in the name of 'continued support.' Castro didn't allow them to do that here, thank goodness, otherwise by now we would have been another state of the union, or at the very least another Puerto Rico."

It was an effort to preserve the fig leaf of plausible denial and I let it go without responding to his statement. After a while I got the impression Max was trying to maximise my thought processes and that perhaps he was an Agent of Influence from DGI, *Direcciòn General de Inteligencia*, the Cuban secret police. I only thought that because he did so well at what I used to do. But I let that go too. It was like fishing a bit, as I deliberately kept missing the nibbles from the tiddlers while I awaited a wallop.

The jigging of his lines kept coming regularly and I refused to succumb to a bite. Though I took the baited hook once and spat it out almost as soon as I had my mouth around it.

It had happened when Max said in a rare moment of seriousness, "Self-employment helps economic growth but the psychology of private producers leads to individualism, and is not a source of social awareness."

I'd quickly replied, "Castro keeps swimming against the current, refusing to accept that all rivers flow into the ocean of capitalism." Then I'd got off by stating quickly, following with a white lie, "Government by the few for the few has remained a constant elsewhere while here it needs to generate major opportunity for the majority."

It forced a smile of victory of sorts on the face of Maximiliano Garcia. I let him savour that too. It was becoming a game of smarts whenever we talked about weighty subjects.

I had agreed with the "man with great lungs" completely (as Castro was sometimes known by because of his long speeches), when he said "Cuba had the blessing of starting 20 or 30 years late in tourism." I could see it had been preserved from rapid plundering development by its past hardships. It has the opportunity now to learn from the madness of modern indistinguishable others, who have lost the very character that set them apart in the first place. Too many once exotic locales looked the same these days with the expansion of McDonalds, Burger Kings and other US fast food operators.

We drove north along the coast the whole way and I found myself spending hours gazing at the television set of the window; in a world of my own. For certain seafood, Cuba was one of the planet's pantries. It's live-for-the-moment attitude reflected in its cuisine. Nature was the uncontested ruler. Here the natural drama unfolded before my eyes. Perhaps making me a bit closer to the person I'd like to become. Obedient to the invisible, internal rhythm of the silent sea—I swam in it daily. I prayed its special quintessence wouldn't die of abrasion by the sudden onslaught of the human race.

Out of the blue Max intoned the feeling by saying, "If we're not careful the country will be doomed to the same fate as the charming vacation hideaway that was ruined once word got out. So we play the subtle game of maintaining a balance; the fine line between feeding our families without gross profits for the few. I for one do not want it oversold by whoremongers."

I must admit that the gap locally had been filled beautifully with sustained growth by building more hospitals and schools, not just more hotels and bars, in the planetary treasure called Cuba. I saw it with my own eyes.

Max eventually surprisingly agreed with me that "paradoxically recent spurt in tourism had helped expose problems in Cuba."

While I thought that last statement was a negative, he thought it was a positive. When he admitted that, I thought I'd won the mind war with him.

We finally arrived back in Havana in the heat of the night. The girls were out in force. I recalled us both staring at one who vividly reminded me of a younger version of the old-looking hooker at the sanatorium I'd met.

The trip around the country had been an eye-opener in more ways than one. Cuba indeed does have the facilities to back up its health tourism modalities and it is equipped to offer fast and efficient tests performed by highly trained medical personnel, using the most modern diagnostic and treatment techniques available. Indeed I wish the rest of the world was the same and would not believe so much medical dogma to the contrary. It is a much more equitable society health-wise than most despite the negative western propaganda.

Castro has clearly created a world that is entirely his own. He shows how our existence in the present is made bearable by memory; either real or imagined. Even if I did have to endure for five days in a row hearing schoolchildren begin their day daily singing, "We Will Be Like Ché."

Despite the one-sided bullshit, dictators can rise to power legally through the electoral process too, after all, Adolf Hitler did.

* * * * * * * * *

Admittance that what exists does not work
is in itself a start of change.

Awaiting the arrival of Michal Molody at the designated place on the night we got back into the capital, Max Garcia and I found ourselves in a smoke-filled bar-café where all the universal clichés were heard. One wag apparently on the next able said, "Addressing atheism's aims in Cuba, the government must not impose the Roman Catholic Church on its citizens and should permit freedom of thinking."

After interpreting some of the overheard junk for me the intellectually advantaged Max finally waved his arms in exasperation and muttered, "Too many complaining for the sake of complaining—a miserable human trait. The Fallopian tubes in their mouths should be locked and the keys thrown into the ashtrays."

As we were laughing and sucking down beer, Mike came in with an older distinguished-looking man dressed in a white suit with a matching white walking stick who looked like he was about to drop dead from old age. We shook hands as he pronounced, "Nicholas, I'm so glad you're finally back in Havana. I trust the tour was most informative." I bent my head.

He seemed overly cautious as he gestured diplomatically to the grey-haired fellow, who had already painfully seated himself across from Maximiliano and I, "This gentleman has been patiently waiting three days for you. Mr Georges Durance, please meet Mr Nicholas Anderson."

Based on my sudden change of face, Mike and Max got the cue to leave us alone, and they did so quickly. Mike simply stated, "If you're looking for me later, you'll find me at Instituto de Medicinatropical Pedro Korea. I'll be with Gustavo Korea, OK?" I shook Max's hand as he departed with Mike with no exchange of words, never to see him again, forgetting to get his number.

For some reason, I don't know why, but I stood myself up then to take the outstretched hand of my lover's husband. I felt like a condemned criminal standing in the dock in front of a stern judge about to be handed a long sentence. Then I sat down for my punishment to be administered.

A long silence passed in the din of the establishment. We were just eyeing at each other; transmitting basic understanding. He was about my Dad's age and could have rocked my crib. Finally I said, somewhat incoherently, "How did you find me?"

I was surprised at the bounce in his voice springing from such a deteriorated body. "Oh, that's not so hard when you have connections, you know that, young man." The "young man" dig hurt and I'm sure I winced visibly. He had a right to wound me back, I reasoned with myself.

"My wife told me where to find you upon her return from Egypt," Durance said. "But I have since discovered we have one other link from the past—not through my wife—but also family-related." The wife and family parts tore into me too. He was doing a good job of smacking me around mentally.

"Your father and I never met, but we communicated with each other by telephone and telex many times. He was the British MI6's Foreign Office liaison with the French government when a Russian defector called Yuri Krotkov first disclosed that the Soviets had managed to pilfer our countries' original joint-blueprint for the supersonic Concorde. As a result, the Russians managed to make their Tupolev-144 Concordski at their plant in Zhukovsky one year ahead of the British Aerospace-Aérospatiale model. It never became public that they did so by blackmailing a married member of the French ambassadorial staff in Moscow with a swallow. You know, a KGB sex slave deliberately introduced to compromise a target. Explicit photos included.

"Fortunately our DGSE *Direction Générale de la Sécurité Extérieure* —the old SDECE, as I was used to calling it—the new name for the French secret service, made certain the Soviets got plenty of free publicity as to the aircraft's airworthiness when they blew it up at an air show at Le Bourget outside Paris in 1973. We were most offended that they would have the balls to premiere it on our soil after stealing it from us. Naturally MI6 leant a hand at making it look like pilot error.

"The incident, however, delayed British Aircraft Corporation's involvement in Europe's new Airbus Industrie consortium until January 1979 as your government naturally questioned our ability to keep secrets. I was at the welcome back party at Toulouse-Blagnac airport, along with the heads from Messerschmitt of Germany and Spain's Construcciones Aeronáuticas."

I cursed internally, wishing Mike Molody had heard all that. He had told me the opposite story about the Concorde when I had debriefed him years and years ago. So many stories conflicted; one didn't know where to start. I was glad I was out of these games of intrigue.

He took a sip uninvited from my second untouched beer bottle, not taking his penetrating eyes off me. "I can see you are what she wished I was now. But I've been a career diplomat in the last half of my life while you've been an active covert operator during the first half of yours. I could never be you."

He was doing a great job of pointing out the age disparity, making me feel guilty for pussyfooting away his younger wife of 23 years difference. I was saying to myself, 'OK, okay, I was to blame and I did commit the misdeed. Hang me now.' I was grateful it was cloudy in there, otherwise he would have seen me blushing.

He pulled a thin file out from inside his jacket and placed it in front of me. "It's not everything but it's something. It contains a single sheet of the pertinent information of your SIS records. Enough to prove your existence. I have, of course, kept a copy for safe keeping. The full details contained inside the file at NATO was impossible to access, even for the eyes of the French government who are supposed to have full ingress to everything but don't.

"I do have to congratulate you on your continued loyalty in the face of such adversity. It's admirable but a classic case of studied gullibility. You didn't realise you were expendable for so long. Your recent activities indicate you probably know at last.

"According to the initial findings from my inside reliable sources, as a result of the sham internal investigation following the Biggs assassination, a Lieutenant-Commander Brennan managed to make a copy of yours and his MI6 files, before they were permanently removed from the in-house SIS records and placed in the 'black room.' It is believed he gave them either to his mother or his wife—I don't know whom—for safekeeping because he didn't know whom else to give it to. While I cannot substantiate it, I also believe his uncle, his name is O'Malley, eventually obtained them and he then handed them over to the IRA, who were officially blamed for the killings in the first place. Precisely where their two copied files of Brennan's and yours are right now is a mystery. Despite the family connection, your Irish Brennan was not an informer and never was, though he was pressured to be at the very end of his life. But he recognised, obviously, that they tried to set him up that day in Dublin when the British ambassador was bumped off. The fact he did nothing when everything else was going crazy around him probably saved his life...which was against the carefully-laid game-plan. I have to assume the other person involved in the affair was you. At the private inquest we conducted of our own, it indicated, at least in theory, you were within geographical range of the activities. Was it you?"

I nodded affirmative, quickly taking the opportunity to ask, "One small question, please, before you continue. Who is 'we'?"

"Very interesting development. 'We', the French government, and I, didn't know for sure until the unfortunate affair came up between my wife and you. Who the other person was shooting at the assassins, was always admittedly, a calculated guess. There are around two-dozen files of British individuals whose names we know of that are in that 'black room' hidden in a vault below a landmark London hotel north of Hyde Park. We only know this because we have, over a decade, asked SIS about these 'notables' only to be officially informed they don't exist. France knows they did exist, so their denial only alerted us to the fact. We simply kept a record of our own over time on the names, but there are probably more hidden under the dirty carpet. But by re-opening some of old files and painstakingly piecing together snippets here and there, coupled by a recent confession by an Algerian terrorist we have in custody, have we only recently been able to understand fully what really transpired on 21 July 1976 in the Irish Republic."

"Well I would appreciate you telling me more please. There has to be a lot more that you haven't told me yet?" I asked politely.

"Yes, of course," Durance proffered. He visibly relaxed and drank some more of my beer directly from the bottle. Seemed his talking now exceeded more than he was used to of late.

"NATO likes to 'fix things' that don't need to be fixed, as you may know... Before I get into that, first, you have to learn something about the slain British ambassador Mr Biggs' background. I knew him quite well from the world war days, when we were young men like you. We were in the same covert Jedburgh group. 'Jedburgh' was the British and US code name for specially trained three-man teams who would work with resistance units behind enemy lines. He was attached to the 'Hubert' team and I was the only Frenchman in Jedburgh team 'Francis.' I had managed to make my way to Britain when France fell to the Nazi's. Durance is not the name I was born with, it means 'imprisonment' in English you know, as I was captured once, and the nickname stuck. My given name is Georges le Zachmeur. 'Hubert' was the code name for members of the *Organisation de l'Armée Secrète*, the OAS—the Secret Army.

"Originally, at the time, the OAS were kind of like the ideological forerunner of the French Foreign Legion. But it evolved into an illegal military body by 1961, adopted by French settlers in Algeria supporting French rule. De Gaulle was in power in France in those days. The OAS collapsed upon the imprisonment of its leader, General Raoul Salan in 1962. It was really a war the French government would prefer to forget from many angles.

"Anyway, back to Biggs. He and I first met at 'ME/65', the cover name for Milton Hall, the Jedburgh training school in Peterborough, England. He was a very brave man, quite content to stare the enemy in the face and slap them if necessary. Unfortunately he lost his right eye in Egypt at *Al Alamayn*, Alamein. There's a huge oil field just south of there now, which was the real reason, at the time, for man's skirmishes over land rights in that region of the world.

"Because of that regrettable incident, coupled with his past work with OAS members, Christopher Ewart-Biggs got the reputation of handling all-things Arabic-related at the British Foreign Office, where he worked after World War II was over. Later, in the early-sixties, he was transferred to Algiers as the British Consul. He was a man with a personal mission.

"The Algerian War, sometimes known as the Battle of Algiers, was in full flow by 1954 and it ended in 1962, on 5 July to be precise—the day of Algeria's independence—a year after Biggs' arrival there. Half a million died as three factions fought amongst each other: the Algerian nationalist population; the French colonial army; and the revised version of the same group I've mentioned, which were known as the OAS.

"Because of his long-term connection to the OAS, he was quickly accepted as being trustworthy. But the new revised OAS was almost fascist in its political beliefs, very right wing. Biggs was by now a committed socialist. Always on the 'side of the people' and, in fact, had become active in the British Labour Party. There was a clear difference in their respective goals. They wanted to colonise and he desired peace.

"Christopher was immediately instrumental in negotiating for the ending of the Algerian War, of which the Algerian nationalists—the people—were declared the winners. Obviously the OAS thought they were sold out by Biggs, and when the jailed Salan got out in 1968 there was a price put on Biggs' head.

"I had met the Englishman again in Algiers, at the Special Operations Centre, around the time of his admirable shuttling between the warring parties. He was obviously the dynamo behind the whole peace process. He achieved a miracle in so short a time span. He was very much in favour of Algeria being independent from France. It was something France also wanted deep down but didn't know how to go about achieving it, nor admit it.

"The British were aware of the death threats to Biggs by former members of the OAS, many of its non-French stalwarts had joined the French Foreign Legion by now. After a few overseas postings and everything had quietened down, the 'Anglos' made a strategic move, transferring their golden boy...to France, where his excellent reputation could be exploited in the best interest of his country. He was made Minister at the British Embassy in Paris in 1971.

"Well, of course, he kicked some bottoms there too. He was an achiever you see, always accomplishing his own benevolent non-violent objectives. Peace in the world was his driving force. In the five years he was in France he managed to piss off, as you English say, the French-born former OAS ultraconservative die-hards time and time again. Many of its leaders, which by this time, had risen in the ranks to the top of the UN and NATO. The latter of which France is only a political member and not a military member.

"So they couldn't and wouldn't do anything against the Briton while he was still operating on their sacred French soil. It would have made France 'look bad' and they couldn't have that, oh no. But when he was promoted as Ambassador to the Irish Republic, it was their opportunity finally for revenge and they did it quickly. The OAS hierarchy hated him with a passion. The rest of it I'm sure you know. I have absolutely no doubt in my mind Christopher Ewart-Biggs would have brought the different Irish parties who were at loggerheads together—in a way everybody would have been happy at the outcome, an acceptable compromise. It was a rare 'something' he had a knack of doing. He'd done it before and he was going to do it again.

"I went to his funeral at Golders Green in northwest London. It was the least I could do to show my respects to this tireless honest man who never sought glory for himself."

I sat there in silence. The pieces fitted the jigsaw. "I have another question for you, if you don't mind," my voice sounded like someone else's. "What was the significance of 21st of July to them?"

Georges Durance looked at me as if I was supposed to know. "On that day in 1954, France surrendered North Vietnam to the communists. It was known as their 'last day of shame.' But it wasn't. Algiers became their 'next day of shame.' The French Foreign Legion were the perceived goats in both sorry affairs. Two shambles within the same decade, *sacre bleu*! A political disaster too! Up to then these men of the illuminati were used to getting their way. The cost of failure became too great since it involved the moral bankruptcy of their power; a beginning of an admittance to weakness in their global structure. The dirty work had to be done to uphold their system. The grey men in suits in the various governments' aristocracy apparatuses make decisions to adverse risk, then the black tricks squads obey them. I should know I've done the dirty work for them myself. So have you. I saw the light eventually but had to keep playing the role. From that moment of truth onwards I have always read the newspapers from both sides of the fence…to know what the enemy were thinking. But I see signs now that you too are starting to 'rumble against the machine.' They also eliminated Brennan I'm sorry to tell you…they have got adept at making such things appear like accidents and/or making others take the blame.

"Nevertheless, I can look back now and regret my part, as I was at one time in charge at the UN for France's interests. Not many of us did consider the option of another way—that's why I admire your resiliency. I hope you succeed.

"As an example of my disgust, the Algerian people *still* are suffering tremendous casualties for the same old reasons. Meanwhile its natural gas and oil flows to the multinational corporations. It only ends when the likes of Biggs and yourself stand up and make a difference, I'm ashamed to admit in my old age."

Durance was deep in thought, then he continued, "If *I* did contribute anything to better this sorry state of world affairs, it was within a year of Christopher Ewart-Biggs' murder. I was at the Diplomatic Conference on the Reaffirmation and Development of International Humanitarian Law Applicable in Armed Conflicts—a long title—and I vehemently fought to add two protocols to the Geneva Convention, the international rule-making device for the laws of war. The first protocol brought irregular forces—meaning terrorist and rebelling factions—within the full scope of the law of armed conflict, thus making them 'legally accountable' in any nation. Protocol II concerned the protection of victims of non-armed conflicts. What this means is: no longer can it be acceptable for the world's governments to arbitrarily try to solve any kind of disagreements they may have on other countries' territories."

"But," I said, "all these rules and regulations are fine and dandy but are still being ignored by the powers-that-be when they feel like it. They change the laws to fit the crime as they go along."

"Not exactly," he said, "this is a button preventing them from getting out of the loop the next time they try to abuse our world's basic human rights. It puts a cog in the wheel and so gives peace a chance to work. Right now organisations like the United Nations and NATO are our only international judges and juries, making decisions on behalf of the people of the world, while ironically still actually fulfilling the functions the illuminati want them to. But I think world opinion is slowly turning against them as a result of exposure to awareness, which surround a handful of events like Biggs' and Brennan's elimination's. People are starting to sit up and notice all the 'worming' that's going on. It's a beginning at least. The Americans and their British representatives in Europe are obviously the worse violators, as you well know. France is not that far behind."

I posed him the questions of, "What next? Where do we go from here?"

"Well, I have delivered you the document you wanted. I've upheld my part of the deal. If there is anything that can be returned as a favour, I'm certain my country will thank you for it. For example, perhaps you can divulge to me, the results of your recent trip to the Sudan...?"

I thought pensively for a while as he sat there quietly in front of me. This was my chance to get back at those I gave my all for. I didn't deserve their betrayal, nor did Davy Brennan and Christopher Ewart-Biggs. It sickened me. "Yes, I can take care of that right now, Mr Durance. You will be happy to learn the *exact* whereabouts of Carlos the Jackal, a man who is wanted in France, and has been tried and found guilty in absentia. He is still there in the Sudan. I can provide you with his precise location."

The first thing he said in response to that stunned me. "Our satellite HELIOS, with its SPOT satellite imagery system, can verify that precise location tomorrow." Of course, I thought, his wife had told me years ago that he was the person in charge of setting up France's spy birds. It was from him that she got into the habit of reading newspapers covering both ends of the political spectrum and talking the same way to mask her real affiliation.

He quickly wrote down all the particulars as I related them to him—I threw in the titbit about Arab militant funds coming via a New York City ice cream shop's bank accounts, perhaps it could be used for politic advantage. I was surprised at his nimbleness of hand for such an aged fellow. When his Mont Blanc fountain pen was capped and back in his pocket, he hesitated, then announced, "I take it also that your fling with my wife is over too..."

I could only agree with him, and sheepishly bowed so as I sat there. *I strongly felt my pretty lady Ursula's palm pressed flat momentarily against my beating core before it pulled away.*

"That reminds me of something else," I said, recovering. "Operation Yellowbird. What do you know about it?"

He smiled broadly for the first time, shaking his head as if it meant a great deal to him. "Ah yes, this is what we teasingly called the Chinese variation of an earthworm. The French government partly-funded the project, working closely with the Hong Kong triad crime syndicates. I'm afraid all I can tell you is that the underground tunnel served both our purposes. They got their Chinese dissidents out; many came to France, in fact, while we got our spies in to China. A nice arrangement indeed, good for their propaganda and great for our...our..."

He stopped and cleared his throat, then added, "To tell you more will be to violate state secrets for which I am under lifetime non-disclosure. I've already told you more than you need to know about other subjects, as it is. Sorry."

"Yes, that's the problem these days, "I said. "I'm so tired of the photo opportunities and noble rhetoric—the so called nationalist agenda."

Tipping the rest of my beer bottle into my mouth, I prepared to leave. As I stood on my feet, we held each other's hands at length, warmly. Durance still sitting was holding my eyes too for long seconds, and then said, "I meant to ask you, Nicholas, what is it that drives you? World peace was Ewart-Biggs' target, what's yours?"

I didn't miss a beat in answering that. It was an easy one. "I was in love with a wonderful Danish woman called Vibeke Brink. We'd been together for eight happy years. She used to travel the world in the course of her job. When the time was right, she was going to be the mother of my children.

"While overseas on a trip, she received an emergency blood transfusion after badly cutting her arm while trying to get the cap off a bottle of a cola drink. The blood was tainted with a disease that her hometown's doctor in Denmark didn't recognise. Her health deteriorated quite quickly and she died one year later. It was twelve months of anguish because I didn't know the answer. Nobody did at the time.

"I still recall, vividly, going for a winter stroll together on the deserted North Sea beach for the last time as I pushed her wheelchair. She died the next day at her parents' farmhouse in my arms. How I cried! We both knew on that last sad walk north of Thisted, that it was the end, but the frustrating part was we didn't know *why*. She went to her grave not knowing. That was what was the hardest part for me being the survivor all those years. It was a living hell.

"Then a year and a half after her death, AIDS was officially diagnosed in Uganda. That was the same country where she cut herself. When I looked into it, I found out it was all a cover-up. I have since found the first HIV-related infection was traced to a man living on Uganda's western border with (then) Belgian Congo, some twenty years previously. For two decades, it was kept from the public. The deeper I delved, the more insanity I kept unearthing. It can't continue in this day and age. It has to change eventually. I'm doing my best to make it happen. It was the main reason why I wanted to go there recently. A catalyst of sorts for me, if you like."

I wiped a tear and paused for breath. I had more to say.

"The bottom-line is this, in chronological order: 1959—Man discovers this unknown viral disease and studies it in labs for five or six years and later tests the effects of the virus on its own unsuspecting people; 1964-65—the same viral research programme was implemented on a wider area in Uganda; 1975—a renown scientist with a conscience informs the world that 'something' is about to occur worldwide from a 'virus that causes cancer'; 1980—my girlfriend received a blood transfusion in Uganda, after accidentally cutting herself; 1981—her doctor says she's dying; 1982—she passed away; 1984—the medical hierarchy announces AIDS has been found...in Uganda of all places. What am I supposed to think? Purely circumstantial? I doubt it. It seems almost too ironic to my liking, and my suspicion remains. On this subject, I have always wanted to disprove my findings, but I have failed. This *is* my compelling conclusion." Durance sat still like a stone.

I paused to reconsider, sighed deeply, then continued, "It is *my* utmost sincere understanding of the truth as I conceive it to be."

I'd had enough of the finagling of the world today. I picked up my one-page file and prepared to leave. As an after thought, I turned and said to the Frenchman, "Thank you for keeping your end of the bargain, by the way."

I waved the folder in acknowledgement, kissing it. "Who knows? I'll probably write a memoir in the form of a novel about it one day. It's easier nowadays for a larger market to understand non-fiction in that mode of presentation."

"In France, we call that *un conte autobiographique*—an autobiographical tale—a narrative which goes 'beyond the thing itself but where everything originally is real,'" proffered Durance. "If you do eventually get around to writing anything about this, please—of course—do not use my real name, Lieutenant Commander."

I could only agree. "Roger that, sir," I confirmed. It was a wishful statement on the spur of the moment. Writing anything down was the furthest thing from my mind. Publishing the real names of people could invite a whole bunch of newer problems but sometimes it was subjective and substantive…so long as I would be accurate to the spirit and the letter of what transpired…

The wise old man had a final statement as I gave him my last farewell. "What's right and what's true are different."

I shook my head again in agreement and turned away for good.

When I walked out into the bustling raw Havana *avenida* where a *mardi gras* of sorts was in progress with the *jineteras* (hookers) dancing *salsa* with tourists, I was in a quandary. Should I go back to Los Angeles, a city of no limits, home of the mouse that whored? Or should I continue my decades old fight for the truth?

I would have to hide to accomplish the latter even if it may not be the politically correct thing to do.

Which way to run?

Writing is a way of explicating ideas, expounding upon experiences. Language is stretched. It is the backbone of society, the armature. It is the record-keeper of the world's adventures.

Accretions

The World—What pisses me off no end is that, sometime between quitting SIS in 1983 and returning to help out in 1992-93, my country had the same opportunity as France to build its own spy satellite version of HELIOS. The project was codenamed ZIRCON. For reasons I'll never know exactly, Britain's government mandarins (another tool of the illuminati, while half of them actually *are* the same entrenched élite I describe, never mind which major political party is elected into power) made a disastrous decision to scrap the idea. Instead they persuaded "Attila the Hen"—a.k.a. Margaret Thatcher (British Prime Minister from 1979 to 1990)—to buy into the US' ECHELON global satellite communications spy cosmos (knowing full well Britain wasn't going to get access to all the information it generated), at the same time, agreeing to allow its main overseas listening post to be installed on the top of the UK's Yorkshire Moors at Menwith Hill. Other participants in this scheme are: Australia, Canada and New Zealand. To this day, along with these three other English-speaking countries, the British government continues to pay good money for the privilege of being abused when the urge takes hold of our American master across the pond. ECHELON and other spy satellites are operated by the US' National Security Agency through its Tordella electro-magnetic supercomputer centre at Fort Meade near Laurel, Maryland, that in turn is supervised by its military managers, the Pentagon's National Reconnaissance Office in Washington, DC. ECHELON and its crypt-analysts can code-break and scan two million electronic communications—e-mails, faxes and phone calls (secure and unsecure, war and commercial industries)—per hour, and of that figure approximately 13,000 are cross-examined further by computer and from the read-outs some 2,000 end up in the hands of human sigint analysts. Originally designed for the Cold War the three departments fighting communism (A5, B6 G4) were consolidated in 1992 under one name: Z Group. Now the decryption methodology is used for catching designated criminals but really useful for unethical political and economic gain. Note: I am pleased to know that the NSA and NRO past successes were based on collecting unlimited data through eavesdropping and imagery satellite communications from low-tech, analogue-based, fixed-position targets but today their nation's capitalist agenda has come back to haunt them. The global mobile tele-communications businesses it largely created and bankrolled have installed the cheaper high-bandwidth fibre-optic cable under-sea and -ground plus digital-ised, which due to the wide routing system of a modern world on the move, severely restricts identification of the location of the source.

The long and short of this historical disaster, nevertheless, is that the United Kingdom has slowly but surely agreed to become another state of the United States—the 51st to be precise. In less than a decade the British Prime Minister has effectively become the Vice President of Europe reporting directly to POTUS (US Secret Service code for President of the United States). Everything I fought for in the Cold War—so-called democracy—went to hell in 1991 shortly after the collapse of the Soviet Union.

France on the other hand is an exception. While she has her own fair share of power-hungry groups, too, she does know they exist—which is more than I say about a lot of countries' people who seem to live in a fog about such matters of dominance. She continues to battle to maintain her own heritage, generate her own exports and generally make her own way without outside influence—even generating her own secret intelligence without depending on others.

While France is not perfect, I greatly admire that determined individuality. It's what I believe I'm all about too. I now live there. By not residing in a crypto-fascist plutocratic country nowadays *I now have the freedom of my life from the outside.* I detest anything totalitarian and refuse to be a computerised statistic. There's nothing creative in this kind of bland enveloping extremity at all.

Internationalisation is great for the people of the world but globalisation is nothing but a US-designed imperialist programme to make themselves richer and everybody else poorer. It's actually a lot worse than communism. Certainly it isn't freedom or at best it's too much freedom.

But put in a simple sentence though: *All Governments Lie.*

* * * * * * * * * *

Dr E. Michal Molody—(I've protected his real identity herein) has guts. He'll come through eventually and hopefully will win a Nobel or a similar recognised award…he has to for all us ordinary people who want a choice when choosing how our sickness and health is to be determined. For BENNY to win would be to stick a rude finger or two up to those that tried to prevent achievement.

Of course, presently, western health organisations (by necessity) have begun the practice of big business, and in order to protect their profits are going to refute my claims and that of the details within. They are going to activate their impressive public relations campaigns. They are going to knock down and claim that no clinical trials were ever conducted; no controlled human studies; no animal safety data is available; efficacy was based on clinical experience; and anecdotal reports of individual cases—*all of which is absolutely true*—and blah-blah-blah…in order to justify their non-action and active resistance

You see, in the West, the system revolves around placebo—with the admirable exception of Germany, Russia and Cuba. In these three countries, placebo-free studies are conducted simultaneously.

Why can't all countries legitimately do *both* placebo and placebo-free studies without sacrificing the legitimacy of our experimental designs? Is it really that hard to do? In the West, pre-determined old policy by the ruling medical Establishment has dictated that it *must* be one way. Large powerful pharmaceutical institutions govern them, and so be it. [Guess who own millions of stock in them too from the first day of trading? Yes, the illuminati (entrenched élite).]

But why can't placebo-free testing be used with patient consent when the patient has limited options? If the patient is educated correctly and is able to make an informed decision, we avoid the ethical question of the morality of withholding treatment. We can always perform mechanistic studies afterwards and thus directly address the science in two smaller tests rather than one big one; in essence preventing being taken directly one-stop to the top floor by stopping on each level on the way to discover what was there. In this manner we preserve the inalienable human right to be completely informed at the ground level. Why should we be told just one option and deliberately be denied the other? There is a moral and philosophical obligation to tell the public both sides of the coin without pre-conceived bias. Open your minds and subsequently that of the public you serve and we can go where we want...unless you don't want us to stray off the course...?

Another aspect which I find almost comical: What is labelled "alternate care" by the West that uses "traditional medical methodologies", is in fact known in the East by the reverse. The cheaper proven practices in the East have been developed over several centuries as compared to the West's couple of hundred years. One regards health as a human right; the other sees it as a right to make money on illness and death

I also find it sick that more than 25% of modern drugs are derived from just one per cent of plants "looked at"...yet there is so much western political opposition to "alternative medicine". Go figure.

* * * * * * * * * *

Dr Leonid Viser—Still in Russia, unfortunately...or fortunately, the authorities changed their minds on processing his application to emigrate but told him they valued him more staying there then allowing him to leave for Israel. But, I understand, at least his standard of living improved dramatically and he got more pay.

* * * * * * * * * *

Colonel Boris Kokorin—I would like to add that I have since found out that this former KGB officer at its old Political Education Department, which at the time was responsible for indoctrination of communist ideology, was a top graduate of Moscow's Marx-Engels Institute (the "school for spies"). Nowadays he is a high-ranking FSB (*Federalnaya Sluzhba Besopasnosti* or Federal Security Service) official and he and I are quite friendly. He even officially loans me a 9-mm Makarov pistol with the comfortable leather holster to fit my back whenever I stay in the wild frontier of modern Moscow but I have never got to use it, thankfully. When I leave I must return the items to him, without fail.

In Moscow whenever Kokorin and I are out and about together, driven by *Mr* Smardz of course, we always dig each other in the ribs when we see the distinct red British or American diplomatic licence plates on cars. They are identified as D-04 and D-01, respectfully, and are almost all Jaguars or Cadillacs too.

When I was last in Moscow we both saw a badly dubbed counterfeit of a James Bond 007 movie at an underground video arcade in the city centre. We did laugh heartily at his antics as it was too far fetched from our own realities and personal experiences.

* * * * * * * * *

Major Irena Puchovskaya—I never did come across her again though, I have to admit, that at one time I would have liked to.

* * * * * * * * *

Ilya Smardz—Smardz is Smardz, same as always.

* * * * * * * * *

Christopher Ewart-Biggs—Old-style diplomats the world over are still clinging to traditions of the last two centuries. They have forgotten that the 20th century was one of the bloodiest ever. They still adhere to this outdated notion of sovereignty that is absolutely obsolete and it guides their thinking.

Thankfully there's always an exception to the rule. The Englishman Christopher Ewart-Biggs, a ranking diplomat, had the rare ability to make certain that enemies stayed in the same room talking to each other…and made them actually listen. It's akin to making the water stay in a bottomless jar. I commend you sir, even in death.

* * * * * * * * *

Paddy O'Neill—(Not his real name) is still running the IRA's Irish ops part-time from the US, though I understand he spends semi-retirement time now in Pittsburgh, Pennsylvania.

* * * * * * * * *

Ilich Ramirez Sánchez a.k.a. Carlos the Jackal—It used to be known as snatches but today it's known as rendition. I can confirm that French commandos abducted the larger than life Venezuelan from the Sudan 10 months after I provided his whereabouts to the government of France and six months after some erstwhile Frenchmen saw him close-up for themselves after inspecting their precision satellite pictures. The US claimed they sent a team of black undercover Americans to check too but if that's true then why didn't they lift him out? After all the French got the idea to do so from the number of times the US government had captured wanted persons from other nations with the same impunity. Ilich Ramirez Sánchez was subsequently found guilty for murdering two French policemen and jailed for life. Carlos the Jackal was really guilty of much more than that as he was responsible for so many deaths all over the world. (I have much more to write about him and will. But guess who was mailed the sole copy of his uncompleted manuscript at a Moscow address and will get around to editing it from the Spanish and publishing it in English eventually. No question mark entered please notice. Many strange things have happened in my life but this is one of the strangest.) Today he is the permanent resident of cell number 258187 in Le Santé prison in Paris.

* * * * * * * * * *

Dr Ralf Marczewski—Frankly, I think the *Bundesnach-richtendienst* (the West German federal intelligence) man takes the cake. It's not his real name, mind you (only because I never knew what it really was to start with). Years after the incident I described in Poland, he organised and smuggle a whole uranium hexaflouride-manufacturing nuclear plant to Pakistan as part of his million-dollar deal. He bought the parts and pieces in several European countries, assembled them in Bavaria on 60 lorries and had them driven to Pakistan in the late-70s. To add insult to injury he had the gall to declare it at all investigating customs stops as "an experimental laboratory". You have to smile at his cheek, really. Today Pakistan is a nuclear power, largely thanks to his contribution.

* * * * * * * * * *

The Author—I was granted a dishonoury in 1983 when SIS knew I was in the frame of mind to quit without notice or deliberately get myself fired (but that's a whole separate story that I'm keen to tell in *NOC Twice*). As well as signing the UK's Official Secrets Act, which I have wilfully broken now, and in return for accepting a public interest immunity certificate*—effectively a gagging order (that was presented to me upon retirement)—I was then given my six-figure gratuity in one payment in cash, this was legally owed to me after 12 years service but I was told right there and then that I was no longer eligible for pension. However, at the time I was quite happy to leave it at that, seeing the pay-off was quite substantial. It should also be noted that during my services career numerous other documents were proffered and duly signed by me to release the British government from culpability should I be in the wrong place at the wrong time. I was never given copies of these.

Although I was officially disgraced, two years after retiring, I was informed via my parents that I was to be awarded the Companion of the Order of St Michael and St George, which ranks just below a knighthood. I respectfully declined it as it meant sod all to me and in doing so did not get to meet Queen Elizabeth II of England in person, which disappointed my mother greatly.

Subsequently due to extreme unforeseen circumstances, which occurred over 20 months during 1992-1993, I obviously did not abide by the rules and chose this route of pseudonymity. But what triggered me to *start* writing was being detained in January 1994 at Miami Airport soon after my return from a trip to the Caribbean. I was informed by secure encrypted e-mail from London that my already secret file had been physically withdrawn internally and officially re-classed as "unavailable in perpetuity". *That* spurred me to commence writing my manuscript. Even if and when the British freedom of information bill becomes law, it does not mean that my account will ever be declassified so as to then qualify as so-called freedom of information in the first place. It has to be accepted that so many orders were issued verbally only and not actually put on paper up front so they

---

* PII (Public Interest Immunity) certificates are a UK legal mechanism exclusively signed by the Foreign Secretary via a written submission that allows any applying British government service to block the release of any documents that may be assessed as "damaging national security" (which in this case pertains to the author's entire career at SIS and Royal Navy Fleet Air Arm) being disclosed to the public, media or law courts. Once issued it is expected that matters are closed forever. No appeal is permitted whatsoever.

cannot then be declassified… Anyway, it would appear now that my record are sealed forever so please accept this unofficial version as the gospel truth.

* * * * * * * * * *

—4 November 2002, Milan, Italy—over nine years later…

I had flown to Europe from the Caribbean just the day before for a business convention. This day I was walking inside the magnificent haloed high-ceiling landmark of the Duomo, having crossed the cobblestone main square outside the cathedral in the city centre, when I caught sight of a very pretty woman coming in my direction. It wasn't until our paths crossed that a frisson of lightning zigzagged down my back…I was momentarily thunderstruck.

The sun's reflection off the stained glass ceiling gave her face a liquid gold complexion and the butterflies started to dance in a rolling thunder that only I could hear. But the mirage kept gliding away from me and was 10 paces away before I was able to croak, "Ursula."

She stopped dead in her tracks, turned slowly and stared as that unspoken electricity snapped, crackled and popped back to life again across the invisible wires of the divide. Then she whispered, "Nicholas." I resisted the urge to run and grab her as we cautiously stepped towards each other and politely kissed continental style. An internal light of power miraculously came on inside me then, that's all I can say.

She had herself only just arrived from France the day before too. I was also to quickly learn that her husband, Georges Durance regrettably had passed way 18 months after I saw him in Cuba. While she was telling me this it was a second moment of clarity when absolute realisation presented itself: Vibeke was smiling down for the first time ever and was blessing this nexus.

I believed at the time Ursula and I were destined to meet again. It was fate, some kind of law of karma.

Well, it's a long story really, enough to write another book I suppose…we lived happily ever after but *not* with each other, which is about par for the normal course of events throughout lifetimes in this day and age but we're still friends!

Epilogue

I made a living from recognising cognitive dissonance—in others as well as myself. So in the interest of truth I offer these insights on intrigues, many of such result in infuriation and inadequacy, with the outcome being passivity by the people in the know. *I have found that factual accounts of real happenings have been much more bizarre than fictional storytelling.*

My four-decade cycle of travel, travel, travel, travel has fashioned me into a professional foreigner—in Japanese it's called a *gaijin*—and I now place that terrestrial experience into good use for a small step or four in the right directions by hopefully jogging some rigged standpoints in this Epilogue. I personally do not, for the most part at the on-set, look at anything from the point of view of bias. I believe I'm as neutral as could be. Opinion is based on facts as it presents itself to me. Up to that moment, I did not have a position either way, and will convey as such to all and sundry.

However, there are many people divided against and/or extremely pro themselves. I am not one of those. I am my own worst critic when I divert off the centre without first conducting reasonable research.

A stranger once said to me about herself, "The more countries you travel to, the wider your perspective of the world becomes." I think there is a lot of historical truth to that. The stories from my life's adventures in their metaphorical language and its focus on certain individuals hopefully gives page-turning insight on those rare people and their unusual tales from the far remote corners of society.

The tapestry woven I hope this published account gives the reader a realistic recitation of how I experienced my own intimate time in the undertakings. There's an element of fictional secret for obvious reasons: I don't want anyone dropped into an imbroglio. Others have been mentioned purposefully because they are already in the public domain. Insiders will know who you are. That's why this book is A Documentary Novel. *Remember, none of this actually happened...*

Authoring is not a particularly fastidious occupation, more an examination of what was already presented to the mind. By penning a life story in fictional form I feel like a war correspondent within my own sphere. It is the opposition's version of a polarised society from the point of view of a former insider who focused on taboo subjects as determined by the political class who have applied pressure outside the law, thus making him an outsider. And their actions triggered his responses, that way around. So when I put pen to paper or finger to keyboard or speak on the phone, I commence from the basis that my communiqués may be accessed. But I don't care now if they know because publishing my book is and was the only tool I have. So I persevered. I'm proud of myself to not give up against all odds.

Sadly I am also cognisant that history has a rhythm of stressing framework over the fact of foundation; an opinion preferred over the reality.

If it seems I contradicted myself at times, so be it. Nothing is perfect. The lives we live are often diametrically opposed based on a different set of circumstances on a fresh new day. Sometimes disbelief is good for the mind because it presents a substitute to stick-in-the-mud belief and subsequently it makes one think more about another method to the madness.

There are many obscurities and circumlocutions for my own *raison d'être*. In my bluntness, this is not admittance. It's just a bare fact of life.

I have always seen truth as being similar to one of those mirrored globes that reflect light. Everyone admits its existence but they see its rays shine from different angles and in a multitude of ways. It's like chasing revolving shadows bouncing off that glass ball. The same is true of the planet's 200-plus nations on how they view the same problem, project or person, as they are observing it from their respective positions on the different pages of the ball of an atlas. Many aspects overlap each other, sometimes in a pre-determined pecking order of access to knowledge and put in that order by the same ones who dominate the first few single-digit pages on a list of names not necessarily in alphabetical order.

The genesis of ideas, like everything else, has been democratised. We are all equal, and none are more equal than others. People find inspiration in the drama of a visionary labouring alone to make the vision a reality...this person with defiance and faith that recognises that a revolution is about to occur. Then the crowd follows. It was always that way from the beginning of time. More openers of the gates are invited to venture forth on this path. *If you think you are too small to make a difference, you've never had a mosquito bite you!*

In a time increasingly dominated by technology, when we doubt our very ability to master the complex organisation of the society in which we live, the thought of a private vision working its way to public consciousness—altering the contours of reality—seems all the more appealing for being such an unlikely scenario.

Thinkers today believe in their capacity to change the world while others are daunted by the challenge of understanding it. There's a powerful link between creativity and politics: Writers subtly prose the imagination in print; dancers translate enchantingly by gracefulness; painters camouflage their ideas behind brush strokes; and musicians conceal messages with songs laded with hidden meanings. All provide boundless spiritual beauty and inspire. It's about ordinary people having the collective power to break down international barriers and speak up and be heard and seen in their own way. Anyone not prepared to take risks cannot create.

I am of the former. I choose to write in the hope that those finely tuned individuals, seeking a difference across the developed world, can discover these hidden downtrodden lands and spread delicious words by mouth to the similar thinking amongst them. For me it is the best form of communication. Therefore one must also consider who controls the printing presses, broadcast networks, film studios and telephone communications today, and where, even why.

Crime in the western world has declined markedly of late as the police can subpoena your mobile/cellular phone provider to find out where you were at any given time. Is this good or bad, I can't decide, it's a grey area. It's a fine balance between solving transgression and invasion of privacy. Thank goodness for watchdogs that watch those that are watching unsuspecting us, and that they continue to be a pain in the arse on our behalf.

Support their efforts please because without them your liberties will be eroded without you even realising it.

Your Internet service provider (ISP) can run an indent damon on you when you are logged-on and can reveal all sorts of information on you. Even more disturbing, and indeed to all who post to any public news groups, is the fact that everything you've ever written from day one is completely readable from a monster database by everyone on The Net. Thank goodness for the advancement of free encrypted software for the public available by secure e-mail that makes it harder to be spied on. Most of the ISPs in this specialised arena, it should be noted, are situated in democratic nations where freedom of speech is revered to the hilt.

It has also been said that the worldwide web has consumed everything in its path. I do find this line interesting in that the number of folks with access to the Internet in the world, a decade and a half after it became available, hovers around the 750 million mark—a minute minimal per cent—of the global population. (Even by tripling the millions it is still negligible.) Sadly, most mortals on the planet haven't even made a phone call yet nor knows what a telephone looks like, forget the thought of them knowing what a computer is and does.

On a positive note: I'm glad to see that the Internet, if used properly, is feared by those that fear it because it is an equaliser, one of the few forums in which people can be judged solely by their words instead of looks, dress or accents.

In this written work in your hands I undertook the conflict between deeds and conscience, which relate the personal to the political. Challenging the values of a developed society. I am unafraid to speak out in timorous times (even though I have to keep my face concealed for my own protection). I will always from now on act on behalf of the vulnerable and the wounded in a western-dominated world that only prizes success, an idea mistakenly fostered mainly by the US. I invite you to step out of the safety zone and find some way, somehow, your own non-violent way to effect change. Those not willing to consider this…please go back to watching your brainless Hollywood-style programming. One day you may eventually realise our own real lives are a form of soap opera…but it only becomes so when you decide to be actively involved in positive change. I hope my story will encourage others with suppressed stories to venture forth. You must not be wary anymore of truth. I no longer am.

When greed takes precedent over special needs; the bottom line has dropped too low.

Our planet we call home needs to re-focus itself because the disparity in income and standard of living is too wide a labyrinth. A large number of populaces from the "global south" (the third world), they—most of the present leaders that care—know so because their people are the ones falling into the deep crevices. The income per head between the seven richest and the seven poorest nations gets appallingly wider, and more than doubles every decade. The same sad story as the rich get richer and the poor get...yawn...are you one of overweight westerners in general, eating ice cream while filing your nails and chatting on the phone? Hello?

If we shrank the Earth's population to a village of 100 people, pre-serving all human ratios, we'd have 57 Asians, 21 Europeans, 14 from North and South America, and 8 Africans. Seventy would be non-white; 70 would be non-Christian. Half the world's wealth would be in the hands of six people—five of them US citizens. Only 30 people would be able to read; half would suffer from malnutrition; and 80 would live in substandard housing. Only one person would have a college education. (Figures may not be exact but it's a flow chart in words for better comprehension.)

Capitalist propaganda states this is "democracy", in another words "you are free". But it's never a freedom to do what you want—devolution from control perhaps but not revolution towards progress. With communism dying out I can see capitalism being untied too. Hopefully this scrunched hard knot of green paper around the few inside the cocoon will be unravelled in my lifetime.

After this temporary tirade of text I do suggest a similarity between my book and the Internet in that you may have found what you were not looking for because you did not know it previously existed. Prised outside the comfort zone you are now more knowledgeable about certain inner workings, hopefully.

I would like to see the ugly underbelly of the world dug up and its flesh bared to clean air. The legalised pharmaceutical trade available in chemists bears a remarkable similarity to its illegitimate cousin, the leisure drugs available from your local street corner bum, in that the profits are in epidemic proportions. After the tobacco criminals have been locked up then it'll be these boys, then after that the weapons industry war-mongering hypocrites. All in the business of making obscene profits from people dying.

I have smiled often on how issues, which have sprung forth, have been nothing more than a vehicle for exploring how much some people will do to protect their reputations while the objective is to continue as before. They succeed admirably with their protective layers of lawyers, accountants, bankers, diplomats and slanted media coverage—all tools of the illuminati: keepers of the pigs' cash, gold, stocks and secrets.

We live on an unapologetic aggressive Earth with more takers than givers, seduced by the spoils, afraid to plant seeds. Even the peat smoulders in anger. The earth itself has become a non-entity in western civilisations' universe. The "Marie Antoinette" issue of our days *is* the environment. Local sustainable development should be the new name for peace in the world. Otherwise we can pump more air into the atmosphere to make it expand bigger or start euthanasia instead, the "good death". *No country can continue where the helpline number can simply be dialled to correct a problem.*

Over two decades and billions in expenditure later, spent just by the US alone, after starting their war on AIDS, has produced no drug nor vaccine…you'd think that all the brains in charge would seek to look beyond the telescopic field at something else outside the narrowing view…but no. Victims of their own industry's constant drum beating they answer any questions relating to our health that it must be a drug or vaccine and nothing but. *The world must also grasp that both the major political parties of the United States are rightwing, i.e.: the conservative right of France is philosophically to the left of the most liberal of American democrats. The people of the US have nothing to compare to even though they are brainwashed into thinking they do.* The end result is always on the same side no matter what: *Having everything is as cancerous as having nothing.*

Meanwhile in the non-western world the spectre of fundamental Islam is raising its ugly head higher, leading its followers backwards. I do understand its noble philosophy but it doesn't realise that if it succeeds its people will be swallowed whole into the expanding capitalist quicksand. *Power without principle is barren but principle without power is futile.*

The world's problems constantly change and cannot be frozen at some arbitrary point in time. Advancement will proceed as its more fiery proponents chip away at the real enemy: The block of granite called the Establishment, the promoters of religions, drugs and war for gain. Gradually its defences will be eroded with the opening of minds.

I am not naïve...I can feel it coming slowly, already—all things considered. I could continue my constructive criticism but I won't for perhaps I have misunderstood what the machine is about having being blasted through its tunnel. I am a British former Secret Intelligence Service officer who evolved into a citizen of the world. I bring those perspectives and limitations from those experiences to the forefront. I do not have a political agenda and I have remained mostly myself, in that I have operated in a straight line for the common good of humanity believing where there is no division, possibilities multiply.

The comas, semi-colons and full stops should speak nice and clear; otherwise its just waste of time writing them. Words should ricochet like bullets...but not the metal kinds as I have learnt to my personal costs.

Is the human race apparently not yet ready to move forward as a species—does a bit more of the selection processes need to take place? Perhaps we need to smile at each other more... "The smile is the shortest distance between two people," somebody once quipped. I believe it!

Look into the eyes of youth, see the flare that burns as brilliantly as the world's desire for peace and be thankful for that midsummer's day beam that knows it will come.

My daughter when she was a pre-teen attended an international festival on lands afar from her own and met young Bulgarians there. I looked into her sparkling eyes as she related her tale accompanied with photographs. When I had spent many years spotting the solemn-faced enemy through binoculars and gun sights, it's hard to look at their celluloid genuine grins as they stand innocently besides one's own beloved. Years later I met a recently married couple also from Bulgaria on a plane to Belize. It becomes difficult to talk to them even after the rifles have been confiscated and it is proclaimed we are now friends. The fact that my kid can relate her fun and that man and woman sitting next to me could converse in harmony...was worth it. In both cases I had to excuse myself to go into transitory seclusion and let my pain ebb in silence. Then I returned ebullient, encouraged by my small contribution to the progress.

[In 1989 Bulgaria destroyed 130,000 sensitive communist archives out of the 280,000 they had. Today, my time ensnared there then officially doesn't exist. I also know that NATO's Military Committee doesn't exist either, sic.]

In my own particular way, my life's training has been shaped whereupon my physical and mental self has become worthy of the spiritual self and it has already taken up residence within me. I won't go so far as to say it is a version of *gomo rimpoche* (Tibetan for attaining "total enlightenment" or "nirvana") but certainly I consider my experiences *rimpoche* by itself. I am to myself, an "enlightened one".

Coming to the end of my years of writing this account, I now feel I am leaving home instead of coming home. *Res ipsa*, I hope this book "speaks for itself". I did not write about what I did not know and to embellish what was already my story. I thank you for completing it with me.

A journey inspired by the search for answers can never be repeated.

THE END